Breal

The Sterling Shore Series,

Book 5

C.M. Owens

Breaking Even
The Sterling Shore Series

Chapter 1

Brin

No, no, no, no! Not today! I'm so sick of this!

He has his side of the street, and I have mine. All he has to do is park on his side of the damn street.

Our subdivision doesn't allow driveways—a stupid rule that I don't understand—but the streets are very wide and made for curbside parking. Everyone parks directly in front of their house. It only makes sense. Maggie and I park in front of our house.

But this jerk, for some reason, refuses to park his car on *his* side of the road—in front of *his* house.

The end of the cul-de-sac has a family with three teenagers, so they take up the entire arch for parking. Maggie and I already have to squeeze in. I have to park close to her so that our next-door neighbors have plenty of parking room in front of their smaller house. The jerk across the road has a wide open space directly in front of his large house, but he's a dick.

Every night he gets here after my neighbor, Mr. Morgan, goes to work for his twelve hour shift. He takes his spot and parks right on my bumper in case Mr. Morgan comes back and needs room. I could park across the street—in his spot—but that would be admitting defeat. And I refuse to be defeated.

Today he has really screwed up.

I'm not going to spend twenty minutes backing up and pulling

1

forward numerous times in an effort to get out. Not happening. If he insists on parking on *our* side of the street, the least he could do is leave a respectable gap. It's a common courtesy. Apparently he'd rather piss us off as opposed to pissing Mr. Morgan off.

I have to work. His lazy ass sleeps half the day. He revs his engine at all hours—when he leaves and gets back. He doesn't show the slightest ounce of concern for anyone else. Enough is enough, and I've had e-fucking-nough.

Before I lose my courage, I stalk across the street and bang on the door. A gentle rap might have been polite, but I'm not worried about manners right now. This bastard loves blocking me in. Today he'll move his car or... or... I'll do something, dammit.

Silence.

I almost lose my nerve, but I pull out my best big-girl guts, and I pound on the door again, longer this time. I hear a string of curse words being spewed as someone stumbles inside the house, bumping into walls and crashing into things.

I steel myself, ready for a fight. I'm anything but confrontational, but this dick has pushed me to my limit.

"What the fuck?" he gripes, swinging the door open to reveal something I wasn't expecting.

I knew he was gorgeous—I have eyes. Hell, Maggie and I call him Mr. Sexy for a reason, but... um... wow. I hate him for being *wow* right now.

His dirty blonde hair is still messy from the bed, but in the sexiest way possible. His perfectly golden skin is almost hypnotic, and his numerous tattoos might as well all say *bad boy*. And don't even get me started on the piercings—one in his eyebrow and one in his nipple.

I've ogled him from across the road before. He loves going out shirtless, so I've had plenty of opportunities to drool.

After numerous stolen gawks, I was fully prepared to be met by the Mr. Sexy that lives here. I thought I was, anyhow. What I wasn't prepared for was for him to be in his boxers—only his boxers—and standing at full attention like a good little morning soldier.

My eyes dart straight down, taking in the ungodly bulge. Thank God it's hidden by the thin fabric.

That does very little to my ever-wavering confidence. What happened to my fury? Why was I even furious? Why did I come here?

As my mouth flops agape, he raises his brow, seeming amused.

"Gotten your fill yet? I was trying to sleep," he says through a sexy drawl that floods me with numerous conflicting emotions.

Hunger, excitement, humiliation, then anger. *Anger*. Yes. Finally. Bring on the crazy bitch.

My eyes snap up when my brain decides to start functioning again. "Move your damn car!" I bark, letting my rage run over my skin with an almost tangible glow.

His eyes widen, as if he's shocked by my early morning intrusion. Well, he can get over it. After a breath, his confused expression turns bored.

"No," he says simply, leaning against the doorframe.

Really? That's all I get? Are you kidding me?

"Move your damn car now! I have work, and I'm not going to

spend twenty minutes trying to get out of the small space you left me with."

"Then you shouldn't have parked so close to the other car," he says with a shrug, crossing his arms over his expansive, defined chest as he gives me his best I'm-too-fucking-cool-for-this-shit smirk.

I glance at Maggie's red BMW just in front of my car. She stays up late, pounding away on her laptop to finish all her numerous projects for impatient clients. I can't go wake her up to move her car or find her keys. I refuse. Besides, those are *our* spots. I have to park close to her so that Mr. Morgan has room enough to leave for work. This jerk just steals the gap every night—to hell with everyone else.

If this is the way he wants to play, then let's play.

"Fine," I hiss, making his eyes darken and his triumphant grin spread before I turn to stalk back toward my car.

"Knew you'd see things my way," he calls out from behind me, sounding so damn smug.

He mutters something about me being crazy, oh, but he hasn't seen crazy yet. He has no idea just how *crazy* I can be. I'm sick of stupid men, heinous egos, and insatiable desires to piss me off. Well, mission accomplished. I'm very thoroughly pissed.

He starts to close the door right as I hop in my car. I smirk when I see him watching, possibly planning to mock me in my sad attempt to break free from the tiny space he's left me with.

Without hesitation, I crank the car, throw it in reverse, and slam on my gas. My head jolts forward before I even hear the sickening impact of my rear crashing into the front of his Porsche. The alarm on his car wails, sounding as though it's crying after my *very* provoked attack.

I hear him yelling loudly, probably calling me every name in the book, but I don't give a damn.

Take that, asshole.

Serves him right. Now his pretty little black Porsche has been kissed by my white Camry. Well, I suppose it's more than a mere kiss. His car has officially been fucked by mine.

My car lurches forward when I toss it in drive, slamming on my brakes inches away from Maggie's BMW, and then I slam it in reverse again, smashing his front end even more. My neck pops this time from the jolt.

His car continues to bellow, agonizing over the damage I've caused, and a wild, hysterical giggle bubbles through my lips.

"You crazy bitch!" he roars, gripping his head in disbelief while standing in the middle of the street with nothing on but his boxers.

All of our neighbors have come out to play spectators for the psychotic scene, but I don't care. I've been run over, tossed aside, and walked on for too long. This morning something has snapped. I'm sick of being a doormat.

"Fucking shit!" Maggie says loudly, laughing wildly from the front porch of our home, wearing her robe and a look of fascinated horror.

I hadn't gotten her keys because I didn't want to wake her up. *Sure*, it made a lot more sense to simply wreck my car and his.

Now that my adrenaline high is coming down, I suddenly feel a little mortified, but I refuse to show that to him. So, with a daring glint in my eyes, I act unaffected.

I offer him a wave and speed out of the larger gap I've made, heading toward work, while the rest of the neighborhood trips over themselves to go see what craziness just erupted.

Rye

"What the hell happened?" Wren asks, walking up with two coffees in his hands.

His eyes are pained as they stare at the crumbled hood of my car. I had to have the damn thing towed here after that lunatic smashed into it. Over a parking spot? Really? So over the top.

"My neighbor went psycho," I growl, bending down to examine just how bad this really is. Fortunately it seems to be limited to cosmetic damage.

"What the hell did you do to her?" he asks.

Craning my neck, I narrow my eyes at him. "I never said it was a girl."

He gives me an incredulous look that I happen to find a little offensive.

"If you pissed someone off bad enough to destroy their car against yours, it was a chick. A guy would have just punched you."

Again, I'm offended. "You really think a guy is stupid enough to try to punch me?" I challenge, making damn sure my muscles are flexed.

Wren rolls his eyes as he walks over and hands me the second cup of coffee. "Down, Cujo," he jokes, and I glare at him as he circles the car, taking it all in.

"When's the insurance company coming out?"

"They're not coming," I mutter, cursing my easy-to-piss-off neighbor when my hood refuses to open.

"You didn't call her insurance company?" he asks, sounding confused.

Crazy girl ran off without waiting for the cops. I could be a dick and get her arrested for a hit-and-run, but I won't. Even though she deserves to be scared out of her fucking mind.

But I'll do something to get even. I may not want her in jail, but I sure as hell want revenge.

When I saw my short, somewhat nerdy little neighbor standing at my door in her long skirt, oversized white button-up shirt, and ugly-as-hell shoes, I just assumed she was trying to find an excuse to talk to me. Then she had rolled her shoulders back, stood as tall as she could, and barked at me while her light, brown hair sat in disarray on her head.

Would it kill her to try and look a little appealing?

I might have lost my cool and acted like a dick during the heat of the moment, but she woke me up too early. This isn't... this is ridiculous. You don't bash in a guy's car—his pride and fucking joy—over a parking spot. Especially not before coffee.

"Hello," Wren prompts. "Insurance company? When are they coming?"

Obviously he's not going to drop this.

"Nah. Insurance companies piss me off. Besides, I just bought a few new tools to play with. Might as well experiment on my own car," I say mildly, pretending as though it's no big deal while secretly plotting my badass revenge.

Wren looks around my massive garage as all my guys work their asses off. It's a busy week with all the new clients. It'll be a pain in the ass to try and work my own car in.

"When's the magazine coming?" Wren asks.

"They're doing their article in a few months, so it might be a while."

"Is it on just this one shop, or the entire franchise?"

"This one is the main focus of the article. The franchise will get some attention. They had the columnist come out and take a look at the place. She was impressed," I say with a suggestive tone, and he rolls his eyes.

"Figures."

Leaning back and ignoring my poor baby, I stare at him. "Didn't fuck her, if that's what you're insinuating. She's doing an article, so that would mean drama. But you shouldn't act so appalled by the thought. In fact, you should be mixing things up by now. You're single. Erica isn't sitting around mourning the loss of your marriage."

He grimaces, and I frown. Maybe that was too harsh.

"I know," he says through a slow exhale. Then he sips his coffee while trying not to get lost in thought. "So what'd you do to piss her off?" he asks, looking back up while lazily gesturing to my car.

I guess we're not allowed to talk about the fact he's not doing anything besides sitting around. I don't want to tell him I took her

8

parking spot. He'll ask why, and then there will be a hellacious amount mockery that follows.

"Nothing, really. She's just bat-shit crazy." At least that's the truth. And I'll make sure the punishment is fitting.

Brin

Maggie whistles low, chuckling as she shakes her head in disbelief. I groan as I stare at the rear of my car that I'll have to spend a fortune to get fixed.

Maggie came to meet me at work, curious about what happened to set me off this morning. I've spent the morning in knots, unable to face work after my *little* breakdown. The museum can wait. I have a big-ass mess to sift through.

My boss will just have to do his own job today, because I'm taking a personal day. I don't care if he's already seen me standing in front of the museum for the past two hours just staring blankly at the mutilated rear end of my car. I'll have to work overtime to pay for my rampage.

"Was it worth it?" Maggie asks, still smiling as a piece of one of my taillights falls to the ground, shattering a little more to punctuate the tragedy it has suffered.

My crumpled Camry's rear still looks better than the front of his destroyed Porsche. I dread going home. Maybe I'll get lucky and he'll stick to his side of the street. I never see him outside of the subdivision. We barely even see each other outside in the yards.

Shit! I can't believe I stood there and drooled over him this morning—then went crazy and smashed his car. Now that the anger has fled, the humiliation and dread are ruling me.

"I just... snapped. I don't know. Maybe it's because of hormones or whatever. I'm almost twenty-six, so it could be an early midlife crisis or something."

She snickers while shaking her head. "Girl, I'm twenty-nine, and I've never mowed down a Porsche."

I decide not to remind her what today is. I've talked about it enough this past year.

"I'll start calling around to get some price quotes on fixing this. I hope he doesn't expect you to fix his Porsche or sue you," she sighs, slapping me in the face with reality.

Ah, hell. It was a hit-and-run. "Or call the cops," I add, exasperated as I flop my head into my hands.

Why was I so stupid? I should have just called in and stayed in bed this morning. I've destroyed a car, and now I could quite possibly be going to jail. Great. I don't take good selfies, so I can only imagine how I'll look in a mug shot.

Chapter 2

Brin

I made it through the night without seeing Mr. Sexy or enduring his wrath. Thank goodness. His Porsche was gone when I got home, per the usual. He usually comes and goes during the late hours, and he almost always wakes me up with his obnoxious returns and departures.

If he came and went last night, he didn't rev his horrible engine like normal. I'm lying in my bed instead of a cot in a jail cell, so he apparently never called the cops. No mug shots just yet. I pray this isn't just the calm before the storm.

Rising slowly, I head to the kitchen, ready to make some coffee. I groan inwardly when I think about all my nosy neighbors. Why did I cause a scene?

Maggie's door is shut tight, her music is still softly playing, and there's no crazy lady crashing into cars this morning to disturb her. I'm sure she pulled another late night.

I tiptoe through the house—my morning routine—and finish getting ready for work. When I walk out, my jaw drops. My car is blocked in—again. It's not the fragile Porsche behind me this time, though.

There's a large, black Range Rover with a black-painted brush-guard that is almost touching my falling-apart bumper.

Un-frigging-believable. That ass did it again! I don't know where he keeps his vehicles, but I know he has several. I've seen him drive this one before.

As I stalk to my car, I glance at his house, willing it to burn to the ground with him in it. My mind doesn't grant me the pyrotechnic show I crave, though.

I gauge the few inches he has left me with, and I scowl. I'll have to get Maggie's keys, move her car, then move mine, then move hers back, then get in mine and leave. All because he's a jerk who can't stay on his side of the street.

A string of profanities leave my mouth too loudly, and Ms. Morgan looks over at me while weeding out her dead flowerbed, offering me a disappointed glare. If she wants to point that glare at someone, it should be the dick across the street—not me.

He's so lucky Maggie is anti-gun. Otherwise... I won't go there. I need to get violence out of my head. I've pissed off my neighbor, who is now trying to piss me off for pissing him off.

Headache.

When I make it back inside the house, I see Maggie was wise enough to leave her keys out. She has better foresight than I do, because I sure as hell never saw this coming. Why provoke the crazy woman who bashed in your Porsche's brains? Does he not realize I've lost my mind? There's no telling what I might do in the heat of the moment.

I rush back out to move Maggie's car, but I'm frozen to the ground when I see a smirking devil propped against his doorjamb. I'll no longer refer to him as Mr. Sexy. From now on, he's Mr. Dead Meat.

He idly sips his coffee, his twisted, wicked grin growing ever so slightly as he watches me, waiting for me to show my ass again. Today he's wearing dark denim jeans and a black T-shirt that says "Nirvana" on the front.

I offer him my best I-want-you-dead glower, and he raises his coffee cup in a toasting motion, proving he's proud of his little payback. I hate him. Mr. Dead Meat can go to hell. I'll not be driving into his car today. Mostly because it wouldn't do a damn bit of good, and because my car might fall apart this time.

After playing musical vehicles, I head off to work, praying I don't file anything wrong. I'm sure my boss is going to make me work over just to make up for yesterday.

Just as I park at the museum, something familiar catches my eyes. Then a sickening feeling consumes me as the scene registers in front of me. My heart stops when I see the only man in the world I wish would disappear off the face of the planet.

It's him. John Abbott. The son of a bitch who made me a divorcee just after I turned twenty-five is here, and he's not here alone. A gooey-eyed blonde is draped on his arm, staring happily up at him as he walks out of the museum—where I work.

What's he doing here?

I watch as he unfolds something, and my heart constricts. It's then I realize he's sliding a ring on her finger. He's proposing here? At my work? What... the... hell is going on?

Not that I've been keeping tabs, but I know for a fact they've only been dating for three months. Everyone who knows us always fills me in on his life, even though it should be obvious that I don't want to hear it.

This is too soon. Has he lost his mind? Or is she just as stupid as I was to think the creep is capable of truly caring about her?

I scan the parking lot for his truck, hoping I'm not parked anywhere close to him. God must be busy, because he doesn't answer my prayer. I'm parked two cars down from him.

I try slumping down in my seat, but it's too late. His eyes lock with mine, and then he tilts his head. At first I think he's going to pass by, pretend as though we're two acquaintances who barely knew each other once upon a time, but then he stops just as he reaches the back of my car, his eyes locked on the rear. Horror spreads over his face, and he drops Barbie's arm to rush over.

"Brin! What the hell happened?" he demands, his eyes pinned toward the back, and I huff loudly when I realize what kept him from just walking on.

He's what happened. I was too pissed to think straight because of what yesterday was. The ignorant, selfish, stupid asshole. Now I have to face him and only humiliate myself further.

I slowly climb out of the car, wishing I had gone to church more. Maybe then God would have helped me out. Why does it feel like I'm being punished?

Brin

"So he was there getting her ring appraised?" Maggie asks in disbelief, referring to my son of a bitch ex-husband and his shiny new toy that has the Sterling sparkle.

"Yep. And I showed up just as they were leaving. He actually used my name to call in a favor and rush the process along, and they did it for free because he and I are *friends*. Can you believe the nerve? My life sucks," I groan, cursing as I drop to my bed.

His fiancée must know what a prick he is if she's forcing him to get the ring appraised. It wasn't a flashy diamond, so it can't possibly be worth more than a thousand dollars. Pointless appraisal if you ask me.

Maggie starts to speak, when we hear a loud, terrifying cracking noise, and I squeal loudly as my bed shifts and breaks. A stupid girly scream passes through my lips as the right side collapses, slanting my bed at a terrible, unforgiving angle that drops my ass in a rolling motion to the hard floor.

I land awkwardly and a grunt is forced out of me. After peeling myself up, I look around, still a little stunned.

"What the hell?" I groan, looking at my large bed in disbelief. My poor, poor bed. The ache from my pummeled rear reminds me the bed wasn't the only one injured. My poor, poor ass.

Maggie is wide-mouthed as she comes to gape at the crazy damn thing that has just happened. "How did your bed just fall apart?" she asks, and I look at her as if she's joking.

"Sorry," she mutters, realizing that was a stupid question. But as she examines the bed closer, she gasps. "These legs have been sawed through. And the other two are completely intact. Someone did this on purpose."

Shocked and completely bewildered, I try to process that. Who

15

would break in and saw my bed down? No. That's preposterous.

"How could anyone even get in the house? Maybe we've got beetles or something."

That's when she turns pale and takes a step back. But within seconds, her horror turns to fits of laughter. Um... What's going on?

"Oh damn. It appears you've started a war," Maggie says, not making a damn bit of sense.

"What?" I ask slowly, suddenly questioning her sanity.

Her laughter tapers off as she slides down the wall until she's sitting and leaning against it, putting her eye-level with me.

"Mr. Sexy came over earlier today because our pipes burst outside. I never saw it. I should have possibly questioned that, but hell, he had tools, and I know nothing about pipes or tools—no pun intended. Anyway, my days are always busy with client calls, and I had to leave him alone numerous times. I heard noises, but I didn't really think much about it. You're so fucked if you've started a war with him."

Her laughter resumes while my mouth remains unhinged, dumbfounded by this turn of events. That asshole is paying me back? Why? He frigging sawed down my bed?

"I only ran over his car because he had our spot. Again! That was us breaking even. This... this is him getting back up by one shot."

Maggie tilts her head as an amused smile crosses her lips. "What are you going to do about it?" she dares.

I scowl as I finally climb back up to my feet, and I grab my phone and keys from the nightstand. Is there a hardware store nearby?

"First I'm going to find a saw so I can knock down the other two legs of my bed to make it level, and then I'm going to google revenge."

Her laughter returns just as I walk out, and I glare at the neighbor's house across the street. When I see his Range Rover behind my sad little car, I stalk through the darkness.

The second I reach the door, the bastard swings it open before I can even knock. "Yes?" he drawls, having the audacity to seem bored.

How dare he answer shirtless and attempt to distract me! Those tattoos aren't intimidating me right now, though. He lives in a subdivision, so he can't be too dangerous. I don't think. Maybe, anyway.

"I need your saw," I growl.

He tries not to grin, but fails miserably as he reaches beside the door and pulls out a hacksaw, as though he was waiting on this. How did he know I'd come over here when I only decided it seconds ago?

"I'd give you the electric one I used, but you might cut one of your fingers off. Looks like you'll have to do it the hard way," he gloats.

I narrow my eyes at him while snatching the saw away. "Thank you," I hiss, and then I turn to walk away.

You really told him off, Brin.

"Oh, and now we're even," he calls through the darkness, humor and triumph lacing his every word.

"No. We were even when I screwed up your car," I growl, never slowing down. "This means war."

His throaty chuckle puts unwelcome tingles throughout my entire body, but I shrug them off as my speed quickens.

"Bring it on, Darlin'," he says to my back.

17

Famous last words.

Rye

"You're kidding," Wren says just as I lock the door to my office.

He follows me out to my car, and takes the passenger seat. I've finally succeeded in talking him into going to Silk, but I have to swing by my house and change first. I refuse to let him back out, and he will if I don't drive him there myself.

"Nope. And now she's threatening war."

I can't help but laugh. What's she going to do? Try to run over my car again? I'm not driving anything but this beast for a while. Besides, her car wouldn't survive another attack.

"Did you just laugh?" he asks, his eyes wide in disbelief.

"Don't look at me like that. I do laugh on occasion."

He snorts derisively. "On a very rare occasion, and nowhere nearly that loud."

Grinning, I shrug. "Must be the adrenaline high."

It's later than I meant for it to be, but we finally finished this week's ungodly load. Maybe I can start on my car tomorrow. And with us being caught up, the guys can handle taking care of the grunt work alone.

As I crank the car and pull out onto the road, Wren sinks back in the seat.

"You're fucking crazy, dude. The girl could be one of those chicks that cuts a guy's balls off in his sleep or something."

Hadn't thought of that. And I really wish he hadn't just put that thought in my head.

"Then I'll sleep with one eye open. I couldn't let her get away with smashing my car and not do anything about it. It wouldn't be... me."

He tilts his head, and I keep my eyes trained on the road in front of me because I refuse to see the scrutiny in his eyes. "Then call the cops. The girl hit your car and drove off. Don't sneak into her house and saw her bed down."

My laughter escapes before I even realize it, and Wren's eyes widen again. Christ. You'd think I never laugh at all. Okay, so maybe it is rather rare, but that just means I'm not an easily entertained fool.

This is more fun than I realized, and I might have laughed a long time ago if I had known how fun it was to piss someone off as well as I've pissed her off.

I would have loved to have seen her face when she crashed to the ground after that bed collapsed. As high as that bed was, it had to have gone into a forty-five degree angle the second it fell.

We turn onto my road, and I grow curious when I see people walking down the sidewalk in mass quantities. It's rare I see more than a few joggers. These are regularly clothed people in suits and casual wear, all of them walking as though they're on a mission.

Just as I near my house, I quickly whip into the spot that will piss her off in the morning. I can't help my smug-as-fuck grin.

"Holy shit!" Wren says through a cough, his gaze going across the street to my house.

It's then I realize my lawn is littered with people who are dying laughing, and a projector screen is playing on the side of my white home. What. The. Hell?

It's a scene on repeat, and it's not exactly something I want my damn neighbors seeing.

"What the fuck is that?" I screech, irritated by the unusual octave of my voice.

I climb out of my SUV, wondering why there's guy-on-guy porn on the side of my house.

"What the hell is this?" I growl as soon as I near Leslie Marks, my neighbor from down the road.

"It's *Broke Back Mountain*," she says through a chuckle, and I cringe as the scene starts back over, apparently playing on a loop as two cowboys in a tent breathe a little too heavily.

"Ah, hell," Wren says, walking away from me like he doesn't know me at all.

I'm going to kill her.

I rush over and grab the projector, and then I stomp the fuck out of it as the sounds and images end.

Everyone is laughing, but I tune them out as I zero in on the girl sitting on her porch, grinning as she absently stirs a straw in her glass. My stride turns into a sprint, and she squeals while jumping up and running inside, dropping and shattering her glass in an attempt to escape me.

The door slams and locks seconds before I reach it, and I pound fiercely as the neighborhood continues laughing at my back.

"Who is it?" she asks in a singsong voice, a mocking lilt to her tone that proves she feels cocky and safe inside her house.

"Open the damn door!" I bark, and her laughter pours out to taunt me.

"Not happening. Consider us even."

Even? "You've got to be fucking kidding me!"

She only laughs harder, and I glare at the door like I can blow it to pieces with the sheer power of my enraged mind. Unfortunately, all that happens is the abrupt promise of a migraine.

"Fine. You want to play this game? Then consider this a declaration of war. Just remember you started it."

"Bring it on, Darlin'," she says in a playful, deep tone, recycling my words from yesterday.

There will be hell to pay for this.

Brin

"Shit!" I yell as the blue dye drips from my body.

Maggie's laughter rolls out, and I turn to glare at her as the blue continues to soak through my clothes.

"Damn," she chuckles as I close the refrigerator door.

"It's everywhere," I groan when I look at my body, the kitchen floor, and the wall behind me. Oh, and my poor, pitiful hair.

Maggie's laughter only grows. How did he rig my refrigerator to explode blue dye packs the second I opened it? And when the hell did he do it?

"Did you let him in again?" I growl, giving my murderous glare to the possible traitor.

"No," she chuckles, shaking her head. "He must have found a way in."

"And disarmed the alarm?" I ask skeptically.

"Must have," she says, lying her ass off.

"How could you?"

She only laughs harder, grabbing her side as though she's in pain. I glare at my *ex*-best friend, and she leans back, trying to catch her breath.

"He's dead," I hiss, doing all I can to come up with something as equally destructive to do to him. "Right after I get this damn blue off me. It had so better not be permanent, or you'll be the next one to suffer my wrath."

Instead of cowering in fear—as she should—she only continues to laugh, and I storm into my bedroom to shower and plot my revenge.

Brin

"It's not so bad," Maggie lies, biting back her grin as she looks at the remnants of blue that are still staining my hair.

"It looks like I have a lot of graying hair." I could cry—if I knew how to cry. The blue faded to be a duller, lighter color, but it didn't all wash out. My clothes are ruined, and my hair... I'll kill him.

"It's really not so bad. Besides, I can make you a hair appointment with my girl. She'll have this fixed up in no time."

She gives me an apologetic smile that I don't particularly find sincere. She's helping the enemy. How could she?

"Well, I have a date to get ready for," she says when my scowl loses its effect. I suppose it can't lose its effect if it didn't have one to begin with. "So you're on your own with Mr. Sexy for the rest of the day."

She turns to walk away just as I say, "You have an early morning date? So this is getting really serious?"

She grins as she walks into her room, not bothering to answer. It's barely six in the morning. But I have more important things to worry about than her breakfast date.

I quickly rummage the cabinets and see the baking soda. Genius strikes.

When I hear Maggie slip into the shower, I quickly make my way out the front door and across the lawn. Hopefully he's not up yet. As long as he's not waking up to gloat about my new dye job, I should be able to get in without detection.

He doesn't have an alarm on his house—I don't think. He swung the door open as soon as his footsteps made it there the other morning when I banged on his door. And I know I've seen him climb through the window before when he apparently locked his keys in the house.

Geez, I sound like a stalker.

Moving to the window I've seen him climb through three times, I push up, smiling when the window lifts without sounding an alarm. It's a little high, but fortunately I'm able to hoist myself up and fall in like the worst covert operative ever.

Staying still, I listen for any rustle of movement to say I'm busted. I look around at the living room I'm in. Damn. It's twice the size of ours. And it's really, really clean. So not what I was expecting.

I wish I had more time to snoop, but I don't. I have to hurry before he finds me.

His massive kitchen is easy to locate, and I take a second to marvel at all the marble surfaces. It looks like a picture Tuscany would envy.

Surprisingly, the copper accents and fixtures actually look good alongside the sleek stainless steel appliances. Guys don't deserve kitchens like this. I would love it, take care of it, and treat it with so much respect. It does smell good in here, so maybe he's utilizing it at least a little.

With a wistful sigh, I open the fridge, and that's when I melt a little more. It's something people should sing about. Crisp vegetables along with numerous other things are perfectly organized within the fridge. I want to move in and move him out.

Grabbing the ketchup, I offer one last look to the fridge, and then I sneak back out. This is going to be good.

After managing to get out the window with more grace than I entered, I sprint across the yard and head inside. It takes the ketchup a while to run to the top, but I wait patiently, never moving my eyes until the last drop has slid down. Then I flip it back up. Just as I grab the baking soda, Maggie walks in wearing nothing but her towel.

I ignore her as I focus on the task at hand.

"Why are you pouring baking soda into our ketchup bottle?"

Ah hell. This is making a mess. My excitement has caused my hands to shake and some of the baking soda spills over.

"It's not our ketchup," I mumble absently.

"Whose is it? And why are you pouring baking soda in it?"

"Have you ever seen one of those baking soda and vinegar

volcanoes people used to do at school?" I ask distractedly, still dedicating the majority of my attention on my revenge.

"Yes. Why?" she asks slowly.

"Do you know what the main ingredient is in ketchup?"

I screw the lid on with a proud smile on my face as the red coats the white and hides it from sight.

"No," she says, acting as though she's worried about my sanity at this point.

"Vinegar," I murmur, grinning bigger as I carefully move to the window, looking to see if anyone is outside that could tattle on me.

"And?" she prompts.

I turn around, my twisted mind reveling in the sheer excitement. "One thing that is very predictable about our jackass neighbor is that he barbeques every third Wednesday of the month. I can smell the burgers cooking from over here. I always feel hungry all day because of that damn scent. Tonight, he'll have a surprise."

"The ketchup?" she asks, still seeming confused.

"Yep. Just like anyone else that uses a bottle of ketchup, he'll shake it first."

She walks over just as I open the door, and she asks, "What happens when he shakes it?"

Rye

Wren and Tag deal the cards again just as I bring the burgers in.

Dane is sitting next to Maverick, though I don't know why either of them came. Dane isn't my biggest fan. But Tag and Wren keep trying to put us together.

Girls.

"Your luck has to run out sooner or later," Tag growls, glaring at me.

"He wouldn't be winning if Raya was here," Wren points out.

"She's banned from the poker tables," Dane says idly, picking his cards up.

"I refuse to even watch her play poker anymore," Tag grumbles.

I just laugh. It feels good to finally have Tag over. He rarely gets out of Ash's ass these days.

I pull out more beers and all the shit we'll need to start making our burgers.

"Where's your girl?" I ask, putting the spread out on the kitchen island.

Maverick hops up to grab a plate while Tag answers.

"She's hanging out with Rain and Raya tonight. Raya and Kade have been on the rocks since his grandfather's death. So Ash and Rain took her out to cheer her up."

That's why Tag came. His girl wasn't at home.

"Ketchup?" I ask Maverick as he turns around.

"Nah, it's not my thing. I don't eat anything red," he says suggestively, forcing my stomach to roil.

I roll my eyes as I put my bun on the plate and reach for the ketchup, shaking it before continuing my conversation with Tag. "So that's why you came over—"

A loud *bang* halts my retort as something wet and cold slaps me in the face, and I jump back while trying to see anything but red. Fucking ketchup is every-damn-where.

For a brief moment there is stunned silence, then suddenly there is nothing but riotous laughter as the scene around me registers to everyone.

"I guess red *is* your thing," Maverick jokes.

Dickhead.

Tag and Wren are laughing hard enough to be in stitches right now. *Assholes.* I'm still trying to wrap my head around what the hell just happened as I wipe away the red goop from my eyes.

Ah, fuck. The shit even got on my ceiling.

Then anger bubbles up as realization sets in. She couldn't have. How would she have gotten into my house? No. I'm giving her way too much credit.

"What's wrong?" Dane asks, trying his damnedest not to laugh as my fury seeps through every feature on my face.

"I'm going to kill her," is my simple response.

Brin

I'm not surprised to see him stalking across the yard, muscles flexing as his jaw ticks. But I am surprised to see him still covered in ketchup.

All the streetlights illuminate him, but I swear he's angry enough to glow on his own. His dirty-blonde hair is smeared with red, and he looks as though he just walked out of a massacre.

My laughter breaks out before I can do anything about it, and he stops and looks through the window where I'm gripping the ledge for much needed support.

"That's what I fucking thought," he growls. "Okay. Remember this shit."

He turns around and walks away, and I drop to the ground to pray for air. But I'm just laughing too hard. It was a shitty day at work, but having this to look forward to made it bearable.

"I take it the ketchup volcano worked?" Maggie asks, amused as she struts out in her formfitting dress.

More like a ketchup bomb.

I nod when words can't form, and my laughter infects her, making it impossible for her not to join in. She rolls her eyes as she grabs her purse.

"I have to go meet Carmen. Try not to get the house burned down while I'm gone."

It physically hurts to breathe right now. I love it when my plans come together.

Maggie waves while shaking her head, a small bit of laughter still lingering in her wake. I'm glad she's found someone to date, even though she's constantly gone now. I'm actually looking forward to my date tomorrow. I almost wish it was tonight. It sucks to be here alone with nothing to do, but at least I got my nemesis back.

He's going to come back with something terrible, so I have to be prepared. I shouldn't be enjoying this as much as I am, but it's the most fun I've had in years.

Just as I grab my remote, the TV cuts out, and the power dies to the house. Did he really just do that?

My humor fades quickly, because this is crossing a line. I storm out of the house, ready to go bark at the idiot and form some boundaries for the war, when he bursts out of his door, stalking in my direction, barely recognizable under the sliver of moonlight when he gets closer.

It's then I realize the entire street is blacked out, and he looks around to notice the same thing.

"Was it her?" a guy asks from inside his house, laughter lacing his words.

"No," Mr. Sexy growls. "Whole damn neighborhood is blacked out. Let's take this to someone else's house."

He starts to say something to me, since I'm standing here at the edge of his yard and staring for no particular reason. He's still wearing ketchup. I can say that's why I'm staring, even though it's really too dark to see it.

"Can't. Just got a text to pick up some diapers. I need to go," a male's voice says—and it sounds familiar, oddly enough.

"I should go, too," another says, and they all speak over each other as bodies filter out. All I can make out are their silhouettes before I turn around.

I head back to my house, feeling a little weird just staring in the dark. It's been a while since this neighborhood has had a blackout. It's usually the bigger cities in the summer that blackout because of the heat and everyone using their air conditioning.

It's not anywhere nearly that hot, so I don't know what's going on.

Just as I settle down on my sofa and pull out my phone to call Maggie, there's a knock at the door. I start to answer, but I know who it is.

"Not in the dark," I murmur, shivering a little. He'll torture me if he finds out I'm creeped out at night when I'm here alone.

"I'm not here to get revenge just yet," he says through the door. "You have a gas hot water heater. I've fixed it for Maggie before. Mine is electric, and you've hosed me down with ketchup. It's only right you let me in to use the shower."

He's good at sounding harmless. Too bad I'm too smart for his tricks.

"Sorry. But no. You have plenty of friends' houses you can go to."

"They all just left. Most of them have shit to do tonight. Some of them aren't really friends. And besides, I'm not getting into my car with this shit all over me."

I purse my lips for several long minutes, and finally, with a reluctant sigh, I do something he's bound to make me regret.

"As long as you call a temporary truce," I say through the door, my hand hovering over the doorknob.

"Truce until I'm out of your house. Then the war resumes," he says quickly.

I doubt I can trust him on that, but I still let him in. I gasp when he rips me up from the ground and crushes me in a... hug? I'm really embarrassed when my legs try to wrap around his waist, because he drops me back down to the ground and laughs as he walks into my bathroom.

"I've got first shower," he says, shutting the door behind him. "By the way, love the new hair color."

It's then I realize what he's done. The bastard has covered me in ketchup, and made fun of my horribly bluish-gray hair. I go to pound on the door, wishing I had the strength to beat the hell out of him.

"You said truce!" I yell, glaring at the door like I can see through it.

"Believe me, that wasn't revenge. That was just a taste of what's to come."

I wish he meant that dirty. I hate him for making me wish that. Especially since I know he'd never see me that way. Guys like him go for girls like Tria Noles or Ash Masters or even Raya Capperton. They don't go for girls like me.

Instead of fuming at my bathroom door or throwing myself a pity party, I grab some clothes and head to Maggie's room. I'll just shower in there—a cold shower. Maybe he'll be gone by the time I get out.

Rye

Does this girl buy anything other than white or black cotton panties? No lace, no satin, no other color. How can someone so feisty manage to be so dull in every other way? There's no way she's getting laid if she's wearing this stuff.

She has a thousand candles, like most girls, and they're all lit throughout the room and the house, giving me a view of the sad life she leads. I should have snooped when I was cutting down her bed.

"What the hell are you doing?" she yells at me, slapping my back and then dancing around while clutching her hand as she scowls at me. "That hurt!" she barks.

I look at her as though she's lost her mind while I close her sad underwear drawer.

"You hit me," I remind her as she glares at me.

Her hair is wet and dripping down the front of her red shirt. That wouldn't be so distracting if I had gotten laid in the past few months. Damn work.

"Yeah, but you're looking through my panties!"

"That's what you call them?" I ask, sounding intentionally disappointed as I point over my shoulder, gesturing to the drawer of the dreary.

Her eyes rake over my naked chest and fall down to the pink towel clasped around my waist. Good thing I'm sexy enough to pull off any color.

She blushes while attempting to scowl, but she's too busy getting lost in her fantasies. While she's distracted, I walk by her, pretending as though I didn't just break the cardinal rule about personal boundaries. You learn a lot about someone by their underwear drawer. Poor girl has no life.

No wonder she started a war with me. It's probably the only excitement she ever gets.

"Why were you looking at my panties, and why are you wearing my towel?" she asks as she follows me out.

"Let me go grab some clothes and we'll go get something to eat," I say instead of answering her question.

Her footsteps pause, and I fight back my grin.

"Why would I go to get something to eat with you?"

"Because I'm starving and you interrupted my food, which is too cold to eat by now, and I have no way of warming it up. Get ready."

"I'm already ready," she says as I turn around.

Her hair is still wet, she's wearing very little makeup, and her clothes are two sizes too big for her. Did I mention her hair is wet?

"Just thought you might want to wear something that fits. Or maybe dry your hair."

"I prefer comfortable stuff," she says, an angry, defensive undercurrent to her tone. "And I can't dry my hair without power. I'll look like a clown if I attempt makeup by candlelight."

Sheesh. She blows my kitchen to hell with her ketchup bomb, and she's pissed at me. Hell, I didn't even point out the makeup bit. Not aloud, anyway. Well, I don't think I did.

"Fine. I'll be back in five."

I jog over to my house while still wearing her towel, and ignore the numerous whistles and mocking catcalls I hear in the darkness. At least they can't tell the damn thing is pink.

It doesn't take me long to pull on some clean, ketchup-free clothes—even though the fact I can't see a damn thing makes me uncertain about what I'm even wearing.

Several flashlight beams are littering the sidewalks when I come back out, and my feisty little neighbor is standing in my yard, her back turned to me as the moonlight gives us all the light it can produce— which isn't too much tonight.

"You could have come in," I say as I shut and lock the door.

She turns around and her arms fall to her sides.

"I'm still trying to figure out what you're about to do," she says, her eyes probably oozing skepticism, but it's too dark to see.

That's when the lights come back on, and the neighborhood comes to life as all the interrupted evenings resume. She looks up at the streetlights, and she shrugs.

"Looks like you can heat your food up now," she says while walking off.

It's like the life has suddenly been zapped out of her, but I don't say anything as she crosses the street. Well, until I see her car is still crumpled up. Now I have to speak.

"You need to get your car fixed," I call out.

That shit is dangerous. No brake lights or taillights are there right now.

"I'm working on it," she sighs, and then she disappears into her house.

Oh well. So much for eating out. At least now I have plenty of time to plot my next attack.

Chapter 3

Rye

She's going to be so pissed when she finds the little surprise I left for her. My stupid grin only grows. I feel like a kid right now.

I hate early mornings, so it's rare that I ever go in before ten. But this morning I have too much to do, so I'm heading in at the ungodly hour of six. I'm already running late, but I can't leave until I hear her—

"Shit!" she screams, a loud clattering following her squeals of terror as her feet scurry in panic across the house.

Fuck yeah!

I bought the nastiest looking tarantula I could find at the pet store after I ate my reheated burger, and then I put it in her room while she was sleeping. Maggie is quickly becoming my favorite accomplice. I think she's enjoying watching this little war.

I'm sure as hell enjoying partaking in it.

My laughter comes out in thick spurts as I make my way across her lawn, and her door jerks open as she yells at me. "Bastard! I let you borrow my shower, and this is what you do?"

I just laugh harder as I make it to my car.

"Sorry, tiger. Couldn't resist."

"Come get it out of my room. It's on my bed!" she yells, standing there with her hair a complete wreck while wearing the most embarrassing pajamas known to man. Are those unicorns on flannel? Oh good grief.

"Not happening," I chirp while opening the door to my car. "Have fun with your new pet. I named him Killer."

She runs to grab the garden hose from beside her house, and I crank the Range Rover and toss it in reverse, trying to hurry before she gets me, and laughing my ass off the whole time. When I throw it in drive, I glance in the rearview mirror to see her running with that hose in her hand until it reaches its limit and jerks her backwards.

My laughter only pours out harder, and I finally turn on my air to kill the heat trapped in my car.

"Fuck!" spews out of my mouth as the pink flecks from hell blow out and cover me.

Glitter? Fucking glitter? How did she get glitter into my air vents? My car stays locked!

I can't go back home because that crazy girl will be waiting. She probably prepared for my return. No. I refuse to give her the satisfaction of seeing me wear this... fucking sparkling shit, or shooting me with her damn garden hose.

I curse like a madman as I drive to work, groaning every time more glitter falls from my body. My ride is going to be a bitch to clean up.

I park quickly, hoping no one sees me like this... But my shitty luck continues.

Tag is here, waiting for me. I forgot I was supposed to take in Ash's car for upgrades today.

The grin that unfolds on his face taunts me before his merciless laughter.

"What happened to you? Just get back from Never Never Land, Tinker Bell?"

I hate him.

"Don't start," I growl, which of course makes him laugh harder as he follows me into the garage office.

He stands at the doorway, doubled over in laughter, and I turn to glare at him as more pink glitter falls to the floor. Christ. That shit is going to be everywhere.

"Are you coming, or are you going to stand here and laugh all fucking morning?"

He has to grip the wall when his body buckles from his laughter.

"Go on without me, Tink. I'll just follow your pixie dust trail. Peter Pan might need your help."

I roll my eyes while clenching my fists.

"Fuck you," I grumble, watching his body continue to shake with his mocking roars.

"Easy, boy," he taunts. "Someone needs to calm down, and *think happy thoughts*," he says, singing the last part in a child's sort of tone.

Even I have to stifle my grin. The girl is crafty. I underestimated her. How is she breaking into all my stuff?

"Are you done yet? I thought you came here to get work done to your wife's car." I cross my arms over my chest as he slowly straightens back up, his laughter only barely tapering off.

"As long as the Lost Boys can spare you, then yes. I'd like some stuff done to Ash's car before her birthday."

I groan while rolling my eyes, and he laughs harder while taking a chair.

"I take it she won this round?" he asks.

By comparison, my tarantula prank sucks. And I was proud of that, too. Damn it.

"Yeah," I grumble. Especially since I didn't see it coming.

We've been going back and forth, but she had to have planned this before she found the spider, considering I was there when she found the damn thing. Shit.

I refuse to let her win this prank war, and right now, the numbers are in her favor.

Rye

"What the hell is that?" Wren asks, wrinkling his nose as he walks in.

"Mayonnaise and donuts," I answer, looking at him as though it should be obvious. I squeeze in more of the nasty filling, imagining the look of pure disgusted horror she'll have when she takes a big bite.

The donut swells, and I take the tube out to move on to the next.

"Are you using a calk gun to do that?" he asks through a snicker.

"I didn't exactly have anything else on hand." I shrug, glancing around my office like that should be obvious, and then I look back down to resume the task at hand.

"So the girl puts a dirty movie on the side of your house and blows up a bottle of ketchup in your kitchen, and your idea of revenge is to give her gross donuts?" he asks, shaking his head in disappointment. "Weak."

He doesn't even know about the glitter explosion.

The donut idea is weak. But I need time to fully form something massive.

"The donuts are just part of the prank," I lie, trying to save face. "There's more to come. What are you doing here?"

I look up from my sad donuts that now don't feel good enough for the war. Damn him for ruining this for me.

"Just walked out on the blind date from hell. I love Tria and Ash for trying to get me back in the game, but I swear they are terrible at picking girls. Besides, I'm not really ready to date yet."

Considering his ex-wife screwed his brother, I get that. What I don't understand is why he married her if he couldn't get past it.

"Better get a date for the weekend. Ash will have several girls at their party to set you up with otherwise. She does it to me every time, and she's terrible at picking girls. The last chick she set me up was smoking hot."

I pause as I move a donut around, and Wren assumes that's the end of my statement. "Sounds brutal," he mutters.

I laugh while getting back on track with filling all twelve of the surprise desserts.

"Her looks weren't the problem. The girl had a voice like she was on helium, and if I said something that sounded like the line of a song, she'd sing the whole song. This happened about every ten minutes. I was drunk and still couldn't tolerate it."

Wren snickers while sitting down in front of me, and I close the lid on the pathetic prank. I'll come up with something better when I have more time.

"Well, she keeps setting me up with *nice* girls. It doesn't matter how they look as long as they're nice. I'm not shallow by any means, but I don't want to go out on a date with a girl who has more muscle than I do no matter how nice she is. This last girl could have bench-pressed me."

I burst out laughing while leaning back in my chair, and he continues. "The girl before that had an issue with the number four. I don't know why either. But she'd count her steps and jump over the fourth step as though there was an invisible hole in the way. And I couldn't say four words or words that had only four letters. That did it for me, because if I want to say *fuck*, then I'm going to say fuck. Oddly enough, she told me it wouldn't work between us because my name only had four letters. Yes, I was dumped by her."

My laughter grows while he smiles. Ash is a sweet girl with a real big heart. She just tries too hard to make us find what she and Tag have. She keeps having faith in me when no one else does. It's sweet, but she's crazy if she thinks the love they have is for everyone.

What they have would give most people hope. But I've seen the nasty side of love, the dark side most people don't even whisper about. Love isn't something I want or need in my life.

Besides, my life is good—no rules, no drama, no problems. I can get what I need when I need it, but I don't have to have someone in my house all the time.

"Which is why I'm here," Wren says, confusing me as I pull out of my silent reverie.

"What?" I ask, showing him how puzzled I am. What were we even talking about?

He blows out a breath while propping his elbows on his knees.

"I'm supposed to go out with another *nice* girl tonight, but I can't. I have something else that I really need to take care of. Something big. But you know how Ash is. She'll ask a thousand questions if I call and cancel, because they're planning to meet me at Silk in thirty minutes. Sorry for the short notice, but I need to take care of this, so I need you to go in my place."

The humor that was in his face earlier has been washed away by something else. He looks tense, and he's a little pale.

"What's going on?" I ask, all my humor fleeing as well.

"Something I don't feel like talking about. Will you go on the date in my place? I'll fill you in later if anything comes of this. Ash will let me off the hook a little easier if you're there."

I nod as he stands, and I stand, too.

"You know you can call if you need me," I say lamely.

Wren didn't even look this defeated when he and Erica got divorced. It has me worried.

"I know. And I will call. But only after I have details. Try to have fun. Maybe this girl allows four-lettered words," he says, forcing a smile.

I puff out a laugh as he walks out, and then I dial Tag.

"You'd better not have fucked up my wife's car," he says distractedly, the keys of a laptop rattling in the background.

"Your wife's car is still getting fucked up as we speak," I say mildly, earning a small laugh from him. "Looks like I'm filling in for Wren tonight."

The keyboard rattling stops, and Tag lets out a sigh that tells me he knows more than I do. That sucks. I know they're closer, but Wren and I are close enough for him to trust me with this. I've trusted him with all my fucked-up shit, and there's nothing he could tell me that would even come close to what he knows about me.

"He said he was going to get someone to take his place because he doesn't want Ash knowing anything is going on. I don't think this girl is really your type, so you'll have to work hard to play nice."

"What the hell does that mean?" I ask, closing the door to my office.

At least I was able to shower the glitter off me—mostly. I'm thankful the locker rooms I had installed have awesome showers. And I'm also glad that I had a few changes of clothes on hand for the sake of an emergency.

This girl will have to deal with jeans and a T-shirt. I don't have time to go home and change.

"Here," I say, handing Jessica—my assistant—the donuts. "Take these to the house across the street from me and leave them with a girl named Maggie."

She nods as she walks away, and I return my attention Tag. "Well," I prompt when he still doesn't answer.

"Sorry. I was trying to get this email typed and sent before leaving. What I meant was, this girl isn't a Victoria's Secret supermodel."

Ah. "So she's a dog."

He chuckles as I climb in my car. I have it cranked and moving down the road as he instructs his workers about what to do next. The suspense is killing me. At this rate, I'll be at Silk before he can answer.

"No," he says at last. He's closer to Dane's famous club than I am. It's too early to be at a damn club. It'll be hard to give the girl the slip when she gets on my nerves if the club is empty.

"Care to elaborate?" I ask as he talks business a second longer.

"Sorry. It's crazy this week. But she's not a dog. She's cute, but that's it. She's sweet and possibly too nice for you."

Too nice for me? I play that over in my head, trying to decide if I should be offended or not.

"What the hell does that mean?" I growl, deciding to be offended.

"That means you like the wild ones, and this girl is the definition of... well, sweet. She's not the kind of girl who is going to tie you up and steal your wallet in the middle of the night. She's going to make you breakfast in bed. Ash thought she was perfect for Wren."

So Wren gets the sweet girls with a good heart, and I get the crazy girls with a banging bod.

"Maybe I like breakfast in bed," I mumble like a sulking baby.

His laughter pisses me off as I pull up at the club, and seconds later, I see his Mercedes pulling up. He talks to me on the phone, even though I can see him.

"She's not the porn-star babe you normally go for," he says. "That's all I'm saying."

I put my phone down as we near each other before I say, "You have *no* room to talk. Your wife looks like every guy's fantasy."

43

He glares at me as he decides how to answer, and then he shrugs. "True. But she's also pretty fucking incredible. She's more than a pretty face."

Fucking dick. He gets it all, but I'm shallow for expecting as much of my dates?

"Sounds like a double standard," I grumble, following him into the loud club.

He just laughs as we make our way through the crowded bodies. It's only eight at night, but you'd think it was midnight with this many people crowding the place.

"Why are there so many people here?" I yell, letting my voice carry over the music.

I didn't notice that many cars parked out front. Then I hear him— Tag's cousin. Base Masters is jamming away on the stage, and I shake my head as to say *never mind* when Tag turns to answer.

Base's group, *The Fallen*, are always a big draw for this area.

"Hey," Rain Sterling, the sexiest blonde I know, says as she comes closer.

Dane Sterling is an ass for having her, but she comes with drama tattooed on her forehead. "Hey," I say as Tag walks off, leaving me behind.

"Ash said you were coming. I'm surprised she thinks you and Brin will be a good match, but I'm proud of you for getting your head out of your ass and wanting a real woman instead of one the shallow girls you've been dating."

Glad her opinion of me is so high.

"Thanks," I mutter dryly, not bothering to mention that I'm merely standing in for Wren.

"She's so sweet and so pretty," she says, and that makes me cringe.

Girls only call other girls *pretty* when they're ugly as hell. Wren owes me for this.

"We're taking a break. You guys are awesome," Base Masters says into the microphone, waving at his crazed fans as he hops down from the stage. I can't believe Tag didn't tell me his cousin was in town.

"There they are," Rain says, guiding me toward the group standing at the bar as Dane talks to them.

Dane eyes me when he sees Rain's hand on my arm, and I do what I can to move away from her grip. Rain Sterling—who used to be Rain Noles—is one girl I've never tried getting with because of that dick. Even when we were kids I knew better. Ethan—her cousin—always told me she and Dane would end up married.

The only body in our group that I don't know is the one with her back turned. Her waist is hugged by a semi-tight dress. It stops mid-thigh to show her short, lightly tanned legs. But it's her perky ass that gives me the most hope.

Her hair is down and shoulder-length. It's a light brown that I don't normally care for, but I can play nice for a night.

"Wren had something to do," Ash says to the girl as the club DJ prepares to play music and kill the silence. "But Rye is cool."

I'm cool. Wow. That's like saying they see no hope in this going anywhere. Not that I'm looking for a relationship, but I'd like for Ash to build me up a little better than that.

45

Tag walks over and hands me a Corona, and I take a long sip, reaching for the ability to bite my tongue.

"Rye," Ash says with a smile.

The girl beside her turns around, and my beer spews from my lips, soaking Tag who curses me. You've got to be fucking kidding me.

Brin

Ah, hell. What did I do in a past life for karma to punish me so brutally?

Staring at Mr. Sexy who is just as shocked as I am, I almost cry. I should have known better than to think someone like Wren Prize wanted to go out on a date with me. But I had no idea he'd be affiliated with someone like Mr. Sexy—er, I mean, Rye.

Rye? What the hell kind of name is that? Is this the same Rye I've heard them talking about?

Of course it is. It's highly unlikely this group knows two guys named Rye.

"You two look... shocked," Tag says, smiling with mild amusement. "Do you know each other?"

Rye wipes his mouth with the back of his hand, still somewhat coughing on the drink that strangled him when he saw my face.

"Yeah," he says dryly. "She's my neighbor."

Tag looks from me to him several times, and then suddenly his laughter pours out just before Dane Sterling joins in, his laughter roaring out as well.

"The guy who put a spider in your room?" Ash asks, her lips

46

curled in amusement, at the same time that Dane asks, "The girl who left you the ketchup bomb?"

"Yes," Rye and I say in unison, glaring at each other like the war is about to take place here and now.

"Fucking unbelievable." Tag laughs harder, doubling over. "So the girl who turned you into Tinker Bell is Brin? Sweet little Brin Waters?"

It's doubtful Mr. Sexy even knew my name. I didn't know he was Rye Clanton. Hell, I've heard them talk about him numerous times, and never had a clue it was the same guy who lived across the street from me.

"She's not sweet," Rye growls, his eyes narrowing on me as everyone else joins in on the heckling.

Apparently they think I'm this sweet little girl who couldn't possibly break into a guy's house, steal his keys, and blow glitter through a hose and into his air vents. That took hours to do, by the way, and I still have glitter tickling the back of my throat when I inhaled by accident.

It looks like he got rid of most of it, but every so often the light hits his hair just right to show a few shimmers are still in there.

"Need a drink?" Rain asks me, moving her perfect blonde hair out of her face.

"I need a really strong drink," I mumble, moving past her to get it myself.

I feel so stupid. It was bad enough before he showed up. Now Rye knows Wren didn't want to go on a date with me. The last thing I need is my enemy knowing I can't even get a date when it's set up for me.

"Vodka. Straight up," I say to the bartender, hoping I'm saying it right.

I never drink liquor very often, so I have no idea what to order. The guy works quickly, considering there are a slew of people calling out orders. He hands me mine, and I reach for my purse.

"Put it on my tab," a deep, familiar voice says over my shoulder.

"Yes, sir, Mr. Clanton," the bartender says with a nod.

I turn to see Rye just as I take a sip of my vodka. Oh wow. This is the good stuff. I still make a face, but usually I spit alcohol back out.

"I can pay for my own drinks," I say to the man who is studying me too hard.

"You're supposed to be my date," he replies with a shrug.

He motions for me to walk in front of him, and I take another sip, praying it drowns out the humiliation. I need less attractive and less rich friends. Maybe then something like this wouldn't happen because I'd be on my own playing field.

"I'm supposed to be Wren Prize's date. I guess he sent you to deal with the riffraff."

I aim for casual, but I sound wounded. Shit. *Show no weakness, Brin.*

"Wren had shit to take care of. Though he didn't feel as though he could confide in me. I'm here because he didn't want you to feel stood up. How the hell do you know everybody?"

He continues studying me, and I take a deep breath. I got as dressed up as I felt comfortable with for this date, trying to look like I belonged in this crowd. I wish I had my jeans and T-shirt on right now. He looks so casual and at ease, and I'm wearing a black dress I

48

borrowed from Maggie.

It's hard to be me when I'm dressed like someone else. I really need to buy new clothes. Since my divorce, I've lost a good deal of weight, and now all of my clothes are too big—as Mr. Jerk Face pointed out.

"I met Tria a while back, and she sort of introduced me around. I don't really know their men very well, but I know the girls."

I look around just as the music dies down, and the band takes the stage once again. The lead singer is young, but incredibly sexy.

"Too young for you," Rye says, drawing my attention.

He motions toward the stage with his beer to let me know what he's talking about. One look at the guy all the girls are screaming over, and I laugh.

"I realize that, but I'm not exactly old." Even though I feel forty. Then I turn to face him better.

"You don't have to hang out with me. You had no idea your date was going to be the troll across the road. Go have fun. I'm about to sneak out."

Just as I drink down my last few sips, he tugs my elbow.

"Nope. You're not going to go play Ms. Hermit. You're staying because Ash will think I said something to piss you off."

Great. He thinks I'm a hermit. He'd be horrified if I told him my favorite part of the day has become our pranks.

"Don't be nice. It makes me feel pathetic."

He laughs as he drops his arm over my shoulders.

"It's a temporary truce. You loaned me your shower; now I'm

making you have fun. Besides, you made me eat alone after you promised you'd have dinner with me."

I would have killed for one of those burgers, but the second the lights came on, I stood there feeling awkward, and he said nothing. I just excused myself to make things more comfortable.

Is he trying to be my friend right now? Or is he just being friendly?

I hate my life.

"Rye Clanton," a girl purrs from somewhere close by.

I turn to see her just as her chest is jutted in my face. She has a good five inches on me, making her at least 5'8.

Rye grins while facing her as well, his eyes flicking down to her chest to see her very exposed cleavage. She's got me beat there, too. I'm lucky to fill out a handful. As if she needs anymore perfection, her hair is as long and shiny blonde as it can be.

I hate her already.

"Cassandra," he drawls, running his eyes over her body.

I almost gag. I so don't have to be here for this.

I start to walk away when she scoffs, "It's Cassie."

That makes me stifle a smile. He's about to get a drink thrown in his face. Just to watch the show, I turn back around.

"I thought Cassie was just short for Cassandra," he says, recovering from his slip as though it's effortless.

This time I do gag.

She looks at me, appraising me with a skeptical eye.

"And your friend?" she asks, obviously convinced I'm not his type.

Damn. I thought I looked pretty good in this dress. I may not meet supermodel status, but I look better than usual. I just wish it was in my comfort zone.

"This is Brin," he says, pulling me back to him. "She's my date for the night."

Yeah... I'm as shocked as she is that he just said that. Her eyebrows are trying to hit her hairline right now.

"Didn't know you were seeing anyone," she says dryly.

"First date. I should get going. I'll catch up with you another time." He puts his arm back around my shoulders and guides me toward the rest of the group.

"You didn't have to do that. I repeat: I'm not really your date."

"Stop saying that," he scolds lightly. "Tonight I'm your date. And despite what you might think, I don't ditch my date to hit on other girls."

My eyes move to his lips, and I stare for a fraction of a second too long. "Let's dance," he says, smiling down at me.

Since I love dancing, I don't hesitate. I may not can wow a stage with my graceful finesse, but that doesn't matter here. In a club like this, dancing is just sex with clothes on, and I can handle that.

Rye

Cassandra... Er, Cassie looked ripe for the picking, but Brin would have taken it personally. The girl needs to have fun and enjoy life. I wonder if she ever dates.

I should kick Wren's ass for bailing on her and not giving her a reason.

We make our way to the center of the floor, and I pull her to me as I start to move. She doesn't hesitate to grind her hips against me, and it shocks the fuck out of me. Christ, she can move that body. There's nothing *sweet* about her right now.

When she turns and presses her ass into me, I might groan. A little. I wasn't expecting my feisty, cute little neighbor who dresses in clothes too big for her, and tortures the hell out of me to be grinding on my cock right now. I certainly wasn't expecting to be hard as a damn rock.

She pushes against me and stretches her arm up, wrapping her soft hand around the back of my neck as our bodies writhe together. There's no doubt that she feels what she's doing to me, and I'm starting to worry there's a prank in here somewhere.

My arms go around her waist as I bend over, pulling her to me, and we dance like we're not both scheming for the other's next disaster.

She's always been my quiet neighbor until this past week. Then she turned into my enemy. Then it became a fun war that excites and infuriates me in the same breath. But until this moment, I've never thought about her as anything more.

There's something about touching her, feeling her body fold to mine as we both squash our feud for a few songs… My mind is in *all* the wrong places. And that can't happen. We're neighbors.

I have two rules: Don't fuck where you live or where you work. I'm not breaking those rules because of how good her ass feels against me right now, or because she knows exactly how to drive me out of my fucking mind with her hips.

I never expected this, and I'm kicking Wren's ass later for putting me in this mind-fuck.

My lips brush her ear as the seductive music drives us. I don't dance. I fucking hate dancing unless the promise of sex is there. Why did I even suggest this?

She's so short that I have to bend every time I want my lips to touch her, and I stick to her ear because it seems safe enough. "You want a drink?" I ask when I come too damn close to taking her neck instead of her ear.

"Yeah," she says, grinning as she turns around. "Then you have to dance with me some more. This is fun."

I can't help but smile, because I've never seen someone so happy about something so small as dancing. If I could move without being in pain, I'd dance with her all night. But my cock needs a break.

"Come on," I say, laughing when she starts dancing all by herself.

I take her hand and we weave through the crowd to where our group is gathered in a corner booth. Unfortunately, two familiar faces are walking up to join them. Shit. Now Kode and Tria are here. He really hates me.

"Brin!" Tria says excitedly, waving and drawing the attention of blonde douche as well. Crap.

Kode's eyes narrow on me just as Tria pulls him behind her to meet us when we reach the stairs to the elevated area. Brin and Tria hug and talk, both of them smiling. Then Ash calls to her.

Brin takes the shot glass handed to her by Ash, and she shoots it quickly. But her adorable scowl forms, and I can't help but stifle a laugh. Tag hands me a glass of whiskey. Correction, scotch.

"You two sitting down or dancing some more?" Ash asks, her grin growing.

They're getting the wrong idea. Brin might be making me hard, but I'm not fucking her. She's just my neighbor.

"Dancing," Brin says with a laugh, tugging my hand and forcing my drink to slosh over the edges. I'm forced down the stairs by her surprisingly strong grip, but I don't fight her.

I chuckle as I follow her, wishing I wasn't having such a damn good time. It's so... easy right now. Since I'm not trying to fuck her, there's no pressure to be suave or persuasive. I can just dance and pretend as though the growth in my pants isn't painful.

This would be a lot more fun if her ass didn't feel so good on my crotch. When she laughs for no reason other than the fact she's having fun, I can't help but smile. I don't know if I've ever seen her smile when she wasn't torturing me. It's actually a damn good smile.

Rye

After forty minutes, I'm sweating and my dick is begging for mercy. We've downgraded from liquor to beer, both of us holding our fresh bottles while we dance on the floor. I lean down just as Brin turns around.

"Ow!" she screeches while grabbing her head.

I mimic the reaction, rubbing the sore spot she left on me after our skulls collide. Fucking hell. As if the alcohol wasn't going to leave me with a painful enough headache.

"We called truce," she growls, staggering a little from the large amount of alcohol she has put inside her small body.

"You think I did that on purpose?" I ask incredulously.

She steps toward me, her spiteful little glower almost making me laugh. Almost. I'm distracted when she presses her tits against me in order to try and be intimidating.

She's not intimidating. Not even a little bit.

She looks past me, and then glances down at her watch. "Ah, hell. I didn't realize it was so late."

I glance down at my phone to check the time, and frown. It's not even ten yet.

"Late?" I ask as she staggers again.

"Yeah. I have to be at the museum at five in the morning to catalogue a new exhibit. Shit. I should go."

She starts walking, and I follow. She's crazy if she thinks she's driving in this shape.

"You can't drive," I say loudly, trying to shout over Base's loud singing.

"There are always cabs waiting out front. This place is easy pickings for fare."

She comes here often? I've never seen her here, and I come regularly. Of course, it's usually well after *ten* when I get here. Damn early bird.

I follow her to the booth, and she starts hugging the girls, bidding them all farewell as I hang back and sip my still nearly full beer. She then turns back to me and her smile actually does something fucked up to me.

I've had too much to drink.

"Thanks," she says sweetly. "For dancing with me, I mean."

I shrug, acting as though she hasn't given me the worst hard-on ever.

"No big deal. Dates dance," I say casually.

Of course I usually fuck after dancing—on the rare occasion that I dance. Not tonight. Not with her.

She starts to walk away, and again I follow, until she stops abruptly and I have to do one hell of a maneuver to keep from running over her.

"What are you doing?" she asks as she turns around.

"Walking you out and paying for your cab."

What does she think I'm doing?

She laughs as though I've said something funny.

"That's not necessary. I paid for a cab here, and I can pay for my cab home. I don't trust you. I might end up in Arizona if I let you anywhere near the cabby."

"Fine," I say again, even though it's irking the hell out of me. "Then… I guess… Well, I'll see you at home… Er… I mean… You know what I mean."

I curse myself for suddenly sounding like a nervous kid. What the hell is in my beer?

"Yep," she says with a growing grin. "And something nice will be waiting for you."

For a second, that sounds dirty, but in the next breath, it sounds terrifying. What has the devil woman done now?

I start to speak, when she slaps the bottom of her beer against the top rim of mine, and my beer starts foaming and bubbling out, distracting me as I try to pull the bottle away from me before my drink gets all over my clothes. When I look up, her head is thrown back as she laughs and walks away.

Tag comes up beside me and sips his beer while joining me in gazing after the little pain in my ass. He's not scowling like me, though. Now I need a new beer.

"I can't tell if you want to fuck her or throttle her," Tag says, the smug bastard sounding amused.

My eyes land on her ass that suddenly seems so much more tempting than it did yesterday.

"Yeah, well, that makes two of us," I mutter dryly, hoping he didn't really hear that.

Watching her hips sway like I'm entranced is actually pissing me off. She'd better not ever wear a dress again. Any dress at all.

I really don't like this.

Chapter 4

Brin

"So you went on a date with Mr. Sexy?" Maggie asks in disbelief as I slowly peel off the high heels that have tortured my feet all day.

She was gone when I got home last night, and she was still asleep when I left this morning.

"Well, only because Wren Prize realized he was way out of my league before I even got there. He probably googled me."

She snorts out a laugh as I collapse to the chair, too tired to move. I hate new exhibits.

"Believe me, that can't be the case. I've met his ex-wife. She was a moody bitch. One day she'd be incredibly sweet, and the next she'd be a total snob."

With this crowd, it's all about the total package usually. They want the shell to be just as pretty as what's inside. I'm surprised he married someone that cheated on him with his brother, but I'm not surprised that she was a beauty queen.

I'm just… me. A little plain and certainly nothing extraordinary. I was never the girl that drew the men in, especially if there were any other girls around. Sterling Shore is frigging loaded with girls who look like they just stepped out of a Paul Colton fashion magazine. I married one of the three guys I dated in high school.

"But she had all the Sterling sparkle," I sigh, glancing over to see a very tempting box of donuts.

I'm starving. I haven't eaten since breakfast. But they're so far away, and my feet hurt so badly. And since when does Maggie buy donuts? She's a health fanatic.

I start to ask when she says, "You can always get the *Sterling sparkle*, too."

This time I'm the one to snort out a laugh. "And be someone I'm not? No thank you. I'd rather find a guy who likes the real me. Plastic surgery is so out of the question. Some girls are born to be beautiful and wear dresses like the one I borrowed from you, and some girls are like me. I like going out without a lot of makeup, or sexy hair, or high heels, or even anything special. That's who I am. I wish I was like you, or Rain, or Tria, or Ash, but I'm not. I'm also fine with that."

I once thought I found a guy who loved me the way I was. And then he decided he wanted a life full of the glamorous things. He didn't cheat on me, but he sure as hell made me feel like an idiot for ever trusting him. I guess people change.

Donut. I need a donut.

Using more energy than I care to admit, I heave myself off the couch and wearily strut to the kitchen counter that is holding the tasty promise.

"When did you get these?" I ask, opening the box.

Oh, heaven has found me. Cream filled.

"Last night. Not too long after you left," she says mildly. "Did you ever catch the monster spider?"

Stupid, big, scary spider.

"No, but at least I found out that it's not poisonous. I looked it up. I wouldn't have been able to sleep if I hadn't."

I pick up the first donut as I walk back to the chair, ready to unwind and eat the delicious morsel in my hand without any guilt.

"So was he good as a date?" she asks, sounding all too eager for details I don't have.

"He was nice enough. We danced, drank, and enjoyed the fact that it's a damn small world. But other than that, nothing special. He probably went after another girl that did have the sparkle after I left, but he was polite enough to pretend to be my date for the night. He's apparently not as big of a dick as I thought," I say, and then I bite down into the glazed heaven that—

I start gagging and coughing as something gross ruptures and coats my mouth. What disgusting hell is this?

Maggie starts laughing as I dive off the chair and rush to the sink, spitting out a glob of the white nastiness that is mingling with bile. Then I turn the sink on and put my mouth straight under the faucet, praying for a reprieve from the offensive substance.

Is that... mayonnaise?

Maggie's cackles are only growing louder as I continue to rinse, spit, and repeat. Once most of the grossness is gone, I grab a banana from the bar and start chomping on it, praying it hurries and gets rid of the lingering taste before I vomit.

I glare at the traitor who is rolling off the couch, heaving for air as her body writhes from the riotous laughter.

"You did this?" I ask through another mouthful of banana.

"Of... course... not," she says through her chuckles.

Then I glare at my front door, contemplating doing something foul right now. I was too busy to do anything to him today. Damn. Next time I'll make time.

"That's it. If you want to be a part of this war, then I'm about to start including you," I growl.

She stands and shakes her head, still laughing. "Oh no. I'm Switzerland. I don't want to be involved."

"Being Switzerland means you're neutral. You're not frigging neutral. You're a traitor—Benedict Arnold."

She only laughs harder while sitting back down on the couch, clutching her side as though it hurts.

I'll pay him back. I just need to think of something good. His mayonnaise donut prank was actually lame compared to my glitter prank. I'm still out in front. I think. Well, his blue dye trap did make me go to the hair stylist before my *date*.

"I'm going to take a shower. Then I'm kicking your ass," I mumble, ignoring her snickers as I head to my room.

It takes less than two minutes to strip down and get in the shower. Stepping under the warm water after a terrible day is always comforting. I've been in a stiff skirt, an itchy jacket, and a ruffled blouse all day. I look drabber than a ninety-year-old librarian when I go to work.

After washing the day away, I step out, wrap a towel around me and my wet hair, and set to work finding something comfortable to wear. As soon as I open my panty drawer, a scream bubbles out as a hairy beast stares at me.

61

Perverted spider!

"Shoo!" I urge, acting like the damn thing has a clue what I'm saying.

It runs toward me, and I leap backwards, stumbling and falling onto my grounded bed. This guy is going to be the death of me. But I'll be the death of him first. Game on.

With cautious and careful maneuvers, I grab a glass from my dresser and time my attack just right. With a quick slam, I've got the monster pinned under the glass, and a sigh of triumph graces my lips. Now I just have to get him out of my room.

How the hell do I do that? When it jumps under the glass, forcing me to squeal, I consider giving it the damn room and moving out.

"You okay?" Maggie asks, sounding so damn entertained.

"Just caught Killer," I announce, keeping a wary eye on the spider that could just be pretending to be captured.

"The spider?" she squeaks.

I should transport this thing to her panty drawer and let it terrorize her. But I don't need two wars going on at once, so I refrain.

"Yep."

I'll deal with the spider later. Right now I just want to dry my hair, collapse onto my broken bed, and then maybe read or rest.

Nah. I'll be scheming. That's what I want to do.

My smile grows as I head to the bathroom and unwind my hair from the towel. I grab the hairdryer and turn it on, but another stupid scream leaves my lips, forcing me to inhale the vicious white powder that sprays me and the rest of the bathroom.

I'm going to kill him!

"What'd he do?" Maggie cackles, relishing every second of her spectator's seat.

The distinct smell tells me it's baby powder that just attacked me. Asshole. I hate baby powder. How did he get it into my hairdryer?

Maggie's laughter grows louder when she's suddenly in the room with me, looking over my tragic state. My hair is spattered, and with it being wet, the powder is matting against it. That's going to be a bitch to get out.

My eyes are barely squinted slits that are surrounded by the white hell that is covering my face, and only a thin line of my lips is visible.

I really wish I had dried off better. The water just made it stick to me too well. I hate him. Hate him. Hate him. Hate him.

"Are you growling?" Maggie asks, and I glare at her.

"Maybe." A puff of powder blows away from my lips with the word.

She turns away, her snickering lingering in her wake, and I reach under my counter for supplies. Tomorrow is Saturday. I don't have to work, which means the ultimate revenge will be mine. And I won't stop at one prank. Nope. Not tomorrow.

Tomorrow I'll show him what war really looks like.

Brin

The shower is steaming up the bathroom, and only a small amount is escaping through the crack left by the window. I finish pouring out the last of the baby oil on the tile floor. The off-key humming is annoying, but I ignore it as I go on about my task, making sure every last drop of the second bottle comes out.

My phone buzzes as I slowly shut the door, quietly letting it click into place, and then I tie the rope to the doorknob, checking that it's securely attached to the bed at the other end. I make my way toward the front as my phone starts buzzing again.

Seeing no reason to leave the way I came in, I unlock the front door and stroll out without a problem. Then I head to the cracked window as I answer the buzzing phone in my pocket.

My supplies are waiting, and I start assembling my arsenal as I talk.

"Yeah," I say without looking at the phone.

"So, we're having a party tonight," Ash says, surprising me. "We were supposed to have it last night, but it was cancelled because of the possibility of rain. But Wren's going to be here. Can you come? He really does want to meet you. Especially now that he knows you're the one tormenting the hell out of Rye."

I start pulling the zip ties on all the bottles of trigger-pull air fresheners—making sure they don't start spraying just yet—and I answer, "Ah. So knowing I'm a little crazy turns him on?"

She laughs as the humming continues, and I prop against the side of the house, waiting patiently.

"No. He wanted to meet you the other night, but he had someone call him. He's a little bummed, but I know seeing you will snap him out of it. I think it has to do with Erica. Tag won't give me details. He's loyal like that."

It's been a year since my divorce and I'm just now ready to start dating. It's just been a short period of time since he and his ex split up. Even less time has passed since the actual divorce. Is he even ready to date? Or is Ash pushing me on him?

"Um... I don't—"

"Please," she interrupts.

I sigh hard as the humming changes, and I smile when I recognize the song. Base Masters sung that song the other night—while we danced.

"Sure," I say finally.

She rattles on about the time and place, and I nod as though she can see me... until the water shuts off.

"I've got to go," I whisper. "But I'll call you back later."

I hang up before she can grill me, and I wait until I hear the sound of a yelp and a crash before I toss in the first air-freshener grenade. I grab the second, pulling the zip-tie until the spray comes out continuously, and toss it in.

Yells and threats ensue from inside the bathroom as my laughter bubbles out, and I continue throwing them, one right after another.

"Fucking stop!" he yells, as though I'm going to listen. "What'd you do to my fucking floor?"

The baby oil keeps his feet from finding traction, and I hear him crashing and thudding as he yelps in agony with each fall.

"This is for the baby powder," I gloat, tossing in two more cans. "Now we're even!"

Several things crash to the ground, and he curses more as the cans continue spraying.

"Damn you!"

I cackle while running away, ignoring the numerous curious looks from the neighbors as I make my great escape. I made sure he didn't have any scissors or knives to cut the ties, and that's the only way to shut them off once those things are tightened.

He can take as many showers as he wants, but he'll still smell like seven different fragrances for a while. I love revenge. It's not bittersweet; it's fucking delicious.

I shut and lock the front door, still laughing as I go to the window.

"What'd you do?" Maggie asks, joining me and acting just as excited as I am.

"Febreeze grenades," I say through my laughter, almost dancing from side to side as I watch his bathroom window. I'm so glad it's on the front of the house.

We both watch in anticipation, and then the moment I've been waiting for happens. The bathroom window goes up, and a body with a towel drops out.

Hey! That's my pink—

"Why does he have a pink towel?" Maggie asks, laughing.

"That's my towel," I pout. Damn. Now it's going to stink like too much air freshener. He can keep it.

"Pink's really his color," Maggie muses, and I tilt my head, appreciating his failed attempt to keep the towel around him as he tries to get up, his body glistening from the baby oil bath. But he does get it reattached before I can get a full frontal.

His back has just as many tattoos as his front, and when he faces us again, the sun glimmers against the piercing in his nipple.

Oh damn. This wasn't supposed to be sexy.

"Drooling," Maggie says in a singsong voice, grinning at me, and I clap my mouth shut.

Rye looks around, his eyes glaring in my direction. Mrs. Patterson smiles and waves at him as she walks her dog, taking small, slow, very hesitant steps as she openly gawks.

Rye shakes his head and walks back toward his front door where he pushes against it, only to stumble backwards. Yep. I locked it on my way out.

I'm a genius. Or a maniacal fiend. Depending on what kind of mind frame you have.

When his head drops back in exhausted defeat, I might giggle a little. His only option is another window, which he moves to. I left it unlocked. I'm very considerate like that.

After shoving it up and drawing more attention from the neighbors, he hoists himself in. One problem... the pink towel falls off, and I get a very mouthwatering, heart-stopping, incredible view of his perfectly sculpted ass as he throws himself inside.

Mrs. Patterson loses the hold on her dog's leash, and Skip runs off, barking at nothing as he rejoices his freedom.

I'm still staring just like the perverted lady on the street, both of us gawking at a window he's long since abandoned.

"After a show like that, Mrs. Patterson is going to need a new pacemaker," Maggie jokes, eliciting a small snicker from me. "You know there will be hell to pay," she adds.

I narrow my eyes, glaring at her with as much menace as I can muster.

"And you'd better not help him."

She shrugs, putting her hand behind her back. "I won't."

Juvenile as it is, I swear her fingers are crossed behind her back.

He'll come for me. But it'll be worth it. I just set the bar a little higher.

Rye

"Why the hell do you smell like you just left a bridge party at the retirement home?" Wren asks, swatting at the air around me as his nose wrinkles.

I mutter a few curses while taking a sip of the dark beer. Why are there only dark beers here? I prefer Corona. I should have brought my own.

Twelve damn showers couldn't get that smell off me—and I had to shower in my guest bathroom. My throat still burns from inhaling that shit, my bathroom floor is still slimy, and my eyes are bloodshot. I so owe her, and I'll have my revenge. Just as soon as I think of something that is just as good.

"I don't want to talk about it," I mumble, prompting him to laugh.

"She got you again, eh? Damn. You're getting your ass kicked."

"I've done some ass kicking, too," I defend, pissed that he thinks I'm just taking it and not dishing it out.

He rolls his eyes as he walks over to join Rain and Tria, taking part in whatever conversation they're having.

I look up just as the devil steps out, wearing a casual pair of white shorts and a red tank top. The other girls here are all in sexy, tight dresses, including the girl Ash has set me up with, yet my tormentor is here looking like she's ready for a day at the beach.

She takes in everyone, and frowns, apparently noticing the same thing. Ash waves her over, smiling happily as she turns to me and mouths, "Get Wren."

Poor Wren. He's in for a night of hell.

"Your date's here," I grumble while moving over and slapping Wren on the arm, my eyes still on the girl I'd like to throw in the pool.

That's not good enough. I need something epic after what she did to me earlier.

He turns around and looks at her, smiling as he says, "She looks like the only one here that came to relax."

I frown as I try to understand his meaning. Is he complimenting her or putting her down?

"What do you—"

"Wren," Ash interrupts, smiling as she guides Brin over. "This is the girl I've been telling you about."

Brin looks down, acting as though she's a little shy or awkward. That's sure as hell not the girl I know.

"Hey," she says bashfully when she finally peers back up.

"Hey," Wren says back, giving her a smile he barely uses.

I still don't know what's going on with him, but I can tell he's not really at this party. Well, physically he is, but his mind is a million miles away. He's going to hurt her feelings if he doesn't act right.

69

"Hey," I mock, rolling my eyes before glaring at her.

Her smile morphs into a real one and grows as she looks at me, and then she bites back the taunting grin. "You smell... odd," she says coyly, and I narrow my eyes at her.

"Wonder why?" I growl, and her laughter breaks free.

I don't care how cute her damn laugh is, she's still going to have one hell of a reckoning the second I find the perfect revenge.

"You two are still warring, I see," Tria says, chuckling as she walks up.

Kode comes to rest a possessive hand on her hip, staking his claim as though I'm interested.

"She broke into my house and baby-oiled my floor, and then bombed me with air freshener," I gripe, and everyone starts laughing, including Wren.

Her smile is aimed at me as she says, "We're even. Truce for the night?"

Even? Ha! "We're not even close to even, but yes—truce for the night. We need some boundaries."

She nods, agreeing with me. I'll regret that if I see something I could get back at her with. But for now, I'll give her a damn temporary truce.

"Hey," Ingrid says, sidling up beside me as she tries to interfere with our conversation.

Apparently *hey* is all anyone else wants to say tonight. At least this girl is completely normal, unlike some of the others Ash has introduced me to.

Brin's eyes scan the long legs of the blonde attached to my arm, and she appraises the skin-tight dress that is glued to the body of the bomb-shell. I almost release a smug smile when she tugs at the ends of her shorts, obviously feeling uncomfortable. At least her shorts fit for a change.

That ass better not looks as good as it did the other night.

"Sorry," Brin says, looking at Wren and away from me. "Ash said a barbeque, and, well, I didn't realize it was a dress-to-kill barbeque."

Everyone snickers as Wren moves closer, shrugging. "You look good to me. We can take a walk later, and you can tell me all about your future plans to torment Rye."

I glare at the traitor who only sniggers at my expense. Brin forces a smile that doesn't come close to reaching her eyes. Now I feel like an ass because I realize she feels really uncomfortable.

In all actuality, shorts and a tank top do make sense for a barbeque.

"Care to help me find a drink?" Ingrid asks, tugging at my arm.

"They're at the bar," I say, motioning toward Tag's big ass setup he has on his pool patio.

I should hang out at my beach home more often, but I love my suburb house during the off season. Even though it never really gets cold here, the wind at night this time of year is pretty chilly. All of these girls will be regretting their clothing soon.

Ingrid frowns as Wren offers Brin his arm. What is he? Eighty?

"Need a drink?" he asks her.

"A beer would be nice."

71

She grins up at him, fooling him with that sweet smile that masks the devil's wicked grin underneath. She could fool the CIA, but she can't fool me.

"You know her?" Ingrid asks as she returns with a glass of some fruity concoction.

"Yeah," I mutter vaguely, not enjoying the way Wren is resting his arm around her waist. He doesn't know her well enough for that. He might pull back a nub if he accidentally crosses some arbitrary line the way I did.

I'm not sure he can handle her.

"You going to stare at the girl wearing shorts all night?" Ingrid asks, sounding a little annoyed.

I suppose I'd be offended if she was staring at a guy while on a date with me, but she's taking this out of context.

"Would you rather I gave you all my attention?" I ask, giving her my most charming smile, which she quickly dissolves under.

Predictable.

Her grin splits her face as she takes a sexy-strutted step toward me and puts her hands on my chest, running her fingers down to the tops of my abs.

"Yes. I would," she says, trying to sound as provocative as one can.

"Rye," Tag calls, looking over his shoulder as he mans the bar in the absence of his bartender.

"Yeah," I say, walking away from my ready-to-please date.

"Grab the salt, and come do shots with us. It's in the kitchen. Top

72

right cabinet."

What am I? The fetch-it bitch?

"Sure," I mumble, feeling a little distracted when a small, reserved giggle comes out of Brin.

That's not her laugh. Her laugh is either maniacal or carefree. That's the most forced laugh I've ever heard.

Why the fuck do I care?

Wren's a good guy. She'll be fine. It's not my damn place to worry about whether or not she's fine.

I make my way inside the house and roll my eyes. Tag's directions suck. There are at least ten *top right cabinets*. Dick. It's not like I've never been in his kitchen before, but I've never had any reason to dig through his damn cabinets.

After opening and closing several, I finally find the one that hosts the salt, but something else catches my eye. Red food coloring.

Reflexively, my eyes dart to the French doors and land on Brin. I could so get her with that dark beer and this red food coloring.

Ah, hell. I can't. We called a truce for the day.

Sulking, I start to close the cabinet, but then I swipe both bottles of red food coloring instead. I'll just play with Ingrid. One person is just as good as another and this opportunity is too good to pass up.

As soon as I make it outside, Ingrid is waiting and I'm handing Tag the salt.

"Can I do shots with you?" she purrs, back to being all over me.

I grin as I take her red, fruity drink. Perfect. "Sure. You do the first one."

She giggles like a fool hands me her drink. When she looks away, I pour a whole tube of the stuff in what little bit of drink she has left. The red blends in with the differently shaded red drink—enough to pass a drunk girl's inspection.

She chugs the shot, and I happily hand her back her drink to chase the tequila with. She takes large sips, finishing it off, and I grin in anticipation.

"Was the shot good?" I ask, reaching for one of my own.

When she smiles, I can't help but burst out laughing. Her teeth, tongue, lips... her whole damn mouth is blood red. Girl could pass for a freshly fed vampire right now.

"What?" she asks, but I can't speak because I'm laughing too hard.

I look around for Brin, hoping she sees it too, but she's down on the beach with Wren. Really? She's missing the fun stuff.

When my laughter continues to be belted out, Ingrid turns and looks at Tag who leans back, cringing.

"Damn, girl," Tag says, just as Dane sees her and chokes on his shot, laughing as soon as he coughs his drink down.

She jerks her head toward the windows of the house, and a shrill scream of horror escapes her before she starts spitting the red out—well, trying to spit it out. Damn, this shit is awesome.

She's almost crying, so to relieve her panic, I manage to form words. "Relax," I say through my laughter. "It's just food dye."

Her eyes widen as she looks up, a long, red spit string still clinging to her lips. That's gross.

"You did this?" she almost yells.

Yes. A little fun is about to begin.

I just nod, proud of my little prank. Her face turns a furious red that rivals the stains in her mouth, and she twirls around angrily to stomp out.

That's no fun.

"Way to lose a date," Dane chuckles, acknowledging me without any hint of distaste.

At least he's warming up.

Hmmm. Ingrid's reaction was not the result I expected. In fact, that's the opposite of what I wanted. I think I've laughed more in the past few days than I ever have in my life. I really should have started doing this sooner.

"I wish Brin hadn't made me call a temporary truce," I grumble, now feeling bored as Wren and she slowly make their way back toward us.

"You can hold off on torturing her for one more day," Tag snickers.

It's Saturday. I had a lot of shit planned for our war.

"They won't work," I say mildly, tossing back a shot of my own before gesturing toward the beach.

"Why?" Tag asks, sipping his beer now.

"Wren and Brin? How dorky is it to have rhyming names?" I ask incredulously.

I thought that would be obvious.

Dane growls for some weird reason, and Tag turns his head to snicker. Oh. Shit. Rain and Dane. Oops.

"My bad," I mutter as Dane walks off.

And we were just starting to make progress. Oh well.

Brin and Wren walk up the steps together, and I notice her beer is low. It's just low enough for this little bottle of red to do some damage.

I glance down, weighing my options, and shrug. Fuck it.

Brin

Wren is sweet, but he seems so distracted. I feel like I'm boring him to death, and every time I think he's telling a joke, I try to laugh. But I have no idea what the hell I'm doing. I haven't tried dating since high school.

This was so stupid.

"You need a shot," Rye says from behind me, grinning while giving me a wink.

He's embarrassing the hell out of me right now. Knowing he's told everyone here about our war—mostly Wren—is mortifying. Wren probably thinks I'm a two-year-old.

Though liquor is the enemy, a shot would be perfect right now.

"Thanks," I murmur with a tight smile, growing more nervous by the second.

Wren is texting someone. Again. That's what he's done for most of the time we've been out here. The walk on the beach consisted of him texting, or cursing under his breath, or apologizing for ignoring me.

I've never felt so uncomfortable.

Rye takes my beer as I absently grab a lime wedge and stare at the shot, trying to gather courage. Then I chug it down, suck on the lime, and reach for my beer. He hands it to me promptly while grinning. I'm sure my face is screwed up in disgust. That was nowhere nearly as good as the shots at Silk.

"Thanks," I say, sucking in a breath as I finish drinking the rest of my beer, and Rye covers his mouth with his hand as he shakes with suppressed laughter.

Surely my face wasn't that distorted.

When I turn back to Wren, he's putting his phone away and apologizing for the hundredth time tonight.

"It's fine," I say with my same, fake smile, but his eyes widen in horror as he stares at my mouth.

"What the hell?" he asks through a strangled cough.

I frown, and then wipe my mouth. When red appears on my fingertips, I gasp, worried about where the hell I might be bleeding from. But when I hear the roaring laughter coming from my asshole neighbor, I realize that dick is behind this.

"We called a truce!" I screech, which only clues Wren in, and he joins in on the laughter.

Rye stumbles backwards when I dive for him, and he narrowly dodges my foot that is aimed at his crotch. Bastard!

"So much better," he says through his snickering, even though that makes no sense to me.

I chase him around the pool, fighting back my grin when he grabs Ash and uses her as a barrier between us.

"Oh hell no!" she says, even though her smile is growing. "I so don't want in the middle of you two."

I glare at him, trying to grab at him, but he keeps the brunette beauty between us, even as she tries uselessly to escape.

"Tag," she calls playfully, "help! I'm going to end up with food or alcohol all over me."

He just laughs while shaking his head, and Rye continues to chuckle as he keeps himself shielded.

"Sorry to break up the fun," Wren says with a sad smile, drawing my attention, "but I need to be going. There's something I have to deal with right now."

Crap. I'm busy chasing Rye and acting like a kid. I've probably just ruined all my chances with Wren. Not that it matters. I wasn't all that into him anyhow.

"It was nice to meet you, Brin," he says so cordially, making all of this seem suddenly... boring.

We're supposed to have another date tomorrow. An actual date where we go out to eat. Now... I feel like he's changing his mind. I wish he'd just tell me now and get it over with.

"You have my number," I say while tucking my hands into the tops of my pockets, a nervous reaction.

"I'll call you. Have fun. Don't let Rye drive you crazy." He winks at Rye and then he hugs Ash before walking out.

Rye walks out from behind Ash and heads over to me, dropping his long arm across my shoulders as though he didn't just... Ah, hell. I've been standing here talking to everyone with a damn vampire's mouth.

I hate him.

I glare at his hand as it comes to rest just off my body, hanging casually as he guides me over to a table.

"Guess it's just us now," he says as we make our way to some seats.

"What happened to your date? Too charming for her?" I muse, trying to sound annoyed instead of nosy.

"No," he says, laughing. "She didn't deal too well with the bloody mouth bit."

I can't help but laugh. I bet the beauty queen flipped the hell out if he did that to her. I just want massive payback. And I will have it. When he least suspects it.

We sit at the far back and just watch all the happy couples, and the Sterling men who have brought equally designer women. Why the hell did I think shorts and a tank top would be okay? Oh yeah, because it's a barbeque!

"Why haven't you gotten your car fixed yet?" he asks just as Tag comes over, carrying something odd and fruity to give to me.

I'm thankful for the interruption.

"It'll get rid of your food coloring. Hopefully," he snickers.

I roll my eyes while mumbling a thanks, trying to keep my mouth as closed as possible.

"And this is for you," Ash says, coming up and handing Rye a glass of whiskey on the rocks.

We're going to be trashed at this rate. Liquor is the devil.

He thanks her as they walk off, and then he returns his gaze to me as I drink my weird fruity drink with a straw. I'm trying to decide if I like it or not. I've never been a fan of frozen drinks. Brain freeze is a bitch.

"Well," he prompts, leaning up on his elbows to stare intensely at me.

Crap.

I shrug as though it's no big deal. "Haven't had time."

He mutters something about safety and me being an idiot. I choose to ignore him.

"I'll have it taken to my garage. It'll get fixed quicker there."

I've heard of his garage—through the others. It's supposed to be the place where *all* of the rich and famous around here go. There's no way I can afford that if I can't even afford the scrubby piece of shit garages.

"It's fine. I have something lined up," I lie, taking a bigger sip of my drink.

"You're lying. Your whole body just stiffened. If it's about money, don't worry. Your insurance will cover it. I'll make sure the deductible isn't an issue."

Shit. Shit. Shit.

"I... uh..."

"You don't have insurance?" he asks, his voice hitting an angry note.

I give him a sheepish grin while shrugging. "Liability only. It's fine. I'm working overtime at the museum. I'll have the money in a couple of weeks to cover it."

Maggie has already volunteered to pay the full amount of rent on the house and utilities just so that I can get my car fixed, but I can't let her do that. I'm still paying off some of John's credit cards that were in my name. It'll take a while, but eventually I'll get it all caught up.

"And you wrecked a Porsche? That's not very smart," he grumbles, leaning back while taking a deep breath.

"It was a bad day. A really bad day. It was... You're right. It was stupid. But you pushed me. Why are you parking on our side of the street? Your side has plenty of room."

He frowns as he takes another sip of his drink.

"Kittens," he says randomly, and I give him what has to be an unbelievably confused stare.

"Kittens?" I ask, trying to look for a code to decipher. Nothing.

"Kittens—several that are just a few months old. They're living in the storm drain of the gutter. They climb up in your engine, and when you start your car... Well, it's not pleasant. Animal control is behind and they haven't come out to remove them yet. All of my neighbors are getting as far away from that damn opening as possible."

I bite back a grin. He doesn't want to be a kitten killer. That's what started all this.

"Aw," I saw teasingly, enjoying the way he narrows his eyes at me.

"I'm allergic to cats. That's the main reason," he lies, and I work really hard not to smile mockingly. Okay. Maybe I don't work at all.

"Stop smiling," he grumbles, sipping his drink again.

"For a bad boy, you're actually a pretty big softie."

His lips curl up in amusement as his eyebrows raise. "Bad boy?

What makes you think I'm a bad boy?"

I squirm uncomfortably while absently stirring the straw in my drink.

"You have tattoos all over your upper body. Your nipple is pierced. So is your eyebrow. And you have a motorcycle."

He lets go one of those throaty laughs that always makes me smile, and I just let the vibrations rattle through me.

"And that qualifies me for bad boy status?"

When he says it like that, it sounds pretty stupid. Instead of making myself look like a bigger idiot, I shift the subject.

"Why do you only have one nipple pierced?"

His grin slowly changes into one of more mockery. "Because I wasn't *bad* enough to get the second one pierced," he jokes, making me feel like a jackass.

Jerk.

"Really?" I ask, playing along.

"The shit hurt a lot worse than I thought it would," he says while chuckling, still sounding as though he's making fun of me.

From there, conversation just flows. I detail my very demanding yet low paying job, and he tells me all about his garage. His career is by far much more fascinating, and I actually enjoy listening to him speak so passionately about it.

I laugh when he tells the Tinker Bell story and how Tag still taunts him. And for a little while, the rest of the world gets shut out. It's... nice. And a guy who looks like Rye Clanton should not be so easy to talk to. It just isn't fair that he's so damn perfect.

Brin

"You're such a horrible drinker," Rye says through a laugh, helping me out of the cab as soon as he finishes paying.

I just giggle, because right now, everything is spinning and it's all hilarious. He laughs, too, finding the world just as amusing as I do.

When I start to fall, he bends and scoops me up as though I'm weightless and carries me the rest of the way to the house.

"You're right," I murmur while resting my head against his chest.

He smells so terrible. I wish I hadn't bombed him because he'd probably smell so good right now.

"About?" he asks while fumbling with my doorknob.

"You're a terrible excuse for a bad boy."

He laughs again as the door swings open, and I squint against the lights inside to see a grinning Maggie.

"Hey!" I exclaim, half singing the word, and she starts snickering.

She must be drunk, too.

"Liquor?" she asks as Rye steps in, carrying me toward my bedroom.

"Lots and lots of liquor," I answer, beating him to the words.

He navigates my house too well, and gently places me on the bed. "Might want to get her some water," he says while grinning.

"On it." Maggie disappears as Rye slides my shoes off and pulls down my covers on the other side of the bed.

He moves me to be there once he finishes, and then he moves my hair from my face as I nestle in.

"I take it you had fun with Wren?" Maggie asks, fishing for information.

Rye takes the water from her and forces me to sit up enough to drink it against my silent protest.

"Wren was completely uninterested in me. We're supposed to have a date tomorrow, but I'm pretty sure he's planning to cancel," I say flippantly.

Maggie frowns, as does Rye.

"Why do you say that?" he asks, forcing me to take another sip.

As my glass comes back away from my lips, I answer, "Call it women's intuition. Can I go to sleep now?"

He chuckles quietly and leans down to tuck me in while setting my glass of water on the nightstand.

"This war resumes tomorrow," I mumble, earning another snicker from him.

"Your ass is mine," he teases.

I just grin as my eyes grow too heavy to hold open another moment.

Chapter 5

Brin

As expected, Wren sent a text during the night to cancel our Sunday date. That's fine. He's really not my type. Though I'm not actually sure what my type is. Well, Rye would be my type if he wasn't so far out of my league.

"I think it's cowardly to break a date via text," Maggie growls.

She's been badmouthing Wren all morning, but it's not necessary. That spark wasn't there, and we both knew it. Everything felt so... forced.

"It's fine. I need to run to the store. You want anything?" I ask as I pick up my keys.

"Donuts would be nice," she teases, and I glare at her.

That reminds me... I need to do something to get back at him for the red mouth. I'll come up with something while I'm at the store.

When I walk out, my mouth falls. My car... It's gone! Who the hell would steal a wrecked car? An old wrecked car.

"It's at my garage," a deep voice says, prompting me to look up just as Rye crosses the street, his jean-clad legs taking long strides on his way to me.

Why does he look so good even under the influence of my cruel hangover? "I'm on my way there now. I just need your keys."

My mouth opens and closes a few times, and then panic sets in. I can't afford his garage! I told him this already.

"No. You can't fix—"

"It's fine, Brin. It's seriously no big deal. We happen to have a surplus of the parts, and this gives me a reason to get rid of them. Besides, I can't torture you if you get yourself killed in that thing. You can drive one of mine for a few days until you get yours back."

He reaches me and pulls my keys from my hand and exchanges them for his Range Rover keys.

"I can't drive that," I hiss, pointing to the SUV that costs more than I make in three years. Or more. He's crazy.

"It's harder to tear up. Don't worry," he says while winking. Then he turns around and walks away, leaving me in my stupefied state as my feet cement themselves to the ground.

A black motorcycle is parked in his yard, and he throws one long leg over it before pulling on his helmet. The beast roars to life, and he rocks it back until he can drive off the grass and onto the street, leaving me to wallow in my humiliation.

"That's so fucking sweet," Maggie says from behind me.

I turn to see her grinning while sipping her coffee, and I glare at her. "It's not sweet. He feels sorry for me. I can pay for my own car to get fixed."

She snorts and rolls her eyes. "You can't pay for his shop. And his is the best."

So she knew where he worked this whole time?

I frown as I look at the black Range Rover at my curb. He's loaning me his car while he fixes mine. And all this after I wrecked it into his. What a twisted, weird world we live in.

Rye

"Engine looks rough as hell. Sparkplugs are going bad, brakes are shot, rotors are fucked, tires are bald—"

"In other words, it's a piece of shit," I interrupt, flipping through the interview questions for the magazine reporter that will be coming.

"Yeah," Wrench—my lead mechanic—says.

"Fix it all," I say with a shrug, cursing at how personal some of these questions are.

Why do they need to know about my home life? This is about my garage, isn't it?

"Don't you need to call the owner? That's going to be a chunk of cash, and it's a Camry, and not one of the snazzy new ones, either. It's an old Camry—talking dawn of the dinosaurs here. There's a cassette player, dude. The owner may not have that kind of dough. In fact, I don't think I've ever seen a blue-collar car in here."

That makes me sound like a rich asshole. I charge a lot because I have the highest quality workers, but still.

"This one is on my tab. Do whatever needs to be done."

I can actually feel his surprise, so I don't bother looking up. Brin can't keep driving that thing around, and she'd have never let me take it if I hadn't had it towed without her knowledge.

"Alrighty then," he says at last, and then I hear him talking to a familiar voice in the hallway.

"Hey," Wren says as he walks in.

I look up as he comes to drop onto the chair in front of my desk.

"Shouldn't you be getting ready for your date?" I ask, glancing at the clock on the wall.

I don't usually work on Sundays, but it's been so busy that it was necessary to do. I really have to get my new guys trained properly so I can let this place run without me a little better.

It sucked to call Wrench in, but I know Brin will be impatient while waiting on her car. And I won't dare let anyone besides me or him touch it. Since he's even better than I am, I want him to take care of every detail.

"I canceled the date," Wren says, bringing me back to the here and now.

I could strangle him. She just finished saying he was going to do this.

"Why?" I growl.

His eyebrows go up as a daring grin forms. He has no idea how close I am to slapping his grin off.

"Dude, if you liked her, all you had to do was use *Star*. You didn't have to dye the girl's mouth red."

Star? I've never used Star. It's a code we came up with a long time ago after a battle over a girl named Star went on between two of our friends. If you ask a guy about Star, it means you're calling dibs. I'm not calling dibs on Brin.

We are friends. Nothing more.

"No need to use Star. Pranks are just our thing. You know the only two rules I have."

I look back down to the interview questions, and then I groan when I see all the even more probing questions. Why do they need to know the length of my longest relationship?

No wonder they send you a pre-interview list. They're letting you know ahead of time that they're about to bend you over and fuck you hard. It almost makes me want to cancel.

"Whatever you say," Wren snickers. "It was obvious you didn't like the idea of me dating her."

His eyes are on me expectantly when I give him my attention again. "You don't make a good couple. But that doesn't mean I want her for myself."

I'd sound like an ass if I told one of my best friends that I didn't think he was good enough for Brin. But he's not. He proved that.

"It's fine, Rye. Honestly. You're right. We're not right for each other."

That just pisses me off.

"What the hell is wrong with her? You don't think she's good enough? Because she—"

"Whoa!" he says laughing, holding his hands up for me to stop. "First of all, put your fangs away. Secondly, I didn't mean anything bad by that. She's cute and sweet, but we have nothing in common, and there was mostly heavy uncomfortable silence between us the entire time we tried to talk."

"That's because you were too busy staring at your phone instead of paying her any attention. She's easy as fuck to talk to."

His grin only grows. "I'm sure you're right. Anyway, I've sort of got some shit of my own going on right now. And dating isn't exactly on the agenda. Turns out… I'm a father."

I think my jaw just hit the floor. What. The. Hell?

His grin is gone as the weight of the world settles into every feature he has.

"When the hell did Erica have a child?" I ask in a rasp whisper. Am I that oblivious to the world around me?

He lets go a sad, bitter laugh while shaking his head. "Erica didn't have a kid. This kid is six-years-old. I met the mom long before Erica and I got together, and I had a one-night stand. I used a condom, but… apparently shit happens. Condom broke, and I didn't even remember our night together until she said something about it."

I can barely breathe, so I can only assume he's suffocating.

"Damn. And you're sure? That's it's yours, I mean."

He nods slowly, his eyes cast downward as he struggles to digest it all.

"Yeah, it's legit. I have a daughter. Just got the results back from the paternity test yesterday. That's why I left, and that's why I was texting. My lawyer has been working hard on this. I seriously have a daughter named Angel."

Still a little in shock, I ask, "Is she living here?"

"Yeah. The mom's name is Allie. I met her one of the times I was in Cancun. Turns out she was living four hours from here, and moved here to be with one of her friends. Now she's a nurse at Sterling Memorial. She wasn't sure about telling me, but the kid kept asking about a father, and then we literally ran into each other at the grocery store. She took it as a sign that she needed to do the right thing."

Holy shit. "And she didn't think to do the right thing years ago?"

He frowns as he leans over and rests his elbows on the desk. "It was a one-night stand. She didn't know my last name. She only came to Sterling Shore to meet me once she saw me in a magazine article with Tag. She started to call me several times and kept chickening out.

"But she ended up landing a good job at the hospital, and now she's living here. She's been trying to find the courage to approach me for the past three months. I want to know my kid, but she's made it clear that I'm not allowed to give her money or see her outside of Angel. Apparently I was a major asshole to her that night. It was a bad year for me, and I fucked her and walked away. I don't really blame her for not being too happy with me.

"I begged Ash not to set that date up with Brin last night, but you know how pushy she is. Tag hasn't told her what's going on, so she didn't know any better. Then I felt like a jerk for being such a horrible date, and I wanted to make it up to her by asking her out on another date. But the truth is, I'm seriously not in a place to date right now."

I can't blame him for that. Hell. That's wild.

"Sorry, man. I wish I knew what to do."

He blows out a harsh breath as his hands shake. I don't know how he's holding it together. "Allie is going to let me meet Angel eventually, but it might take a month or two. She wants to ease her into the transition. A month. I might have to wait an entire month to meet her. My lawyer says he can make sure I see her within a week. But Allie is already terrified of me using my money and influence against her.

"I'm afraid if I push her too fast, she'll flee and I'll never get the chance to know my daughter. So I'm playing this her way. She wants time, so I'll give her a little time. In the meantime, Tag's helping me get my house ready for a kid. There's a lot of shit to being a dad, and I'm honestly freaking the fuck out a little."

"I'd be freaking the fuck out a lot," I murmur, reaching under the desk and pulling out the bottle of whiskey to hand him.

He raises and shakes his hand in one motion, refusing the alcohol. "I have to go to Mom's right now. She still doesn't know. I'm about to break the news to her, and hope she doesn't beat the hell out of me. I can't believe I didn't give her my last name. Hell, I think she said I lied about what it was."

That doesn't sound like Wren at all. But we all do stupid shit from time to time. Just turns out that his one time being shitty ended up altering his life. Now he's missed six years of his kid's life.

"If you need me or just need someone to get shit-faced with, you know I'm here."

He laughs sadly while scrubbing his face with his hands. "I might take you up on that offer real damn soon. Tell Brin I'm sorry, but don't tell her why."

I wave him off like he's ridiculous for even thinking I'd share that. But Brin is going to think this had something to do with her.

"I'll take care of it. You just worry about you and your kid right now."

He sighs hard. "That sounds so strange. *My kid*. Erica wanted kids and I told her no. Not because I didn't want them, but because she and

I were never going to last, and I knew it before I married her. I'm so stupid. Who marries someone they don't even really want to be with? Am I really ready for a kid right now? What if I fuck her up?"

I'm the worst possible person for this conversation. I've never even had a serious relationship. A kid? I don't know the first thing about this.

"Wren, you're the most level-headed, mature, and grounded one of us. You'll be an excellent father."

He smiles, and I mentally pat myself on the back. Good. I said the right thing. And I believe that he will be a good dad.

"I need to go, but I'll catch up with you later."

I nod as he stands, and then I reach for my phone. It's rare that I spend a Sunday night at home—since I enjoy living instead of being a recluse—but tonight I'll make an exception. I have a ton of shit here to do, but there will be one girl who has a major complex if I don't head over now.

And I can't show up empty handed.

Brin

"You sure you don't want us to come hang out with you?" Maggie asks over the phone as I flip aimlessly through the channels.

Why isn't there ever anything on when I try to watch TV?

"I'm beyond positive. You two are in a new relationship, so you'll constantly be saying disgustingly sweet things and making out. It'll make me sick with envy. Go. Have fun. I'm a big girl."

She sighs as though she doesn't want to relent, but she does.

"Fine. But don't sit at home in your pajamas. Go out and have fun. See if Rye is busy."

That's hilarious. I doubt very seriously Rye Clanton has nothing to do. I'm positive he doesn't want to hang out with me. The blonde on his arm yesterday is probably over her moment of anger, and now she'll be in his bed.

I hate men.

I decide not to say anything and just hang up. Tria sends me a text asking if I want her to come over. Apparently she heard Wren cancelled as well. Sheesh. It's not like he broke my damn heart.

I send her a quick *no,* and resume my boring night. After ten more minutes of finding nothing on TV, I stand up, still wearing my pink hearts boxers and smurf T-shirt, and head to the kitchen.

The great thing about staying at home instead of going out on a date is the fact that I don't have to match my clothes or care if my hair is pulled back in a ponytail. And I can eat junk food while drinking whatever I want instead of the proper wine that goes with my uppity dish.

Beer it is.

Just as I get settled back on the sofa with a bag of marshmallows and my beer, someone knocks at the door. Damn. Can't I just get a little peace?

"No war tonight," I say, knowing damn well no one else would be knocking. It sounds more like he's kicking the door rather than knocking.

"No war tonight. Let me in. I have food."

Food? Why does he have food?

I jog over to the window and look out, making sure there's no trick behind the door. Sure enough, he's holding a pizza box with several large bags on top, which explains the kicking. But what's going on?

When I open the door, he blows out an exasperated breath. "Finally. Move."

I follow behind him as he starts unloading the numerous cartons of food onto my coffee table.

"What's this?" I ask, motioning to his ungodly amount of takeout.

"Food."

"For the entire neighborhood?" I ask incredulously.

"I don't have your number, and I had no idea what you would want, so I grabbed Chinese, pizza, sushi, vegan shit, and Thai food. Pick something and eat it," he answers while pulling out a DVD.

"I'll pass on the vegan shit," I say with a small grin.

He snickers while popping open the DVD case.

"And that?" I ask, admittedly amused when I see the cover of the movie—*Batman*. Is he making sure I'm fully stocked for my night in?

"I refuse to watch a chick flick, but I have a big ass selection of movies. I just grabbed one. Sit. Watch. Eat."

Bossy.

"You're watching a movie with me?"

"Yep. And then we'll discuss you taking better care of your car. It's probably a good thing that you ran all over me."

I frown as I reach down for a slice of pizza, and then I tilt my head. What if he has put laxatives all over this thing? I wouldn't put it past him.

"What's wrong with my car? Other than the smashed rear, obviously."

He comes to sit down beside me on the couch as the movie starts. An alien movie? Really? That is so not what the box said it was. Batman sounded much, much better.

"Everything," he grumbles, sounding annoyed.

"You don't have to stay. It's obvious you're cranky. I know you have better things to do than to hang out with me just because my date fell through."

He glares at me as though I've said something wrong. "I'm cranky because you had no brakes, what little bit of oil you had was disgusting, and your tires have wires sticking through the bald slicks. It's careless and dangerous. Especially when you live right across from a mechanic."

I bite back a grin when his ugly scowl grows. He's pretty frigging cute when he's pissed.

"Sorry. John usually took care of that stuff. It's about all he was good for. Before that, my dad did it. I just... I didn't really think about it," I murmur absently, pulling the piece of pizza up to inspect it a little closer. It looks harmless enough, but I reserve the right to be suspicious, considering Rye is the one who brought it.

When I look back at him, his expression has changed. "Who's John?"

I shrug at his question, focusing the majority of my attention on my level of courage. To eat the pizza, or not to eat the pizza; that is the question.

"My ex-husband."

He coughs as he chokes on nothing but air, and I give him a quizzical look while mocking offense.

"Is it so preposterous that someone would marry me?"

He slaps his chest as he tries to catch a clean breath, and it takes a concentrated amount of effort not to laugh at him.

"Just... I didn't... You're so young. You've been married?"

"I'm no younger than Ash. Hell, she's younger than I am. I'm twenty-six. We got married right out of high school." The second he groans, I roll my eyes and add, "Cliché, I know. But everything is romanticized to the nth degree when you're eighteen. Sometimes people find the real stuff that young. Sometimes they get the watered down generic version. I had the latter of the two."

He leans back as the movie plays, and I keep the pizza just far enough away to tease my lips. It's just too risky to take a bite without knowing if he's done anything to it or not.

"How long ago did it end?" he asks.

I wasn't expecting him to ask that, and much to my surprise, I grin. "The day I ran all over your car was exactly one year."

His mouth forms an "O" and he half laughs. "Makes sense. Doesn't mean I'm going to go easy on you. I still owe you for the damn air freshener ambush."

I chuckle lightly while putting the pizza in front of his mouth. "Take a bite."

"Why?" he asks skeptically, arching an eyebrow at me.

"Because I don't trust you."

He thinks about that for a second, tilting his head as though he's weighing that answer. "Fair enough." He bites into the pizza, and I breathe out in relief. I'm starving.

"Got anything to drink?" he asks with a mouthful, digging through some of the other choices.

"Beer," I say with a one-shoulder shrug while standing.

"Beer works."

After leaving him and grabbing us both a beer, I return to see him eating out of a Chinese carton, his chopsticks holding noodles as he watches the gory movie. While he's distracted, I eat the bite he has suspended in the air, and he gives me an I-know-you-didn't-just-do-that look.

"I was about to eat that," he mutters dryly.

"I know. That's how I knew it was safe to eat."

He rolls his eyes and resumes eating, and I just watch him for a minute. He really isn't anything like I thought he was.

Brin

"No," he groans, trying to back away from me as I force myself on him.

"Please," I beg, almost whimpering.

"Damn it, no! I refuse. I can't. I'm already going to regret all you've made me take."

I straddle him, giving him my best pleading eyes, and he actually laughs at me.

"Hell no. It's not happening. You'll just have to do it yourself."

"That's not going to happen. You have to do it first."

He laughs harder, shaking his head as though he's dealing with a crazy person. I'm not crazy yet, but I will be if he keeps denying me.

"I'm too full to take another bite. If you want to eat the damn cheesecake, you're going to have to take a leap of faith. I'm. Not. Eating. Any."

I sigh wistfully, looking longingly at the forkful of cheesecake that I've been trying to jab into his mouth for five minutes. "Then it must be poisoned."

He continues chuckling as he lies back on my couch, and I do all I can to ignore the very intimate position I've ended up in. Crap. I'm sitting right on top of his crotch and he's lying back, watching late-night TV like it's riveting stuff. It'd be stupid to act like I can feel the erection he has and make this awkward, but *oh my damn*, it feels so good.

I have to be at work early, and it's already after eleven, but I refuse to let him go home. This has been too much fun. We've eaten entirely too much, watched a couple of terrible movies, and now I really want a bite of this cheesecake. Why does he insist on making me beg?

He's acting as though this seating arrangement isn't bothering him, which pisses me off. I'm a frustrated ball of hormones now. It's really not fair.

I should have changed out of my mismatched wardrobe, but that might have made things… obvious and weird.

Of course, straddling him is probably making things weird, too.

"Please," I say one last time, jutting my lip out in an exaggerated pout that makes him laugh again.

His hands come to rest on the fronts of my thighs as he sighs. "Fine. Last damn thing I'm eating for you."

I grin happily and put the forkful of cheesecake in his mouth. He swallows and opens his mouth for me to see that the food is harmless, and I quickly dive into the cheesecake, not bothering to move off him.

Maybe I can get away with it for a minute longer, because he feels really good under me. And it's been *so* long since I've felt anything even remotely close.

Each hard line of his abs or chest is very easy to feel through his thin shirt—not that I've been finding ways to rub against him all night. Fine. So maybe I have been finding ways to rub against him all night. I'm only human.

The muscles on his arms are definitely distracting, and his hipbones have those sexy little lines I want to touch. His shirt keeps riding up, teasing the hell out of me.

The door flies open, and Maggie stumbles to a halt in the doorway. Her eyes widen at first, and then a slow, pleased grin spreads across her face.

"I'll come back later," she says, and that's when I tense.

"It's your house, Maggie," Rye says from under me, taking a sip of his beer. "I'm about to go. Then she's all yours."

"She's not my type, so take your time," Maggie chirps, giving me her best mischievous grin before walking in the rest of the way and

100

BREAKING EVEN

shutting the door. She heads to her room without another word, and I look down to see Rye grinning.

"I think she got the wrong idea," I mumble, ready to throttle my best friend.

"Probably because you're straddling me in a pair of pink boxers."

My face floods red, but I do my best to hold my composure. "Probably," I murmur, casually unraveling myself from him as I stand up. Crap.

"I need to get home. I have some invoices to log before I crash. Long day for me tomorrow," he says while standing.

Then he slaps my ass and shocks the hell out of me. "I'll see you tomorrow. The war will resume."

"War on. But next time only get cheesecake," I joke, knowing there won't be a next time most likely.

"Next time I'm bringing two slices of pizza and that's it." He slides his shoes back on, and rubs his sexy set of abs that are hiding beneath the thin black shirt, but it's hard to look away from the hard ridge behind his zipper. "I won't be able to walk tomorrow, thanks to you."

Maggie chokes on something when she overhears the tail-end of that conversation on her way to grab her laptop.

Ah, hell. That's going to take some explaining.

Rye just laughs and leaves the full explanation on my very tired shoulders. I have to be at work at five, he's just now leaving, and Maggie is about to interrogate the hell out of me.

As soon as the door is shut for a full five seconds, Maggie drops to a chair and stares expectantly. "Details. All of them. Don't leave anything out."

Chapter 6

Rye

"I want to pay you back," Brin argues, following me around my office as Wrench works on her car. I refuse to let her go down to the work area, even though she's begged. Numerous times.

"I've already said no. I told you I had the parts on hand. It's not like very many of my customers have vehicles to match those parts. They'll just be wasted."

It's a complete and total lie. The car would have been fixed by now if I had already had the parts on hand. I'm still waiting on two parts to come in, because I just ordered them yesterday. Wrench keeps finding more shit wrong every time he digs a little deeper. But she can't know that.

"I'm paying. Now let me go see it," she demands.

"Not happening."

"Why?" She acts as though I haven't already gone over this ten times with her.

I walk over to her, lean down so that I'm in her face, and meet her mean little scowl that I happen to find pretty damn cute.

"Because I'm not letting you anywhere near power tools. Insurance thing."

She crosses her arms as I lean back up, and she tries harder to intimidate me with her glower. Not effective.

"Well, I need my briefcase out of the back. It has a file that I need to get back tomorrow."

She's relentless. But I'm not caving. She'd end up killing someone on accident if she got down there. Or she'd hurt herself, and I'd end up spending the rest of the day in the hospital waiting room.

"Fine. I'll go get your briefcase. You stay put. If you try to come down there, I swear I'll haul your ass out of here over my shoulder."

She glares at me but finally looks away, silently admitting her defeat. I walk out and head down the steel staircase to the lower level where we keep the cars. It's an open warehouse space, and the cars are driven in from the lower deck. There's a higher elevation parking deck where the workers park and come in through the office area—my space.

"You coming to inspect my work again?" Wrench asks, an amused eyebrow cocked as I open the backdoor to her car.

Where's the briefcase?

"Nah, I'm looking for a briefcase. Have you seen one?"

He wipes his hands on a towel while shaking his head. "The only thing I've seen are a couple of receipts. I didn't read them, but I put them in the glove compartment so that we didn't knock them out by mistake."

"We?" I ask, my eyes narrowing. "Who else has worked on this car besides you?"

He laughs while leaning back under the hood.

"No one. It's a habit to say *we* because I've usually got a few other guys doing the grunt work. My bad. Any reason why this damn Camry is so important?"

"It's not the car I'm worried about; it's the driver. The rest of the parts should get here early tomorrow morning."

He rises up and tilts his head. "Damn. You must have spent a fortune on shipping to get everything here this fast."

I refuse to talk about this. I could have bought her a new car for all the shit I've had to replace and have shipped overnight. Not to mention the tires. I got her some of the best. And I replaced her hubcaps with actual wheels.

She wouldn't have let me buy her a new car, and she'd flip the hell out if she knew what I've spent. Most people would probably get the wrong idea, since I barely know her. But I have the extra cash, and she needs to be driving around in something safe.

"Come get me if you find anything else wrong with it. I need to get back upstairs."

Wrench nods as I head up to tell the fiery little girl her briefcase must be somewhere else. When I walk into my office, she's sitting on top of my desk with her legs crossed, and an unbidden fantasy rocks through my mind.

I really shouldn't be picturing her leaned back as I pound into her. But all I can think about is her clawing at my back while I make her scream my name.

I blame her. It's all because of her straddling me last night. My mind hasn't been right since then. I keep picturing her under me, over me, against the wall... It's a long damn list.

It's probably because she made me have fun with very little beer, too much food, and a movie. In fact, it was one of the best times I've had in so damn long, and that makes me sound pathetic. But my mind never wandered off to things I want to forget, just like it never does when I'm with her.

I've gone to resorts for weekend getaways with girls that most men would cut off their left nut just to touch—girls who wear the sexiest, most expensive lingerie and look better than the models who strut on the runway. And yet I can't think of anything I'd rather do than get her back in her pink boxers and smurf shirt while we lounge on her uncomfortable couch.

Brainy smurf. It wasn't even Smurfette.

When Maggie came in, I almost gave her a hug to thank her. Brin had been on top of me, her thighs parted as she put herself right on top of my hard-as-a-rock dick. Neither of us mentioned what she had to be feeling, and every time she rocked forward, trying to put that damn cheesecake in my mouth, my cock tried to spring free from my jeans.

I ate the damn bite, hoping that would get her off me before I exploded in my jeans like an unpracticed virgin. I can't remember the last time that something so small left me so damn twisted up.

"No briefcase," I murmur at last, shifting uncomfortably when my damn cock starts to press against my zipper.

She shrugs, looking bored as she slowly gets off my desk. I bite back a groan when the shorts she is wearing slide up as she slides down. What the fuck is going on?

"It must be in my room then."

She starts walking toward me, and I walk around, trying to keep my body angled away from her. I lower myself to the chair, happy to have my hard-on hidden—

"What the hell?" I yelp as I crash to the floor.

My decimated chair lies in shambles around me as I groan and try to get up. But the hellacious laughter rings out as I peek up from beside the desk to see the face of my enemy.

She uncurls her hand to reveal all my chair's screws, and she giggles loudly while bringing them over to the desk and putting them down.

"That's for leaving my mouth red and for making me beg last night," she gloats.

A throat clearing from behind her startles her into a squeal. A very amused Wrench stands in the doorway, leaning against the jamb, and doing all he can to restrain the insuppressible grin on his face.

"Beg for cheesecake," she adds quickly, horrified. "And it was food dye. That's why my mouth was red."

Her cheeks turn a harsh pink, and I laugh while climbing back up to my feet. Wrench hides his grin with his hand as his body shakes with repressed laughter.

Brin's face turns all the redder, and she rocks back and forth on her heels and toes, looking longingly toward the exit.

"I uh... I... I'm just going to go... die now," she says before darting out the door, hiding her face all the way out.

I just laugh harder as Wrench stares expectantly at me, lowering his hand from his mouth to reveal his shit-eating grin.

"The Camry owner, I presume," he says with thick condescension.

"Yeah. My neighbor."

His laughter sneaks out as he comes to sit down in front of my desk.

"When I was fixing the rear, I noticed the black paint. Perfect match to your Porsche that you brought in all banged up. Did you hit her or something?"

I scowl at him. "No. She ran over my *parked* car."

His confusion is warranted. I shouldn't have opened my big mouth.

"And you're paying for the damages on her car because?" he asks, prying.

"Because she has liability only."

I'd like to knock that smirk off his face. He's lucky he's the best mechanic I've ever known.

"And?" he asks slowly.

"*And* I shouldn't have to justify any of my actions in my own garage," I growl.

He laughs while holding his hands up defensively. "Sorry. Chill. I get it."

Gets what?

"Why did you come up here?" I ask, annoyed at this point.

"To tell you I've done all I can do until the other parts get here. I'm heading out. You staying? I can work on something else if you want."

"Nah. I'm about to head out, too. You had to work all weekend. After the car is finished, you can take off for a few days. On me."

His mocking grin is still pissing me off. "Thanks. See you tomorrow."

A text buzzes in, but I ignore it when I see my dad's name on the screen. He must be getting married. Again. That's the fourth text this week.

Wrench walks out as my eyes move to the window. I don't want to deal with my father or his bridezilla right now. I have no desire to go back to that damn house for any reason.

I need a distraction.

The pet shop is right next door, and my distraction is served up on platter.

Rye

"So this one isn't venomous?" I ask as the snake slithers over the guy's hand, acting like a calm, gentle serpent. That almost sounds like an oxymoron.

"Nope," he says, making the word *pop* as he smacks his gum.

"What happens if it bites?" I ask, now second guessing my master plan.

"Feels like the prick from a briar. No big deal."

That's not so bad. Besides, this thing seems so docile. "I'll take it."

He puts the green snake into a sack that resembles burlap material, but softer, and then he ties it at the top.

"You need an aquarium?"

After I torment the hell out of Brin with it, I'll turn it loose. Snakes in aquariums... Not my thing.

109

"No," I say, shrugging as I hand him the money.

My grin only grows as I pick up my phone. Now I have her number.

"Hello?" she answers, probably confused by the number she doesn't know.

"It's me. What are you doing tonight?"

She pauses for a minute, and my smile becomes painful. She's right to be paranoid.

"I have to run some errands, but I should be back within an hour or two. I'm on my way out right now."

"Good. I'll see you then," I say while hanging up.

Maggie—the good woman that she is—gave me a key to their house and the code to the alarm system. So from now on, I have full access to torture the hell out of Brin.

My phone buzzes, and I grimace, worrying that it's going to be my dad again. It's not him, but it's almost as bad. I groan when I see Ash's name on the screen.

"Yeah," I mumble, knowing damn well what she's about to do. She only calls when she wants to set me up.

"Please tell me you have nothing going on tonight."

Shit. Here she goes.

"I have plans."

"Look, I'm sort of having a major problem, and I was supposed to go out with Hillary Barns tonight for drinks. But I can't see her. I don't even really like her, and if she sees me in this shape, she'll gloat and claim some sort of victory from all of this. You know she has a huge thing for Tag. I realize most women do, but she's so fucking blatant about it."

Is she... crying? Did she just say *fucking*?

"Ash, are you okay?"

"I'm fine. I will be fine. I just... can you please go meet her in my place? She just wants to set up the pool party for Tag, and I really can't deal with her. I've hated her since he hired her, and I refuse to see her. You know everything there is to know about the party. Wren is MIA, so it has to be you. Please. I'm begging you."

Considering she sounds like she's close to falling apart, I sigh and agree. At least it's not a matchmaking scheme.

"I'll have to reschedule it. I have plans, but I'll tell her I'm taking over the party planning so you don't have to deal with her anymore."

"That'll work," she says, a sniffle following.

"You sound rough. Can I do something?"

"No," she whimpers. "I'll be fine."

With that, she hangs up, and I frown. What just happened?

Instead of dwelling on it, I drive over to Brin's house, happy when I see the Range Rover is gone. I really hope she doesn't run over my newly-repaired Porsche with my Range Rover. That would suck.

Once I park—and leave her plenty of parking room—I jog up to her house. Maggie's car is gone, too, so it's just me and the snake in my hand.

That sounds a little dirty.

After unlocking the door, I head into the bedroom and grin as I pull open the cotton-filled panty drawer. But when I spot a few new

111

pairs of satin thongs on top, I'm forced to swallow hard against the instant knot in my throat.

When did she get these?

The snake wiggling in the bag reminds me of the task at hand, and I remove my eyes from the scandalously distracting new underwear to focus on my main objective. I stick my hand in the bag, but I pull it back quickly, screeching like a kid when the damn thing latches on and bites the hell out of me.

"Fucking psycho!" I bark, dropping the bag.

The sneaky bastard tries to slither away, but I grab him by the tail, jerking it back up from the ground. But then the vicious thing turns and strikes at my hand, and there's not a damn thing I can do but cry out like a little bitch.

Briar scratch? That's not like a damn briar scratch! That's like having two searing hot, fat needles jabbed into you. The guy switched the snakes. He had to. The one he was playing with was calm and even... sweet. This thing is a rabid demon.

After it strikes me again, I drop it, and it slithers under the small crack of her bed. I groan as I stare at the impossible mess I've gotten myself into. I sure as hell can't leave this horrible thing in her room. This is a complete and total fail. Instead of doing a victory lap, I'll be playing the snake trapper all night.

Brin

Grocery store, drycleaners, and the gas station. Three more stops and then I can rush home and change. I want to look better than the last time, so I actually bought a sexier pair of shorts. They're still comfortable. They're not as sexy as a tight dress, but they're a step up from my usual attire. They were also cheap because of a sale, so that made it a no-brainer.

"Brin!" Tria calls, waving at me from a restaurant patio. As I move toward her, I see a red-cheeked Ash sitting beside her, sipping from a teacup.

Rain sits down with them just as I near, and then I see Raya Capperton right behind her, a bitter scowl on her usually sweet face. What's going on? And why do they all look pissed?

"Are you guys okay?" I ask sincerely, and Ash starts crying into her napkin.

Oh no.

"We hate men," Raya says while crossing her arms under her chest, her eyes the saddest I've ever seen them. I really thought things would be better between her and Kade by now.

"I can't be in public," Ash says, wiping her eyes as her tears pour uncontrollably.

I stand on the sidewalk as they sit behind the rod iron-fence separating us, and I remain dumbfounded and completely useless.

"We can't go to my place," Tria grumbles.

"Mine either," Raya growls.

"Certainly not mine," Rain says, sighing... oddly.

Shit. I really, really, *really* wanted to hang out with Rye tonight. I have so much fun when he's around, but... Ah, hell. I have to do the right thing.

"You can come to my place. Maggie has a date tonight, so my house will be empty."

I won't cancel on him until I know for sure they are staying for a long period of time.

Apparently all hell has broken loose in the fairytale lives of the Sterling Sparklers.

Brin

When I open the door, I hear a rustling motion in my room, as though there's a struggle. What the hell? Did he set up a prank that moves?

"I can't believe he did this," Ash groans.

I still have no idea what's going on with all of the girls. They rode with me, but they were bashing men without details as to why they were ranting.

Instead of going to my room to find what prank Rye has left behind, I move to the kitchen and decide to make margaritas instead.

"What happened?" I ask as Rain gives Ash another tissue.

"He didn't tell me. He kept it from me, and now... now... I'm going to kill him," Ash growls, her fury sweeping in quickly.

The rustling in my room turns to silence, and I realize that jackass is in there right now. I'm going to kill him before Ash kills Tag. That's why he asked me what I was doing. He wanted to make sure I was going to be out of the house, and like an idiot, I even gave him a timeframe to plot his attack. Stupid. Stupid. Stupid.

"Why are you killing Tag?" I ask softly, serving her the first strong glass of margarita.

"Because I'm pregnant and he didn't tell me!" she barks, and I slide the margarita away from her. Obviously she can't drink that in her condition.

Everyone at the table goes still and silent. Apparently no one knew. But... isn't that something the girl tells the guy? Not the other way around?

"It's payback. For Trip. I know it is. I'm going to kill him," she groans, dropping her head to her hands.

"I thought you were on the pill," Rain says quietly.

"I am. But I had to change my prescription two months ago. Whenever you change your pills, there's a major possibility that you can get pregnant. So, we used condoms during that period of time. One of the condoms broke the last time I got drunk. My fertile son of a bitch husband knew it, but he kept it a secret.

"For two months he's acted differently. He has constantly stopped me from drinking alcohol, limited my caffeine intake, and has even made me eat healthy shit. And he did it all with stealth so that I didn't notice. He's crafty like that. It's one of the things I love and hate about him. But you have to tell a girl there's another body growing inside of her if you're suspicious!"

Whoa.

"You're sure you're pregnant?" Tria asks.

"Positive. I took ten tests. Not one of them said negative. My bladder has shriveled up in fear because I tried to take more tests. One time—the condom only broke *one* time."

She scrubs her face with her hands and glances down to her stomach while we all search for the right thing to say.

"Wow. He really is fertile. Or maybe it's the two of you combined, considering you're the first and only girl he's ever gotten pregnant," Rain says, looking just as shocked as I feel.

Ash's eyes change, anger fleeing as regret fills them. "I'm so sorry, Rain. This is... I'm an insensitive bitch for griping about this in front of you."

I forgot Rain can't have children, and I'm sure this is hard for her to sit in on.

Rain smiles warmly and rubs Ash's hand in hers. "You're not an insensitive bitch. I don't think you know how to be. You were surprised, then a little freaked out, and now you're venting. It's allowed."

Something crashes to the ground in my room, and a series of muttered curses and yelps of pain ring out in sequence. Then I hear the window in my room opening and slamming within seconds apart. Did he just call someone or something a vile bastard?

"What was that?" Ash asks, recoiling in alarm.

"That would be my very annoying neighbor trying to carry out some nefarious plan of revenge. Apparently things went *awry*. Pun intended."

I grin as they all chuckle, and Ash says, "Come on out, Rye. We could use advice from a man right now."

"No thank you. I'll just stay in here until you all leave," he calls back, and I stifle a laugh.

"Does he sneak into your room often?" Tria asks. I don't like her teasing smile right now, because she's giving me way too much credit if she thinks Rye is into me.

I grin while joking, "Usually he waits until after I go to sleep, and then he breaks in and breathes heavily in my ear."

"That's bullshit! I never breathe heavily. I'm afraid it'll wake you up," he says, playing along instead of being defensive, and everyone laughs again.

"I've never heard him joke before," Rain says, her eyes on Tria.

"Me neither," Tria says, grinning.

They apparently don't know him very well, because that's all the man knows how to do.

"Come have a beer," I say to him as I stand and head to the fridge. I return to the table with two beers and a pitcher of margaritas.

With a reluctant sigh, he comes out, eyeing the table full of women. His arms have spots of blood on them, and so do his hands. What the hell has he been doing? He looks like he got into a fight with a thorn bush.

"What happened to you?" Tria gasps, staring at the same red flakes of blood that I am.

"I don't want to talk about it," he mumbles, sulking.

"Did you know I was pregnant?" Ash asks Rye, ambushing him.

He doesn't even act affected by that question.

"I knew about the condom breaking. Shit happens. He didn't know if you were pregnant," Rye says with a shrug. "It's not like he can pee on a stick for you."

"But he knew I could be pregnant," she growls, taking her anger out on the only man in view.

He comes to sit as close to me as he can get and as far away from Ash as he can manage. I'd laugh, but now is not the time.

He picks up his beer just as I take a sip of mine, and then he swaps the bottles and takes my beer instead. I'd ask why, but I already know the answer. Instead of reacting at all, I just start drinking the new beer.

"Someone else talk," Ash mumbles, burying her head in the crook of her arm as she rests it on the table. "I'm tired of being the only one with issues."

Raya sighs hard while staring at her engagement ring, twisting it absently while remaining lost in thought. "Kade won't let me in. He refuses to let me help him through anything, and since Thomas died... He just keeps pushing me away. He won't even look at me right now. I've tried to be patient—give him time to grieve—but I think he's only growing farther away from me with every passing day.

"I left the vineyard three days ago, turned off my phone, and I've been staying in a hotel. We've already moved back the wedding date twice—even though we're weren't even planning the wedding until spring. I'm starting to think he regrets proposing. It's hard to love someone if you can't let them in. And he just keeps shutting me out."

"Have you tried talking to him?" Rye asks, and he's met with a glare I didn't know Raya was capable of.

"No. Why didn't I think about talking to him?" she asks, sarcasm dripping from her tone. "I love the jackass, but he's... Well, I'm pissed."

"Why are men so damn stupid?" Tria growls.

"Men suck," Rain says for the hundredth time.

"I can't believe he didn't tell me I was pregnant," Ash groans.

Tria decides to take her turn after a long, deep breath. "Kode has gotten a little more aggressive lately than usual. He punched a guy last night because the guy's hand might have groped my ass. But I had warned him the guy was a sleaze-ball photographer, and had asked him to keep his cool since he insisted on joining me at my meeting. I needed that guy to use Beauty Graffiti on his shoots. He sure as hell won't now."

"He grabbed your ass in front of Kode?" Rain asks in shock. "I'm surprised Kode let him walk away."

"I love Kode for who he is, but there's a line. My business is the line. The guy was inappropriate, but I was handling it. Kode can't just swoop and give me that reputation. No one will work with me otherwise. I can handle things myself from time to time."

"Sounds like Kode had justifiable reaction to me," Rye whispers, leaning down to my ear.

I have no idea how to respond to her problem. I've never had a guy react that way over me. Twisted as it sounds, I'm actually a little jealous. John would have let a man grab my ass and give it a massage, and he wouldn't have done a thing about it.

I lean over to Rye and tug him down to me so that I can whisper in his ear, as they all go on and on about men being stupid.

"They're leaving them? They're all breaking up at once? Is that what this is?" I ask, confused by the madness going on around me.

"You aren't really leaving them, are you?" Rye asks, suddenly looking worried.

They all stop talking and stare at him as though he has sprouted a second head. "Don't be so dramatic," Raya scoffs, rolling her eyes.

They all say something about him being ridiculous and make fun of him for being a drama queen, and I bite back a grin. "Yeah," I say, adding to the bash-Rye fun by echoing Raya's words, "don't be so dramatic."

He glares at me, and I snicker quietly to myself. Rain hides her smile behind her hand, and I tilt my head. She still hasn't said what Dane has done to piss her off. All she has said is that men suck.

"Why do men have to be idiots all the time?" Tria asks Rye, narrowing her eyes at him, and all the girls stare at him expectantly.

Rye mutters something like hell and high heels under his breath just as the front door opens and Maggie walks in.

"Oh," she says, feeling a little startled. "I didn't see any cars."

"They rode with me. I thought you were already gone on your date," I say by way of explaining.

Very quickly, I go through the motions of introducing Maggie to the girls she doesn't know, and she waves awkwardly, considering they all sound and look miserable. Maggie turns her attention on the uncomfortable man at my side who is getting closer to me every time a girl gives him a threatening look.

"I'm glad you're here. Can you help me get a TV out of my car? It's a present for my dad, but it's a big son of a bitch."

Rye almost leaps out of his seat. "Fucking love to," he says gratefully, and Maggie works hard to suppress a grin when he almost sprints outside.

She walks over to the fridge to pull out a drink, and then she goes pale. I turn back toward the women at the table as they vent and slam men. I don't miss this hell. But when I was married, I only had Maggie to vent to.

"Um... Brin?" Maggie says, her eyes wide as she waves me over.

"I'll be right back," I say to the girls who don't even pause.

When I reach Maggie, she points to the fridge and whispers, "Why are there two things of blood and worms in there?"

"Oh," I say with a shrug. "The less you know, the better."

She rolls her eyes, trying to look exasperated, but then she accidentally smiles. "You two need to fuck and get it over with."

I just laugh. If she had seen the girl he was with at Ash's house, she wouldn't be saying that.

The sound of Rye coming back in interrupts the conversation, and Maggie goes to instruct him on where to put the TV. Once he's put the oversized box away, he walks out of her room, acting like he's going to escape.

"I'll see you ladies later."

I practically fly over to him, and block his path, refusing to let him leave me here alone with this, but he picks me up and moves me behind him. "Rye, stay," Ash says, a whimper in her voice. "We need a man's opinion."

He groans long and loud as he stares longingly at the door. "My *opinion* keeps getting me barked at," he mutters under his breath, turning his glower on me once more.

But he relents, and sluggishly walks back to the table, casting a look of pure hatred over his shoulder at me once more before sitting down. I smile at his misery and take my seat.

A small rapping on wood doesn't even disturb the rant going on in my dining room, and Maggie runs out in her short, sexy dress on her way to answer the door. When she opens it, Carmen walks in. Striking blonde hair, long, tan legs, and a perfect body that is encased in a tight red dress are what makes up the exterior of Maggie's bombshell girlfriend.

Rye's grin slowly crawls up as he takes her in, and the girls all turn to face the new woman in the room.

"Everyone, this is my girlfriend, Carmen," Maggie says, practically glowing as Carmen leans in and kisses her.

Rye's jaw falls unhinged, and I roll my eyes at what a damn guy he is.

"I really should have started coming over sooner," he says, and I slap him in the chest, earning a grunt and chuckle from him.

Considering he's a frigging brick wall, I inwardly whimper while rubbing my hand under the table. Damn, that hurt.

Still snickering, he goes to the fridge but pauses when he opens the door. After a beat, he grabs two beers and returns, offering me one. I'm going to have to restock the alcohol after tonight.

"We should get going," Maggie says, still grinning.

Carmen waves at us, her smile matching Maggie's, and they walk out hand-in-hand. The girls all stare at the door for a moment until Ash finally says, "I think she has the right idea."

Rain starts to grin, but covers it quickly with a serious face. "Yeah. Men suck."

Rye drops his head to his hands while groaning and mumbling something about burying me alive.

Brin

"It's not like I'm opposed to having another child. Tag is an incredible father, and I love the hell out of him. I just wanted us to plan out our next baby," Ash says, drinking her *virgin* margarita. "We'll be fine. Tag should have told me, but he didn't want me worrying. Trip is still in diapers, and he's a handful, so Tag didn't want me to freak out unless I had to."

I'm positive that she's the only sober person at this table.

Rye rolls his eyes and rests his head on my shoulder as he tries his best to keep quiet. He's been saying that for most of the night. But every time he opens his mouth, he's berated by the drunken women. He's like the only metal rod in the middle of a lightning storm.

Ash was stressed about the fact she's been taking her birth control this whole time, worried about the effect it might have on the baby, but Rye assured her that Tag swapped the pills for water pills the second the condom broke. He has a friend in the pharmacy who managed to package them up just like her birth control. Tag really did go all out. And that's why he's still wearing condoms—just in case she wasn't pregnant. I suppose that is rather pointless now.

You'd think the revelation would have been comforting, but she blew up at Rye after he told her—like it was his fault Tag confided in him and didn't tell her. I found the entire tirade rather entertaining, especially since Rye kept tugging on me like he expected me to defend him.

I didn't. At all.

In fact, I might have possibly encouraged her to be madder at him.

I'm also fairly certain that Rye has learned more about everyone's sex life than he ever wanted to know. Well, not my sex life—or lack thereof. I've not once mentioned anything about my past drama.

The girls finally seem to be calming down.

"Maybe Kade will eventually open up to me. He's grieving, and everyone deals with grief differently, right?" Raya asks, earning a growl from Rye.

He said the same thing forty minutes ago, and she unleashed hell on him before she broke into tears. I think he'll have PTSD after this night.

Tria sighs after finishing the last of her latest glass of margarita. "The guy shouldn't have touched me. I mean, I sure as hell didn't want him to, but I was trying to handle it more subtly. Kode can't lose his temper on every guy with a wandering hand, but he only did it because he loves me. Would I really want him to just stand by while some guy grabbed my ass right in front of him?"

Rye glares at her while keeping his head on my shoulder, but he wisely says nothing. Again, he pointed out this same logic less than an hour ago and she told him he was just like any other man.

Someone bangs on the door, and Rye says, "Finally," under his breath.

"It's ope—"

Before I can fully get the words out of my mouth, Tag's body is filling the doorway, his eyes going soft the second they find his wife. Ash gives him a tight smile as more tears fill her eyes, and she stands as he quickly closes the distance between them.

"Ash," he says softly, pulling her to him and looking at her in a way I've never known, "I'm sorry. I just didn't want to worry you and it be a false alarm. But I can't think of anything I'd rather do than have another child with you."

She smiles up at him as he wipes away her tears, and she pulls him down until their lips touch. "No," she says in a reverent breath. "I'm sorry. I just... freaked out a little. I needed... a minute."

He nods, his smile growing. "I completely understand. I've been on an anxiety rollercoaster, but I love you, and I actually want another baby. I get to be a part of it from start to finish this time. It's... exciting. Really exciting."

A soft sigh graces my lips, and Rye raises his head and puts his finger in his mouth, mocking a silent gag. I elbow him, and he snickers quietly as Ash comes over. "I'm going home with my husband. We have a lot to do and discuss."

I feel like an idiot when I start grinning uncontrollably, but it's so frigging sweet to see them together. Then the door opens again without a knock as Kode comes in, his eyes going directly to Tria.

Tag and Ash grin, and they escape as Kode goes and drops down in front of Tria's chair.

"Baby, I wish I could say I'm sorry, but I'm never going to let another man lay a hand on you. You know that. You know me. I love the fuck out of you, and I've changed a hell of a lot, but I can't change that."

The very same thing that pissed her off is suddenly filling her with pride as her tears glisten. I apparently don't understand love. If John ever did anything to piss me off, he didn't apologize. We would eventually just go on like nothing ever happened. There was never a grandstanding apology that melted hearts or resolution of any sort.

"I know. I... I love you. All of you. And I'd probably slap a bitch if she touched you."

He starts laughing as he stands, and he pulls her with him, wrapping her up in his arms. "Can we go home?" he asks sweetly, kissing the tip of her nose.

This is like watching numerous romance movies all at once. I hope Rye has a blood and gore flick ready again. I'm going to need it to bring me down from my high once this is all over.

Raya watches them leave, and she stares at the door as a tear slips down her cheek. Rain pats her arm comfortingly and leans over to take her hand. "Kade is hard to get through to sometimes, but he loves you."

"Yes I do," a male voice says from the door I never heard open.

Kade Colton is staring at his fiancée with a sad, apologetic smile. She starts to say something, but she clears her throat and sits back first. When she feels confident enough, she finally speaks.

"You keep pushing me away. Every time you face any sort of

emotional challenge, you push me away. I'm tired of it. When you do this, I'm worried to death I'm going to say or do the wrong thing and lose you. I don't like walking on eggshells, and I refuse to do it anymore," she says without any emotion in her voice, even though I can tell she'd love nothing more than to cry.

How does she do that?

He nods slowly while walking until he reaches her. He bends and puts both hands on either side of her chair, boxing her in, and he makes sure her eyes meet his.

"You're right. And God knows I'm sorry. This... all of this... you're the only person I've ever had this with besides Granddad. And obviously what we have is very different. But you shouldn't ever be scared of losing me. I'm yours, Raya. All yours. That means you can say or do whatever you want, and I won't go anywhere, regardless of what's going on around us. I love you."

Another tear falls down her cheek and she stands, which forces him to move back and allow her.

"Okay," she says simply, walking toward the door.

"Okay?" he asks, amused as he follows.

"That's what I wanted to hear, and you said it. Let's go home."

His smile breaks across his face, and he pulls her to him before delivering a kiss that I have to turn away from. Rye's brown eyes are staring into mine, and he winks as he avoids the scene just like me.

But those eyes are so close, just like his full lips, and my breath gets a little harsh.

"I think you two should get away for a while," Rain says,

reminding me that she's still here.

I break away from the eye contact that has left me almost dizzy, and look back at the couple that is separating.

"She's right," Kade says, grinning as he presses another sweet kiss to Raya's lips. "Let's go to Vegas."

Raya laughs as she laces her fingers with his. "When?"

"Right now. We won't even pack. We'll buy clothes when we get there."

Her eyes grow wide, and I turn green with envy. All of these beautiful women found the best men the world has to offer. I've never been treated even half as well. And it's actually a little depressing.

"Okay," she says for a new reason, her grin growing.

Kade's smile is almost heart-stopping, and he pulls her from the house before she can even say goodbye.

"Wow," Rain says, acting exhausted as the door shuts. "What a night."

Rye looks at her curiously, as do I. This is the longest she's gone without saying men suck. I start to ask her what's going on, when the door opens once again.

"Knock Knock," Dane Sterling says as he comes in, holding the hand of their smiling daughter—Carrie Sterling. It's official now; Carrie has been adopted, and she has a home that most children only dream about.

Rain smiles up at him and stands to grab her purse quickly.

"You ready?" Dane asks as he comes to wrap his arm around her shoulders, kissing her softly as a greeting.

"Yeah. Just let me tell Brin bye."

He eyes Rye for a moment, and then the little girl tugs on his arm and all of his attention goes to her as his smile warms. He bends down to tie the shoe that has come undone, while Rain comes to whisper to us.

"Sorry. All the girls were bitching, so I thought it would be terrible to say that Dane never does anything wrong. Thanks for having us over."

Mine and Rye's words refuse to form as she waves and walks away, going to Dane's side as she takes over holding the little girl's hand.

As soon as the door shuts, Rye leans back in his seat and takes a long drink of his beer.

"Was it just me, or was this the weirdest night ever?" I groan.

Rye pulls the beer away from his lips just barely in order to answer. "You have containers of blood and worms in your fridge, I tried putting a live snake in your panty drawer, and I'd say we're the most normal people that were in here tonight. What does that tell you?"

I laugh lightly as he stands, and he pulls at my hand, forcing me to stand as well.

"How did they even know the girls were here?"

He smiles proudly as he stretches. "I sent them all a text. I sent one to Kade first, knowing it would take him the longest to get here. Then I waited until the girls started making sense to text the others. And voila. You're welcome, by the way."

"Thank you," I say quickly.

"Let's watch TV and order a pizza. I wanted to go to Silk tonight, but fuck that. I'm exhausted."

He wanted to go to Silk with me?

My dorky grin would probably give me away, so I mask it with a respectable one instead, discreetly clearing my throat. His arm drops around my shoulders as we head to the couch to watch whatever movie he brought over with the snake.

That snake better not still be in my room.

Chapter 7

Rye

A soft, warm body is on top of me, and I wake up as my hands slide down Brin's back. She's sleeping peacefully with her head tucked into the crook of my neck, and the light pours through the window as she stirs just barely.

How long have we been asleep? Is it really morning? And why the hell do I just want to stay under her and go back to sleep?

I can't seem to stay away. Being around her is the best part of my day lately, and that's bad. Very bad.

Her hand slides up my chest as she snuggles in closer, and I smile as I tighten my hold around her waist. She looks so small right now, but she packs a lot of punch. I'm starting to think she packs more of a punch than I realized, because I really don't want to leave her right now.

"Good morning," a whispered voice says, and I jerk a little, quickly trying to get still when Brin mumbles something in her sleep.

I look over my shoulder as Brin continues to breathe evenly, staying asleep.

Maggie is grinning behind her cup of coffee, her eyes alight with an enigmatic sparkle. Oh shit. What time is it?

"She has to get up in thirty minutes to get ready for work," she says, smiling as she sips her coffee.

"I need to get to work, too. We're supposed to get her car finished

131

today," I say while trying to climb off the couch without waking Brin up, shifting her little by little off my chest.

I never go to work this early, but today I'm pretty excited. I can't wait to give her back her car.

"How much is her car going to cost?"

I smile when Brin presses a kiss to my chest. She's pretty damn sweet when she sleeps.

"Nothing."

I finally manage to get her moved to the couch, and I brush her hair away from her face as I stand up.

"Nothing?" Maggie asks, sounding intrigued. "It has to cost something. You couldn't have possibly had all those parts to spare. Along with paint and stuff."

Brin thinks she pays half the rent here, but this neighborhood is ridiculously priced. Maggie has family money, and I assume she makes Brin think she's contributing just as much as she is.

Maggie's a damn good person. Brin's pride won't allow her to think she owes anyone anything.

"Something tells me you understand why I need her to believe I'm not spending a dime on this. I'd appreciate it if you helped me out."

She shrugs, her smile only growing.

"I helped you sneak in to rig our fridge with blue dye. Of course I'll help you with this."

I bend over and grab my shoes, and then drop to the chair across from the couch, trying and failing not to look at the sleeping girl with her back turned to me. I've really got to get a grip.

Rye

"The car is fixed," Wrench says, grinning at me like he's waiting for my reaction.

"You're sure it's ready? No issues at all?"

"Positive," he affirms.

Tag walks in, and Wrench continues grinning. "You two need a minute?" Tag asks, noting the stare-down.

"No," I snap, and Wrench starts laughing.

"The Camry girl needs to bring it in for regular maintenance so this doesn't happen again. Your wallet will appreciate it."

He turns and walks away, leaving that in the air for Tag to pounce on. And he does.

"Camry girl? Brin? You're doing something to her car and paying for it?"

He sits down, eager to grill me. But I don't have time to deal with him. "Ash's car is ready. It's been ready. You were supposed to pick it up a couple of days ago."

He rolls his eyes while grinning. "I've been busy, as you saw last night. I'm here to get it now, but you're deflecting. What's going on with you and Brin?"

Shit.

"I don't know what you mean. We're friendly neighbors who torment each other. Nothing else."

"Dude, you're either talking about her, talking to her, seeing her,

133

or plotting a way to drive her crazy. You've got it bad, or you're just plain crazy. I'm going with option one."

I snort derisively, even as my nerves clam up in my throat.

"I don't have it bad, and we both know I've been crazy for years. She's cool. She doesn't pout or whine when I do something reprehensible. She just plots her own attack, and we have fun. It's completely and totally normal."

"There's not a single normal thing about anything you just said. But if you want to live in denial, fine. Just a warning, though; my dick stopped working for anyone but Ash the second I started falling for her. When's the last time yours worked?"

He's fucking with me. No way is that a real thing.

Jessica walks in, and she struts all the way to my desk. She bends over farther than necessary to hand me some paperwork to sign, and then she struts back out.

"Get anything from that?" Tag asks, looking smug as hell when I bring my eyes back up from all the shit I have to go through.

"From what?"

"The girl just did a catwalk performance to your desk, shoved her tits in your face, and you barely glanced at her. And she's just your type."

My type. I'm getting sick of hearing about *my type*.

"I noticed," I say with a shrug.

"Oh? What color of dress was she wearing? Was her hair up or down? And what did she say?"

What is this? The Spanish Inquisition?

"I rarely notice a girl's dress color, I never pay attention to hair, and she didn't say a word."

He laughs as though I've said something ludicrous, so I lean back while arching my brow.

"You referred to Sarah Jergens as the *purple-dress girl* because you couldn't remember her name. You bitched about Tria dying her hair from blonde to black. And Jessica just told you about a meeting you have tomorrow. So you just answered all three wrong. Care to tell me again that Brin isn't in your head?"

I shift uncomfortably in my chair. I really didn't notice Jessica at all. I saw her walk my way, realized that she bent over too far, but it's like I didn't ever really see her. And she spoke?

"I didn't notice Jessica because she's listed under one of my two rules—I don't fuck people from work. Too much drama."

"You're really hell-bent on denying this, aren't you?"

"Why is it so hard for you to believe we're just friends? Look at Rain and the Sterlings. Proof is there. There is nothing physical going on with the guys and Rain, yet all of them would have paid for her car to get fixed if she couldn't have afforded it. So there."

A challenge brews in his eyes.

"They've known Rain since they were kids. It took years for them to get that sort of closeness with no romantic feelings. But she and Dane were instantly close. Sort of like you and Brin."

I'm going to strangle him. "We're not Rain and Dane. We're Rain and Maverick—friends."

He grins as he leans forward, and I want to slap the hell out of him.

"Fine. If you honestly don't have any feelings for Brin, then I suppose you'll be fine with the girl I'm setting you up with tonight."

Ah, fuck.

"Tonight? No offense, but Ash has the worst taste in women. And I have plans for the foreseeable future when it comes to her blind dates."

He laughs condescendingly, and I glare at him.

"I didn't say Ash has you a date. I said *I* have you a date. And I've got damn good taste. Have you met my wife? She's fucking perfect."

"And you know this girl?" I muse, semi-suspicious since the only woman he ever notices is his wife.

"Corbin Sterling knows her. She's not one of his exes though. She's a sister of a girl he *dated*. He said he was sending you a picture. And the girl knows her cars. She might know more than you."

Doubtful.

I really don't want to go on a damn date. I have plans. I'm dying to see Brin in the kitchen. No one has ever actually cooked dinner for me.

"Why tonight?"

"Because now that the initial shock of the baby is over, Ash is excited and she wants to celebrate with her friends. Of course you know Brin will be there. Ash was calling her before I left."

I frown as his words resonate. "So Brin will be there all by herself." Now it makes sense. "I see what you're doing, and I'm not playing along. You think when I see Brin all alone that I'll drop my date and go to her. Well, you're right, but not because of the reasons you think. We're friends, and I'm not going to ignore her for someone I don't know. It sucks to be around a bunch of couples while you're stag. That's the only reason I let your relentless wife set me up with women at your functions. Thanks, but no thanks. I'm not playing your game."

I really hate his smirk. "No game. Ash said she's setting Brin up on a date to make up for the bad date with Wren. So you'll be all alone if you don't go with the girl I've picked out for you."

What the hell?

"And Brin said yes?" I ask, trying not to sound angry. This shouldn't be pissing me off.

"Yep. So what's it going to be?"

I glance at the time, and try not to let my jaw tick. Before we both crashed on the couch last night, we discussed hanging out at my place. Apparently she's obsessed with my kitchen and wants to cook in there. Then she tells Ash she wants to go out on a date without even canceling on me?

"Fine. I'll meet your girl."

Tag smiles as though he has a secret, and then he walks out without saying another word.

Looking at the time, I decide to head home and get ready for my fucking date. She'd better be as perfect as Tag promised.

A text from the bastard I hate the most comes across the screen, and I groan when I read it. I should have just ignored it. This is quickly becoming the worst day I've had in a while.

Dad: *Found three boxes of your things. Come get them or I'll throw them* *away.*

I just roll my eyes. Any time he gets a new wife, I suddenly have *boxes* pop up. In other words, he wants me to meet the latest gold-digging Barbie of the hour. Now I'll have to make a stop on my way home to deal with Brin.

I knew this was coming, considering how many calls and texts I've ignored recently. Why did I read that message?

I grab Brin's keys and drive the short distance to my father's fucking massive house, and I head through the service entrance instead of the front. Unfortunately, he was expecting that.

"You could send someone a message letting them know you're coming," he says disapprovingly.

I couldn't care less.

"You could just mail my stuff to me. I haven't lived here in years, so I can't imagine what else is left of mine."

"The attic just got cleaned out. Found a bunch of your old photos and trophies. Some of it may be things you might want to go through and throw away. Some things you might want to keep."

Trophies and photos.

"Just let me meet the new wife, and I'll grab the boxes. We both know that's why you really sent that message. How old is she? Is this one at least older than me?"

He frowns while taking a breath. "She's older than you. I'm sorry you seem to be in such a foul mood, but at least try to be cordial."

I cross my arms over my chest as I stare expectantly.

"She's by the pool," he says, finally.

I nod and start walking in the direction, every step making me sicker. I hate being inside this house. The walls are stained with too many memories that only fuck with my head.

Dad can't seem to handle being here alone. But he's never going to learn or care. None of them are ever going to be her. A young ass isn't going to soothe the guilt.

Blonde, big chest, barely legal... There's no way the girl sunning in a bikini and wearing stilettos is really older than me.

"Marilyn, this is Rye."

Of course her name is Marilyn.

She slowly pulls her glasses down, and she doesn't hide her eyes as they hungrily rake over me. Sick. Most all of them do this. Why can't he find one single woman who cares about him enough to not eat me up the first time they meet me?

"Not what I was expecting," she drawls.

My father doesn't acknowledge the typical ridiculous behavior. They're all the same. Hungry for money from him and sex from anyone else. Not me. Fuck no.

"I'd say nice to meet you, but I don't lie."

She growls playfully, and swats her hand like she's using cat claws. "Your father said you were a bit of a rebel with an attitude."

I decide not to respond. She's not worth the breath. Instead, I make my way over to my father, and stop as he turns around.

"I've met her. I'll grab the boxes and go."

He frowns as he looks down. "Good seeing you, son."

139

I don't reciprocate. I'd rather just walk away and leave him stewing in the silence that proves how much I hate him.

I grab my boxes, not bothering to stay here and go through them, and I carry them outside to Brin's Camry. After I toss everything into the trunk, I close it and Marilyn is right in front of me.

"Christ," I grumble, trying to catch my breath.

"Not what I expected you to be driving," she says, stroking the side of Brin's white car with her red manicured nail.

"Didn't come to impress," I mutter dryly.

She wisely takes a step back as I open the door. It's not easy to fold myself into Brin's small car, and I curse it when my knees hit the steering wheel again. My damn Porsche has more room than this.

Marilyn waves at me, grinning as though she thinks I'm on the menu, but I shudder instead of giving her the reaction she expects. I back out and make the short drive to my very dark house.

I distinctly remember leaving at least three lights on. I know I didn't turn all the lights off when I left this morning. There's no way I'm walking into one of her traps without some sort of defense. Besides, I'm pissed at her right now for canceling on me without telling me.

A date. She shouldn't be going on a fucking date.

Brin

"I have to pay him back," I groan. This hour-long argument is getting old. "Especially now. I didn't know he was paying for it himself."

"He wants to do this, and it'll piss him off if you argue. Just let him. It's not like you're taking advantage. He's trying to do something nice."

Huffing, I consider my defeat. I really don't know what to do. I can't afford this if he did too much. It's been in there for a while, and his shop is outrageously priced. I looked it up online.

"So you're doing something together? Again?" Maggie asks with a smile that says too much.

Ash invited me over, and begged me to let her set me up on another date, but I told her no. I've been excited about seeing Rye all day. And he never canceled, so I'm really hoping that means he wants to see me, too.

I'm happy with my selection of a semi low-cut, white shirt and a very flattering pair of frayed, dark denim shorts—short shorts. My hair is actually down and fixed, and I even put on a little more makeup than usual.

"This might sound stupid, but I think he might sort of be interested?" I say, but it sounds more like a question.

Maggie chuckles lightly while giving me a look I can't decipher.

"He *might* be interested? Brin, a guy might be interested if he buys you a drink. If he pays to have your car repaired—after *you* crashed it into his on purpose—then it's obvious he's interested. More than interested. The two of you have been spending more and more time together."

I can't help but grin, and hope I'm not reading all the signals wrong. He slept on the sofa with me, we cuddled during the movie,

141

and his arms stayed around me long after he went to sleep. I almost didn't go to sleep because I was savoring every second of it.

"What are you two doing tonight?" she asks, leaning back in her seat.

"We're hanging out at his house because I told him I want to use his kitchen. Which is true—his kitchen is freaking amazing—but it's better than going out into the real world where all the gorgeous women call his name. And I'm not exaggerating."

"He's not spending the night with *all the gorgeous* women. And in the two years I've lived across from him, I've never seen him have a girl over. And I'm nosy. I would have noticed."

I'm envious that she's lived across from him for that long. I should have moved in with her the second she offered, but instead, I stupidly tried to manage living in hell. Well, my parents' house—same difference. I only moved in here a few months ago.

"Do you think you could—"

The door swings open, interrupting whatever Maggie was going to say, and Rye stalks toward me like a determined man on a mission. And holy shit, it's sexy as hell.

But my excitement is cut short when he sweeps down and throws me over his shoulder, walking back toward the door with me dangling.

"What are you doing?" I ask through a laugh.

Maggie smiles as she watches us, acting as though we're her favorite show.

"I left at least three lights on," he says while carrying me across the yard.

Crap.

"I didn't do anything. I swear. Your window is locked."

"I locked it so you couldn't get in anymore, but I left three lights on, and now they're all off."

I just giggle, but then I see my Camry. Holy shit! It looks brand new. Better than brand new. Are those real wheels? And new tires? And tinted windows? It doesn't even look like the same car, and that's just what I can see under the glow of the streetlight.

"Hey! Let me see my car. It looks incredible!" I exclaim excitedly.

"Sure. Right after you walk me around my house. I don't want to end up like one of the idiots from *Home Alone* with a scalded hand, a burned head, or a nailed foot."

I can't help but giggle. "No trust," I mock, and he snorts derisively.

"Hell no."

He stands me upright when we reach his porch, and he hands me his keys while keeping his front to my back, his body flush against mine.

"Open the door," he says impatiently, and I bite back a grin.

Very purposely, I bend over and make sure my rear rubs his crotch. He doesn't move as I squint in the darkness to try and see the keyhole, taking much longer than necessary.

"Tonight would be good," he jokes, his voice full of amusement as his crotch stays firmly planted against my ass.

"Yeah, yeah," I murmur in a putout tone.

Finally, I push the door open, and flick on the first light. "See?

Your doorway isn't rigged with a blow torch, and your door handle is nice and cool to the touch."

He pokes his head in very warily, and he looks around, cautiously gauging every possible attack point.

"There could still be room for a nail in the foot."

I let him guide me through the house from behind me, but his hands on my hips become distracting. I stare down at them, and he suddenly brings me to an abrupt stop.

"You're about to run over a wall," he says through a chuckle. "It helps to look up when you walk."

He steers me to the right, and we walk through his kitchen, which calls to me. "I really want to cook in there."

"That's what you said last night," he mumbles, not sounding overly enthused.

"I'm not going to poison you, if that's what you're worried about. It'd be too much of a waste to cook a meal in there and then ruin it."

I expect him to laugh, but he doesn't. Instead, he keeps steering me into each room, forcing me to flip on the lights and walk around.

I laugh in between each new shift, but I can't see his expression. He must be terrified since he's being so quiet. That makes me a little proud.

"It's safe," I promise, lying my ass off.

He'll find a few things soon enough. Most of it is in his massive, beautiful bathroom that I really want to play in. The all-tile shower has five showerheads, and they all looked like so much fun. Damn, I love his house.

When we reach his bedroom, my sharp intake of breath is unbidden and embarrassing. I was in here earlier, but he wasn't home, so it didn't really dawn on me how much magnitude this room holds.

His massive, king-size bed barely makes a dent in his ungodly sized room. Kings would envy a room this enormous. Maggie's house is so small by comparison.

"Why do you live in the suburbs?" I ask, trying hard to swallow my nerves as we move around the room, getting closer to his bed.

"I have a house on the beach, but this place is closer to the garage. And it's the one adult purchase I've made since I became an adult," he says with no emotion.

"You had to make an adult purchase?"

"Well, this room seems fine. Now to the bathroom," he says instead of answering me.

After we make it through the bathroom—where he doesn't find either of my traps—we move back through his bedroom, and I chance a glance at the bed. I can't help but wonder if I might make it there tonight.

The very thought almost makes me lightheaded. But he pushes me out of his room and back to the living room, finally seeming pleased that nothing too rancorous is going to jump out and get him.

Now I need to go grab the groceries for our dinner.

"Do you need a ride to Tag's?" he asks. "I have a driver for the night. The car will be here in about twenty minutes. I just need time to change."

Tag's? Do I need a ride?

"We can pick up your date on the way to pick up mine if you want."

The air in my big fantasy balloon is violently deflated as the crushing weight of reality hits me. "Date?" I ask in a hoarse voice that forces me to clear my throat.

"Yeah. Tag set me up this time. He swears it's better than Ash's choices. He said she got you a date, too."

I'm so stupid. I was just in his room planning this night all wrong. I can't believe I really thought I had a chance with him.

"Um. No thanks. I'm good. I should go, though," I say while turning away.

"That's cool. Let me know if you change your mind," he says dismissively.

He turns his back on me and starts unloading his pockets, so I take that as my cue to leave. I don't even bother saying *bye*.

With quick, angry strides, I reach my house in no time and the door slams behind me. Maggie comes running out of her room, clutching her chest as though I just scared the hell out of her. But one quick look at my face, and her fear is replaced by worry.

"What happened?"

I roll my eyes while heading to my room, barely holding back a scream. "He has a *date* tonight."

"What?" she asks in as much disbelief as I am in.

At least I'm not the only idiot under this roof. Maybe there's too much iron in the water and it's making us delusional.

"Yep. Oh, and he wanted to know if *my* date and I wanted to ride with them."

I turn to see the pure shock on her face, and she drops to my sad, pathetic bed. I'm paying him for my damn car. Definitely paying him.

"I so did not see that coming. And what date do you have? I thought he was your date for the night."

So did I.

"Ash offered to set me up with someone at their party tonight. I told her no. He told Tag yes when he offered to set him up. I can't believe I was such an idiot."

I shouldn't cry. It'd be pathetic, and dramatic, and... embarrassing to cry over a guy that I was merely *friends* with. Fortunately, no tears come out, though I'm really not surprised. I stopped crying when I was a kid.

Rye can kiss my ass. I'm done being his friend.

"Call Ash and tell her to make the date happen," Maggie says, bringing me back to the hell I'm in.

I look at her like she's lost her mind, and then I drop to the bed beside her.

"I don't want to go over there. I don't want a date. And I sure as hell don't want to see him on a date. I didn't want to like him. In fact, I wanted to hate him. But he's so frigging sweet, funny, smart, and comfortable. I slept like a rock last night, and I honestly thought I'd sleep even harder tonight—if you know what I mean."

She snickers quietly while reaching over and grabbing my phone. "Set the date up. If you don't, it'll make you look bad. You're too amazing to look like you're pining over him. Go have fun. Or at least look like you're having fun. Otherwise he'll ask questions you don't want to answer."

Why did I ever let myself go to this place? I would be fine right now had I kept my mind in the friend-zone.

Maggie is right. I'll look pathetic if I stay here after that. I guess I'll have to text Ash.

Rye

"You came," Tag says with a frown.

What the hell?

"Yeah, and I picked up Leah. You're right; she knows all her shit about cars. She went to grab us some drinks."

Please don't ask me what color her dress is.

I know she has red hair, a slim body, and a vast amount of knowledge about anything with wheels, but I can't seem to remember what color dress she has on.

His frown only deepens, and his eyes trail over to the back gate to his patio as it opens. In walks the girl who pissed me off, and she doesn't have anyone with her. What dick couldn't go pick her up?

Wren didn't go get her either, but it was planned for them to meet here so that neither of them felt compelled to get along. It put them on neutral, easy grounds. This dick Ash has for her isn't affiliated with our group, so he should have gone to pick her up.

I try not to breathe differently when I see how fucking perfect she looks. The light blue sundress is flowing at the bottom instead of tight like the other girls are wearing. She looks so damn sweet and tempting.

I can almost see her blue eyes from here, like they are glistening as she searches the party.

"So you really went and picked up Leah?" Tag asks, his eyes going from me to Brin.

"It sounded like you wanted me to, so I did. Brin's date here yet? I think she's looking for him."

He mutters something about stubbornness and pride, but I have no idea what. Nor do I care.

"So it doesn't bother you that Brin is here with a date?" Tag asks, fishing hard for something he won't catch.

It's driving me crazier by the second, and she hasn't even met the guy yet. But I refuse to tell him that, because he'll never let us just be friends. He'll keep pushing me until I crack, and Brin's not the kind of girl you have fun with in the bedroom. She's the kind you marry.

Not me. I don't want something that serious, and it would have to be that serious with her—monogamy, steady dinners at a set time, cuddling on the couch for hours, and recording our favorite shows. That's not who I am. It can't be who I am. Some people just don't have the luxury of picturing themselves happy.

Some people have seen the real side of the ending instead of the happily-ever-after fable people want to believe.

"Here's your drink," Leah says, smiling as she hands me the Corona.

I offer her a brief smile, and make a mental note that she's wearing a dark red dress in case Tag asks. It's hot that she knows so much about cars, but it's also annoying. Though I love talking about cars all day, I prefer to be the one educating. I don't like feeling like someone *thinks* they are educating me. It actually pisses me off.

Brin just listens and smiles and asks questions, and that's what I like—someone who I can teach. This girl is making me dread going to the garage because of how dull it all sounds.

"Brin!" Ash calls cheerily as she makes her way toward her with a guy I'd like to punch.

Maybe she won't leave with him. Then I can keep my sanity without making a scene.

Brin

I can't believe I let Maggie talk me into this. It's so much harder than I thought it was going to be.

Rye's date is stunningly beautiful, and even though he looked my way for a while, now his eyes are back on *her*—his perfect date—as he drinks the beer she brought him. He was probably pitying my pathetic attempt to blend in.

What was I thinking by wearing a sundress?

Ash finally makes it to me while pulling the arm of a guy who might as well have douchebag tattooed on his forehead. Great.

"Adam, this is Brin. Brin this is Adam," Ash introduces, and I try to rein in my temper when I see his expression.

There are numerous things a guy can do that I don't understand. There are several expressions I can't decipher. But I know disappointment when I see it.

"Oh," he says, forcing a smile. "Nice to meet you."

Liar.

Right now he's secretly cursing Ash for inviting him here. My shoulder-length hair is light brown, and tonight it's fixed. My eyes are actually a pretty cool blue most days. It's like they shift. This is one of the good days, and he's still not impressed.

Some of my features might be amazing on their own, but all together, they make a girl most guys consider ordinary. I've always been completely fine with that until I met Rye.

"It's nice to meet you," I say quietly, somehow hiding the sigh on the tip of my tongue.

Ash frowns as she looks from me to Rye, but she can't possibly know anything. I'm doing good at playing *fine*.

"Sorry about the sundress," I murmur with a shrug. "I had to get ready quickly."

Ash starts to say something, but douche boy beats her to it.

"I just found out about this ten minutes ago, and I managed to—"

"So," Ash interrupts, "Adam, Brin is the assistant to the director at the museum. She's witty, smart, funny, and completely unpredictable. Brin, Adam is climbing the ladder at Millington Inc. He's an accountant and... um... new to the area?"

She acts like she knows nothing about him, and she turns on her heel to retreat. And what does he mean ten minutes ago? Ash said she had a date for me much earlier than that.

"How long have you been in Sterling Shore?" I ask him as a way of killing the awkward silence.

"Actually, I've been here for ten years, so I'm not sure what she

151

meant by that," he says with a smile that doesn't reach his eyes.

I don't like him. In fact, I can tell what a major turd he is right now. With drop-dead gorgeous girls, guys work hard on a façade that could fool royalty. But with girls like me, they barely even try to mask their real selves.

"Ah, so Ash barely knows you."

He tilts his head, checking out Ash's ass as she walks away. What a dick.

"I met her the other day. She met with us about maybe changing accounting firms. I thought she was inviting me here for her," he says while turning back around to meet my eyes.

Of course he did. This guy is just as average as me, so I'm not sure why the hell he's acting so above my level. He looks a lot like John, and he'd be in the likely pool of datable prospects I could obtain—if he wasn't such an arrogant prick.

In his mind, he looks like the Sterling men. At least I'm self-aware. There was once a time I sat around laughing at all the beautiful people. I should have stuck to that instead of befriending them. It makes life hard.

"Ash is married to Tag Masters," I say quickly, wondering how he doesn't know that if he was going to be on her account. She must have decided early on that she didn't want this prick to deal with.

So why did she set me up with him?

His eyes scan the scene and widen when they land on the beautiful man who is pulling Ash close for a showy, steamy kiss that almost makes my toes curl. Damn.

Rye is laughing with his date as she giggles beside him. Perfect—she even laughs pretty. My brief window of fantasy seals itself shut right in front of my eyes.

Her immaculately manicured nails are painted hot pink, and I glance down to my short, sad, plain nails. Her long, vibrant, red hair is a sharp contrast to my shorter, duller locks. I should have gotten a different color when I went to get the blue covered up.

Stop. I need to stop. I'm me. That's never bothered me before, and I refuse to let it bother me now just because I had a crush on a jerk that I thought liked me.

"Should we sit or something?" I ask the guy who is busy drooling over every other girl here.

"Sure," he says, sighing as though he's bored out of his mind.

This is going to be a long night.

Chapter 8

Rye

I've started to go talk to Brin numerous times. It feels wrong staying away from her. We're friends. Only friends. And I happen to love being her friend, even though I've only known her for a short period of time.

So why do I feel like I can't just walk over and talk to her?

"Do you know that girl or something?" Leah asks.

She doesn't sound annoyed or intimidated, and that sort of bothers me. Brin looks amazing tonight, so Leah should feel insulted by my inability to stop looking. Brin pulls off the innocent thing, even though I know she's not at all innocent.

"Yeah. I do. She's my neighbor and my friend."

She shrugs as she asks a passing server for another Corona. Leah drinks my favorite beer, likes the things I do, and she's a knockout, but I can't seem to make myself interested.

Fuck. This is her fault—Brin. I can't keep thinking about her like this, but every time she forces a brittle smile for the guy she's with, I want to go rescue her and spend the night watching gory movies and talking about nothing. And then I want to do something to torment her.

"You smell like a carburetor," Leah says, grinning.

Not sure how I smell like a carburetor, but okay...

"I showered at the garage before Tag swung by to tell me about the party."

She giggles as she steps closer. "I wasn't complaining. I happen to love it."

I'm fairly sure this girl would fuck me in the work area of my garage, and usually that would have me squealing tires to get us over there, but I keep looking over at Brin instead. The guy she's with doesn't seem the least bit interested.

"Excuse me," I say to Leah, and I make my way toward Ash as Leah says something back.

Ash looks up from her glass of water and frowns at me. "What's that look for?" she asks.

"Who's the guy acting like he can't wait to get out of here?" I retort, glaring at her.

How could she do this to Brin?

She grumbles and groans under her breath, and finally she releases a few choice words.

"An accountant I just met."

"And you set him up with Brin without knowing him? Why would you do that?"

She hesitates for a minute. Then she finally curses again before dropping her shoulders in defeat.

"Fine. You and Brin weren't supposed to come. And if you did come, you were supposed to come together. But apparently the two of you don't give a flying shit about each other the way I presumed—the way we all thought you did. That guy is the only guy I could get over here at the last minute. But I honestly thought the two of you were into each other, and I never thought you—being the alpha jerk you are—would let her show up with another guy. It was a push. A tiny little push, and the two of you shoved back. This was not supposed to backfire."

I'm going to strangle Tag. Now I look like a dick. "So Brin had no intentions of going out with that guy tonight, did she? Tag came and told me she was already coming and that she'd accepted the date offer."

Ash guiltily pouts as she looks toward the very depressed and bored Brin.

"No. That was to force you to face your feelings for her. She told me she had plans when I asked. I was so excited, and then she sent a text later saying that she'd come. I thought you liked her. I wouldn't have tried pushing you two if I had known you would go out with Leah. Tag said if you turned down a girl like Leah, then you were more than likely hard-up for Brin. His words."

I turn and glower at the fool talking to Dane Sterling, but he doesn't notice. I should kick his ass for this. Brin came to my house thinking she was going to cook, and I fucking offered to let her ride with me and my date. She thinks I'm the one who didn't cancel. I should throttle the both of them for doing this to us.

"We're not guinea pigs, Ash," I growl.

"I know," she says apologetically. "It's just... Rye, you smile when you're with her. You laugh. You joke. And you look so damn happy. I've never seen any of that with you until you met her. And it happens every time she's around. I just wanted you to see what's right in front of you. Jealously is a good motivation. Tag and I messed around and wasted so much time. I didn't want you two to do the same thing."

Fuck. Can't we just be friends? It's like I'm speaking a foreign language that no one can understand.

"Thanks to you, Brin thinks I bailed on her to go out with Leah, and now she's over there with Captain Jerk who keeps staring at your ass every time you walk by. Think about that the next time you want to play the manipulation game."

I start to walk over to Brin, but Ash starts crying, and I groan. Fucking pregnancy hormones.

"Shit, Ash. I'm sorry."

"No. You're right," she sniffles. "I'm the one who's sorry. I just want... you... two... to be... happy," she says through harsh, labored, tearful breaths.

Motherfucker. I'm going to hang myself right now.

"You had good intentions," I say while pulling her to me and hugging her. "I'll go talk to Brin and save her from the reject she's with. But it's because we're friends, Ash. I like Brin too much to date her. Do you understand that? I don't date long, but I keep friends for life."

She pauses her sniffling as she looks up, frowning. "Fine. Go be her friend."

Once I'm sure she's not going to break into a sobbing fit, I start to walk toward Brin, but her date is almost at the bar, so I go toward him instead. "Two Coronas," I say to the bartender as he mixes a fruity drink.

Brin's not too crazy about fruity stuff.

"You friends with Ash?" I ask while turning back toward the party.

"Sort of," he says, shrugging as his eyes land on Leah.

The redhead waves at me, and I wave back, suddenly feeling like the biggest jerk of the night. Brin... She had to have thought I was the worst person ever earlier. I'm going to kill Tag.

"Damn," he drawls, watching Leah with too much interest. "You with her?"

He's got a gem but he wants a stone. Dumbass.

"For tonight. Tag set us up."

He scowls at that comment. "You're lucky. All these hot girls are walking around everywhere, but Ash set me up with a girl I could get on my own. I just assumed that I was coming to meet her, but then she explained it was a friend. Didn't know Ash was married, but she's hot, so that means hot friends. Then I get in here, and every girl is banging hot except for mine. Don't get me wrong, she's cute and fuckable, but definitely not someone I'd pick out of this crowd."

I'm pulling my fist down before I even realize I've just knocked him on his ass, and the whole party goes quiet as the wailing grows louder. The cocksucker is on his back, crying as he curls up into the fetal position while his nose pours blood.

Dick.

Tag's mouth is open, but I still see the smile in his eyes. I'll deal with him later. He'll suffer the wrath for him and Ash, because I'm *not* making her cry again.

"What?" I bark at everyone, and they all turn away quickly, returning to what they were doing with forced casualness.

Brin is missing from the table, and I curse while running my hand through my hair. She's probably even more pissed at me now.

"Where'd she go?" I ask Ash, glaring at her.

When her lip trembles, I soften my look immediately, and she points toward the house.

Leah starts to speak as I pass by, but I completely ignore her as I take quick, determined steps to the house. Going through the patio entrance, I end up in the kitchen first, and there she is, sitting on the countertop while drinking her beer.

"Hey," she murmurs quietly while looking through the window in front of her, not staring at anything in particular.

"Sorry, Brin. I shouldn't have punched out your date, but he—"

"Spare me the details," she interrupts on a long sigh, her eyes moving down to her beer. "I have a pretty good idea what he probably said. I don't need the exact words. Thanks for punching him. I'm just waiting on a cab."

I've never felt so sick and pissed.

Brin

This can't get any more embarrassing. I was fine until he went and told Rye all the things he'd silently said to me with just his actions. This is mortifying.

I know Ash didn't put me through this on purpose. Guys put on their best performance around her, so she couldn't have known what a

159

douche he is. But it's the last time I accept her date offer. She should stick to her day job because she's a terrible matchmaker.

"You don't need a cab. I have a driver, so I can take you home."

And the humiliation just keeps coming in the form of his pity. Great. I'm not going to work tomorrow. I'm going to stay in bed all day and pray for good dreams.

"I don't want you to do that. The cab will be here in about ten minutes. Go back out to your date. She seems... I think she seems perfect for you. I heard her talking about cars earlier. She seems to know her stuff. That's cool. And she's really very pretty. I see why you wanted to cancel our stay-in night so badly. I don't blame you at all."

It's hard not to choke on envy or cry. I've never been the girl that hates another girl for being sexy, but right now, I'd love to see *Leah* fall off a cliff.

He blows out a breath while dropping his head back. "Ash and Tag set this all up to try and push us together—you and me. Ash didn't know the guy was going to be a total tool. The only reason I even came here with Leah was because Tag told me you had already accepted a date. I guess he thought I'd storm over to your house and do something."

Just when I thought it couldn't get any worse...

This was all an elaborate setup meant for manipulation. All because they thought the same thing I thought earlier today. I guess Rye proved them wrong.

"Ah," I say with a bitter laugh. "Well, I'll make sure to kick her ass when she's not pregnant. I bet they feel like idiots right now. At least you got to meet someone that wasn't a total *tool*."

I aim for joking, but I sound so resentful. In an effort to help, they only made things impossible.

"I wouldn't have canceled on tonight to go out on a date with a girl I didn't know if Tag hadn't told me you were going on a date. I swear. I just don't want you to be mad at me."

It's sweet, but it's also making me feel pathetic. I'm his friend. I'm always the friend.

"It's fine, Rye. I'm not mad. At all. I honestly didn't expect anything any different. And I'm sorry Ash and Tag thought you had a thing for me. I know that must be—"

I'm cut off and shocked when Rye's lips are suddenly on mine, his tongue sweeping in when I try to gasp. His hands roughly push my legs apart, making room for his body, and he grabs my waist and jerks me to him. It's hard to not to moan when he devours me harder than I've ever fantasized about.

I thrust my fingers in his hair and pull him even closer, relishing the taste of his mouth as my tongue goes to meet his. Oh dear God he can kiss.

When his hands slide down my waist and start pushing my dress up, I don't even think about stopping him. When his hands start sliding up the bare skin of my thighs, I pray he hurries. And when he brings our centers even closer, I wrap my legs around his waist to make us touch, and the friction becomes divine.

He groans and breaks off the kiss while pushing his forehead against mine, his body trembling slightly as he pants for the same breath I can't catch. I'm frozen, stunned, and doing all I can to slow down my erratic heartbeat as my legs drop from his waist.

"You're driving me fucking crazy," he says in hushed tone before turning and walking away, leaving me feeling bereft and confused.

With unsteady legs, I leap off the counter and follow him out, unsure about what I'm going to say or do, but he's gone. He just... left. What the hell just happened?

Brin

"So he punches your date and then kisses you?" Maggie asks, looking just as confused as I feel.

"And then tells me I'm driving him fucking crazy. Don't forget about that part."

I drop my high heels to the floor of my bedroom and try not to think of the delicious smell he's left behind on me.

My lips are still a little swollen from the breath-stealing kiss, and I honestly don't know if I'll ever think about anything else ever again. Why'd he have to go and kiss me?

"Any insight would be great," I mumble when Maggie stays quiet.

"I'm as confused as you are. It's times like these that I'm grateful I'm into women. Men are too fucking weird."

I laugh humorlessly while scrubbing my face with my hands.

"Well, maybe... Hell, I don't know," she says, still at a loss.

What now?

Chapter 9

Rye

"Motherfucker!" I roar as piss splashes all around, and I'm forced to painfully cut it off mid-stream.

Some stupid fucking piece of clear plastic shit is on my toilet, blocking anything from getting in. I knew she did something! Damn it!

Peeling away the disgusting plastic wrap, I finish my morning piss, cursing the entire time. Why didn't I think of that?

I climb inside the shower and flip it on. I'm in desperate need of a good shower now, thanks to the fucking piss bath she set me up for. I use the keypad on the side, turning on all the showerheads at the same time, but instead of a clean shower, I'm met by the damn sticky rainbow from hell.

Purple, orange, red, green, pink... all the colors collide like Lucky Charms just threw up, and I growl as I leap out, covered in the syrupy, grainy shit. What the fucking hell? Is that Kool-Aid?

When did she do this? How did she do this? I locked the window.

I've been trying to forget her, but right now she's making that pretty impossible. After a few more seconds, the fruity rainbow ceases and clear water rushes out in its place. Fucking finally.

My shower takes longer since I have to wash off all the damn Kool-Aid, but I finish up and head straight for the coffee. I refuse to go to the living room until I have to because I know I'll look across the street. She should be gone to work by now, and I can map out my

163

payback plan.

The very thought strikes an uneasy chord in me. Did I ruin it all with that kiss? Can we just forget it happened?

The coffee finishes, and I add the sugar, stirring it absently as I think back to being between her legs, feeling her wanting me just as much as I wanted her. I'm forced to grip the edge of the counter and forget the coffee for a minute.

I've been in that same position numerous times, and I've never walked away. But until last night, I've never wanted anything that badly. And it's freaking me the hell out.

I need liquor instead of coffee, but it'll have to do—since I have work. I chug the cup, but I'm spewing, spitting, and gagging in the very next second. Son of a bitch!

I dump out the foul cup of coffee and grab the sugar. She *did not* just use the oldest trick in the book.

She did. A small taste confirms it; she swapped the sugar for salt.

Unbelievable.

My reflexes have me stalking toward the front door despite the fact that I'm just wearing my towel, but the second I open the door, I remember I can't just show up over there and pretend nothing happened. What have I done?

Then I see her car still parked, looking untouched. She doesn't have work today?

Rye

Why'd I have to go and kiss her? And why can't I stop thinking about it? I could have said anything in this world and confused her less. Fuck, now I'm confused, too.

I feel... I feel stupid.

"You look like shit," Tag says as he walks into my office.

"You look like a betraying bastard," I retort, glaring at him as he sighs and drops to the chair.

He studies me for a minute, and then he finally leans up.

"When I met Ash, I wanted her. But in less than a day, I felt more for her than I had felt for any other girl. Insta-love? No. But I was definitely spellbound. I was a dick that didn't want to feel that. By the time I was ready, I had already pushed her away. A lot of people judge her for her decision to hide our first pregnancy from me, but they shouldn't."

He stands and walks over to my mini-fridge to pull out a bottle of water, and I wait on this drama-fest to end. It's not the same. It's not even close, but he doesn't know the sordid details of my hidden truths because I've never told him. The only friends of mine who know are Ethan Noles and Wren Prize.

Tag continues, and I let him, because I can't tell him how different we are. "I had chances. I could have gone to her at any time. I knew where she was, had her number, and even wanted to see her, but I was too stubborn to admit it. We're creatures of habit, and I think we both know what my habits involved at that time. One woman barely seemed sufficient. But when I finally gave in, I realized that what I thought I wanted was empty. Ash filled a void in my life that I didn't know was there. I was just trying to do for you what no one—including Wren—

did when I was in the same position. Guess I was wrong."

Everyone stood by and watched the two of them fight each other. It wasn't just him, and it wasn't just her. But that's not what's going on here.

"I kissed her," I blurt out, completely shocking us both because I have no fucking clue why I just admitted that. Tag's eyes widen before he laughs.

"Then I guess it wasn't a total waste," he murmurs more to himself than to me.

"But I left. Brin isn't the type you let into your bed for a little while. She's a lifetime commitment, and I'm not a lifetime guy."

Tag smiles, but it seems like he drifts off into memory land. "There was a time when I felt the same way."

I appreciate what he's trying to do, but I'm not him. I wish I was, but I'm not. His old fear of commitment didn't stem from the same dark roots mine does.

I've seen the nasty side of love. I've seen it swallow people and destroy all their hope, their light, and their will to live. I couldn't ever do that to someone and live with myself.

"We're different," I tell him, motioning between us. "Not all people can change."

"If you manage to stop thinking about her, then maybe you're right," he says, offering me a tighter smile. "But if you can't, then you might need to admit defeat. That's all I came by to say. I should go. Let me know if you need anything."

I just nod, and he walks out. I release a harsh breath that has been clogging up my lungs, and I turn to stare out the window to the pet store. Even that makes me think of her now. Brin didn't go to work this morning, and I'm almost positive it's because I fucked with her head last night.

How the hell do I dig myself out of this hole?

Brin

"You're not staying in bed all day," Maggie gripes, ripping the cover off me for the third time.

"Can't you just let a girl wallow for one day?" I growl, squinting against the intrusive light she has let into my room.

"No. You're not doing this. You're too strong for something like this to knock you on your ass for even a minute."

I glare at her before jerking the covers out of her hand and pulling them back over my head again. But as soon as I settle in, she's depriving me of my shield once more, and this time she throws the covers out of my room.

"I used to love you, but you're quickly rising up to the top of my most-hated enemies right now," I say in warning.

She crosses her arms over her chest, her stern gaze pinning me in place. I hate Maggie's pissed look. It's actually a little scary.

"Fine!" I snap, crawling out of the bed and feeling resentment toward her rising.

"Good!" she barks, and then she turns on her heel and storms out, pausing only to grab my covers and drag them away.

"What am I supposed to do? I've already called in and requested a personal day."

"Go out and get some air. I'll prepare our stay-in movie night, and I'll teach you how to properly deal with disappointment. It includes three flavors of ice cream."

That sounds promising.

"Where should I go for air?" I joke, earning a huff from her.

"The beach is ideal. Now go. I'll get everything ready."

With a great deal of reluctance, I start getting my clothes on and I pull my hair back. I frown when I see my keys. Maggie said he brought them over when he got home last night. I'm glad I wasn't here.

Now I have to go see what all he did to my car, and it's going to break my resolve just a little bit more. Any guy who kisses a girl and stalks away is obviously battling with the fact that he doesn't want to want her.

It sucks, but I get it. I know I'm not the type of girl he goes for. I knew it from the beginning. But our chemistry... I just thought he'd get past the superficial bullshit. I'm not that bad, dammit.

In a room full of normal women, I'd be much more appealing. I should move to a new town. One where the gene pool isn't overloaded with the super sexy.

When I finally force myself outside, I stare at my car like I've never seen it before. I only saw it under the streetlights last night, and I took a cab to Ash's house because I knew I'd need lots of alcohol to make it through the date. I was right.

In the daylight, I can see the extreme makeover so much better.

Even the small scratches and shopping cart dents are gone. I half expect a sparkling effect to start up at any moment. I walk around it, noting all the added details. He had to have spent a small fortune on this.

Why? Why do all of this? And he said I was driving him fucking crazy. Well, he's frigging driving me insane.

It takes me a minute, but I finally get into the front seat, smiling when I see that it's all the way back, and I adjust it so that I can reach the pedals. I can't believe this. He gave me leather upholstery? Real leather? And it feels so good. I swear it almost has a new car smell.

There's a touchscreen panel on the dash that I can assume must control my air and radio, since the old turn dials and radio system are missing. Tears fill my eyes. He completely changed my entire car for the better.

I laugh when my car cranks on the first try. It usually takes a few key turns to start it, and it purrs instead of squealing like it's in pain. When I shift it into drive, I almost break the gear stick. Normally it's so hard to put into place, but now it just glides almost too easily.

I can't help but giggle, and a tear escapes my grasp. Pulling away from the curb is so easy because the steering is so much better. Everything is better. The rear isn't shaking when I try to tap the brakes. Brakes! They're not screeching!

I almost do a happy dance when my car stops without sliding a few extra feet. It's a whole new car. The radio starts playing, but it's all in Spanish. I glare at it for a second when I reach the stop sign.

Every time I try to change the station, a box pops up and asks for the password. He did this on purpose, and I can't stop smiling.

Rye. I have to go talk to him. I refuse to let one kiss screw up our friendship. And there's something else I want to do.

Rye

"I've got five-hundred dollars here, but I know that's nowhere close to covering it, so I'll make monthly payments," Brin says, sounding very close, and I almost jump out of my damn seat.

Where the hell did she come from? And how long has she been in my office?

"Um... I told you it was on me," I say lamely, cringing at how juvenile I feel in this moment.

Her hair is pulled back, her shorts are too short for me to ignore, and her shirt is tighter than usual. She would go buy fucking clothes that fit the moment I start having issues.

"No," she says, putting an envelope on the table. "I don't want you doing me any favors. I can pay you back. It might take me a while, but I don't like owing people anything."

She might as well slap me. This is all because I ruined things between us.

"I'm not taking your damn money, and if you try paying me, I'll never talk to you again."

I push the envelope back across the desk, and she glares at me. Christ, I love it when she's angry.

I'm twisted.

"It's not like you want to ever talk to me again anyway. You kissed me and ran off like I had some disease. Which I don't, by the way."

Fuck. We're apparently going to talk about this now. Here. And I'm not ready.

"I'm sure you don't," I mutter dryly. "But I'm sort of at work. Can we talk about this later?"

"No," she says with a shrug, pushing the envelope back toward me again. "Because you won't be talking to me later. I'm paying you back."

She moves to the far corner, putting distance between us when her hands start to tremble. I really don't want to do this right now.

Jessica walks in, wearing a dress she must have been poured into, and Brin's eyes go to her, appraising her. I know what she's thinking right now because I see it in her eyes. And Jessica doesn't even notice the corner Brin is in.

"Your lunch meeting is in twenty minutes, Mr. Clanton," Jessica says with a baby voice. Why do girls talk in a baby voice on purpose? Wouldn't that only appeal to a pedophile?

"Thanks," I say quickly, hoping she gets the hint to leave.

She doesn't.

"And I wanted to know if you need me to stay late tonight?" she asks, going into a sexier voice that has Brin inching toward the door.

Fucking shit. She's getting the wrong idea. Does Jessica always talk to me like this? Am I just super aware of it now that Brin is standing five feet away?

"I can't imagine there would be any reason why you would have to stay late."

"I can think of a few reasons," she says seductively, and I visibly grimace.

"I should go," Brin announces, and Jessica squeals and jumps, startled by the fact someone else is in the room.

"I'm so... sorry," Jessica stammers. "I didn't realize there was a client in here."

Brin smiles tightly, and before I can correct her, Brin starts talking. "It's fine. I'm just on my way out." Then she looks at me. "And I'll send the rest of the payments through Maggie from now on. That way... Well, I'll let you get back to your conversation."

She's gone before I can even get my tongue untangled, and Jessica turns back to me with fear in her eyes.

"I really am sorry, Mr. Clanton. I honestly didn't know anyone else was in here."

I groan while gripping my head, and then I slam shut the drawer to my right while standing up. I need to go for a ride and clear my mind.

"That's not really the issue, Jessica. I hired you for a number of reasons—one being the fact that my clientele is ninety percent men. And maybe I enjoyed the flirty nature at first, but this is work. Work means acting professional. If you can't do that, then find a new job. Cancel my noon meeting. I'm leaving early."

She holds back tears as I walk out. Great. Now I've made another woman cry. Fuck my life.

Brin

"It was stupid, and I don't want to talk about it," I say numbly, staring at the TV even though I have no idea what's on the screen.

"When I said get some air, I didn't mean for you to go see him."

Just the thought of that girl getting ready to strip naked in his office makes me sick. He just sat there, watching me watch them. It was the ickiest experience of my life. My feet felt so heavy, and I still feel like the world's biggest idiot.

"I didn't mean to go see him, but then I got in the car, and it reminded me what a freaking amazing guy he is. *Was*. Now he's slime."

I scowl at the TV like it's Rye, and Maggie sighs. "Well, is the car good at least?"

The glacier encasing my heart warms just a little at the thought of my car.

"It's perfect—which is why I went over there to pay him. He spent way too much, and then I was crying, and I don't cry. I never cry. I didn't cry when John ruined my life and stuck me with all of his credit card bills. I didn't cry when he divorced me. And he sure as hell never did anything sweet enough to make me cry. Rye... I'm so... I don't get it!"

Maggie looks torn about what to say, but she doesn't have to decide because the devil himself walks into our house without so much as a knock. My heart sputters the way my car used to when I look up to meet his serious face.

I don't know if I've ever seen him without a glint of mischief in his eyes until the past two days. I hate it.

"Rye," Maggie says uncomfortably, sitting up in the chair.

"Care if we have a second?" he asks her, but his eyes stay on me as his jaw tenses.

"Um... Yeah," she says uncertainly, looking to me for permission to leave.

I just shrug as she slowly gets up and leaves us alone. I don't think I can get any tenser.

"Brin, about earlier... with Jessica, that wasn't—"

"Don't," I interrupt, sighing. "Please don't. You don't owe me any explanations. I showed up at your office unannounced. She didn't see me. I didn't think... It was stupid. I'm sorry. You don't have to come over here and explain."

I've never felt so pathetic.

He frowns as he comes to sit beside me. I wish he'd just leave.

"Brin, I don't have a thing for Jessica. She works for me. That's it."

I just laugh bitterly. "Rye, go. I don't even know why you're here. Well, I do actually. You feel bad because you kissed me and then ran away. Then I got to witness a girl more your type go for gold in your office. You're decent enough to feel bad about it, but you don't have to. In fact, I'd like it if you'd just stop."

"Brin, I—"

"Stop saying my name. Stop coming over here. Stop playing the pranks." I stand up, turn my back on him, and ignore the fever going on behind my eyes. I will not cry. "Before you started sending me mixed signals, I felt just fine with the way I am. I don't have to look like I just stepped off the runway in order to be happy. I don't have to deal with the sleaze balls who are just looking for sex, because I'm not the one-night stand of their dreams. I'm perfectly happy. Or I was."

"You... you're messing with my head, and that's not okay. I don't like someone making me feel as though I'm not good enough. I want to be appreciated the way I am. I know what I want, and games aren't involved. So please go. I'll crown you king of the war by default. You win. Consider us even."

The first tear falls, and I silently curse it. I've never wanted to be one of the Sterling Shore perfect women until him. And I don't like hating myself.

"You're taking all of this out of context, Brin. I... Fuck!" he yells, slapping something.

I turn around to face him, but he's suddenly right there, and just like last night, his lips are on mine, surprising me with an attack that I wasn't prepared for. Instinctively, my fingers thread through hair instead of shoving him back like I need to do.

He pulls me tightly against his body, even though he has to bend over to kiss me. When his tongue sweeps in, I either whimper or moan—possibly both. A noise escapes him that almost sounds feral, and the kiss becomes even hungrier.

Why am I doing this to myself?

We fall to the couch, and I'm straddling him before my brain can process the shift. His hands are all over me—my back, my neck, my hair, back down to my ass. We're a mess of pants, moans, wild hands, and ravenous needs.

But I stupidly want to do more than what we can do on this couch—with Maggie home. I also want him to stop before my heart gets tripped up and shattered.

"Rye," I mumble against his lips, trying to catch my air and my sanity.

"Please don't get even with me right now," he says, his lips moving down to my neck.

Oh damn. I've never felt lips so demanding—hard and soft at the same time. I want to live in this torture for as long as I can.

"What do you mean?" I ask, trying to push him away, but pulling him closer instead as I gyrate my hips.

He growls, and I move again, doing what I can to drive him as crazy as he's driving me.

"I mean don't stop this to get even with me for last night. Let's call a truce for the night."

I'm torn between smiling and swearing. I'm past the point of confused.

"You want a truce?" I ask breathlessly, curling to him as he continues that divine trail of kisses, dragging his lips across my collarbone on his way down my chest.

"I want a lot of things right now, but we'll start with a truce."

I'm fairly certain my heart has stopped beating or else it is racing too fast to be felt.

"Okay," I say like a crazy girl who is begging to be broken.

He stands with me still wrapped around him, and I'm almost positive he's going to put me down and leave me hanging. Again. So I do what any sane, rational person would do—I clamp my legs around his waist so tightly that they'd need the Jaws of Life to undo me.

Yep. Problem solved.

"What are you doing?" I ask when he starts walking, but his lips refuse to part from mine for long, and he returns to the hungry kiss without answering.

Not that I'm complaining.

Every emotion I have conflicts with each other. I want to stop and never stop at the same time. I still feel us moving, and then I hear the door shutting behind us. It takes so much effort, but I pull back to see him carrying us across the yard.

He tries to go for my lips again, but with fresh air comes some clarity, and I'm able to dodge his attack. But in his soft brown eyes, I see that mischief is back, and his smile is stealing the last ounce of my strength.

"Where are we going?" I ask as we reach his yard.

"Where do you think? You want to cook in my kitchen. And I want to see that... Later."

Yep. I'm putty. All of the sensible is tossed away as madness sinks in and my lips return to his with an almost desperate need. I'll worry about the consequences later. Either way, the friendship is fucked. Might as well enjoy the perks.

His talented tongue provokes fantasies I plan to live out, and I kiss him back with every bit of my desire pouring free.

The door pushes against my back as he fumbles with his keys, but he finally gets it unlocked and carries me over the threshold. I still have a death-grip on his waist, and my legs try to cramp from all the exerted force.

"Christ," he murmurs, breaking the kiss and gasping for air.

"Don't you dare freak out and run," I mumble, moving my lips back toward his as he navigates his house the best he can without being able to see around me very well. "I will hurt you if you do."

He laughs as he meets my lips with a teasing kiss, and then I'm suddenly tossed onto a mattress that angels had to have made themselves.

"I'm not freaking out and running," he says, slowly climbing over me, nudging my legs apart with his knees and then settling into the space he's created. "You're not getting out of here tonight."

The knot that forms in my throat almost chokes me, and my senses become hyperaware of everything around me. Each breath, touch, taste, smell... It's all driving me out of my mind as he takes his time, slowly bringing his lips down to my neck and tormenting me with pleasure.

"You're trying to torture me," I groan when his hands slide up my waist and just narrowly miss my breasts.

His throaty chuckle does that weird thing to my heart, and my legs tighten around him in response. He leans back and tugs his shirt over his head, and my eyes go straight to the hard lines of his chest and stomach, and I lick my lips while staring at all the ink.

His bluish-black nipple ring has my attention, and I run my fingers over it. He watches me for a moment, his breaths heavy and fast as I toy with the warm metal, but then he drops to me.

His sleeved arm comes to rest beside my head first, and then his half-sleeved arm comes down next. I try not to act as out of breath as I am, but he's half naked and he's on top of me. So that makes breathing a very complicated thing.

"Not yet. I'll have time later to torture you. Right now, we're both putting each other out of our misery. Because I can't fucking think anymore. And you're not any better off or you wouldn't be skipping work to huddle up on your couch."

He's miserable? That shouldn't make me grin like an idiot, but I'm twisted, so it does.

"And these shorts are too fucking short."

He starts tugging at my button, and I curse myself. Shit. I should have worn the sexy stuff. As soon as the front is undone, he starts tugging them down, and his taunting grin forms.

"Don't laugh," I groan, covering my face. "You're totally ruining the moment."

He snickers as he tugs my shorts all the way down, and leaves the cotton monstrosities on me. I'll never wear comfortable underwear again. Damn.

"Actually, these suit you," he jokes, leaning down and kissing me right where I want him to, and I almost do something stupid like buck off the bed.

His breath is warm through the fabric, and he grins against me until I hook my thumbs in the sides and shove my panties down to my knees. His breath stops, and I stifle a grin when he seems caught off guard.

He kisses me closer now that there's no fabric in the way, and he pulls my panties down the rest of the way before tossing them to the floor. He runs his hands up my legs as he parts them farther. Every touch feels like fire against my skin right now, especially when his tongue finds that bundle of nerves that has me crying out like a damn virgin.

My head drops back and my eyes close, but he stops. I think I growl. I know a very warning sound comes out of me, and he chuckles while moving up my body and pushing his lips against mine.

"We'll have to do foreplay another time," he murmurs against my lips as he shuffles out of his jeans.

My anger flees as excitement unfurls in my body, and he reaches for his nightstand. When I hear the drawer open and the foil crinkling, I almost get dizzy from the adrenaline rush.

I've been divorced for a year, but it's been so much longer than that since I've had sex.

He tugs my shirt off as he raises up, and I'm left in only my bra. He looks down at me in a way no one else ever has, and I'm left feeling feverish. He wants me. His eyes are on me and staring at me hungrily—the same way Kode stares at Tria. It shouldn't be possible.

He turns to push his boxers down, and that thrill shoots through me again. I mindlessly remove my bra as he turns back around, and my eyes go straight down and stare.

I think I must have done something very, very right in a past life.

"Like it?" he says with a grin I can feel.

He moves over me, and I go to the thing that I'm finding the most fascinating. A silver barbell sticks out from the tip of his cock, and I'm fairly positive this sort of thing could make a girl fall in love.

"You couldn't get your other nipple pierced because of the pain, but you have this?" I ask in a rasp voice.

I touch it, feeling the metal, and he jerks in my hands as a deep rumble forms in his chest. I try to stay only on the metal, not the hard rod that is very happy to be with me. But it's hard not to touch him.

"Don't get too excited. You won't be able to feel it very much with the condom on," he says as he starts rolling the rubber down and hiding the silver.

I really want to feel it. I'm on birth control, but I'm rather certain it is stupid to have unprotected sex this early on. I think. I can't think. Shit.

Once he's fully sheathed under the latex, he looks up to meet my eyes and his slow grin crawls up to capture another piece of the heart I should be guarding. I reach for him and he comes willingly, but he shocks the hell out of me when he thrusts in without any warning.

My breath comes out in a rush as the full, deep, stretching sensation hits me. And he pushes in farther, finding a place inside me that I *know* has ever been touched before.

"Fuck. You feel even better than I thought you would," he groans, acting as though it's a bad thing. I think.

Again, thinking is rather hard to do right now.

He pulls back and rocks in, and my breath comes out again as my body tries to acclimate to him. Even with the condom on, I can still feel the piercing enough. And I love it. In fact, I'm ruined. I'll never want another man without it.

I really hope we stick together long enough for me to feel it without a condom.

My thoughts all run together when he drives in harder, and I pull him down to me, hoping his lips on mine will help drown out the humiliating sounds I'm already making.

He pulls out of me suddenly and then he takes my place while pulling me to be on top of him, both of us sitting facing each other, as he grabs my hips and plunges me down onto him, impaling me divinely.

His eyes roll back as he releases a sound that pushes me to the edge too soon. Our kiss becomes wild as our bodies collide, and he moves one hand to my hair, tugging just enough, and keeps one hand firmly planted on my hip, making our centers hit with force.

It all feels too good. A myriad of emotions and sensations hit me at once as he takes a nipple in his mouth, pushes himself up to let his piercing hit a spot inside me that has been dormant, and his hands... There's something about his hands being on my body—owning me, claiming me, needing me.

I've never felt so sexy in all my life, and I love it.

His name is coming through my lips before I can stop it. My body burns hot and cold, a powerful eruption of mind-blowing perfection goes off, and I fight to stay vertical when my whole body tries to fold under the force of the orgasm.

He keeps going, making it impossible for me to not to whimper from the overwhelming sensations and ecstasy-laced high that I'm still riding out. But then his body jerks under mine just before he stills, and his breath comes out in a hard rush that slithers over my skin with a gentle, warm touch.

He pulls me to him and kisses my neck, his breaths slowly starting to return to normal, and I almost hold my breath.

Now that the moment has come and gone... What happens?

"You can go fix food now," he says through a winded tone.

I laugh lightly while shaking my head, and his lips come up to capture mine in a kiss that means so much more than it did seconds ago. It's only three. We have a while before it hits that awkward point where you don't know whether to stay or go.

Maybe we can have fun for that entire time.

"How am I supposed to walk after that?" I mumble, very distracted by his talented lips and wicked tongue.

All of the groceries are still at my house. There's no way these stems of jelly are going to support me for walking and cooking.

"Fine," he says, breaking the kiss with a grin that gives me too much hope. "You can cook in thirty minutes."

When his lips brush mine and he flips me to be on my back, that excitement floods me again.

"And what are we going to do for those thirty minutes?" I ask, trying not to giggle, squeal, or scream out in joy.

He purses his lips as though he's giving that serious thought, and then he slides to the edge of the bed. All I see is him dropping the old condom into the waste basket beside the bed, and then the nightstand opens again before a foil-crinkling resounds in my ears. I feel the tingles of excitement rock through my body like a live wire has just been set loose inside me.

"I have a few ideas," he says, grinning over his shoulder.

183

When he turns around, a new condom is on, and I can't look at anything else. This day is so different than I thought it was going to be.

"I've always been a fan of show and tell," I murmur distractedly, feeling his grin rather than seeing it because my eyes are otherwise engaged.

"Really?" he asks mildly, crawling back over the bed toward me, looking like a stalking predator. I'll happily be his prey. "Because I've always been a bigger fan of show," he adds, and then his lips come down on mine just as he thrusts deep inside me.

This is my new favorite day of the year.

Rye

Something smells incredible, but it's too hard to move. Opening my eyes seems impossible. But my stomach growls in response to the delicious scent that is getting stronger, and I'm forced to wake up.

Why the hell was I asleep?

I look over at the clock to see it's seven in the evening. Did I really just take a nap?

It's then I see the cute, white cotton panties that are still on my floor where I threw them earlier.

Brin. That's why I took a nap. I never would have thought she'd be so damn ravenous in the bedroom. In fact, I barely kept up. We spent the afternoon doing all my favorite things, and now I feel as though I've spent the day working out.

She's not in the bed, which prompts me to frown, and then I curse myself for being disappointed.

I didn't go over there for this. In fact, I went over there for the exact opposite. I wanted to explain about Jessica, but I also wanted to tell her how much I valued her friendship, even though we haven't been friends for long.

I didn't want her thinking it had anything to do with her, but I'm not the relationship guy. It's not what I want.

Then she had to go and fucking say the shit she was saying, and every time she said something, I wanted to shake her. And she was right—I was fucking with her head. Problem is, she's been fucking with mine, too.

I never meant to kiss her. I never meant to grab her up from the floor or enjoy the way her legs immediately wrapped around me. I never meant to hold her like I wanted nothing else. And I sure as hell never meant to walk over here and fuck her in my house, on my bed, on my floor, against my wall, or in my closet—I still don't know how we ended up in the closet.

But the first taste I had of being inside her was different than anything I've ever experienced. There was more going on than just sex. I'm not sure that even makes sense, but for once, sex was more than just a means of having fun. It meant something.

I'm scared this has just gotten incredibly complicated. What do I do now? Brin is addictive. I never would have thought she could be so damned addictive.

The smell gets even stronger, more divine, so I stand up and grab my boxers, deciding to go investigate. The closer I get to the kitchen, the bigger my smile involuntarily spreads, which just worries me that much more. Why am I smiling? Why the hell can't I stop?

When I reach the kitchen, my stupid-ass grin gets painful. Brin is standing at the stove, wearing nothing but my shirt, and singing quietly as she stirs something in a pan. My shirt looks really damn good on her.

It's hard to tell what she's singing over the sizzles and crackles on the stove, especially since she's doing it so quietly. But I take a seat on the stool behind the kitchen island bar, and I watch the show she's putting on.

Is she singing the Macarena? Does anyone even know the words to that song?

She grabs a pan and moves it to be on a cooling rack on the counter, and I prop up and watch her as she bends over to look in the oven, inspecting whatever is in there. My shirt doesn't crawl up high enough for me to see her bare ass. Damn.

She closes the oven door and turns around, but when she sees me, she screams as though I just said *boo*. I just arch an amused eyebrow to complement my teasing grin, while she gasps for air and covers her heart.

She's brushed her hair and put on a little makeup, something she would have had to do at her house when she went to collect the groceries. That makes me feel like a jerk. She feels like she has to try and look better right after mind-blowing sex.

I don't know how to deal with her—this. Us. But I refuse to think about it right now.

"Don't do that," she hisses, her scowl forming and making me smile harder. I love her angry face.

"Don't do what? Sit at my own bar?" I ask coyly.

She stifles her grin as blush rises to her cheeks. I'm pretty sure she just forgot about what happened in my bedroom during her startle and her little scolding.

"Um... I thought you might be hungry, and I still had all the groceries. I hope this is okay."

I just grin bigger while standing up and making my way around to her. Christ, it's like I can't help myself. This can only end badly. But I don't want to think about it right now.

When I reach her, I pick her up and slide her ass on the bar while I step between her legs, and her breaths go erratic. That makes me feel so fucking good.

"I told you a few hours ago to cook. So I don't mind. Especially since I gave you thirty minutes and you took much, much longer."

This time she's the one that looks amused as she wraps her legs around my waist.

"That's not my fault. You're the one who wanted to try to go through a whole box of condoms."

Damn. This conversation is actually starting to wake up the exhausted appendage that should be in a coma. How is that even possible?

"I didn't hear you complaining earlier," I murmur as I press my lips to her neck, unable to stare into her blue eyes anymore.

Her breath hitches and her legs get tighter around me. "I'm not complaining now. You are. I'm just trying to make you something to eat."

I grin against her neck as my mind goes to the gutter, and she laughs while pushing me back.

"That's not what I mean."

I just snicker quietly, until my eyes gravitate to hers again. I really shouldn't be getting lost inside her pools of blue, but something inside me is all fucked up right now.

"You look good in my shirt," I say as my eyes stroll down her body, landing on the hem I'm pushing up. "Especially since you didn't put your panties back on."

She groans while hopping off the counter, and I frown at her back while she goes to the stove.

She mutters something about thongs and never being comfortable again, though I have no idea what she's going on about. Then she takes the pan off the stove and puts it beside the other.

"You can't touch me until you eat. I've worked hard on getting this ready."

The fact that she told me I can't touch her makes it imperative that I do touch her. Does she not realize this?

"Hey!" she squeals, giggling as I pull the shirt up and start moving my hands all over her body very playfully.

She tries to twirl out of my grasp, but she just ends up facing me, and I lean down and kiss her with a need that scares the fuck out of me. When her tongue sweeps in, my knees try to buckle, and I groan when she jumps up and wraps those sweet legs around me.

With her like this, I don't have to bend over, and I also have her as close as possible. Well, almost. I'll have her as close as possible in a second.

I'd fuck her right here if my condoms weren't in my room.

"The food," she says against my lips, though she doesn't put any real willpower behind getting down.

"Can wait," I say, acting as though I'm finishing her sentence.

I'm rewarded with a grin and a kiss that gets hungrier. I'm going to overdose on sex at this rate.

Rye

"Food is excellent," I say as I take a bite of the chicken.

She glares at me, and I almost choke on my bite when I try to laugh. Even from across the table—which is where she put me when my hands kept getting too close to her during the reheated meal—she looks too tempting.

"It would have been excellent two hours ago. Reheated, it's just barely okay."

"Easy, tiger," I joke, still getting her threatening glare.

She attempts to look angry for a moment longer, but the humor in her eyes and the small smile on her lips destroy that ability. She sips her wine while she studies me. Shit. We're about to talk. About this. About us. I don't know what to say.

"Do you have to go in early?" she asks instead, surprising me.

"No. I rarely do. It's only on occasion. Usually I go in around ten and leave around eight. Well, I prefer to leave around five, but we've been unnaturally busy and I'm trying to get my new staff up to par."

She grins as though she enjoyed something about that answer. Maybe it's because we're having a normal conversation for once.

"You?" I ask.

She sighs hard while nodding. "I have to go in at six tomorrow. Two hours earlier than usual."

This time I grin. I really don't think I've ever had this sort of conversation. Especially not over a dinner someone cooked for me— since this is the first time someone has cooked for me. She looked really good in my kitchen. I'll worry about how all of this is affecting me later. Right now, I just want to enjoy it because it's new. And God help me, I like it.

"Why a garage?" she asks while forking some more of the cold-in-the center chicken.

I bet it really would have been excellent when it was fresh off the stove. Next time.

Fuck me. I'm already planning a next time.

Clearing my throat and ignoring my inner war, I shrug. "I loved cars enough to never grow bored. My attention span is usually small, so for a career, I needed something that would keep me intrigued."

"And you just started it up? That easy?"

I chuckle while shaking my head and wondering if she'd get mad if I came to sit beside her again. Honestly, if she doesn't want to be touched, then she should change out of my shirt.

"No. It wasn't easy. I inherited a lot of money from my grandfather years and years ago. My father put it in a trust fund to keep me from touching it. My Granddad only left it to me to piss off my dad," I say fondly, and she tilts her head. "When I was of age, I emptied a chunk out and built my garage, hired a staff, and started from scratch on collecting clients. For the first year, I spent more than I made, but that second year... Things picked up."

Things picked up so well that I created an entire franchise, but talking about it sounds like I'm bragging. So I end the explanation there.

Her grin returns, and she moves her plate as she stands. I can't fight the stupid smile on my face when she comes to sit beside me again, and I wrap my arm around the back of her chair, letting my hand start playing with the soft strands of her hair.

"You said you bought this house as an 'adult' purchase. What did that mean?"

I still can't believe I even said that in front of her. But the damage is already done, and this isn't exactly the darkest part of my past.

"My dad said I didn't know how to invest, and that I was a kid on a mission to blow through my inheritance. Especially when the garage didn't look to be promising. He was taking me to court to try and have my trust frozen until a later age due to a 'childish' mentality. My beach house was a good investment, but it didn't make anyone think I wasn't spending frivolously because of the partying neighbors that surrounded me. So I bought this place to prove I was spending wisely.

"It's a great investment, considering the location, neighborhood, and property value. Dad lost his case very quickly. This house might have saved me from losing it all. I didn't ever picture myself living here, but I like it."

191

She grins again, and then she leans in and awards me for the admission by kissing my cheek. I don't know if anyone has ever kissed me on the cheek like that. And I know I've never enjoyed such a chaste show of affection.

"What about your mom? Did she agree with your dad or you?"

Not ready for this discussion. Never will be.

"She didn't have any say," I murmur vaguely, not elaborating, and she fortunately doesn't press for more.

"How'd you end up at Maggie's?" I ask, needing off the subject of me.

Ah, hell. She got divorced. That's how.

She just shrugs instead of acting affected. I was worried this was about to take a cold nosedive.

"My parents expect too much out of me, but I moved in with them, thinking they'd leave me alone since I'm adult. They didn't. Maggie had been begging me to come live with her since I had gotten divorced. We've been friends since we were little, even though she's a little older. Our dads worked together for a while. My dad was Maggie's dad's boss."

So she comes from money?

"Maggie comes from a lot of money because of her dad's job," I say, frowning.

"Yep. And my dad has more of it. But I got married at eighteen against my parents' wishes, got a job they didn't approve of, and lived my life the way I wanted to. I didn't want to be a doctor, or a lawyer, or anything else they wanted me to be. They still haven't forgiven me."

I wasn't going to bring up the whole marriage thing, but she mentioned it, so I assume it's allowed to be talked about. It's driving me fucking crazy.

"Why'd you get married and divorced?" I ask in a rush, tensing when she does.

After a long period of silence that seems to cloak the air in regret, she finally blows out a breath.

"Because I was young and dumb," she says through a sad laugh. "I was sheltered and treated like a porcelain doll with a mapped-out life. He was fun and free-spirited. I went to an all-girls private school; he went to public school. I was from a rich family; he lived on the worst side of town."

She pauses briefly while shaking her head.

"It only made sense to get married," she says dryly. "He stupidly thought my father would cover all of our expenses and his life would change for the better once he married me. He kept holding out that hope. Year after year, John thought he had a brilliant idea, and he'd try to get my father to invest. I'm sure he cared about me. You don't stay married to someone for six years if you don't care about them on some level, but I don't think either of us actually really loved each other."

She clears her throat while staring at her plate.

I've had girls confess their love after knowing me for seconds. I've had girls throw themselves at me for all the wrong reasons. But I've never had any sort of relationship that held meaning of any kind. So I can't relate.

"Why do you say that?" I ask, wishing I knew what else to say.

She smiles weakly. "Because I didn't cry."

That... confuses the hell out of me.

"Umm..."

She laughs while shaking her head. "He represented freedom to me. I represented fortune to him. Neither of us got what we wanted. I was content with my crappy job, the small apartment we had, and our meager life. But I didn't have freedom, because I still felt like a constant source of disappointment—just like I did at home. When he told me he wanted a divorce, I felt as though I could breathe for the first time in years. I was pissed that I had wasted my time, and I was pissed that he said I was holding him back, but I wasn't the least bit sad that our marriage was over. The day I wrecked your car, I was pissed over the fact that I ever gave him any part of me, and that day represented all that bottled up anger. But I didn't cry."

I sit silently, feeling like an ass for having nothing to say. But she finally looks up and smiles at me. When she does, I forget anything else exists, and that fear in the back of my mind tries to rise to the surface.

"Why are you grinning?" I ask, feeling confused.

"No reason," she says, shrugging. "Why didn't you call the cops?"

Huh?

"The day I slammed into your car," she clarifies as she slides over to be in my lap, stealing any thoughts I can have as her body straddles mine in the chair, and she leans down to my neck.

I swallow hard when her lips start making small, moan-worthy trails. It really doesn't take much at all for her to turn me on.

"Well?" she prompts, but it's damn near impossible to talk as her

194

hands slide up my bare shoulders, and then move back down as she continues the kissing torture on my neck.

"I didn't want to send you to jail."

She leans back, smiling, and my eyes go down to where her shirt has risen up. I'm getting a view of the part of her body I plan to have again. Very soon. Very, very soon.

I love the fact that she doesn't cover up or even try to. She just lets me look as she runs her hands down my chest. When she bends over and takes my pierced nipple into her mouth, tugging at the metal in a way that has my cock twitching, I bite back a growl.

"Why all the tattoos and piercings?" she asks, dropping my nipple ring from her mouth, but her legs tighten as she squirms in my lap.

I have a feeling I know which piercing is on her mind right now, and I can't fight the smug grin on my face.

"It started as a phase. But tattoos are addictive, and I love getting something new every once and a while. The nipple piercing was on impulse, and it really did hurt like a bitch."

She squirms on my lap once more, and I swallow a groan as her hand travels down to the top of my boxers—the only clothing I would put on. With her on my lap like this, I regret that decision. If my cock strains any harder to get at her uncovered, perfect—

"And this piercing?" she asks, sliding her hand down the front of my boxers and freeing my erect cock.

She teasingly runs a finger over the tip, and then she plays with the piercing, forcing a jolt of desire through me. You'd think I'd be too sated to keep fucking. This is the most I've ever had sex with one girl,

195

let alone one day.

"Another impulse."

"Did it hurt?" she asks, sliding her hand down the shaft of my dick and then back up.

I can't hold back my groan this time. "Yes," I say between harsh breaths.

"Does it hurt now?" she asks, keeping her ministrations slow and steady as she bends back down to kiss my neck some more.

"Very much," I say, feeling her grin against my neck. "I'm pretty sure you could help with that, though."

"Oh?" she asks sweetly, playing along.

I'm not sure what she's doing to me. It's like a fog has invaded my mind, and the only thing visible inside my head is her. It's exciting me as much as it's leaving me terrified.

I don't speak as I try to make sense of all of this. Any minute she's going to ask what we're doing, and I'll have to answer. I don't have an answer. I don't want this to end right now, but I want it to stop immediately. It's so fucking confusing.

"What are you thinking about?" she asks, noting my facial expression as she leans back.

I force a convincing smile and lie. "Counting condoms in my head. By my calculations, we have two left."

Her grin returns, and she slides herself onto me without warning, taking me deep inside her, and moaning as I fill up every centimeter of her hot, wet heat. I'm not sure who gasps louder when our bases meet, and her head falls back as she rocks her hips, moaning again.

She's squeezing me to damn death with her tight grip on my painfully hard cock. I've never been inside a girl without a condom, and right now, I'm not sure that I ever want to wear that thin layer of latex again.

"I wanted to feel it," she says in a shallow breath, rocking again and crying out.

I can't breathe, think, speak, or even move. I didn't know such a small barrier was interrupting such... Fuck, this feels good.

"Feel what?" I ask in a rasp, hoarse whisper that betrays my every fear.

"It. The piercing. It's... It feels so—*Ah!*" she cries out, gyrating her hips once again as she starts a steady rhythm.

I lift her hips and slam her down onto me, and we both make some hellacious sounds that mingle and form an animalistic melody. I do it again, and again, and again, until she suddenly rips away, robbing me of her heat, her tight sheathe, and the best feeling I've ever had in my life.

"We need a condom," she says through a shaky breath, and I almost roar in frustration.

She's right. Fuck, I know she's right, but now I feel spoiled and I want more.

"Yeah," I say tightly, wishing she hadn't just given me nirvana and stolen it right back. "Are you on birth control?"

I have no idea why I'm asking. It's still stupid, but as I stand, she nods, swallowing hard as she stares at my cock that is still glistening from her.

Pushing my boxers to the ground, I pick her up and set her on the table, angling myself against her entrance as her eyes widen.

"I'm clean," I tell her, gauging her expression and waiting for her to stop me.

She's not stopping me or asking questions. I'd tell her if there was anything she should worry about, and I believe she'd tell me. But her eyes just stare expectantly, and I stop thinking.

I push back into her, and her eyes roll back in her head until she cries out again. This is so fucking stupid, but no thought makes sense when I'm with her. I'm not me. I'm some idiot who thinks it is okay to do this thing I can't define. I'm some moron who is picturing things that contradict the reality I have. I know what happens when fuck-ups like me find girls like her.

They leave them broken.

"Harder," she whispers, and I lose it. All restraint is gone, and I pound into her with everything I have, biting my lip when I start getting too loud. It's a moment of pure abandon, and nothing outside of our bubble gets in. I've never made any fucking noise during sex until today, but this girl is driving me bat-shit crazy, and I'll be damned if I don't love it.

My hand slides up her stomach, pushing the shirt with it as I grab one of her perfect tits and squeeze. She moans, proving she enjoys my touch, but I have to let go and return my hold to her hips to drive in as hard as she wants me to.

When my name tears through her lips and echoes through my bones, I explode inside of her, groaning as her muscles clench and milk me. Nothing has ever felt so good, and I'm pretty fucking ruined in this moment.

I drop my head to her chest, refusing to disjoin our bodies just yet, and her hands go to my hair. She runs her fingers through the strands affectionately, and I kiss her skin that is showing, nudging her shirt up farther so I can taste as much as I want to.

"Mmm," she finally says. "I really love that piercing."

I chuckle against her while nipping at her skin, and I pull out while helping her sit up. My table has now been christened just like so many things in my room.

"I've never done that," I admit, enjoying the way her smile crawls up.

"It was stupid," she says, grinning bigger.

"It was. But I want to be stupid again some time."

As soon as the words are out of my mouth, I regret them, because I see hope form in her eyes. I shouldn't be making future promises, because I don't know what's going to happen. This isn't me.

But her grin turns mischievous as quickly as her eyes shed the hopeful glisten, and she hops off the table, letting my shirt slide back down and cover her body.

"You might have to beg next time. My body is a little overwhelmed by all the stimulation. I'm not sure it can handle much more, and right now, I'm pretty exhausted."

She walks back to my room, and a sick knot forms. She's going to sleep in my bed? Fuck. What have I done? I can't just ask her to leave. It's Brin. I've never had a girl in here. I've never fucked anyone in this house... until her. What the hell am I supposed to do about this?

When I make it to the bedroom, she's pulling her cotton panties back on, my shirt is across the bed, and she's leaning down to pick up her own clothes.

She's leaving?

"Are you packing?" she asks, motioning toward the three boxes I've yet to go through. I had put them in the corner, and now Brin is staring at pieces of my past that I don't want to remember but can't seem to let go.

"It's just some old stuff," I say dismissively.

She starts working with her shirt, trying to untangle it. She *is* leaving.

This is exactly what I wanted, but as she slides her arms through her shirt, I feel myself moving toward her. I tackle her on the bed in no time, and I'm kissing her as she giggles against me.

"I need to go. I have to be at work early."

Go. She wants to go. She's not planning to stay, and I should be relieved. But it actually pisses me off. Fucking confusing bullshit.

"What time? I can set my alarm clock." What the hell is wrong with me?!

She goes still in my arms, but after a few seconds, her leg wraps around me.

"You want me to stay the night?" she asks curiously.

No. Yes. No. Fuck, yes. This is really starting to irk the hell out of me.

"Yes. You're already here. You're tired. I'm tired. And I have an alarm clock. Besides, I've seen you eyeing my shower at least five times today. If you stay, you can take a shower in there tomorrow morning."

When she grins, everything makes perfect sense. I can do this. I think. I fucking hope. Shit, I really hope I can do this for at least a little while. I know it can't be permanent, but we can be happy for a little while. There's nothing at all wrong with that.

"I do want to take a shower in there, but I have a feeling you won't get up early enough to take one with me. And that's why I've been eyeing it."

Yep. I'm fucked.

"Oh?" I ask, grinning as she snuggles into me.

"Forget it. I'm spent. No more sex tonight. Still want me to stay?" she mumbles, yawning as her precious body molds to mine, and she tucks her head under my chin.

Something warm spreads throughout my body as she hugs me to her. I hold her to me, feeling so damn comfortable that it's mind-boggling, and I grin against the top of her head.

"Yes," is my simple response. Because I do want her here. I'll deal with all of this confusion some other time.

Chapter 10

Brin

"You bastard!" I yell as the sticky, colorful assault pours from all of the showerheads. Why the hell did I let my guard down?

Rye laughs as he holds the shower doors closed, and I curse him while trying to figure out how in the hell to turn this damn digital shower thing off. It needs a frigging passcode! Who honestly believed so much technology was a good thing?

I try to reach one of the showerheads to shove it away, but the tall son of a bitch has installed all of them too high for me to reach without something to stand on. I had to pull a chair in here when I sabotaged him. I really wish I had that chair right now.

"Payback, tiger," he says, grinning, even though his face is obstructed by the fog on the doors.

Tiger. It's a simple word, and he's called me that before while playing our game, but it sounds different after you've had sex with someone—mind-blowing, phenomenal, life-altering sex.

Does he have to be this amazing? It almost makes me hate him.

"I'm going to kill you," I growl as the sticky mess finally starts slowing down and turning a little clearer, promising me that the Kool-Aid attack is almost over.

He just laughs, and I stand here in all my nakedness as the colors slowly dissipate. I'm scowling, but he can't see it through the even more steamed-up glass.

Finally, the clean water starts coming through, and I get under the flow to start rinsing away the sticky aftermath that is all in my hair. Closing my eyes, I put my head back and get to work on my hair. Poor hair.

I shouldn't grin when his body is suddenly against mine, but I do. I shouldn't angle my neck to give him better access to kiss it, but I do. And I definitely shouldn't let his lips start devouring mine, but I can't help myself. I can't believe he got up this early.

"I'd love to stay in here with you," he murmurs against my lips, "but you'd never get to work if I did."

Work is seriously the last thing on my mind.

I pull him to me and kiss him harder, fully prepared to be late, but he forces me to let him go while he laughs.

"Get finished. I'll make you some coffee."

As sweet as that sounds... "I'll pass on the coffee," I say while glaring at the gloriously naked man in front of me. Does he really think I'm that stupid?

His grin spreads as he shrugs and opens the door. "Your loss. I make an excellent cup."

"I prefer sugar. Not salt."

He just laughs while walking out, and I frown. I really wanted shower sex this morning.

"Fuck it," he says, suddenly back in the shower with me, and I grin in anticipation when his lips come down on mine and he picks me up.

Brin

I expected to get inside the house and tiptoe around in an effort to get ready and hurry to work, but Maggie and Carmen are sitting on the couch, both of them grinning as they stare at me.

"What?" I ask innocently, walking straight to my room.

"Don't you dare get ready without telling me details," Maggie gushes, running into my room as I grab a few things to change into.

"Details? I don't know what you're talking about," I say deadpan, holding back my giddy grin.

"You fucked him! Hell yes! I knew it. So are you two seeing each other again tonight? Did you two talk about why he was being so crazy?"

And these are the questions I wanted to avoid.

"I don't know."

"You don't know? Well, did you ask him what all this was about? He seemed genuinely freaked out about losing you when he came over."

I sigh hard while shrugging off my old shirt and pulling on my fresh one.

"We didn't talk about any of that, and I'm not going to. It'll ruin it. It always does with guys like him—not that I have tons of experience."

Maggie doesn't have to know that Rye is the third guy I've ever slept with.

"So you don't get any answers to the questions you want to ask because it might freak him out or something? That's stupid, Brin. That's not you."

She glares at me, but I roll my eyes. "It was one night, Maggie."

And one incredible shower this morning. "I'm not going to quiz the guy about what one night means. *That's* stupid. If it goes somewhere, great. If not, fine. That's the joyous world we live in. People date to get to know each other. They don't figure it all out on the first night."

She follows me around as I finish getting ready, and Carmen is sipping her coffee on the sofa when we walk out. She does her best not to look at us because this just got awkward—roommate dispute.

"*You* do, Brin. You never screw someone without knowing there is a potential promise of a relationship. You've dated numerous guys for months without giving it up."

"I haven't really dated since high school," I say through laughter. "I'm an adult. And I'm allowed to have some fun. I'm not deluding myself into thinking Rye wants anything more than fun."

She scowls at me. "You're more to him than fun. I guarantee you he has feelings for you that go deeper than the surface."

"Maggie, right now I'm the exotic creature. For once in my life, I'm something refreshing. To him at least. He's used to gorgeous girls throwing themselves at him, and I'm the ordinary girl who smashed his car instead of dropping my pants. Well, before I dropped my pants."

I aim for joking, but her ugly scowl promises I'm not getting through to her comical side.

"Maggie, don't. Don't force me to analyze this. It's fun to be different in a good way for a change. Last night, I felt better than I have in so many years. Don't steal that by forcing me to see it as it is. Not yet. Just let me enjoy it for a little while."

Her look softens, and she blows out a breath.

"Fine. But if he hurts you, I'm roasting his balls on a campfire."

He's going to destroy me.

"I'll be fine," I lie.

I can do this. I can have fun, meaningless, casual sex with my beautiful, sweet, incredible, perfect neighbor that I happen to be falling for too much. I was okay with leaving. But then he asked me to stay. I was okay with it being just one night, but then he referenced the future. I was okay with it just being about sex, but then we talked. And for the first time since John left me, I talked about our divorce without getting angry.

I smiled. I frigging smiled because it felt so good not to give a damn anymore.

Now I'm smiling again, and Maggie is frowning.

"You're already in love with the bastard," she groans.

"Am not," I retort quickly, rolling my eyes.

I'm not sure how deep that lie is, but I know it's not exactly true. I'm pretty sure I've been falling in love with him since the day he stole my car to fix it. But he's not looking for love. And I'm willing to take what I can get, because I settle. I always have. That's how people find a few moments of stolen happiness from an otherwise cold and disappointing world—they settle.

Rye

"You have..."

Jessica keeps talking, rattling off my schedule, but those are the only two words that break through. My mind is only on one thing. I've never slept so damn good as I did last night.

No doubt it was from the exhausting evening. It had to be. I refuse to believe I slept so well because Brin was in my arms. But damn she looks sweet when she sleeps.

I wasn't going to get up with her. I knew I'd end up in the shower with her and doing things that would only complicate our lives, but I wanted to play. She always makes me smile when she gets that fake angry hissing tone. She loves our war.

"And Tag Masters is here to see you," Jessica says, somehow managing to make me hear her again.

I turn in my chair and frown. Why's he here?

He walks in, and Jessica's eyes roam over his body. Nice to see she's recovering from my rejection so quickly.

Tag, of course, doesn't acknowledge her. He sits down in front of me, and she pouts on her way out. That girl is going to develop a complex working here.

"What?" I grumble.

"Rain's surprise party is tonight. I just wanted to know if you want Leah to meet you there. She's called me like ten times, wondering if I've talked to you since the night you left her stranded. Ash is going to kill her if she doesn't stop calling my cell phone. Apparently she's very jealous while pregnant. I'm still learning all this stuff. She's never really been jealous before because she knows without a doubt that I'd never do anything."

I walked out on Leah after kissing Brin, and she wants a date with me? Again?

"No thanks. I prefer girls with self-respect."

I can't tell him about Brin. I don't know what to say or how to explain it. At this moment, I don't even know what's going on. But she'll ask. She'll ask soon, and it'll be the end of us when I don't have the answer she wants.

"Hello?" Tag says, waving his hand in front of my face as though he's been talking and I've been ignoring him.

I clear my throat and try to give him my attention. "I asked if you were still pissed at me or something."

I'm not pissed at him. I'm pissed at me for being such a little bitch.

"No. I'm coming to the party, but I'll bring my own date. No more setups."

He frowns and nods. "Fine. I'll see you there. I need to grab some sort of present. What the hell do you buy a girl like Rain?"

I give him an incredulous look. "And you think I know?"

He shrugs and turns to walk out. I've lived in Sterling Shore my whole life, but there's one place I've never visited—the museum. They don't need me here. I'm no good to them while I'm distracted.

I need to go speak to Brin. Maybe today things will be different and I won't feel like I have to have her close to me.

Then again, I am going to the fucking museum to see her, so maybe my shit has just gotten worse.

Brin

"Make sure that is packaged properly. If it arrives at the owner's home with even one scratch, I can promise you that you won't be buying your kids a Christmas present this year," I say mildly to the men who start taking much better care of the artifacts they are packing up.

Ash is still standing beside me, pouting as she awaits my answer.

"No. I don't want you setting me up. Ever. Again."

I turn and start walking toward the next few crates, taking inventory and making sure everything is here.

"I said I'm sorry. I still feel like the biggest bitch in the world. I had no idea the guy was such a creep. I promise this one is different. His name is George and he has—"

"Whose name is George?" a familiar, deep, spine-tingling voice asks, and Ash turns as I do to see Rye gliding toward us, walking in a way that even has straight men turning their heads to watch. Does everything he does have to be so sexy?

He's wearing a tight black shirt that has a skull and crossbones on it, along with *Clanton Auto* across the top. And I grin uncontrollably, uncaring about what an idiot I must look like. He stops when he reaches us, and my smile slowly fades. He's not touching me or even looking at me. His expectant eyes are on Ash.

"George Carpenter. You know him. He's friends with Billy, and he's a really great guy. He wants to meet Brin. He saw her picture yesterday, and he begged me for a date."

He saw my picture and begged for a date. That sounds... odd. Especially if he knows Ash. Standards are too high around here.

Rye frowns as he looks at me. "You're planning on dating George?" he asks, his jaw ticking.

Is he jealous? Am I grinning again?

209

"No. I told Ash I refuse to be set up by her again."

I try to look at the men who are still packing up the artifacts, but it's hard to do when my eyes keep drifting back to the same man I was pretty much thoroughly explored by last night.

He looks as though relief has just washed over him, but Ash turns her attention back to me, so I don't get to fully study the man on my right.

"I said I was sorry about the creep from hell. George isn't like that. He's nice, and funny, and he's actually pretty good looking. I promise he's not the same asshole the last prick was. Please let me do this. I feel horrible about what happened, and Rain's party is tonight. It's perfect."

Rye bristles beside me and answers before I can. "She's not going out with George."

I bite back my grin as Ash turns a glare on him. "It's not your decision. And she's not someone you have to protect. Brin can take care of herself."

"I said she's not going with George," he growls, and Ash glares at him that much harder.

"And I said it's not your decision," she hisses.

He rolls his eyes as he turns to me, and he pulls me to him, shocking the hell out of me when his lips crush mine. I drop the pen and clipboard in unison so that I can steady myself by holding onto his shoulders. His tongue sweeps in, and my knees buckle, forcing him to hold me up.

"You're not going to Rain's party with George," he murmurs

against my lips, nipping at my bottom lip playfully before pulling back.

"Wasn't planning on it," I say, admittedly a little breathless after that.

"Good." He grins, and we both look up to see Ash with tears in her eyes and her mouth turned up in a painful smile.

Pregnancy hormones must be a bitch.

"You two are together now?"

Sheesh. Why does everyone want to push for some sort of promise of a relationship?

"We're going to the party together," Rye says, and then he shifts uncomfortably before turning to me. "Unless you don't want to go with me."

I fight so damn hard to contain the little girl scream that wants to escape me, but I can't hold off my grin. "I want to."

He nods and turns back to Ash. "Go away. And take George's date proposal with you."

She laughs while wiping a tear away, and then she sighs happily. She waves and walks off, seeming all too chipper.

"You came to ask me out?" I ask, turning toward him. "A phone call would have sufficed."

I'm doing all I can to seem casual. His grin returns as he leans down and kisses me again, but he pulls away before I can deepen it.

"I came to see the museum. I've never been here before. I want a tour."

It's hard for me not to be hopeful when he does and says stuff like this. "Then let me be your tour guide."

He smiles as he puts his arm around me, and I breathe in easily. He makes breathing so much better. But what will it be like when we're in front of everyone who expects him to be with someone like the girls they keep setting him up with?

Rye

"You two look good together," Wren says, grinning his shit-eating grin that might as well say *I told you so*.

I don't say anything as Brin returns with Ash, walking across the dance floor and avoiding the drunken crowd the best they can. Ash gets stopped and pulled toward the bar by someone, but Brin continues her venture toward me.

"How does your car drive?" Wren asks her, a lilt to his voice as she sits down next to me.

I put my arm around her and she leans in, making all the shit I've caught from Wren and Tag worth it.

"Like a dream," Brin says with her adorable grin that makes me swell with pride.

I put that smile there.

I can't stop myself from leaning down and kissing her, wishing we didn't have so many people around. It's not supposed to feel this good.

She kisses me back, but she pulls away when I try to push for more. I frown, and she laughs while wiping at my mouth, probably removing her lipstick from me again. Why is she wearing that shit?

In fact, she doesn't look like she normally does. Her dress is tighter, and it's a bold pink color she doesn't usually wear. Even though it's sexy on her, it's not her. I prefer the cute shorts or innocent sundresses she wears. Her heels are higher, her makeup is heavier, and her hair is styled to perfection with curls that had to have taken hours to put into her very straight hair. It sort of pisses me off, though I don't know why.

"Rye Clanton has a girlfriend. Never thought I'd see the day," Ethan Noles says as he joins us in the booth.

Brin tenses just as I do, but I'm more surprised by his presence than worried about his words. "When the hell did you get into town?" I ask, smiling at the bastard who has been my best friend since elementary school.

"Just a few minutes ago. I'm here for a month or two this time. Dane called and told me Rain's party was tonight. Thought I'd stop by and see my cousin on her birthday. Then I make it through the door only to hear everyone talking about the two of you. Had to come see it for myself."

He looks Brin over, pursing his lips as though he's curious. I refuse to let him ruin this moment with too much reality. Brin is stiff as a board, proving this is making her uncomfortable, too.

"We're not a couple," she finally says, and he tilts his head more, smiling as he leans back.

"Looks like he's wearing your shade," he says, turning his eyes back to me.

I wipe my lips where there's still pink lipstick apparently. I really wish she'd just get rid of that shit. It makes kissing a pain in the ass.

"They're neighbors and friends," an oddly familiar voice says with

213

sarcasm as the redhead I turned down crawls into the booth beside Ethan.

He grins as he looks her over, and I swallow hard. Ah, shit. Drama. There will be drama. I hate drama.

Leah. Can the girl not take a hint?

Wren groans as he looks at me, worried like I am. A woman scorned is never a good thing.

"Looks like someone found Momma's makeup bag," the drunken version of Leah quips. What the hell?

Brin rolls her eyes and starts to back away, but I pull her to me. Ethan's smile disintegrates when he takes in the situation.

"Alright, Red. Looks like someone should be going," he says, pushing her out of the booth and trying to wave over security.

"You turned me down for her? For that?" she asks with disgust, fighting against Ethan who is seconds away from losing his temper.

He'll launch her ass out of the booth if she keeps on.

"Yes I did," I say without hesitation when Brin finally stands.

I start to go to her, but she just walks off. Leah follows immediately, and I stumble out of the booth, tripping over my own drunken feet.

Ethan mutters an, "Oh shit," as he joins me in the chase.

But by the time we catch up, Brin is smiling, leaning against the bar as security drags out the screaming crazed girl. She watches and waves at Leah, and then she turns to grab a drink from the bartender. It's then I notice Leah is soaking wet with a red mark across her face.

Did I just miss the good shit? Fuck.

"Shit," Ethan groans. "How the hell did we miss that?"

I just laugh as I make my way over to Brin, but her smile has lost its depth. It seems forced now. Brittle even. I hate that smile.

"Did you slap her?" Ethan asks, whining almost.

Brin smirks while sipping her drink, and then she says, "Just a little tap. The drink in her face came from Ash."

Ash walks up, moving away from the door where Leah was just hauled out. "I've really wanted to do that since she started calling Tag," she gloats, smiling as she hands her cup to the bartender for some fresh water.

"Damn," Wren says, joining us. "What'd I miss?"

We all pout, but Ash is the only one to laugh. Brin seems a thousand miles away. This is the sort of drama that I like to avoid. She's upset but not talking about it. I didn't invite Leah, but I didn't tell her that Leah was still trying to get me to see her either.

"Why was she even here?" Wren asks, looking at Ash.

"Hell if I know. I certainly didn't invite her. She must have heard us talking about it a couple of nights ago when Tag set her up with Rye."

Brin's lips tighten as she stares down at her drink. I wish I could see inside her head right now. I can't tell if she's pissed at me or just upset about what Leah said.

"Oh, so you two are newly together?" Ethan muses, looking between Brin and me.

She sighs while taking a napkin and wiping her lips, trying to get rid of that terrible shit I've hated all night.

215

"Dear God. We're not together," she growls, walking away from all of us.

"What the hell was that about?" Wren asks, glaring at me like it's my fault.

Drama. Drama. Drama.

"Hell if I know."

"This is the part where you go find out," he prompts, giving me a shove in the direction that Brin went.

"You heard her. We're not together. That's boyfriend shit."

He continues to glare at me like I'm an idiot, but I return the glower. "You're making her feel like she's not good enough," Ash says, interrupting the stare down.

Fuck. "All I did was invite her here with me. She said yes. I've done nothing but—"

"Exactly," she interrupts, looking so damn smug. "You've done *nothing*. You probably haven't even told her what you expect from all of this. If you fuck someone you're friends with, you have to talk to them. That's how it works. Now go talk to her."

Brin

I would cry if it wouldn't give me away. Why do I want to cry? I never cry—unless big, stupid, confusing idiots fix my car. Why won't everyone just butt out of our business?

I contemplate calling a cab, and I even pull out my phone as I stare out at the ocean. My face is mostly clean now. I just spent ten minutes trying to scrub off the pounds of makeup I put on.

What was I thinking?

I know exactly what I was thinking. I tried to convince myself that I could get the Sterling sparkle through makeup, hair, and clothes. It doesn't work that way. I looked exactly the same, only I looked like the girl playing dress-up, and Leah called me out on it.

I still can't believe I slapped her. But when she chased me, yelling over the music that Rye had no standards, that he was a horny dumbass with no brains, I couldn't help myself. I could deal with her slamming me, but my temper exploded when she started badmouthing him. I deserved what she said about me, because I stopped being *me* tonight.

I'm trying to convince the world that it's okay for Rye—a guy who couldn't be sexier if he tried—to want me. Why am I doing this to myself? What am I doing with him? This isn't me.

"You going to keep hiding? If so, can I hide, too?" Rye asks from behind me, and I laugh humorlessly while dropping to the sand. I waited too long to call a cab. Just my luck.

"It's a public beach," I say through a sigh. "It's hard to hide out here."

He smiles tightly while coming to drop down beside me. "The new will wear off and they'll start talking about something other than us. They're just excited right now."

This isn't the conversation I expected. It's actually completely different, and I almost kiss him to thank him. But then he opens his mouth again.

"Brin, I want to be honest." Bubble is popping, reality is coming, and humiliation is waiting to pounce. "I don't want a relationship. I really like this thing between us and how great yesterday was, but I keep things simple. I don't think you want something simple. You deserve a hell of a lot more than that."

Oh. That's the conversation I was expecting. And it sucks a lot worse than I thought it would. But I prefer the hard, cold, brutal truth, no matter how ugly it is.

"It's fine, Rye. You can be honest. Don't start trying to spare me by building me up and putting yourself down. I hate that speech. You keep acting as though I'm going to break every time someone makes me feel small, but I won't. Never have. Never will. So stop."

He smiles at me, and then he leans over and kisses me. He's so damn confusing. His lips work against mine for a moment before his tongue slips in, and then he starts pulling me onto his lap.

"You think I'm lying?" he asks, slowly sliding the bottom of my dress up enough to put his hands on my ass.

Since I'm wearing the thongs, his hands find my skin, and I almost moan.

"I think you're trying to keep me from getting my feelings hurt. Just like you always do. It's sweet, but unnecessary."

His tongue slips between my lips again, and he pulls me tighter to his body. "I'm not lying," he says, barely parting his lips from mine. "I'm not sparing you. I'm telling you the truth. I've never done the relationship thing, and to be honest, I never cared. But you... I wish I could be that guy. I've been struggling with what to do all day."

He takes a deep breath as his hand go to my hair, his fingers tangling in the threads, and his eyes study mine. Then he continues.

218

"But I'll fuck up. I know I will. And then I'll lose you. And I really, really like having you around. So I don't want to make promises I can't keep and have you hate me when I fuck up. I'm simple. You're the girl who wants it all, and you sure as hell deserve it, Brin. I'm just not that kind of guy."

He starts kissing my neck, contradicting his words. I can't tell if he's dumping me or begging me to tell him what he wants to hear. And he frigging claims to be simple.

So I do the only thing I know to do. I lie my ass off.

"I never had the chance to have fun, Rye. That's all I want to do. I've only been divorced for a year, and I got married young. I'm not looking for a serious relationship. Have I said anything like that to you?"

He pulls back and stares me in the eyes again as he studies me under the moonlight.

"Are you being serious?" he asks after an eternity of silence.

"Very," I lie again.

His lips almost bruise mine with the next hungry kiss, and my hands go to his hair. I've just thrown my heart into a blender. It won't be long until the button is pressed and my heart is pureed. But I can't just stop. Not when I've never felt like this with someone.

I don't feel used. I don't feel like a disappointment when he's with me. And I don't feel like the girl someone is passing the time with.

Even if it's just an illusion, it feels like he wants to be with me as much as I want to be with him. And it's hard to let go of something that I've always wanted to feel.

"Can we get out of here?" he asks, breaking the kiss and breathing just as heavily as I am.

"Please."

He starts to stand, but stops, pulling me back down as he tugs at my dress. "And, Brin, don't do this again."

I have no idea what he's talking about. "Don't do what?"

"This. The hair, the lipstick, the dress you don't really want to be wearing. I prefer the real Brin."

That's a relief, because I'm not overly fond of the fake Brin. I notice he doesn't say anything about not wearing the slinky panties again, but I can give him that. Especially since I actually enjoy feeling his hands against my skin.

"I prefer being the real Brin. I just knew everyone else would be questioning why you were here with me. Just like Leah did."

He runs his fingers over my arms, dragging them up and down in practiced motions.

"That's bullshit. You're beautiful when you're just you."

Okay. So that just makes it all worth it. I really don't think anyone has ever called me beautiful, and I know I look like a dork grinning right now.

He smiles as he stands up and pulls me to my feet, but as we walk away, my lie sinks in. I just told him I didn't want anything but fun. Then again, life is nothing but a series of settlements.

I can settle for being his no matter how brief it is. As long as it's just me.

"I only have one rule," I say as we make our way toward his car.

"A rule?" he muses, threading our fingers together.

"If we're having sex without condoms, you can't be having sex with someone else."

He looks at me as though I've lost my mind, but I'm not backing down from this.

"I'm not going to have sex with anyone else. And neither are you."

Relief washes over me, and I'm able to breathe once again. That's good enough. It's almost like he's really mine. Almost.

Chapter 11

Rye

"Is that cake?" Wren asks as he comes into my office.

"Yep," I grumble, looking at the delicious morsel that is more than likely full of blood and worms, considering that's the only reason she had those gross things in her fridge. She never did anything else with them. At least I don't think she did.

I'm going to be sick.

With a regretful sigh, I slide the cake off my desk and into the trash. It had better be a gross cake. I'll be pissed if that tempting thing didn't have anything wrong with it.

"Oh," Wren says through a snicker. "Prank cake?"

It showed up an hour ago. It was just sitting on my desk with nothing attached to it. It had to be from her.

"Can't be too careful." I pout, still staring at the chocolate-frosted wonder that has teased and tortured me. I'll make her fix me a real cake to make up for it, and I'll stare over her shoulder the whole time to ensure it's not tampered with.

"I guess the two of you are still on good terms," he says as he sits down.

Jessica walks in, halting my response, and her eyes go straight to the cake sticking out of my small trashcan. She looks... sad?

"You didn't like my cake?" she asks pitifully.

Ah, hell. "You made that?" I ask in disbelief.

She frowns as she nods. "It was an apology cake."

I just threw away good chocolate for no good reason.

"Sorry. I thought it was from—*Brin*. You're here," I say in surprise as my tiger walks in, her eyes narrowed on me.

Are we about to fight over Jessica? I really hope not. We agreed to be exclusive but noncommittal. If that makes any sense. It does in my head, so I'm going with it.

She eyes the trashcan for a moment, but then her pretty blues come back up to meet my gaze.

"Give me the password, Rye," she growls, and my grin slowly grows.

"Getting tired of maracas and words you don't understand?" I tease, proud of the fact I rigged her stereo. "Should have taken Spanish class."

"Now," she demands, looking hot as hell with that fiery temper of hers taking root.

"Nope." I sigh long and loud, acting so weary, as though this is exhausting, and Jessica slowly creeps out.

I start to apologize about the cake, but I decide against it. That will give Brin doubts, and I don't want that.

"Fine. Then that means I owe you," she says threateningly.

Wren grins as he watches with intrigue, and I sit back while crossing my arms over my chest.

"Or you could consider us even, tiger."

She rolls her eyes as though that's preposterous. "Not *even*, Mr. Ass. Now I need to go google my next plan of attack."

Google? "That's cheating," I say with an accusatory tone.

Only I'm allowed to cheat.

"It's not cheating; it's plotting. And I have plenty of time to plot. When do you get off?"

Too easy. I shouldn't. But I can't resist watching her cheeks flame in front of Wren. "Usually right after you do—the second time."

I'm rewarded when her eyes pop open to be much wider. Wren coughs in surprise, and then Brin blushes fiercely while glaring at me.

Worth it.

"Wow," Wren says through a laugh, shaking his head while Brin looks for… something. Probably something to throw at me.

"Not what I meant," she mumbles, avoiding looking in Wren's direction.

"I'll leave right now if you want me to *get off*," I taunt, only adding to her mortification as Wren laughs loudly.

She bites back a grin while coming toward me, and I swivel my chair over to pull her onto my lap. She doesn't fight me, even though she probably has something sick and twisted planned for me later.

I really like this thing between us.

"You're an ass."

"You're here to see me, so that must mean you like asses," I point out, and she grins.

"You're seriously not giving me the password?"

"Will you call us even if I do?" I ask, leaning over to press a sweet, soft, and very quick kiss to her lips.

"Sure," she lies.

"Then no. I have work to do, so I need you to go and stop distracting me so I don't have to stay later than necessary."

"Fine. I'll go. *If* you tell me why you have an entire cake in your trashcan."

I glance over, and curse the delicious looking thing. Damn war.

"I thought it was from you. Jessica brought it to me to apologize for the shit she pulled in front of you. I think she's worried about getting fired. But I tossed it out because I just knew you had something gross as the gooey center. Something like worms and blood."

Wren wrinkles his nose in disgust while Brin laughs and stands.

"Glad I've made you paranoid. I'm going home now to think of something much better than worm and blood cake. My worms died, and the blood did something weird. So I had to scratch that plan."

Most people would probably find this conversation… disturbing, but it's as natural as talking about the weather between the two of us.

"So I'll see you after you get done plotting my demise?" I ask, smiling like a fool as she bends and presses her lips to mine once more.

"Yes," she says sweetly, too sweetly. She's already plotting. Damn.

I watch her ass with appreciation as she leaves. How in the hell did I find a girl as cool as her? I just wish it could be more than it is.

The second the door shuts, Wren leans up on the desk.

"You really like her," he observes, his eyes on me very intently.

I don't want to talk about this, so I shrug. Before I can ask him anything about his kid, he continues. "But you don't plan on getting serious with her."

It's not a question, because he knows me well.

"We're having fun. That's enough for me and her. For now. Eventually she'll want more, and the fun will end. But until that time comes, I'm going to enjoy it while it lasts. I've never had this before."

I hate the pity in his eyes. "But you could enjoy it for longer. There's nothing stopping you from trying."

I'd love nothing more than to punch him. Brin left me in a great mood, and Wren is destroying it. If she's not pushing, then why the hell is everyone else?

"You know exactly what's stopping me. Don't pretend as though I'm some normal guy capable of being what Brin needs. Just... don't. Things are fine, better than fine, and until they're not fine... Well, I'll deal with it when the time comes."

He frowns but nods slowly. He knows I'm right.

Jessica walks back in, her usual smile gone as she carries another cake toward my desk. This one looks... store bought, though. That sucks. Homemade cake is always better.

"What's this?" I ask, looking up at her as she turns to walk out.

"A cake," she mutters, sulking as she exits.

"Sounds like you've pissed her off," Wren says, amused.

Damn drama.

"Eat cake and shut the hell up."

He rolls his eyes as I grab two plastic forks from my desk stash, and I open the lid to the chocolate beauty that pales in comparison to the last one. She could have at least taken it out of the store box.

"Is the icing moving?" Wren asks just as I pull a bite to my lips.

I pull it back and stare at it. Sure enough, the fucking icing is wiggling, and I turn a little pale when I see a slender, disgusting, slithering thing squirming around just under the icing.

She didn't. She couldn't have.

I drop the fork full of cake, and Wren gags as he steps away. I glare out at the pet store that is two shops down from the bakery. She did. She's out there beside her car, and she's fucking waving. That conniving little—

"She's quick," Wren says, half gagging, half laughing, as he draws my attention back to him.

For some reason, that makes me smile. "She's pretty damn awesome."

I drop the cake to the second trashcan in my office, and I shake my head. She's definitely baking me a good cake now.

"The two of you are pretty damn perfect for each other, if you ask me," he says, and my smile vanishes.

Too perfect. This almost seems like a cruel joke. Fate has a sadistic sense of humor if that's the case.

Brin

I squeal and dive into my room, locking the door behind me, but he's at the window instead of the door, and the damn thing isn't locked. It's too dark to be running around the frigging house!

"Stop! I said I'm sorry," I say through a laugh, but he just keeps coming.

"Your ass is mine!"

I giggle while darting out the door, and I run into Maggie's room, barely getting the door slammed in time. Like a child scared of a closet monster, I dive onto Maggie's bed and pull the covers over me.

"Maggie? Why are you already in bed?" I whisper, but the pounding on the door makes me scream, and I hear another scream that seems to echo.

When I jump back, trying to get closer to Maggie, my hand hits the smooth skin of her side and I grimace.

"Let me have her, Maggie!" Rye roars, and at the same time, I ask, "Are you naked?"

A throat clearing emerges from beside me, and a giggling sound comes from the other side of it. I give her side a light squeeze, prompting her to speak.

"This is a little awkward," Carmen says, and I squeal, because it's her naked side I'm holding—not Maggie's.

Maggie's laughter rolls out, and Rye goes silent at the door.

"I'm so, so, so, so, so, sorry," I groan, ripping my hand off Carmen like it's on fire.

"It's fine," Carmen says, a small bit of her own laughter in her voice.

"Carmen is in there?" Rye asks with a lilt to his voice. "And they're naked?"

Oh good grief.

Carmen and Maggie both groan in unison, because they hear this sort of thing from men all the time. As though their relationship is meant to turn guys on. Idiots. But that's not what Rye is doing. He's just being a playful jerk, because he's heard Maggie rant about it this past week.

"Can I come in?" he asks softly, trying to sound hopeful. Maybe he is being serious. After all, he is still just a guy.

We all start to say no, but I tilt my head and beat the other two girls. "They said yes. You can come in."

In the pitch black of the room, I can hear it, but I can't see when their heads whip around to me.

"I need a distraction," I whisper.

Nothing gets said, but they both sigh.

"Really?" Rye says after a beat.

"Really," I affirm, and I get up to go open the door and usher him in.

"Come on in, Rye. Get an eyeful," Carmen says, playing along.

I really like her right now.

As soon as I peek my head out, the look he gives me proves this was a mistake. A really stupid mistake.

"Rain-check," he says, grabbing for me.

I try to dodge him, but I'm not quick enough. Maggie laughs as Rye holds me to his body with one hand, and closes the door with his other before wrapping me up in an unbreakable hold.

He grins down at me, warning me there will be hell to pay, but I go on the offense and push my lips to his. When the surprise makes him part his lips, my tongue slips into the gap, and his hold on me becomes different as I wrap my legs around his waist.

"You're cheating," he murmurs insincerely as his hands slide down to only cup my ass.

He walks me back toward his house, and I grin against his lips.

"Oh?" I ask, feigning innocence.

He doesn't even acknowledge that as we stumble back into his house. He drops me to his bed, and I grin up at him. I know a way to make him forget that I just figured out how to reprogram his shower to where he can only get cold water to come out.

Okay, *maybe* Wrench—whose real name is still a mystery—came over and helped me out. He's quickly becoming my favorite accomplice.

"You're going to give me the new password," Rye growls as he pulls his shirt over his head.

"Suuurrre. Right after you give me the password to my car's stereo."

I could have just gotten Wrench to fix it instead of hacking his shower, but where's the fun in that?

I grab at his loose track pants and shove them to the floor, freeing the very excited part of his body. I love the fact that I'm the one who turns him on.

"I mean it, Brin. I love my hot showe—*Fuck*."

The last word hisses through his lips when I take him into my mouth. He was so busy ranting that he didn't even see what I was up to. Now he's standing in front of the bed as I sit on the edge and own him.

The piercing slides over my tongue, teasing me with the power it has, and Rye's hands go to my hair as I give to him what he gave to me a few hours ago. His mouth is a rare find, because he knows how to slay me in the best possible way with his tongue.

More air hisses through his teeth when I get him closer, taking him as deep as I can while clutching his hips for support. He rocks into me as his muscles tighten, giving me fair warning about what's about to come—no pun intended.

"Brin," he whispers hoarsely, warning me verbally, but I keep him firmly planted inside my mouth, refusing to stop my ministrations until I make him feel just as sublime as he made me feel.

Then the warm, salty flavor invades my mouth, and I swallow as quickly as I can while his whole body goes limp and he drops to the bed. I climb over beside him, glowing proudly as he wraps me up. He kisses me, even though he's out of breath and it's a weak kiss, but I can't help but feel a little powerful.

"Stay the night," he murmurs against my lips for the third time this week. We've been doing this thing for a week now, and he really wants me to sleep over every time.

"Nope," I say, making the word *pop*.

I can't and I won't. It'll confuse the already blurry lines.

We haven't even had sex tonight. We've just talked and made out like teenagers, then there were a few exchanges of small pranks until he found his shower, and now I've just done this to him, just as he did to me earlier. I'd love to have sex, but I think I want to leave things the way they are—for tonight.

"Then let me spend the night over there with you," he says while running his fingers through my hair and yawning.

He adjusts himself to put his head on my chest, and I begin

running my fingers through his hair just like he was doing with mine.

He's sweet when he's sleepy. His eyes are barely staying open, his breaths are already slow, and his grip on me tightens every time he thinks I'm going to move.

So I get still and quiet. Within a few minutes, he's fast asleep with his head resting on my chest and his arms wrapped around my waist. I kiss his forehead, but he doesn't really move.

There's no reason why I can't stay here long enough for him to rest peacefully.

As soon as I'm sure he's not going to wake up, I uncurl myself from his grip.

Just as I'm walking out of his room, his phone buzzes on the table in the hallway. I look—reflexively, not because I'm prying—and a touch of disappointment cloaks me.

Wren: *She's good for you. I think you should tell her everything. She could…*

That's all the preview shows, and as much as I want to read the whole message, I refrain. But I can't help but wonder what there is to tell. I like the fact that the friend he trusts is telling him that I'm good for him. Maybe…

I can't think about *maybe*. It'll hurt too much.

Chapter 12

Rye

My name tears through her lips like a curse, and she rakes her nails over my chest as I continue fucking her from underneath. I kiss her hard, swallowing her sounds of tortured pleasure, waiting for the second orgasm to sweep through her body.

The second her walls clench around me again, I find a dizzying release, holding her to me as my legs stiffen, and I thrust up and hold myself deep within her.

"You're going to be late for work," I mumble against her cheek as she pants heavily on top of me.

"You woke me up an hour early," she groans. "I'm not going to be late. What are you doing in my bedroom so early? Again?"

I frown as she slaps the alarm clock that is just now going off.

"I thought you had to be in at eight," I say as my hands start sliding up her body.

I never wake up early, but that has changed these past few weeks. She rarely spends the night. Usually I have to trick her into it, but I love being in bed with her when she first wakes up.

So, I keep showing up, dragging my ass out of bed with the sun, and watching her sleepy eyes open when I jar her awake. The reward is always worth the grumpy girl I get afterwards. Right now, I'm still inside her, and she's still coming down from her orgasm.

It's been a month almost, and I still can't seem to get enough. I love it and hate it at the same time, because I'm a little bit consumed by her even when she's not around. Which is the main reason I take two or three days here and there and go silent—no calls or visits. It keeps her from forgetting what this is, and she never calls or texts me on those days either, which lets me know she still understands.

I kiss her neck and start moving inside her again, but she almost jumps off me and abandons me on the bed. "You're going to kill me with sex," she groans, going to her bathroom, and I sit back and admire the view of the very naked hips swaying from side to side.

"Sounds like a damn good way to go, if you ask me. Why aren't you going to be late?"

"Because I don't have work today," she says as the water in the shower starts running.

I frown as I get up and follow her into the bathroom, already naked. When I join her, I'm met with the sprayer head she's holding, and the cold stab of the water almost steals my breath as she shoots me with it.

"Damn!" I yelp, leaping out, and she laughs behind the curtain while I fall to the floor.

"What was that for?"

She continues laughing, and I glare at the curtain.

"For waking me up on my day off. It's Saturday, jackass."

Oh. Shit. It's Saturday?

"Good. Then you don't have anything better to do than spend the day with me. Let's go get breakfast and go for a ride on my bike."

I stand up and rejoin her in the shower—after making sure she

234

isn't waiting with that damn sprayer head still in her hand.

"Not today. I'm going to the vineyard to see Raya. She's got a thing going on, and she invited me."

I didn't get invited, and that sort of pisses me off.

"And you don't want to take me?" I pout like a five-year-old, but she just laughs.

"I would, but that would be awkward, since it's all girls. Maybe you and I can see each other tonight. If I make it home."

She's trying to piss me off. "*If* you make it home?"

She shrugs as she washes the shampoo out of her hair, and I do all I can not to concentrate on the water cascading down her body.

"There will be a lot of wine involved. I want to get really, really drunk. It's a shame you won't be there for me to take out my drunken fun on."

She sighs wistfully while offering me a teasing gaze.

"I want to go. So what if it's all girls? I survived that night when Ash and them came over and ranted about hating men all night. I can survive a few hours of women drinking."

She turns toward the shower, facing away from me, and I slide in behind her.

"I would let you, but I don't think Raya would like it. She just wants girls there, and I was among the few invited. Besides, I'm sure the guys will be calling you to do something with them."

This is really pissing me off. It's been three days since I've seen her. We never go longer than the three day period of silence. Usually it's just two days, but I needed an extra-long dose of separation this time. But four days is too damn much, especially since I won't be able to see her much tomorrow.

"Then at least let me drive you out there. I want you on my bike."

She turns to me, and her tight, barely-there smile spreads to be bigger and more genuine. "You've never put me on your bike. In fact, you said *no girls allowed.*"

"I've changed my mind. So can I drive you out there?"

Why is she making this so hard?

"Yes," she says, finally wearing that smile I love seeing her use, because she only ever uses that specific one for me. "If you promise to let me drive. Just for a little while."

"Hell no," I scoff, and she shrugs while stepping out of the shower and grabbing a towel.

"Then no deal."

My mouth drops open as I follow her out of the shower, shutting off the water as I reach for a towel.

"You can't be serious. I've never let a girl ride on my bike. I'm not going to let one drive it."

She carries on with grabbing a second towel and drying her hair, ignoring me as though this conversation is over. It's not.

"I'm driving you out there," I say with finality.

"Not unless you let me drive your bike for at least ten minutes."

"Not happening."

"Then I'm driving my Camry."

We'll see about that.

Brin

"Where are my keys, Rye?" I ask, glaring at him as he leans against my Camry. His motorcycle is parked in my yard with two helmets ready and waiting.

His smirk is almost sexy. Almost. "I'll give them back after we get to the vineyard. Hop on."

He motions toward his bike, and I groan while walking down the steps of my porch, even though I'm secretly hiding my grin. He's not a morning person, but he shows up over here all the time—unless he's taking one of his *breaks*. Those are pissing me off.

I know he's trying to remind me this isn't a relationship, and that's really the only way to do it. But he's the one who is calling all the shots, and I'm just letting him. One thing is for sure, he doesn't want this turning into more.

How can this not turn into more? It has to. He's stealing my keys and begging to drive me three hours away for a girls' night because he can't go more than three days without seeing me. Hell, he usually can't go more than two.

Personally, it always pisses me off, because I can barely go a few hours without seeing him, which reminds me how much more I care about him than he cares about me.

He comes toward me after picking up a helmet, and he fastens it to me, double checking to make sure it's safely secured, and then he presses a sweet kiss to my lips before putting his on.

He throws a long leg over his bike, looking too sexy and graceful for words, and I come to join him on the back. As much as I'd like to punish him and deny his demand to drive me, I can't. It feels too good to be pressed up against him.

I hide my grin as I say, "I'm doing this under extreme protest."

He just laughs while cranking up the beast, and it roars to life as my arms go around his waist. I get as close as I can while propping my feet on their designated perches, and he rubs my hands with his before he takes the handlebars and drives out of my yard.

I don't mean to giggle, but a thrill shoots through me. I knew he wouldn't let me drive. And I didn't even want to drive. I just didn't want to cave too easily. It's all an elaborate game of strategy and war, so I've started using it to my benefit.

For miles and miles we ride, and I frigging love it. It's freeing, exciting, exhilarating... It's amazing. Motorcycles are now among my favorite things.

We drive straight through, only slowing down for him to show me things, and I soak it all in like I do every moment we're together. We talk all the time. *ALL* the time. He calls me at work, shows up at work, and I do the same to him. I've kept him from screwing me inside the museum, but he won the battle about his office. Now his desk has been christened.

I'll never forget the surprise on Jessica's face when she caught us kissing. It doesn't bother me what people think anymore. And Rye doesn't give a damn about who sees me wrapped around him.

When we finally reach the vineyard, I almost pout. But he has to come back and get me. Maybe he'll talk Raya into letting him stay.

We pull up to where we see all the cars, and he turns off the motorcycle just as Raya comes out with her arms crossed over her chest.

"You too? Is it impossible for a guy to let his girl come to a damn girls' night without him?" she growls.

"It's not night," Rye says unapologetically, but he doesn't correct her about me not being his girl.

We've avoided hanging out with everyone since the Leah disaster. I forgot why until this moment.

Dane steps out onto the porch, waving at us as he walks to his car. Did he drive Rain out here?

He grabs a purse from the car and hurries back in. I just frown. If he's staying then—

"If Dane is staying, then so am I," Rye says as he climbs off his bike, taking my hand and helping me off, too. With a few quick motions, his helmet is off, and his hair has that sexy, messy look I love.

"Might as well. They're all here. I just called Kade to come back, but he was already on his way."

She tries not to grin, but she can't help it. That girl is so in love. Must be nice.

"I've got it," Rye says when I struggle to get the helmet off.

He moves my hands and removes the helmet for me, and then he bends and pushes his lips against mine, earning a smile from me. I wrap my arms around his neck and giggle when he picks me up, carrying me toward the house.

"You two are so damn gross," Ethan says from the porch, and Rye grins against my lips while releasing me.

"Why the hell are you here?" Rye asks, still smiling.

I'm not overly fond of Ethan. I can tell he doesn't understand Rye's fascination with me. And I'm sure he expected them to be hanging out more than they are. Rye is the one who keeps showing up and kidnapping me from my house. I'm not twisting his arm to keep seeing me when he does.

"I came out to see Kade, and apparently stumbled into a couples' night. What the hell?" Ethan mumbles.

He looks at Raya and shakes his head, but I don't know why. Raya is gorgeous—perfect for the Colton Prince.

"Not what I expected to find," he murmurs under his breath.

So he's not impressed with Raya either? It's not just me?

Rye doesn't let go of my hand. Instead, he pulls it up to his lips and kisses it, and then he bends and kisses me again. My smile is as instant as always. This is different from the last time we were all together. And I don't feel so on edge.

"Let's get in and start tasting the wine," Ethan grumbles.

"It's too early to start drinking," Raya says as she follows us in.

"I'm in couple hell. It's a perfect time to start drinking."

He goes straight toward the wine, and I roll my eyes. "You look windblown," Ash says as she walks over, smiling while drinking a bottle of water.

"She looks sexy," Rye says, wrapping his arms around my body and pulling my back to his front.

"You rode his bike?" she asks, apparently doing the math.

"I stole her keys," Rye says with a shrug. "Speaking of which..."

He pulls my keys out of his pocket and hands them to me, and I roll my eyes while tucking them into the pocket of my shorts.

"You want wine? They've got an excellent merlot here. I can't have it, but I can live vicariously," Ash says.

"Brin likes white wine. But she can't drink so early because we haven't really eaten. It's only like noon. And I'm starving."

He remembers what kind of wine I like. Why is that so sweet?

"So, where are you from?" Ethan asks me, but his eyes are on Rye, so I'm assuming the question is for him to answer.

"She's from Sterling Shore. Why?" Rye asks, his grip getting tighter.

"Just curious. Never seen her around before."

"She went to private school upstate, and doesn't hang out at the socialite functions. Problem?" Rye asks.

Is this about social status? My father is a wealthy man, but not compared to people like Rye's father—Rygan Clanton, who I've only heard about through the others. My dad certainly doesn't have the money the Sterlings have. So we never went to the upper elite parties.

Even though Ethan is a Noles—one of the most prestigious old names and old money families in the city—he doesn't dress the part. He looks as rough around the edges as Rye, so I only assumed he was the type to brush off such superficial titles.

"You two seem to know each other pretty well. It's cute. I'm not being a dick, so get that ugly, threatening look off your face," Ethan says flippantly.

I look up just as Rye relaxes his expression, and I lean back against him more, forcing him to return his attention to me as he looks down. His smile forms the second his eyes meet mine, and I feel a little powerful to have that sort of effect on him.

"The cheddar is phenomenal. Try it," Raya says to Rye as she pulls out platters and platters full of mixed assortments. Cheese and wine are commonly put together, and I can't help but grin, especially when he shifts uncomfortably behind me.

"He can't have cheddar," I joke, laughing at him when he scowls at me.

"Wow. You told her about that?" Tag asks as he joins us.

"I didn't mean to. She made some weird casserole the other night, and the damn thing had tons of cheddar in it. It sort of... came out."

"No pun intended?" Tag asks, amused, and I burst out laughing as poor Rye glares at him.

"You lactose intolerant or something?" Ash asks, intrigued and working hard not to laugh.

"No. I'm not. I can eat any other cheese and drink milk. Cheddar is just a mean bitch. I don't want to talk about this."

He starts sulking and I turn to face him while wrapping my arms around his neck. He kisses me on the forehead as he clings to me like a shield from their laughter.

"How about bread? Are their certain breads that make you fart?" Raya asks, poking the bear a little more.

He groans while dropping his forehead to mine, and I grin as I hold onto him. Everyone watches us, and it starts to become obvious that we're both causing a scene.

"You work at the museum?" Ethan asks me, so I turn away from Rye to answer.

"Yes. For a few years now."

"What do you do?"

"Everything," Rye says before I can answer. "She's supposed to be the assistant to the director, but she should be the director, because that lazy dick never does anything. It's always her. She's the one who handles all the exhibits, the shipments, the inventory, the special showings, the event planning... All of it. I haven't seen her lazy boss get off his ass yet."

I can't help but smile again, and suddenly it doesn't matter if we're giving them a show that contradicts all of our denials. I kiss him, and I don't hold back. Neither does he.

"Where's that wine? I need something dry to counteract all the damn sweet shit they're spewing," Ethan says, but we both ignore him.

I'm a little scared to drink. My father always said not to drink when you had secrets to keep. You never know what might come out.

Chapter 13

Rye

"This sucks," Ethan harps as Brin moves off my lap and toward the wine.

"What sucks?" I ask, my eyes transfixed on her as she pours a new glass.

"All of you."

She hasn't had but a few sips. I keep drinking the whole damn glass the second she gets back with it. This turned out to be a very good day. I needed this.

And Brin is perfect. She's held true to her word, and she hasn't pushed for anything more than what we have. And tonight she's laughed, flirted with me, and kissed me in front of the world without giving a damn about their constant meddling.

If Ash had her way, Brin and I would be getting married right now. But we've learned to ignore all of them.

"Why do we suck?" I ask absently, still watching Brin as she laughs with the very drunk Raya.

"I came back expecting to get to hang out with some of you while I'm here. Kode is up Tria's ass—which is still fucking crazy to me. They hated each other when I left, then they were in love at Rain's wedding. Dane and Rain are married, which is bizarre, considering they weren't speaking when I left. Kade is engaged to Raya, which is freaking me the fuck out. I never expected him to settle down. Wren is

MIA. And then you. You're the biggest shock of all."

My brow hits my hairline as I turn to face him. "What does that mean?"

He frowns as he wobbles in his seat. He's too drunk to speak right, but he's still sober enough to piss me off.

"Dude, fess up. You're in love with that girl. You barely keep your hands and eyes off her. I'm surprised, really. She's so damn sweet. I picture her being with Wren more than you."

I frown as Brin starts to come back, but her eyes go between me and Ethan before she turns back and starts talking to Tria instead.

"Brin's awesome, but I'm not in love. You and I haven't hung out because I'm choosing sex over beer. Sorry. Priorities," I joke.

I shouldn't tell him that there have been days where I hung out at my beach home alone, just to keep from running across the street to see Brin. If he knew I had days off from her, he'd expect me to hang out with him, and that would lead to him wanting me to chase women with him. And there's only one girl I can focus on.

He rolls his eyes. "You're not choosing sex over beer. You're choosing her. Just admit it. It's no big deal; it just sucks to finally be back and suddenly everything is different."

I don't like what he's saying, but when Raya introduces Brin to one of her cousins—her male cousin—I flinch. This party expanded once guys started showing up. Now it's a houseful of Raya's friends and family, along with some of Kade's friends and family. And I don't like the way this guy is looking at my girl.

"I'm not in love," I say to him, but I'm reminding myself. Love is complicated, messy, and fucked up. Love is a relentless bind that drowns you and holds you down. Love is the last thing a guy like me can endure, because then it all becomes real and the fun is gone. Love is a bitter, cold-hearted bitch, and I don't want it. Not to mention, I can't have it.

"You want another drink?" Ethan asks as he stands.

"Bring the whole bottle," I murmur numbly. I need to drink this conversation away, because I don't want to think. Why'd he have to go and ruin this for me?

Brin

"You're drunk," I giggle, smiling as Rye dances with me, his grin only growing each time he puts a sloppy kiss on my lips.

Normally drunk guys are annoying, but I love drunk Rye. Then again, I love Rye any way I can have him.

"You're not drunk enough," he slurs, picking me up and making me laugh harder as he keeps my feet off the ground.

"I can drive us back," I say, choosing my words carefully. I almost said *home*.

"I'm not that drunk," he says, even as he staggers. "But I'll let you call a cab."

People don't keep secrets when they're drunk.

I hate to do this, but I can finally ask him what I've been dying to know. It may suck, but he'll be honest without worrying about hurting my feelings.

When he puts me down, I tug at his hand. I stifle a grin when his mischievous smile comes up. I keep tugging at him until we're outside, and he cages me in against the railing as his lips come down on mine.

"Rye," I murmur, trying to break the kiss as he works harder to kiss me deeper.

"Don't ruin it," he says, confusing me.

"I just want to talk," I say, pushing against his chest.

"What is there to talk about?" he asks, his lips still battling to get to mine. "I know everything about you. You know everything about me. Let's just have some fun tonight."

My heart flutters, and I finally manage to push him back. "I don't know everything."

He tilts his head curiously. "I've pretty much told you the main points. Even some of the ugly stuff. I don't want to talk about my mom. If that's what this is about."

His mom? What's he talking about? What ugly stuff?

"What about your mom?"

He shakes his head. "That's too much. Too dark. Too ugly. I've told you everything else. Isn't that enough?"

His smile has vanished, and he looks to be hurting. I don't know what's going on, but I also don't want to press him on that. Not yet. But I will. When he's ready.

"You haven't told me the truth."

His brow furrows as he studies me. "I've never lied to you. Not even when it was something embarrassing you asked."

In the next breath, I lose my courage. I promised him I wouldn't do this, and I told myself I'd settle for what I could get. He's already giving me more than I thought he would.

"You're right," I say, and his drunken, sweet grin returns. "Can we go back in?"

"Nope. I want to show you the vineyard," he says, picking me up again.

"I've seen it."

"Not with me. I have a feeling it'll look a lot different."

I laugh even as the heaviness settles over my chest. In a fleeting moment of vulnerability, he spoke about his mother. He's never said anything about her other than the first night we were together. It's worrisome. Especially if he's drunk and still won't talk. Drunk people always talk.

I'm not even drunk and I almost told him I love him.

Chapter 14

Brin

Rye pulls up to my house, and he smiles as he turns and unfastens my helmet. The sun is too bright after so much alcohol. I gave in and got drunk. Fortunately I didn't say anything too terrible, but we ended up crashing in one of the guest rooms and staying enveloped in each other all night.

"I wasn't even planning to drink last night," he says while pulling me to him, and I force a laugh. He was worse than drunk. I'm surprised he's not still drunk ten hours later.

"You staying for a while? I can make us some brunch, and then maybe we can grab some movies."

We're both taking a walk of shame, still wearing our clothes from last night. His fingers thread with mine as he kisses my head, and I lean into him. This is good. I can handle this. I just need to forget the labels. Forget the future. It's all about living in the moment.

"I have some errands to run, and I'm going out with Ethan tonight. I think he's jealous of you," he jokes, but I don't laugh.

Ethan hates me and hates the fact that Rye is with me.

"Cool," I say.

Cool? How outdated is that? But it's all I can think to say.

"Cool?" he asks, amused.

I shrug as we almost reach the door to my house. "The two of you could have gone out yesterday. I told you I had a girls' night."

He frowns, but I don't look him in the eyes.

"It turned into a couples' night," he says.

And I want to scream *we're not a couple!* But I don't. Just like always, I nod. "Well, have fun."

"You're mad," he says, narrowing his eyes at me.

"Not at all. I'm actually going out with Maggie tonight. I forgot that she asked me to do that. We're going to Silk. Carmen is out of town."

"Silk?" he asks, suddenly seeming less thrilled about not seeing me tonight.

"Problem?"

His jaw tenses, but he shrugs. "Nope. None. I'll see you later tonight. I can swing by when we get done."

So cheap. I'm so cheap.

"We'll be out late, but if I'm home, then sure."

Again, his jaw tenses. "What are you doing, Brin? Trying to make me jealous? That's not *cool.*"

"Did I say anything about going out with a guy? That would be the only way to make you jealous. And besides, we're not together so what good would it do to make you jealous?"

He takes a step back and studies me.

"We said it would only be each other. We're not using condoms. That was your rule."

"Rye, I'm going to Silk with Maggie. I'm not going to hook up with a guy."

He blows out a breath while running his hand through his hair, and then he pulls me to him and kisses me hard, imprinting more with that kiss than words ever could. But then, he'd never say the things he makes me feel.

"Fine," he murmurs against my lips. "I'll see you tonight, though. Just call when you get back. You've got work tomorrow."

He grins like he has me, but I shake my head. "Museum is closed for renovations for the next two days. I can party like a rockstar."

I can tell he doesn't like that the second his lips tighten. He feels it. So why won't he just admit it?

"I'm definitely seeing you tonight, then," he says, grinning once more as he leans in and gives me one last kiss.

Then he strides across my yard, leaving his bike parked in my spot. I won't hit that bike, though. I love it. It represents something, even though he won't admit it. I'm the only girl he's ever let ride with him.

Rye

I drop the flowers on the ground, along with the birthday present I always bring her. She loved those stupid coffees from the gas stations. Why? I don't know. But she preferred it over gourmet coffee, so I bring a cup every year.

"Figured I'd find you here," Ethan says as I stand up from the grave.

I smile weakly at him. I hate this day. Always have.

It's a day full of guilt, fury, and what-ifs. But today the guilt outshines all else, mingling with a little sadness that I don't usually feel. For some reason, my anger is absent, and I wish it would return. I don't like being without it. I've grown used to having it to lean on like a crutch.

"We still on for drinks?" I ask, turning back to fix the fresh flowers in front of her tombstone.

Lilies. She loved lilies.

"You know it. I'm surprised Brin isn't with you. She seems like the super supportive type. I didn't expect to find you here alone."

Brin… It's getting too serious. She wanted to say something last night, and then she backed out. I was drunk, but I remember it. And then today she started in with trying to get me to admit something by making me jealous. Silk is always crawling with people who want to find a girl for the night, and she's heard me say that before.

"Brin doesn't know about this. And you need to back off of it. It's not serious, it's not going anywhere, and she and I are just having fun. That's it. You of all people should understand that."

He frowns as he glances at the grave, and I pull the last present out of my pocket. The tombstone was made with a locking frame and bulletproof glass—to keep someone from breaking it. I unlock it and change the picture out, just like I do every year.

This time it's her sitting with me when I was five, reading me the Dr. Seuss story of the week.

"Just for fun?" he asks as I finish locking the case back up.

"Yep."

He sighs out heavily, and he joins me as we walk away. The coffee cup sits proudly beside her grave, and I give my mother one last look before turning away.

"Is this because of your mom? Because it's not healthy to—"

"Don't finish that sentence," I warn.

He frowns, but wisely doesn't say a word as we make it back to the road. "I'll meet you there in ten," I say, climbing inside the car.

As he drives off, I wipe away the stupid fucking tear that falls.

I really hate this day.

Brin

"So he thinks you're at Silk with me?" Maggie asks as I start sifting through the mail.

"Not yet. He thinks we're going to Silk, though."

"Should we really go?"

"Nope," I say, finding an unusual letter that is from John's address, but it's not his handwriting.

Curious as to what shit he's done now, I open it. When I start reading it, I get sick. That stupid son of a bitch! I'm going to kill him.

"What's wrong?" Maggie asks.

"John. The bastard took out a loan against my car title, and now they're threatening to come take it if I don't pay the full amount within two weeks."

Maggie stands and rips the letter out of my hand, and then she curses. "This can't be legal. How did he get your title?"

I groan as I try to think, pulling the letter back from her hands. "I don't know. I assumed it was still in some of my unpacked boxes in storage. My car title wasn't high on the worry-about list. How can he do this to me? I'm still paying off his fucking credit cards."

I could kill him right now. That bastard is determined to ruin my life.

Grabbing my keys, I head for the door.

"What are you going to do?"

I glance across the street, wishing I could use Rye to punch John right in the nose. He'd do so much more damage than I can. But I can't do that. That's not our relationship. And besides, this is a little humiliating. And knowing him, he'd pay the money without my knowledge.

My envelope with five-hundred dollars keeps magically appearing in my room no matter how many times I try to leave it in his house.

"If the police ask me for an alibi—"

"You were with me all night," she says with a grin.

I won't really kill him. Maybe.

Brin

John curses from inside the apartment after I continue to bang on the door for a full five minutes. I can't help but wonder who sent me that final notice, because it sure as hell wasn't him.

How did he convince the pawn shop it was in his name? Because this was originally addressed to him.

The door swings open, and the asshole I once stupidly married is standing there with tight lips.

"Before you freak out, I'm just going to say I'm sorry," he says, his dark hair in disarray and tossed around his head like he just woke up. Apparently he has knowledge that I got that final warning.

I barge into his small apartment, and he lets me through without protest. I don't want his neighbors to witness his murder.

"That's my car, John! You had no right. How did you even do it? The title was in my name."

He frowns and then makes some unintelligible sound, telling me more with a grunt than he could have with words.

"You forged it and made it look like I signed the title over to you, didn't you?" I bark, reading between the lines.

"I had no choice. The money went toward my new internet business. I was going to pay it back. It was just a thousand dollars to go with the other money I had scraped up."

"Then why the hell do they want six-thousand in return?"

He curses as he drops to the worn sofa that sits off to the side. I look around, wondering where his shiny fiancée is.

"Because their interest rates are fucking ridiculous, and all the late fees—"

"I can't get an apartment on my own because of the damn credit cards you got in my name—you've ruined my credit. All I can pay on them is the minimum. Twenty-thousand dollars you owe, and all I can pay is the minimum. That barely covers *their* interest rates. Now you've pawned the title on my car? You stupid, selfish son of a bitch!"

He jumps up from the sofa and glares at me. "I thought I had the right formula. The business was an internet launch, and I just needed a little funding. It crashed, though. I can't help it."

"It always crashes, John! Always! When will you just get it through your head that you're not going to be rich? Just settle for the life you have and find a way to be happy. And quit ruining my life!"

I turn to leave. I don't even know why I came here. I knew it was pointless. He's broke, so he can't pay to keep my car from getting swiped out from under me.

"Settle? Like you do? No thank you. I want to be happy."

"Money won't make you happy. Believe me, I know. I was born richer than most people, and I was pretty fucking miserable. Thanks to you, I still am."

He laughs bitterly, and I turn to glare at him as I reach the door.

"I'm not trying to be rich. I just want to succeed, Brin. And you don't know how to be happy. You settle. That's all you do. You accept life and never fight back or even try to find real happiness. So don't you dare try telling me how to be happy. Because God knows I'm not taking your advice."

I pick up the closest thing, which happens to be a lamp, and I launch it at his head. It barely misses, unfortunately, and he ducks before I can throw the next thing—a shoe.

I wish I had better aim right now.

"You'd better hope I figure out a way to save my car. I swear, I'll make your life as miserable as you've made mine if I can't."

I turn and walk away, battling back the depressing new reality I'm in. It's sad to know I have a rich family that wouldn't loan me six-thousand dollars even if I had the audacity to ask.

It wouldn't matter if they would give it to me, because I won't ask.

I'm going to lose my car.

Brin

"What did he say?" Maggie asks.

If I tell her the truth, she'll beg to loan me the money, but she'll never let me pay her back. I can do this on my own.

"He said he's going to give me the money tomorrow. So don't worry about it."

She gives me a look that swears she doesn't believe me as she puts her purse on. "I'm going to meet Carmen. But we're going to a restaurant outside of town—since she's supposed to be out of town."

I just nod, hating that I included her in on my lie. I just didn't want Rye to know how pathetic I was, and I refused to let him think I'd be sitting at home and pining for him.

As she leaves, a tear tries from to escape from my eyes when they water. Not because of the fact that my life sucks, but because my bastard ex-husband said something I wish didn't ring so true.

I settle. I don't know real happiness.

I settled for him. I settled for our loveless marriage. I settled for living here with Maggie instead of fighting the credit card bills that he put in my name and destroyed my credit with, making it impossible to get my own place. And now I'm settling for what Rye *allows* me to have.

I settle for what he'll give me. I allow him to call the shots and make the rules, because that's the only way to keep him.

I want a real relationship. One where I can call him my boyfriend and spend the night with him without trying to keep my heart guarded. A relationship where I don't stay in knots, worried about it ending at any second because he doesn't want a commitment. A relationship where I can just breathe—the way I felt when we first started dating.

But he'll never give that to me. Even though all of his actions say he's falling for me, he keeps his walls very high. He only trusts me enough to tell me the things he wants me to know.

I'm tired of being everyone's safe-zone. If he wants to be with me, he has to say it. He has to prove it. And this has to go deeper than it is right now. Or he has to tell me goodbye, because I can't walk away from him.

It's not his fault that I fell in love. He told me from the beginning this would never be a real relationship, but he made it impossible not to fall for him when he wouldn't stop. He never stops.

When someone knocks at the door, I half expect to find him standing there, but instead I'm met by the pretty girl I once saw in the museum parking lot.

John's fiancée. What the hell?

"Can I help you?" I ask through gritted teeth.

She gives me a tight smile. "I came by to make sure you received that final notice. John freaked out when I told him I mailed it to you. I was worried he'd try to intercept it."

So it was her. Well, isn't that just icing on the cake.

"Why did you send it?"

She frowns as she looks down to her ring, and I let my gaze fall to it as well.

"Because he's an ass that wouldn't have told you until after it was towed away." Stunned, I keep silent, and she starts playing with her engagement ring before speaking again. "If I give this back to him, he'll pawn it and keep the money. If I give it to you, then you can pawn it and get the money. I think it makes more sense to give it to the woman he has screwed over even more than me."

Wasn't expecting that.

She takes off her ring to hand it to me, and I accept it warily. "It's only worth seven-hundred dollars, but you can put it toward some of the money owed to you. I made him appraise it because I wanted to know it was real. I should have known no one would buy such a small diamond unless it was real. He should come with a warning label: Douchebag Liar."

I laugh and nod, and then I open the door wider. John apparently showed his true colors to her as well.

"Do you want to come in? I'm probably the only other person who completely understands what you're going through right now."

She looks around, and then she shakes her head. "I would, but I'm meeting my father. John is trying to borrow money from him to pay for a new startup business. I'm going to make sure Dad ruins him. He'll never find anyone in this town to fall for his shit again."

Good for her. I wish I could have done that. But if I could rewind time, the first thing I would do is get my frigging car title.

Before she walks away, Rye comes walking up the sidewalk in all his sexy glory, his short-sleeved shirt showing off his sleeved arm and half-sleeved arm of tattoos.

The pretty girl on my front porch grows wide eyes when she sees him, and I bite back a grin.

259

"Hey," he says to me, coming close and pressing a kiss to my lips. I let him, because it might be one of the last times he kisses me.

"Hey," is all I manage to say as he pulls back.

He looks to the girl still gawking at him, and he drops his arm around my shoulders.

"Rye Clanton," he says while sticking out his free hand.

She shakes his hand, though she's almost trembling. "Heidi Mills."

"This is my ex-husband's ex-fiancée," I say to his questioning look.

His eyebrows raise in confusion, and he tilts his head, still wanting more. It's too long of a story to go through. And he'd swoop in like a knight in shining armor.

"She came by to pay back some money he owes me," I say as a vague explanation, pushing the ring into my pocket.

Her mouth finally closes, and she swallows hard while returning her attention back to me.

"It was nice meeting you. I didn't really get to speak to you last time. I wish I had. You might could have talked some sense into me."

I smile weakly, thinking back to that day in the parking lot when the rear of my car was smashed all to hell. It seems like so much longer ago than it actually was.

"It wouldn't have mattered. Some things you have to learn for yourself."

She nods slowly, probably agreeing, and then she turns and walks off, glancing over her shoulder one last time at the man who is leaning in to kiss me again. Is what I want really worth losing him if he says no?

Yes. I want more than he's ever going to give if I don't say anything. *No more settling, Brin.*

"You didn't go to Silk?" he asks, looking over my pink boxers and black tank top.

Sighing, I shut the door, and then I drop to the sofa. "No. Never planned to. I just didn't want you thinking I was sitting ready whenever you felt like coming over and getting some."

He grins, but he shouldn't.

"That's cute," he says while sitting down beside me. "I was about to head over to Silk and find you."

My heart beats a little faster, and I prepare myself.

"Why?"

He bends over and kisses my neck as his hand goes to my waist. "Because I wanted to see you. I saw you at the door, so you made this night much better by already being here."

I push him back, and he tilts his head. "I don't want to be the feel-good girl all the time. I'd like to be someone you want to see for more than sex."

"Brin, I'm pretty sure we do a lot more than have sex, considering the vast knowledge you've accumulated about me over the past month. And don't act like I treat you like shit or something."

I groan in frustration while clutching my head in my hands. "You don't treat me like shit. At all. I just feel like shit because you think this is something completely different than I do, even though I don't understand how."

When I look up, he's already moving away from me, putting some distance between us.

"So you're starting to want something. I told you this was for fun. You said you didn't want anything serious."

I laugh humorlessly while staring at the ceiling. "I lied. Just like I always do when it comes to trying to be with you, because I'm stupid like that." When I bring my head back down, his jaw is tense, but that doesn't stop me from continuing.

"I've wanted more since the day you towed my car to fix it. I wanted more the night you slept on my sofa with me. I've definitely wanted more since the day you carried me over to your house and made me have the best night I've ever had. So yeah. I want more. Every day I want more."

"I told you it had to be simple," he says, running a hand through his hair.

"Simple?" I ask incredulously. "This thing between us hasn't been simple since we met. You're the most complicated, contradictory, annoyingly frustrating person I've ever met in my life. You show up over here because you miss me, you can't stay away unless you make yourself, and you talk to me like we're best friends. That's a relationship, Rye. You just don't want me to fall in love, but I—"

"Don't," he cautions, a hard edge to his voice that I've never heard before.

I've never seen him look so angry.

"I knew better. You swore this wouldn't happen. I told you I didn't want it, and here you are trying to force me into something I don't want. Something you knew I didn't want. I don't want a relationship, and you don't know jack shit about being in a relationship any more than I do. So don't try telling me that's what we have. Because it's not. Never was."

I can't believe him. Who the hell is this jerk?

He starts walking toward the door, but I jump off the sofa to grab his arm. "I don't know anything about a relationship? I was married!"

The icy eyes that glare into mine aren't the warm orbs of brown I love. "Yeah, and your marriage turned out real damn well, didn't it?"

I drop my hand from his arm just as he shrugs me off, and then he walks out of my door, slamming it behind him and destroying me. I just stare at the door like any minute the man I know is going to come in and apologize for the asshole that just left.

But he doesn't. And when the first tear falls, I'm not surprised. I finally fell in love, and now I know for a fact I've never been in love before Rye Clanton, because this hurts. This hurts so damn much.

Right now I hate him more than I hate John Abott because I wish I never fell in love at all.

Chapter 15

Rye

"Thanks for coming over," Dad says as I step in.

"It's too soon for you to be remarried, so I assume you have something of real importance to say."

I can't even look at him right now. I can't look at myself either. Shit. I should have never gotten involved with her.

She's right. I fucked with her head the entire time. It should have been strictly sex, because I complicated the hell out of things. We both did. It was messy from the beginning.

I shouldn't be thinking about this. I *can't* think about this.

"I have a few things to go over with you. Mostly financial stuff. I've just reworked my will, and everything is going to you when I die."

If we're not talking about his loose love life, then it's something morbid like this. But this conversation is moot because people like him never die. Unless the wicked kill themselves, the good are the only ones to die, and they die too young.

I'll live for-fucking-ever.

"I don't want anything. Leave it to *Marilyn*."

He sighs as he pinches the bridge of his nose. "I'll be getting our marriage annulled soon. Marilyn doesn't deserve my life's work. I barely know her."

Another failed marriage. That's not exactly newsworthy.

"Then find someone else who does want it. It's guilt money. And I don't want it. Ever."

When a tear falls from his eye, I'm actually surprised.

"You're going to blame me forever, aren't you? You're going to hate me forever for being a simple human. I didn't know your mother was struggling, son. I didn't know she was capable of doing that with you in the house. I would have gotten her help."

Memories flash around my head, and I shut them down. Just like I always do.

"She was struggling because she was married to a self-absorbed workaholic that didn't give a damn about her because he was too busy being a coldhearted son of a bitch."

His jaw clenches, and he glares at me. "Don't you dare blame me for her illness! It was a fucking chemical imbalance. My actions did not cause her issues."

"No. You're right. Your actions are just the reasons she slit her wrists."

I turn to away from him, ignoring him as he follows and calls my name. I don't have anything else to say to him. He never tried hard enough. Just like I didn't.

I was just ten, and she didn't care that I had to be the one to find her—to slip in her blood, to cry over her cold, still body. She didn't love me enough to live, but she loved him enough to die.

Love is a coldblooded murderer. Love is a blanket of lies and spared truths. It's a calculated monster that drains you of everything you have until you're a husk of the person you once were.

"She didn't kill herself because of me. It wasn't like I was the only man she loved. She killed herself because of the disease that ate away at her mind. I could have gotten her help if I had known."

I pause at the door, both of my hands fisted as the words process. *It wasn't like I was the only man she loved.* "Don't ever say that again."

"You know it's true. You can blame me all you want, but it's not my fault. It's not her fault. It's just something terrible that happened too long ago for it still to be ruling you."

I don't have the energy to fight with him right now. My anger is still as absent as it has been lately, and all that is driving me is the pain I thought I had buried long ago. I just want to get the hell out of here and go home—where it's quiet, peaceful, and smells like the girl I should have pushed away much sooner.

Rye

"So he said your mom cheated on him?" Ethan asks.

Wren sits back in his chair while I dump another one of the boxes on my bed, scattering the contents as I stagger and take another sip of the whiskey.

"Essentially," I say, staggering again while throwing a trophy across the room.

I hate trophies.

They both stare as the pieces fall from the wall, carrying a few chips of sheetrock with it on the way to the floor.

"Did you punch him?" Wren asks cautiously, just as I grab a baseball from another box.

I throw it across the room, and it goes through the sheetrock and disappears into the wall.

I hate baseballs.

"Nope," I say, reaching for the bottle of whiskey and refilling my glass. Ah, fuck it. I'll just drink from the bottle.

"Do you believe him?" Ethan asks unsurely as my hand hovers over a picture frame.

The picture inside is of me at Little League. I take a painful breath, and then I pick the picture frame up and throw it across the room, watching it as it shatters against the wall.

I hate pictures.

"I don't have to believe him."

For the first time since I was a kid, I think about the dark side of my mother. The things I've always felt guilty for remembering. Her memory is supposed to be treasured, not tainted. She's not here to defend herself, and in the end, I was the one who failed her the most. She deserves me to defend her now.

"What does that mean?" Wren asks, his voice quiet, acting as though he's worried the next thing will be aimed at his head.

I don't hate Wren. I don't feel like shattering his skull.

Yet.

"It means he already knows she was cheating," Ethan says, and my jaw clenches.

They both take a deep breath, and I grab a book of baseball cards and throw the entire thing against the wall. It doesn't do any damage. It just drops to the ground with a loud *thud*.

I hate baseball cards.

"Are you okay?" Wren asks just as I throw a basketball.

They both duck when it ricochets off the wall and barrels toward their heads. Ethan catches it when it tries to bounce off the other wall, and he puts it beside him.

I hate basketballs.

"I'm fucking great. Can't you tell?" I mutter dryly, grabbing two golf balls.

I hate golf balls.

Brin

The first sound of something crashing startles me awake, and I sit there and listen, trying to see if I was just dreaming. But the loud banging at the door, proves that something is going on.

My tears are even falling in my sleep, so I'm not surprised that my face is wet. I try to dry my eyes as much as I can on my way to go answer the loud, persistent banging.

I'm shocked when Wren Prize is the one looking at me the second I swing open the door. Maggie comes running out of her room, tying her robe, and Carmen is right behind her, tying a robe as well.

Wren stares for a second, tilting his head as he studies them with far too much interest, and I snap my fingers in front of his face.

"Why are you banging on my door at midnight?" I whisper. Though I don't know why I'm whispering. There's no one else to wake up.

"We need a first-aid kit," he says, sighing regretfully as he looks back to me. "And Rye doesn't have one."

"Why do you need it?" Maggie asks as she goes to the cabinet.

He looks at me and tightens his lips for a second, and then he answers reluctantly. "Rye sliced his hand open when he was beating up his car."

What the hell?

"Why was he beating up his car?" Carmen asks.

"Because it's been a rough day."

I take the small box from Maggie, and I barge by Wren on my way over to the dumbass's house.

"I can handle it, Brin. I'm sure you don't want to see him. Especially like this."

I don't want to see him at all. That's why I've spent all day in my room. Since he walked out of here yesterday, I've wanted to stay as far away from him as possible.

"Especially like what?" I ask, ignoring his hand as he tries to help me off the curb.

I'm not ninety. I can step off a damn curb without help.

"He's drunk off his ass, belligerent as hell, and a little violent right now."

For a fleeting second, I worry it's about me, but for some reason, I know it's not. This is something much, much bigger than me. Especially considering he never really let me in enough to cause this sort of meltdown. *He* walked away, after all.

No. This is behind the barrier—the place Rye won't let me see.

I thought I had learned all there was to know about him, which was foolish. You don't learn a lifetime of things in a couple of months.

269

But I didn't know how little I actually knew about him. Yesterday, I realized I didn't know him at all.

Ethan is standing in the living room when we barge in, and Rye is on the couch, blood pouring from his hand.

"Shit," I growl, dropping to my knees beside the couch and examining his much-too-deep wound. "Grab a towel and keys. He needs stitches."

"We can't take him to the ER like this. I know a nurse," Wren says with a grimace and heavy hesitation. "Maybe I can talk her into coming."

He walks away, and Ethan rushes over to me with a towel. Rye groans and mutters something completely unintelligible, and I start applying pressure, doing all I can to limit the amount of blood he's losing.

"Someone want to tell me what the hell is going on?" I ask, looking up at Ethan since Wren is still missing from the room.

Ethan frowns as Rye reaches over and tries to grab at me. He's so drunk that he only misses and falls back to the couch.

"I'd tell you, but I'd rather not end up looking like his Porsche."

Poor Porsche. That thing just needs to give up.

"Why is he beating up his Porsche?"

"Because he's beating up everything right now. Trophies, baseballs, baseball cards... the list goes on and on. Then he went outside, and the next thing I know, he has a crowbar and he's taking his frustration out on the pretty Porsche. But he sliced his hand on the glass."

I start to speak, but Wren returns, putting his phone away as he frowns.

"She's coming, but she won't be very nice."

"I don't care if she's nice. I care if he stops bleeding," I grumble, but suddenly a hand is in my hair and pulling at me.

"Brin," Rye whispers, and a piece of my heart melts.

I hate him, I remind myself.

He keeps pulling, to the point it's almost painful, and I'm forced to rise up to go with him, keeping a strong grip on the towel and the wound.

"What?" I ask, hoping he'll let me go, but he keeps pulling until I'm forced to fall on the sofa with him, my body resting on top of his.

"Someone want to help me?" I hiss. Rye's lips find my cheek, and I curse as he keeps his uninjured hand tangled in my hair.

"I'm not messing with him while he's like this. I took a shot to the face last year. He won't hurt you," Wren says, taking a step back.

"He'd hurt me if I tried pulling you away," Ethan retorts, stifling a grin when Rye tries to bring up his wounded hand to hold me still.

I stop fighting him just so that he keeps his arm still. Great. This is not how I envisioned our next encounter. I wanted to be inflicting pain—not healing it.

For twenty minutes, Rye cups my ass with his good hand, kissing my neck the whole time, and I fight a battle of misery while keeping his wounded hand elevated and still.

"You're back," he says, trailing his lips down to my chest.

"Shouldn't he be passed out by now?" I groan, feeling tortured and pissed.

"Rye won't pass out for a while. He'll slowly start sobering up. He seems to be finding a rhythm with groping your ass," Ethan says, amused, and I glare at him.

Finally, someone knocks on the door, and relief washes over me.

"Thanks for doing this," Wren says as a pretty girl with soft, strawberry blonde hair walks in.

She looks like she's one of the sparklers almost, but she also looks like me. A mixture of the two—ordinary and extraordinary. If that makes any sense.

Who can make sense after being jarred awake at midnight to deal with the man who broke her heart?

"It's not a big deal. I've done more for worse people," she says coolly, but she smiles when she sees me.

"Girlfriend?" she asks as she drops down and pulls out a kit of her own, her eyes scanning the ever-wandering hand that is brazenly moving all across my ass.

"Ex-friend that he only used for casual sex," I say, smiling tightly as she lets go an accidental laugh.

"You're more than that to him and you know it," Ethan says, frowning at me like I'm the one that ended things.

He's as damn confusing as Rye. Maybe it's the entire male populace that I can't understand.

"No. I'm not." I turn my attention back to her as she starts breaking out her packs of sealed sutures and needles. Or whatever they're called.

But Rye starts moving his hand when she goes to touch him.

"Did you pack anesthesia in there?" Ethan asks her.

Wren hasn't said a word since the cold greeting the strawberry blonde delivered. I have no idea who she is, but they apparently aren't on great terms.

"That would be illegal. It's not really my place to stitch him up either, but I suppose some things can't be helped. Can you keep him still?" she asks, looking up at me. "I can deaden the place around the wound to keep it from hurting so much, but I need him to be still while I do that and stitch him up."

I groan as Rye continues to be combative, and I hold his head with one hand as I look into his eyes. "Can you be still, please? We have to fix your hand."

"Kiss me and I will," he slurs.

He's got to be kidding.

"We're doing this to help you. Just be still."

He moves his hand again, and Wren and Ethan both curse.

"Just kiss him and hold him still," Wren growls.

Both the nurse and I turn to glare at him, and he quickly walks away, cowering as though we just pointed guns on him. She turns back to me while rolling her eyes. "Care to help?" she asks, her words meant for Ethan.

"He'll hit a guy. Especially one that gets too close to her right now. Sorry. Not taking that chance."

She looks at him at the same time I do, and he runs away, too

"Worthless men," she grumbles. I wish I could call Maggie to come help, but he won't let anyone touch him right now but me apparently. My confusing hell only seems to grow hotter.

"You'll be still if I kiss you?" I ask him, and he immediately goes still.

"Yes," he whispers, and that's when I see a tear fall from his eye, breaking my heart in ways I didn't think were possible.

I really wish I knew what was going on, but I don't. And I never will. But he has to get his hand stitched up, and I never got to give him a goodbye kiss.

Looks like this is as close to closure as I'll get.

My lips go to his, and I feel the nurse tug my hand away as she goes to work. Rye's tongue slips into my mouth with familiar, expert ease, and his good hand goes to my hair as he pulls me closer, devouring me in a way that only destroys me more.

I always confused his passion for love. And now I remember why it was so hard to be strong around him.

My hands tangle in the soft strands of his short hair as I say a thousand words with this one kiss. Everything I've felt, everything I've wanted him to know, and every ounce of pain I've had all go into this kiss, and he moans while tugging at my small, thin shorts.

"Just a kiss," I murmur against his lips, ignoring the tang of my salty tears as they start to invade.

He nods and moves his hand back up to my hair, and he kisses me harder, as though he's saying all the same things I am. And it hurts. It hurts so damn bad that it feels as though the pain is manifesting into a physical mass inside my chest, pressing against me with a heavy force, and making it hard to breathe.

All I want to do is run out of here and cry. And I will. The second I leave this room, it's going to be a painful, breath-stealing, heart-achingly, agonizing cry that rivals a wolf's mournful howl at the moon. And then I'm never going to speak to him again.

This is it. This is our goodbye. He's drunk as hell, his hand is bleeding, and he has no idea what he's doing, but right now he's giving me the closure I need, even though it only makes it hurt worse.

"Brin," he murmurs against my lips. "Stay tonight." It's a whispered plea that sends an ache too deep inside me and almost decimates my resolve, because he's so sincere right now. But in the morning, everything would be terrible—worse than it already is.

My tears don't wait until I'm out of the room to start dripping harder; they burn down my cheeks with a feverishly rapid succession. I move my lips back to his, hoping it's enough to keep him quiet. I love him and hate him with every breath we exchange, but I hate myself the most.

I did this to myself. I was fine before him, but I'm ruined now.

"I love you," I whisper just as the nurse finishes up.

"I know," he groans, turning his head away. "But you can't. Love is temporary, and it's a bitter bitch when it leaves. I can't be responsible for your happiness like he was hers. Like I was. I can't handle more guilt, and I'll fuck up again."

I have no idea what his drunken words mean, but I stand up as he tries to move. I don't bother learning the nurse's name, or thanking her for all her help. I can't. I can't say another word. Rye is okay now, and I have to go before I fall apart in front of everyone.

I sprint across the yard as he calls my name, yelling for me. And I hear the first punch someone takes. I hope it's Ethan. I look back in time to see it is Ethan, and I almost smile, but that smile fades with all the weight of my misery.

He's drunk. He'll break my heart in the morning because he's drunk enough to love me tonight. But when he's sober...

I keep running down the street with no idea where I'm going, but Maggie pulls up beside me in her car, and I hop in the back seat.

"Saw the drama. Feel like pancakes?"

I just laugh and sniffle at the same time, and she drives away. She and Carmen are still in robes, and I'm not even wearing a bra.

"Don't worry," Carmen says, smiling softly. "It'll get better."

I doubt it. But I don't bother arguing. There's nothing left to say.

Chapter 16

Rye

"Why the fuck do I have stitches?" I growl, glaring at my throbbing, swollen, and bruised hand. The crisscrossed stitches seem to be professionally done, but I'm still wondering if Dr. Frankenstein broke into my house last night and played mad scientist on my hand.

Everything is too fuzzy, and all the memories are hidden under a thick veil of fog.

"Because you're a clumsy bastard," Ethan groans, raising up from the sofa that's in my room.

His black eye gives me pause. "Why is your eye black?"

He laughs as he stands up, stretching as he shakes his head.

"Because you're a clumsy bastard with a mean right hook."

I slowly get out of bed, cursing my aching right hand when the internal throbbing grows to be more vicious. And damn, it itches. But the itch feels like it's under three layers of very tender flesh.

"You don't remember anything?" he asks as I follow him out, ignoring all the damage in my room.

"Nothing after the boxes I shouldn't have ever opened," I say while blinking and trying to stop seeing things in a fog.

"Figures. Your Porsche is going to need more work. You beat the hell out of it last night."

Ah, hell. My poor car.

"And my hand?"

"You cut it on the window after you broke it. Wren's child's mom came by to fix your hand. Yeah. That shocked the hell out of me. No one thought to tell me he had a kid?"

He turns to glare at me, and I shrug.

"Not my secret to tell." He rolls his eyes while leading the way to the kitchen, and I drop to a stool as he starts making coffee.

"Why'd I punch you?" I ask, still trying to put all the blurry images together.

"Because I stopped you from chasing Brin out of the house."

He turns to face me as all the color drains from my face. "Why the hell was Brin over here? And why was I chasing her?"

He breaks down all the details, and I get sicker with everything he says. She kissed me to keep me still. She came because I was hurt. And she left here in tears because I'm the world's biggest asshole.

I made her cry. Her ex-husband never made her cry, but *I* did.

"You shouldn't have involved her," I snap.

"We didn't. She came because she cared. She kissed you because you refused to be still any other way, and she stayed on top of you because you wouldn't let her go. Pretty sure any other girl would have prayed you bled to death."

She should have let me bleed and stayed away.

"I need to go apologize to her."

He props up as I try to stand straight, but things are still a little warped, and it feels like I'm suffering the after effects of a bad carnival ride.

"For what? For breaking her heart or for being a drunken ass?"

278

I don't even want to think about the shit I said to her the other day. It was too harsh, too stupid, and too damn cruel. She didn't deserve anything that came out of my mouth.

"The list is too long to detail. I'll be back," I mumble, stumbling toward the door.

"Tell her I said thanks. We couldn't have handled you without her help last night."

That just turns the knife in my heart a little more. I can't believe she came over here after what I did.

Not bothering to put on a shirt or even shower, I head across the street. I'm barefoot and still wearing my blood-splattered jeans from last night, but she's waited long enough for an apology. Before I even reach the door, Maggie is swinging it open, and she looks pissed—nuclear warning pissed.

"What?" she barks.

She's definitely not on my side anymore. I don't blame her. I'm not on my side either.

"I just want to apologize for... well, everything. Can I please come in and talk to her?"

She blocks the doorway with her small body when I try to come in, so I take a step back.

"She's not here. She had to go to work."

I glance over my shoulder, wondering if my mind is playing tricks on me. Her Camry is still parked.

"Her car is here," I say, turning back around just as the door slams in my face.

That went worse than I thought, and I didn't even get to talk to Brin. I knock, and then curse when I use my injured hand. The throbbing intensifies, punishing me for forgetting about it. Swapping to my left hand, I knock again.

"Go away, Rye. She's not here. She took a cab because she didn't have any gas in her car and she was running late," Maggie says through the door.

No gas in her car? I can at least take care of that.

Shit. When did my life get so messed up?

Brin

"Is he gone?" I whisper from my doorway, wiping away the streaks of fallen tears.

Maggie stares out the window for a moment, and then she sighs. "Finally. Yeah. He's walking across the street." She turns to me with the most apologetic eyes I've ever seen.

"Are you okay?" She cringes and quickly adds, "Don't answer that. It was a stupid question. Of course you're not okay."

I sigh while coming to drop down to the sofa.

"At least the museum had to stay closed for a few extra days. The renovations hit a snag, and the building can't be reopened until next week now."

She hands me a fresh box of tissues, and I smile up at her very gratefully. "Thank God I have you," I murmur, and she smiles as she comes to sit down beside me and wraps me up in the hug I need.

"You've been with me through some of the worst breakups ever. I can be here for you the one time you actually need a shoulder to cry on."

She looks toward the window, and then her eyebrows scrunch. "Is he pouring gas into your car?" she asks, and I look out to see the same thing.

Shit. I have a full tank.

He figures that out when the gas starts pouring out of the jug and onto the ground instead of going into the car, and his eyes move to the house again. Through the thin curtains, we can see him, but I don't think he can see us.

He puts the jug down, and starts walking this way, and I run to my room like the coward I am. "Don't open the door this time," I whisper, and Maggie walks over to the window just as the banging on the door starts.

"What now?" she asks, playing dumb.

"Her tank is full. Let me talk to her. I know she's in there. I just saw her running out of the living room."

Crap. So much for him not seeing through the useless curtains. We need blinds.

"She doesn't want to see you."

"I have a key," he warns, and my stomach knots up.

Maggie flips the newly-installed chain lock into position, and I breathe out in relief.

"Go home. She doesn't want to talk to you. I think you've said enough. Don't you?"

I sink to the floor, still trying to catch my breath, when suddenly there's a loud beating on my window. I jump and scream when I see Rye's brown eyes staring expectantly.

Definitely buying blinds for every damn room in the house.

"Please go away," I groan, standing as I wipe my eyes.

"I just want to apologize."

"Fine. You've done so. Now go away," I say, keeping my face out of view.

"You're crying. Let me in so I can talk to you. Please."

Why is he doing this?

"Do you hear yourself?" Maggie barks, coming into my room on her way to my window. "This is what is breaking her. You and your damn contradictory, befuddling ways. Just go the hell home and leave her alone. You're just confusing her more with everything you do. Fuck! I don't even understand you, so I can't imagine how she feels."

I look over just as he backs away from the window, looking so pitifully defeated. It almost feels like a hand reaches in and painfully squeezes my heart, because I hate seeing his eyes so sad.

"You're right. I'm sorry," he says softly, looking away from me.

"So you said. Now go," she snaps.

This time he listens, and he walks away with his head down. I exhale a long breath before climbing up and getting into bed and pulling the covers over my head.

"I'm staying under the covers no matter what you say this time," I grumble, but one corner folds down, and suddenly Maggie is under the covers with me.

Her eyes hold unshed tears for my pain, and I remember why I've loved her like a sister for all these years.

"I'll stay under the covers with you," she whispers, and her tears sneak out as a violent sob breaks free from me.

Rye

"I don't understand you," Wren growls as he picks up his phone.

"What's not to understand?" I ask while taking another sip of whiskey.

"It's fucking two in the afternoon and you're already wasted. You had it. You had *it*. You had what Tag, Kode, Kade, and Dane have found, but you'd rather sit around and sulk instead of just loving the girl. Just because you don't say it, doesn't mean you don't feel it. What you found with her… Trust me, Rye, it's not something everyone gets to have, and you're an idiot for ignoring it."

He sounds like a bitch. I hate bitches.

Instead of punching him like I want to, I curse him and roll over on the couch.

"I guess that means you're not going to the garage today."

"Nope," I say in a clipped tone that tells him to shut up.

He groans and then walks over to open the door. I wait for it to shut, praying he leaves me with my silence while I search for the anger I need to get past all this. I'm sick of this feeling, and I need the one constant that has been there for most of my life so that I can get back to who I was before *her*.

"Hey, Brin," Wren calls loudly, and my body is off the couch and racing toward the door before I even realize it.

Brin and Maggie are getting into Maggie's BMW, and I start running across the street. Maggie cranks the car just as I reach them, but I'm on the passenger side and banging on the window with no plan.

Brin won't look at me, but I can tell she's still crying. She never cried over the husband she had for six years, but she's crying over me. Again. Has she even stopped?

"Please talk to me, Brin. I'm begging you. Just let me apologize."

She takes a slow, steadying breath, and then she turns her tear-streaked face toward me, crushing my heart by allowing me to see the pain she's in. I did that. I caused that pain.

Her window rolls down, and Maggie curses as Brin's red-rimmed eyes lift to meet mine. "You need to deal with whatever issues you have. Obviously, I wasn't the person to help you through it. I hope you find that person. You deserve an Ash, or a Rain, or a Tria—someone who makes you stronger. Someone who makes you better."

She's trying to cut my heart out right now. I wasn't expecting her to say that. Gravity pulls me toward her, and I start to lean into her window, needing to touch her.

"Stop," she whimpers, and I do.

She takes another breath, and then her glistening eyes find mine again. "I don't know what's going on. I wish I did. But you deserve better than you're allowing yourself to have. And I deserve better than you'll ever give me. I'm tired of settling for what I can get. I just want to be happy."

Maggie steps on the gas as I stand there stupefied. Settling for what she can get?

She wanted me. And I only gave her a piece. But she doesn't understand. Fuck! Why did she have to move in right across the street?

Wren is standing at my front door, looking just as confused as everyone else these days. I walk by him on my way inside, ignoring his scrutiny.

"Why is it that you don't want to be with her, yet you can't leave her alone?"

I swallow hard as I think back to everything Brin said to me. I am confusing and contradictory. I want her, but I don't want all of her. I want her to have me, but not all of me. I'd tell her to keep it simple, and then I'd complicate the hell out of everything with my actions.

"Because I love her and I don't want to. I can't. You know I can't," I finally say in a whisper. It feels like I'm taking my first breath ever as that admission travels free. I drop to the couch, stretching my legs out while staring at the ceiling. "When I'm with her, I forget. I forget it all. And it feels so damn good to just have her with me. It feels too good. And then I freak out, and I worry what I'll do to her. It's so much responsibility to have. I've already failed once."

I can't stop it. I don't want to fucking cry like a girl, but I can't help it. Wren drops to a chair in front of me, and nods slowly.

"Your mom suffered from a mental disease. What she did to you and herself was not her fault. It wasn't your dad's fault. And it sure as hell wasn't your fault. Stop searching for something or someone to blame. And stop letting it destroy your life. There are five stages of grief. I'm pretty sure it's time to move to stage five."

His hand on my shoulder is less than comforting, but he tries. Then he walks out, and leaves me with my drunken tears and dark reality.

I want to be angry. It's better than being miserable. I need that anger, and there's only one person that can give me what I need.

I grab my keys, stagger outside, and get into my sad, tragic looking Porsche.

Rye

"Are you drunk?" Marilyn asks as I barge by her, but I ignore her as she practically purrs behind me.

"Dad!" I yell up the stairs, seeking an attempt at retribution.

He comes down the stairs promptly, and his eyes catch mine. He frowns while looking over my shoulder.

"Give us a minute," he says to Marilyn.

The clicks of her heels promise me the bitch is leaving, but I never take my eyes off the man I hate the most in life.

"You're here to blame me some more, I see," he says, nodding. "Whatever you need to do or say, go ahead. But be prepared to hear the hard truth in return."

My teeth grind as I move toward him, but the anger… Where the fuck is the anger?

When misery is all that clings to me and anger denies me a reprieve, I break. Years of repressed memories clutter my mind, and I fucking fall apart.

"Eight days. You were gone for eight days one time."

His eyes water, and he takes a step backwards as my own tears fall. I can tell he wasn't expecting that, and I sure as hell wasn't expecting to bring it up. But there it is. I need him to make me angry, and he will. He always does.

"How could you not know she needed help after that?" I ask, my voice crackling.

He slowly lowers himself to the stairs, and the tears start dropping. "I thought... I didn't know she did that to you until... It was already over by the time I learned everything. You know that. I had no idea, and you never told me. I never would have let her do that."

The darkness of this house still consumes me and suffocates me every time I'm here. Being trapped, screaming for help, and feeling terrified and hungry for days at a time is something you never forget. You can bury it, but it claws its way to the surface and gnaws on you from the inside.

"She loved you. That's all she'd ever say. She'd lock me in there and then say she was sorry, but she needed time. I was too much to deal with because she needed time to herself."

When he starts sobbing, I back away. Where is my motherfucking anger? It's still leaving me alone with the pain, and I don't understand. I can't breathe. It feels like my chest is trying to cave in on itself.

I roar like a fucking animal, gripping my hair as I stumble around.

"I don't blame you for blaming me, son. I blame myself most of the time," he says through his choked tone. "But I swear to you that I didn't know she was sick. I would have gotten her help, and I would have never left you alone with her."

My back slides against the wall as I sink to the floor across from the staircase.

"I prayed for her to die," I almost whisper, and his head snaps up. The silence is almost deafening before I continue. "The last time… I prayed for her to die. Thirty-two days later, my prayers were answered."

Until now, I've never spoken those words aloud. My father stands, preparing himself to come toward me. But I hold my hand up, silently pleading for him to stop. I need to get out of here. This isn't why I came here. I don't want to talk about it; I want to forget it. I want to hide it, lock it away, and I want to be pissed.

Before I stand, Ethan walks in, and I roll my eyes.

"Did you follow me?" I grumble, staggering back to my feet.

He narrows his eyes. "Little bit. You're kind of a loose cannon right now."

Great. He's worried I'm going crazy. Maybe I am. I don't even know when he started following me.

I feel lost without the rage that has driven me for so long. It's almost like having a piece of me ripped out, and now there's nothing occupying the place where it once was—nothing besides misery. A void rests inside me, and I have no fucking clue what to do about it.

"I'm leaving," I murmur—or slur would be more accurate—but Ethan stays behind.

I hear him talking to Dad, but I ignore them as I stumble back out to my car. I'm too drunk to be driving, so I wait on Ethan to come out.

He motions toward his black BMW, and I climb in on the passenger side.

I thought I'd feel better; I thought he'd make me angry and give me back what's missing so I can cope. But it is still missing, and I only feel worse. Death is easier when you have someone or something to blame—something tangible you can yell at or hate. It's hard to hate a sickness you can't see, one you can't even definitively name. It's a lot easier to hate yourself.

Rye

"Feel better?" Ethan asks as he hands me some Tylenol.

I take the pills gratefully, and stare up at my ceiling. Five days. I'm through being drunk.

"I feel… tired. Miserable would be more accurate. Has her car moved today?"

"It has moved the past two days. By the way, I feel like a creep when I'm constantly staring out the window."

I laugh lightly while sitting up. Oddly, I do feel a little better. Maybe five days of hangovers are enough.

"Thanks. I just wanted to make sure she's not staying at home and—"

"And acting like you?" he asks, arching a brow at me.

I frown as I look around my trashed house. It probably smells like death in here. *I* probably smell like death.

"You still don't want to try to win her back?" he asks.

I'd give anything to have her back, but she's right. I'm nothing but a pile of confusing contradictions. And she was also right about deserving better.

But as I stand and let my eyes go through the window, the Camry returns, and the girl I wish I could let go steps out. All she wanted was to be *it* for me. No one has ever cared about me like this.

She's all I think about. Wren met his daughter for the first time, and I couldn't even force myself to ask him questions, because I knew my mind would only be on one thing—Brin. She's still consuming me.

She drops her purse, and I can't help but smile as she curses to herself. At least, I assume those beautiful, soft, tempting lips are cursing.

"I honestly… I want her back. But I'll never be the guy she wants me to be."

He sighs as he walks toward the door. "Well, you'd better be sure. Ash is trying to set her up with someone. Just thought I'd give you a heads up."

A flash of red consumes me, and he grins like he just said the magic words.

"Don't worry. She's still saying *no* for now," he adds, mocking an attempt to placate my murderous glare. Then he smiles as he adds, "Not sure how long it'll last though."

I can't help but be pissed, but it's not the form of anger I want. I need the old anger, not new rage. I'm not ready for her to move on, even though I know I should let her.

As she stands and walks toward her door, my heart breaks just a little more. She never even glanced this way.

Brin

Work sucks. Again. But at least I don't have to worry about seeing Rye at the window here. Yesterday he and Ethan watched as I dropped my purse in my attempt to hurry. It's easy to see him out of the corner of my eye now, due to several days of practice. It's also pathetic that I'm as good at it as I am.

"Brin?" Harvey Dexter says—my boss and the director of the museum that does nothing.

I look over as he and a man in a suit that screams money walk toward me. Who is this?

He's older, but he's also tall and handsome for his age. His hair is barely dusted by time, and his shaven face is a clean, crisp, version of something familiar. Too familiar. Rye familiar.

Great. Now everyone makes me think of Rye.

Damn it.

"Yes, sir?" I ask, turning my full attention on them and putting my back to the newest exhibit that is slowly wrapping up.

"I can take it from here, Harvey." The unknown man dismisses the sweating Harvey as though he works for him. Weird.

As Harvey walks off, he throws a questioning look over his shoulder. But I don't have the answer he's searching for.

"How can I help you, sir?" I ask, wondering why Harvey didn't even bother introducing us.

The man smiles as he looks at me, almost seeming proud for some reason. And this is only getting weirder.

"He's a bit of a worm, isn't he?" the man asks, looking back just as Harvey turns the corner.

I bite back a grin, but I don't respond. How can I?

"Um… I'm Brin Waters," I say instead, sticking my hand out for introductions.

He grins slowly as he takes my hand and shakes it. "So you are. You're exactly how I pictured you."

Completely, totally, utterly, awkwardly weird.

"Excuse me?" I ask as he walks toward the Egyptian exhibit with curious eyes.

"I'm the largest silent contributor for this museum. They need my money, so that's why Harvey was so rattled."

Is he trying to intimidate me? Because it's working. I just got nervous as hell. I really can't afford to lose my job right now.

"Is there something I can do for you?"

I don't know why I bother to keep asking questions, because he's apparently only saying what he wants to when he wants to.

"Yes. There is," he says, surprising me when he finally answers a question I've asked.

He faces me and smiles warmly, still seeming a little too happy to see me for my comfort level.

"My name is Rygan Clanton."

Pretty sure I just got sick. I know I'm pale, and judging by the look he's giving me, I think it appears like I'm close to passing out… Because I am.

"You love the hell out of my boy," he says with a grin that touches

292

his brown eyes—Rye's eyes.

How does he know that?

"Why are you here?" I ask in an embarrassing, rasp whisper.

He motions toward a bench at the far corner, and I follow him, happy to sit before my legs give out. He waits for me to sit down first, and then he joins me as he stares straight ahead.

"My son is going to come after you. He won't leave you alone. When he wants something, he usually gets it. But you can't take him back."

Weirdest. Morning. Ever.

"He's not trying to get me back. He's only trying to smooth things over between us so that we can be... um... friends again."

I'm so not laying out the sordid details of my screwed up relationship with Rye to his father.

He smiles weakly. "Ethan called me this morning. Rye is breaking down. It'll start soon. But until he's ready to tell you everything—to completely open himself up—this thing between the two of you won't work. So if you love him, you'll make him break. Otherwise, you'll stay in this loop—he'll hurt you, you'll cry, he'll return, and you'll take him back. It's a vicious cycle. I've been in a loop of my own for years. You're the only hope that boy has, and I want you to do what no one else can."

What the damn hell is going on?

"What is that?"

He looks at me with tears in his eyes, and says, "Make him forgive himself and move on."

He stands suddenly, and he leans down and kisses my head while I sit in a silent stupor.

"He loves you already," he says on a sigh. But I know this. Rye just won't admit it. He doesn't want to love me, and that hurts worse than him actually not loving me. "But he won't be strong enough to embrace it until he's strong enough to forgive."

Damn Miyagi bullshit. What does that even mean?

"You're wrong. He doesn't want to love me, and he's never going to try. It's not me. I'm not his *one* person. I tried to be. I wanted to be. But I'm not." He wouldn't be able to fight me if I was.

He swallows the knot in his throat as a tear rolls down his cheek, and my heart clenches at the sight. He doesn't have to worry about me taking Rye back too soon, because I wouldn't take him back even if he begged me. I'm ruined as it is. I'd be a shadow of myself if I went through this hell more than once.

"If his formative years had gone better, he would probably already be proposing to you, and none of this would be going on. Trust me. He loves you just as much as you love him. He came to see me on his own, and he talked. He didn't just yell; he opened up and shared something that must have been killing him for years. That's the first time he's ever done that. He wants to move on. Until you, he's never wanted to move forward. For the first time, he sees the future instead of just the past."

I sit back as he leaves, but I don't say anything. I'm so damn confused. What is it with the men in their family?

Brin

As always, I avoid looking at Rye's house, not even looking at it through my peripheral, but I don't have to look over there. He's on my front porch, standing as I walk up my sidewalk very slowly.

This day sucks.

"Hey," he says softly, tucking his hands into his pockets as I near him.

"Hi." The simple, short, clipped response is a warning to just go back across the street.

"Can we talk?" he asks as he comes closer, ignoring my warning tone.

I choke back a sob and shake my head as the tears try to fall.

He exhales a slow breath while coming to stand directly in front of me, and he takes both sides of my face into his warm hands as he tilts my head up to meet his eyes. Those browns aren't icy anymore. This is the Rye I love. It's also the one who I don't want to be in this loop with, because I won't survive it.

He tried getting rid of me that night on the beach. He tried warning me over and over. But I fought and lied and clawed my way into his life. Now I have to fight just as hard to step out.

"What's there to talk about?" I ask, trying to look away, but he holds my face still in his hands.

"You and me—we're both miserable. I miss you, Brin. So much."

His father knows him pretty damn well. But I made my resolve long before Rygan Clanton offered me his advice. He just cemented my decision.

"I miss you, too. But until you're ready to tell me what's fucked you all up, then what's the point?"

I'm proud of the strength of my voice, and I'm really proud of the fact my heart stays in my chest when his eyes sadden. But it hurts to see him refusing me before the words even come out.

"None of that matters. I just want to be with you. Can't that be enough?"

I want to scream *yes* and roar *no*. My own mind is becoming as contradictory and confusing as he is.

"I wish. Do you love me? Will you ever allow yourself to love me? Will you take off for days at a time when you feel yourself getting too close?" I ask, and his hands drop to his sides.

"Go out with me tonight," he says, intentionally ignoring my questions. Like father, like son. "Just the two of us."

"No," I say, pushing by him on my way to the house.

"Why not?" he growls, following me to the door.

That should be rhetorical, but I answer anyway. "Because you can't tell me this is going anywhere."

"Does it have to be all or nothing?" he asks, trying not to sound angry, but it's there in the undertones.

I pause, slowly digesting his words.

"It doesn't have to be all or nothing. It just has to be *something*, Rye. Something more than *simple*."

His frustrated groan reverberates through my chest, piercing my heart. "Why?"

I turn to face him, barely managing to hold myself back from pulling him to me. "Because I love you. And I won't settle for something less than I want—or deserve—again."

The pain on his face only breaks my heart. Seeing him this upset about my confession only sets another fire to my already flaming pit of misery. I turn away and push through the door. And he lets me go without a fight. Again.

His father is wrong. Rye Clanton is never going to want to be with me. He may love me, but it's under extreme protest. I don't want to fight for a man who's not willing to fight for me. All Rye does is *fight me.*

For once, I want someone else to work for a relationship. Because I'm sick of carrying the weight.

Rye

"What are you doing?" Wren asks as I grab the roses from the countertop.

"I'm going to go get my girl back," I say as I head out the door, and I feel his smile behind me.

She won't fight me forever. She doesn't understand what she's asking to know, or she wouldn't be asking. I can pretend she didn't tell me that she loves me. And she can pretend that this is still simple.

We can do this.

I knock on the door, and Maggie swings it open immediately. She hates me now. And she's a little intimidating with that whole hands-on-the-hips stance while scowling thing.

"Can't you leave her alone?" she asks, groaning as she tilts her head back to look at the ceiling.

"Can I just give her the roses?" I aim for the most charming tone I have, but Maggie is a rather strong fortress.

"No," she says, slamming the door in my face. I hate guard dogs.

Instead of attempting to reclaim my dignity or risk knocking again, I go and stand by her car. Eventually, she'll have to come out.

Luckily for me, I don't have to wait long. I'm fairly sure my heartbeat is in my chest when she walks out in a sundress, wearing small heels, and letting her hair fall down to almost reach her shoulders.

I just want to touch her.

"Hey," I say, grinning as she walks down the sidewalk, and her eyes pop up in surprise to meet mine. Then her gaze drops to the roses for a fleeting second before coming back up.

She wants to say yes.

"How's your hand?" she asks in a near whisper.

"It hurts a little, but there's no nerve damage. Should get the stitches out soon."

She nods, not looking at me. I continue speaking while pushing the roses out toward her. "These are for you."

She doesn't look up, but she draws a heavy breath. "I have to go," she says, stepping around me.

"Go where?" I ask, moving faster and blocking her path to her car door.

"I have a date," she says, still refusing to meet my eyes.

Bile rises to my throat as I numbly move to the side, and I watch as she disappears into her car. This is not how this day was supposed to go.

She pulls out of her spot, and I continue standing and staring. But I can't take it.

My bike is in my yard, and I drop the roses and rush over to it. In seconds, I'm on the road and following behind her at a safe distance.

When she cuts into a restaurant parking lot, I sit at the curb like a fucking stalker. Christ, she's destroying my mind. And I think she's doing it on purpose.

Once she's inside, I wait. But the waiting is driving me crazy. So after about twenty minutes of torture, I go in. It's not very crowded, so scanning the tables is easy work. I spot her and the infamous *date* in a matter of seconds, but she's not at a table with a young guy. This guy is too fucking old for her. What the hell?

I stalk through the restaurant, ignoring the hostess calling for me to wait, and I move in behind Brin just as the prick from across the table finishes his sentence.

"…You made your bed. Lie in it." Then he looks up at me as I come to put my hands on either side of the table, caging Brin in with my arms.

"Little old for you, don't you think?" I ask her, putting my lips close to her ear, but she doesn't even act surprised. She mutters a few choice words as she turns around to look up at me, forcing me to lean back and tower over her.

"Rye, meet my father," she hisses, and I might trip backwards— and possibly stumble over two or three chairs.

She stands just as the waitress brings the food, and she rolls her eyes while turning back to her father.

"You're not going to stay and eat?" he asks her dispassionately.

"Lost my appetite," she grumbles, and then she starts retreating toward the door.

Her father?

He glares at me and the tattoos on my arms before he rolls his eyes. "Never going to learn," he mutters under his breath.

I don't bother saying a word to him. I thought Brin hated her parents. So why is she lying to me about a date and meeting her father?

By the time I reach the outside, she's already driving away, but she's not crying. She's just pissed.

I really know how to fuck up like a pro.

Brin

"This is worth at least seven-hundred dollars," I argue, groaning as the man behind the glass case shakes his head.

"I realize that, but this is a pawn shop. I can't give you what it's *worth*, because I have to sell it. It's business. I've told you; three-hundred is my highest offer. I have to turn a profit. People don't come in here to pay full price. I'll be lucky to get six-hundred for it."

Damn. "And you won't let me pay this now and pay more next month? For my car?"

He frowns while shaking his head. "You've got a sad story with no proof. I hear sad stories all day. I can't cut you any breaks. I'd be broke if I took pity on everyone that had the same bad luck as you claim to have."

This day sucks. My life sucks. This pawn shop sucks. My father sucks. Rye sucks. Rye's father sucks. Everything and everyone frigging sucks.

I can't believe I went to my dad for help. But I thought he might give me my old jewelry to sell or pawn. Nope. I'm still not allowed to have anything that used to be mine because I refuse to go back to college and choose a career that satisfies him, even if I prefer working at the museum.

Well, fine. Fuck them all.

I can't believe Rye showed up. Well, I can believe it, but I wish he hadn't. I shouldn't have lied and told him I was going on a date. I knew better.

I leave the pawn shop without any success. My options are dried up. My car is going to be taken away tomorrow, and there's not a damn thing I can do about it. I've lost this war, too. I'm the worst soldier ever.

Brin

Everything passes by me slower than usual, because I take my time driving home. How can one person have their life so thoroughly screwed up in a matter of a few years?

When I get home, there are several vases of roses, and all of them have balloons attached that say *I'm sorry*. I just want him to hold me. More than anything, I want to be in his arms, because he makes the worst day better. I miss being able to breathe.

But until he's ready to admit this thing can go deeper, we'll be stuck in limbo. And I'll only ever know the parts of him that he wants to show. That night he broke me, I realized there's so much more to him than he'll ever share with me. He'll keep me at arm's length, and I'll never have him. Not really.

He's in pain, but he lives in denial. Just like he denies his feelings for me. I just wish he'd stop fighting the truth. But I know he never will, even though I'm still foolishly holding out hope.

"These have been coming all day," Maggie says, motioning to the roses as she steps out onto the porch. "I've started making them leave 'em all out here."

She looks over my shoulder at Rye's house, but I don't. I know he's waiting for me to do just that.

"I need liquor. Lots and lots of liquor."

Rye

Brin's car has been gone for two straight days. Where the hell is she?

I'd go to the museum, but I'm afraid she'll cause a scene and lose her job. And then she'd really hate me.

"What are you doing?" Wren asks as I walk back into my house.

"Just got back from delivering a few goodies," I say with a careless shrug.

"Pranks? You think that's a good idea under the circumstances?"

"Roses haven't worked, jewelry would be insulting to her, and… I'm going crazy without her, Wren. I just want her back. This is how I

302

got her the first time."

He sighs as he looks out the window with me. "Then maybe it's time to face how you really fucking feel about her. I won't pretend to understand what all you went through, but maybe Brin was dropped off across the street from you for a reason. Ash healed Tag. Dane healed Rain—and the other way around… Maybe Brin is what is going to heal you."

"Gee, Dr. Phil, any more great wisdom to share?" I ask with a sarcastic lilt, and he rolls his eyes.

"Just trying to fucking help."

Wren becomes a forgotten fixture when a cab pulls up, and Brin steps out after paying the guy. What the fucking hell is going on?

I'm running across the street before I know it, and she's turning to face me just as she unlocks the door to her house.

"You need to shave," she says, surprising me for long enough to get the door almost shut before I can speak.

"Brin, where's your car?" I ask, shouldering through the door before she can lock it on me.

She curses under her breath and glares at the door like it just betrayed her. I give the two of them a moment, but she finally turns back to me as I stare expectantly.

"It's getting some work done."

All the worst possible scenarios rattle around in my head as the gut-clenching feeling invades.

"Did you wreck? Are you okay? Have you been in the hospital or something?"

She sighs as she drops her purse to the floor, and then she comes over to me. I glance down at her work attire, and a little relief settles in my bones. She wouldn't be at work if she was hurt.

When she grabs the back of my neck, I almost bash my mouth into hers for the kiss I've been starving for.

My hands are on her, my body pushes against her, and I can't get enough of her taste when she gives me what I've been desperately missing. She jumps up and wraps her legs around me, and I groan into her mouth while pushing her up against the wall. This is so damn right.

Her tongue toys with mine, and I start trying to figure out the best way to get my pants down. But before I can, she pulls back, drops to the ground, and pushes me away when I try to resume the perfect kiss. My mouth opens in disbelief when she goes to open the door.

"Go. I'm fine. Just a bad few days."

I stand my ground and give her an incredulous look. "What the hell? You just kissed me."

"Confused?" she asks, crossing her arms under her perky breasts that jut out from the motion, but it only distracts me for a second.

"Pretty fucking confused, yeah," I growl.

"Good. Welcome to my hell. We're even. Now go."

I try to say something, but I have no idea what to say. She just kissed me, put her legs around me, and now she's kicking me out just when things were getting good. Is this really how she feels right now? Because I think my head is going to explode.

Chapter 17

Rye

Maggie steps out of her car and walks toward me with a frown.

"Why was it so urgent we meet?" she asks, standing beside my bike as I knock down the stand. Slowly, I stand up, crossing my arms over my chest as we move to the sidewalk and out of the city street.

"Because something has obviously happened to Brin's car and I want to know what. No one else can fix her car better than my garage. So tell me where it is."

She rolls her eyes as she fidgets uncomfortably.

"Do you even go to your garage anymore?"

"I'm there enough. Where's her car? I'll have it towed to my place. I don't want some hack mechanic touching the vehicle she drives. I don't understand how it tore up to begin with. We replaced—"

"It didn't tear up," she mutters, inhaling regretfully. "Pawn shop took it. Her ex pawned her title for a grand, but the interest added up when he didn't pay for it, and Brin couldn't pay the six grand in time. She refused to take my money or tell me which pawn shop. I even went to several trying to find the right one."

"How the hell could he have pawned it without taking it in for them to appraise the value?"

It's sure as hell worth more than a grand now that I've added all that shit to it.

"She was missing her spare keys when she moved out. More than likely he had them. All he'd have to do is borrow it from the museum parking lot for long enough to get the appraisal done, and he knows her work hours."

What a fucking asshole.

I climb back onto my bike, and strap up my helmet as Maggie calls the jerk a string of unsavory names.

"Where does her ex live?" I ask, already turning on my bike as she gives me the address. It's not too far from here.

"Don't kill him," she says loudly, trying to reach my ears over the roar of the engine.

I pretend as though I don't hear her, because I'm not making any promises.

Rye

As soon as the door opens, my fist is connecting with the prick's face and he's falling backwards, yelping in surprise as blood spurts from his nose.

He's not really what I expected. Brin needs a real man, and this weasel is curled up and crying. How did she live with him that long?

"Which pawn shop?" I growl, glaring at him.

"What the fuck are you talking about?" he gasps, trying to crawl away from me when I near him.

"Where'd you pawn Brin's title?"

I raise my fist up, but he throws both hands up while turning his face away. "Shit! She knows which one it is. It's the one on Belker Street. Fuck!"

"What else do you owe? Is she paying off any more of your fucking debts?" I snap.

"Just my credit cards. They're in her name though. Her name, her problem."

I'd love to throttle this weasel all day long. But Brin needs her car. He's fucking lucky she needs her car.

I step back as he warily stands, and I make my way toward the door. But it just seems too easy.

"Ah, fuck it," I mutter before turning around and punching him one more time. As he falls to the ground, tears pouring from his eyes, I smirk. "Fuck with her ever again, and I'll make sure it hurts a lot worse next time."

With that, I turn around and head toward Belker Street.

Chapter 18

Brin

"Sick!" Maggie screams, spewing her coffee everywhere. "When the hell did he do that?"

I shouldn't be grinning because Rye exchanged the sugar with salt.

"I don't know, but there's baby oil in the soap dispensers. And I found a rubber snake in my panty drawer. Also, there's a present in the living room that I'm scared to unwrap. He left it at the front door."

I stare at the pretty disguise the present is wearing. Maggie tilts her head with me, and we both gaze curiously at the innocuous looking gift.

He's not letting me go. He's fighting. Maybe this is close enough? I'm sick of waiting on him to really let me in, but am I strong enough to let him keep me just close enough?

Maggie curses her cup of coffee as she drops to the couch. "Would it be too cliché to go borrow some sugar from one of the neighbors?"

I laugh lightly, but my eyes don't move from the present. There's no telling what masterminded prank lies beneath the red wrapping paper.

"What do you think it is?" she asks, both of us eyeing it very cautiously.

"A wicked jack in the box. A food bomb of some sort. Or maybe a dead rodent," I say with a shrug.

"Why are you grinning?" she asks, smiling just like me.

I lean back and look through the large window at the house across the street.

"Because he still hasn't given up. Now he's trying to get me to come to him. He hasn't bothered me since the other day."

His bike rolls up in his yard, and a myriad of feelings wash through my stomach. But I frown when I see it's Ethan stepping off. Why is Ethan driving Rye's motorcycle?

Then I see my Camry pulling up to my side of the curb, and I'm almost positive my heart leaps into my throat. He didn't. He couldn't have.

"I guess he beat it out of John," Maggie says with a grin I can feel.

I turn to her, and sure enough, her smile is broadly pasted onto her face. "John? He went to see John?" I ask, feeling sicker by the second.

John is dead. Rye is going to need an alibi.

"He asked what happened to your car. I told him. He found the pawn shop somehow—meaning he had to have gotten it out of John. And here he comes."

Shit. I'm crying. Again. I hate crying, but this confusing bastard does so many crazy things to my heart.

I open the door before he reaches the top of the porch, and I'm in his arms before he can even tell me what he's done. He smiles as he hugs me and kisses me on the head, but then he puts distance between us as he backs up.

"You're not mad," he says in relief, his whole body visibly

relaxing.

How can I get mad?

"You didn't have to do this," I whisper, scared of speaking in any other tone.

He stares at me for a moment, and his eyes change. They look different than I've ever seen them before. Then he clears his throat and nods toward the car.

"If you have any more problems, let me know. Don't ever deal with your ex directly again."

That's... worrisome. John really might be dead.

"What did you do?" I ask while following him, trying to keep up with his long strides.

I only get a glimpse of his smirk before it vanishes.

"Handled it."

I glance down to his knuckles, but they show no proof of problems.

"He'll sue you if you hurt him. He's a money-hungry son of a bitch."

He laughs as he slows down and tosses his arm around my shoulders. My heart does that freaky fluttering thing as he guides me toward my car.

"If some psycho charges into your home and punches you, then you might call the cops. But not if you've forged your ex-wife's name on a title transfer. Not to mention, someone once told me that the tattoos make me look like a bad boy," he says while winking.

Heart is still fluttering.

"How did you know—"

"Pawn shop guy told me everything. He's a regular at my garage." He pauses as we near my car. "I took it by the garage and had Wrench check it out. Looks like everything is still working good, but if it acts up, call me. I'll come get it and take it back."

If it wouldn't be completely crazy, I'd kiss him right now. If he didn't love me, he wouldn't do this.

But he doesn't try to do anything or even hint at anything. I miss him. I miss him so damn much.

Rye

Staring up at my dad's house for the third time this week is a little disconcerting, but I think I'm finally ready to see him.

Dad opens the door and steps out, surprising me. He never comes outside very often. He rarely goes anywhere at all anymore. Not since Mom died. He even dates online before marrying his gold diggers.

"You want to talk to me?" he asks, coming closer. He stops when he reaches the gazebo outside, and he takes a seat on the swing. "Or are you just going to keep coming by and staring up at the old house?"

With a burdened breath, I go to join him. For a long time, we both just sit here, staring into space. I finally break the silence.

"Did you go to see Brin?"

"Yes," he says without hesitation. "And you did good. That girl loves you. You know it's the good love when you can see it in their eyes. All I had to do was introduce myself and the girl nearly fainted."

I wish that didn't make me smile. I love and hate the fact that she loves me.

"Did she tell you?" he asks, looking off into the distance.

"No. Ethan mentioned it. Apparently he saw you leaving the museum. He was going to talk to her that day, though he wouldn't tell me why."

He also didn't stay after he saw my father leaving. That's bugging me.

Dad just grins for a moment before covering it with a serious face. "Probably for the same reason I went." Before I can ask questions, he adds, "She's why you're here." And it's not a question.

"Part of the reason," I murmur, sitting back just as he does.

The swing rocks us back and forth, and several more long moments of silence pass between us.

"I punish myself, too," he says, leaning his head back. I don't have to ask him what he means, but he elaborates anyway. "I marry women who hate me, because I'm scared of having a woman who loves me. But it's so empty when I look at them, that I have it annulled right away. Usually. Or I never marry them and just let them live here until I can't stand it anymore. But the house is always so empty without anyone here."

More silence. There's nothing I want to say about that, because we'll end up arguing.

"You love her, don't you?" he asks earnestly.

I love her so much that I'm miserable without her. But it doesn't change anything, does it?

Since I'm not ready to share that, I keep it to myself and stare at my motorcycle. All I can think about is Brin on the back of it, squeezing her thighs against me while she laughs excitedly.

"I'm worried about what will happen when I fuck up. Most people haven't seen love the way I have. I guess that goes for you, too."

He nods slowly, his eyes trained on an imaginary spot on the ground. "It tends to fuck someone up." I almost smile when he says that. Almost.

It feels weird to sit here and have a conversation, but for the first time since I was ten, I don't feel angry. Not at him. Not at anything. I'm just... well, I have every emotion except for anger right now. It's different... Refreshing now that the loss of my anger is not so scary.

"I've already fucked with her head. I didn't even mean to. I kept saying everything I needed to at some points, but sometimes I'd say things that I didn't mean to. I kept giving her hope with those few slip-ups, and I kept contradicting myself with my actions. With her, all the lines were blurred and I trampled all over my own rules. And then I stomped all over her heart in the process. I'm just as confused as she is, and it's all my fault. She was never anything but perfect to me."

His lip quivers, but he steadies it quickly. "That's the really good stuff. When you can't force yourself to detach from someone, you've got something rare. You become consumed in the most maddening way, but it's the best damn feeling there is out there."

I look at him, feeling hope slip away. "So you had that with Mom but lost it?"

He frowns as he looks down. "I had it with her, but she didn't have it with me. She loved me, but she didn't love me like that. Even before she got sick, she never loved me like I loved her. But I took what I could get because I knew what I felt for her was rare. It's even rarer if you find someone who feels that way about you. It's a beautiful thing that slips through your fingers if you aren't paying attention. And believe me when I say it's hard to ever find again."

I lean over and prop my elbows on my knees as I try to absorb his words. This is the first time I've ever been able to speak about my mother without feeling knots packed with anger. But my body is relaxed and that odd new peace is still coursing through me.

"Brin felt the same way. I don't know if she still does, but she felt it. And she had to hold it back because she was worried about pushing me away. She kept giving, and I did nothing in return. I filled her full of angst and constant confusion. As shitty as it feels for me, maybe I did her a favor."

He frowns as he looks over at me, but then he turns his face back straight. "If she felt that way about you, then I doubt you're doing her any favors by pushing her away. Because I can assure you a feeling like that doesn't disappear very quickly. She still feels that way about you. Probably always will. If you give it up, you'll chase that feeling for the rest of your life, but it's really unlikely that you'll ever find it again."

Drama. I've tried to avoid it for so long, but right now, it's in my every path, no matter which direction I go.

"I don't think I'm ready for that."

He laughs and shakes his head. "No one ever is. And you get there with someone; you don't get there by yourself. If you're waiting until you're ready, you'll die waiting."

I actually let that sink in, fully digesting that thought.

"What should I do?" I ask quietly when it all seems overwhelming.

His lip quivers again, and he's forced to wipe a tear away from his cheek while clearing his throat. This is the first time I've ever asked for his advice.

"I think you know what to do, and I pray you make the right decision. I've always held out hope for you. You're on the right path to recovery. Finally. I just hope you don't wait too long. Life's too short. Misery is eternal if you allow it to be."

Life is too short. It's a cliché line that almost everyone uses. I've heard it all my life, yet it's never struck a nerve until this moment.

Misery. Not anger. No anger at all. Just misery. Painful, heart-wrenching, soul-stealing misery.

"When's the last time you saw the girl?" he asks, turning his head to look at me.

"Four days ago," I mutter shamefully.

I had a chance to try and get her back, and I know she would have caved after I brought her car home. But I didn't want to use that against her. After meeting her sorry excuse for an ex, I don't blame her for expecting more. She deserves it. I've always known that she deserves more, but I never thought I'd be able to give it to her.

But the smile she gave me when I showed up with her car... I wish I could see her smile like that every day. I doubt she knows about the fact her credit card debt is paid off. And I don't want her to know. Yet.

She might kick my ass over that one.

"You're smiling," Dad says, and I turn to see the tears in his eyes as his own smile forms.

My grin only grows as I think about Brin's temper, her feisty attitude, and her smile that is only reserved me. No one else sees that smile. They only get the generic smile that she gives everyone. She has a special one for me.

The misery ebbs with every good thought. She's the misery. It's all her. Not this. Not my dad. Not my mom. Not my guilt. It's Brin that's making me feel this shitty. She stole the place of my anger and replaced it with her own miserable trap. Ah, hell.

"I need to go. I've got something that needs to be done," I tell him, and he nods knowingly as I stand.

The first thing I need to do is make a phone call, but as I look at my phone, fucking Hillary Barns's name is flashing across my screen. Shit. I forgot I'm supposed to be having lunch with her to discuss Tag's party since Ash hates the woman.

I'll make my call after I make up some bullshit reason for being late.

Brin

I pick up my phone the second I see Ash's name. If she's calling to set me up on a date, I'm going to hang myself.

"Do not mention a date," I grumble by way of answering, and she huffs.

"I'm calling about Tag's party Saturday. You're still coming, aren't you?"

This does not fit in with my plan to avoid Rye. Since he brought my car home, he seems to be avoiding me. If he's avoiding me, then I need to avoid him.

I think.

Maybe.

Ah, hell. I don't know what's going on anymore. Up means down, stop means go, front means back… Everything is so confusing around him. Now not even my own head makes sense anymore.

He's stolen my sanity. Yep. It's gone.

"No. Not this time. Sorry, Ash. I'll try to make the next party."

I can actually hear her pouting from the other side of the phone as I cross the street to go to the drycleaners.

"I have a date for you. It's not going to be awkward. I can promise Rye will be on his best behavior if you're worried about seeing him."

"No," I groan. Relentless matchmaker. Terrible, terrible matchmaker.

When I finally reach the other side of the street, my eyes lift up, and my heart sinks to my toes, cementing me to my spot on the sidewalk. Rye is about fifty feet away, and he's not alone.

On the patio of a restaurant, he's smiling and eating with a woman. And she's leaning over, touching his arm, and biting on her lip very suggestively.

Sick. I'm so, so, sick.

I knew it would happen eventually, but I really didn't expect it to happen just now. This soon. Four days ago he went and punched my ex on his way to get my car. Now he's here. With her. A woman more suited for him than I ever was.

"Brin? You still there?" Ash prompts as I stare mindlessly at Rye.

He moves his arm from her grasp only to grab a bite of the dessert in front of him. He stands and moves toward a waiter, and I just watch. I watch as he talks to the guy and grabs the check. I watch as he hands him cash. And I watch as he returns to say something to the woman who stands.

I don't watch him touch her, because I turn away from the sight and move toward my car again, abandoning my mission to collect my dry-cleaning.

"Brin?" Ash prompts again.

"Go ahead and set me up," I murmur softly, holding back the onslaught of tears that are beating against the backs of my eyes.

"O...kay. Um... Great. I'll see you in two days."

I don't say anything as I make it back to my car, and I hang up the phone. Once I drop to the seat, I put my head on the steering wheel, and I listen to the roar of a familiar engine. I look up just in time to meet his eyes, and he brings the bike to an abrupt halt.

Once upon a time I was a plain girl in an unimpressive car that no one ever noticed. But this man sees me even when I try to hide.

He pulls into the spot behind me, and I contemplate gassing my car and speeding down the street. But there are too many crosswalks, so a speedy getaway wouldn't work out.

He pulls his helmet off and walks around to my window that I reluctantly roll down. He drops down to where he can see in, and I force a smile.

"Hey," he says softly. "You just get into town?"

"I need to go the drycleaners," I tell him, keeping my lips sealed about the leggy brunette I just saw him with.

"I'll walk you," he says while opening my door.

Shit.

"I can walk myself," I grumble, but he ignores me.

Just as we go to cross the street, his date comes riding by in her Mercedes, slowing down as she approaches. I really want back in my car.

"See you at Tag's party," she says with a smile.

He nods and puts his hand on the small of my back as she drives off, and he guides me across the street. I don't speak. Nothing would come out very friendly right now.

"That's Hillary Barns," he says, even though I didn't ask.

I don't want to know anything about her.

"She's pretty," I mumble, trying and failing to not sound bitter.

"Pretty what?" he asks, rousing my curiosity and prompting me to look up just as he looks down. "Pretty annoying? Pretty vain? Pretty odious?"

I want to laugh, but I'm too confused.

"She seems like your type." The words are out of my mouth before I realize it, and I start to apologize, but he shrugs and speaks before I can.

"Not my type at all. I had to meet with her to finalize the plans for Tag's party. I've had to meet with her three times now, and every time she tries to touch... things." He shudders and I almost laugh. "It's exhausting to constantly find polite ways to escape her grasp. I'll be glad when this damn party is over. You coming?"

Shit. Shit. Shit.

She wasn't his date? Double shit. I told Ash I'd go on a date.

"Yeah. Ash was going to set me up with someone, but—"

"That's good. Probably George Carpenter. Nice guy."

He pauses in front of the drycleaners as I choke on my heart that has flown from my feet to my mouth and back down to the pit of my stomach. He wants me to go out on a date with someone else. And he's not the least bit jealous.

"Oh," I say, unable to keep the disappointment out of my tone.

He looks around and shoves his hands in his pockets. "I have to go, but I'll see you at Tag's party."

That's two days away. And he wants me to go with a date. This day sucks.

Brin

"I could show up for moral support," Maggie says as I walk toward the back gate of Tag's enormous home.

It's a pool party tonight. They have a heated pool that battles the cold—which is good, since there has been a chill at night. I chose the sexiest bikini I could find, to hell with it all.

"I may call you if things get bad. Or if I get drunk," I grumble, and she chuckles lightly.

I hang up before putting my phone away, and I take a deep, calming breath while heading into the party. Brazenly, I only wore my bikini and a tiny, see-through sarong. Oh, and of course my flip-flops.

When I walk through the gate, I cringe noticeably. Dresses? Every single girl here is wearing a damn dress—and there are a lot of girls. Really?

I almost want to stomp my foot right now. I know she said *pool* party. And she meant it literally—I asked.

"Damn," Ethan drawls as he walks over to me, tilting his head as his eyes rake over my very, very exposed body. "This is going to be interesting," he adds, looking around as though he's searching for someone.

I could die.

He's wearing his swimming trunks and no shirt, revealing the fact that he has almost as many tattoos as Rye. It seems that only the guys are dressed to swim. All the girls are dressed to kill.

Ash comes up behind him, and her eyes widen in surprise when she sees me. "Wow. Love that bikini," she says, eyeing the small red shards of my top that give an eyeful.

Her eyes trail down to the see-through red sarong that stops mid-thigh, and comes up to my waist on the other side. The black bikini bottoms have red strings that tie the sides together, making it a little skimpier. But with everyone else all dressed up, I don't look sexy; I look trashy.

"You said pool party," I hiss, and she bites back a grin.

"It is a pool party. I don't know the rules on swimming while pregnant. Rain doesn't know how to swim. And the other girls don't want to get their hair wet since it's a little chilly. Sorry," she says, sounding sincere.

"You need to start sending out a dress code for your parties," I growl.

Ethan laughs while walking away, and I huff all the way to the bar, putting my purse on top. I can't help but scan the place for Rye, but I don't see him.

"Where's my illusive date?" I ask mildly when Ash walks up and takes a virgin daiquiri from the bartender.

"He's here somewhere. He was just out here." Her eyes scan the party, but she smiles over my shoulder just as two familiar arms wrap around my waist. "Ah. There he is."

My heart does a few flips as I turn around in the large, toned arms to see Rye smiling down at me. He looks over my bikini, and I try to ignore the sexy tattoos all over his bare skin. His low trunks hang on his hips, exposing that ripple of muscles that form that sexy V.

"You're my date?" I ask hopefully, looking back up to meet his golden brown eyes.

His smile melts all the barriers around my heart as he winks at me. "You didn't really think I'd let you come to be with someone else, did you?"

Relief pumps through my veins, and I slide my hand up his chest as he grips my bare sides and fully appraises my attire.

"Fucking perfect," he says with a grin that only grows. "I knew you'd show up dressed properly, and I've been looking forward to the big reveal."

I grin bashfully while leaning into him, and he bends to kiss my forehead. "So you schemed to get a date?" I ask softly, trying not to melt.

His hair gets ruffled by the fingertips of the wind, and he bends low to press a sweet kiss to my lips.

"I did. And I have something to show you when we leave here. But for now, let's just enjoy a date."

I really don't want to read too much into his words, but for tonight, there's nothing I'd rather do than be his date. To hell with the consequences. I'm ready to take what I can get when I can get it at this point, because I miss him too damn much.

His arm drops to be around my shoulders, and I can't wipe away my grin. He worked hard for this date, and it makes it feel as though maybe there really is hope for us. I almost feel like I can breathe again, and for the first time since we ended things, I don't feel like crying. Which is such a relief.

"Let's swim," he says, even though no one else is in the water.

"I'll look like an even bigger idiot than I already do. No other girl is swimming."

He smiles as he brings me closer to the pool, and his arm goes around my waist. "You're the only girl who doesn't look like an idiot. You came dressed for a pool party."

I really love him.

"I still don't know if—"

Before I can finish that sentence, I'm being hurled into the pool by his strong hands, and a squeal falls through my lips before I suck in chlorine-tainted water.

Rye

I'm laughing when she surfaces, and her beautiful, mean little scowl turns into that smile that's only meant for me—the smile that changed everything.

I dive in, and swim under the water to her barely covered body. She came to torture me, and I know it. Even though she thought she was meeting someone else, I know this bikini was intended for me. And every intention I originally had for this evening seems to want to be delayed.

I don't want to waste tonight with the heavy shit. I want to enjoy this—her smile, her eyes that are glued to mine, and her legs that are wrapping around me.

"So is this a first date?" she asks.

She wants to know what's going on, but she's still not pushing me. Underneath her smile is uncertainty. She deserves to push me all she wants.

"I think this is more like our eighteenth date or something," I say teasingly, and she looks down with her shy grin that I rarely see. I like that smile, too.

Her arms stay around my neck as she keeps her body flush against mine. It feels perfect and right—so damn right.

My lips brush hers just barely, but she refuses to let that be all she gets. And I can't help but smile when she takes control and kisses me hard, pushing her sweet tongue into my mouth and giving me exactly what I've dreamt about for so long.

I kiss her back, but when her sexy little sounds kick in, I have to stop. I'm going to damn burst in the pool if I don't.

I break off the kiss to push my forehead to hers, and she loosely hangs on to me as I walk her around the pool. We can both feel the eyes on us, but I don't care. Right now, it's just the two of us because nothing and no one else exists.

"Where did you want to go after this?" she asks when I start walking out of the pool.

She shivers against the wind, and I walk over to the table where I have two oversized beach towels. But I carry her all the way over there, not really giving a damn if anyone thinks it's ridiculous.

When I sit down, she's still in my lap, and I wrap a towel around her body before hugging her to me. To create some heat through friction, I rub her back with my hands, sliding them against the towel.

"We can go now if you want to. I know you pretty much just got here, but—"

"Let's go," she says while grinning.

Her hair is wet, her face is glowing, and her sweet body is all mine for the taking. I wish I could just take her home right now.

"Let's go," I echo, trying not to sound as nervous as I am.

Ash glares at us when she overhears, considering the party is just starting, and a lot of planning went into the Luau portion of it. But then she shrugs instead of commenting. I suppose she understands.

After we bid everyone an early goodnight, Brin grabs her purse and we head to my Range Rover. She shivers a little, and I open the door for her to climb in.

As soon as I reach the driver's seat, I'm pulling a shirt over my head. It's dark, so this is probably going to creep her out, but it needs to be done.

"Where are we going?" she asks excitedly.

I have a feeling that excitement will be gone soon. Very soon.

"You'll never guess," I say while reaching over and taking her hand as I pull out of the driveway and head down the street.

When she squeezes my hand, I take an easy breath. There's that peace. She's the reason it's there.

Brin

When we pull up to the dark, creepy cemetery, I look at him like he's crazy. This is not a good prank.

But the tension radiating from his body makes me realize this isn't a joke. What's going on?

"Rye?" I prompt, reaching back over for his hand. "What's this?"

He looks over at me, and his lips thin. Finally, he takes a breath and pulls me toward him. I climb over the center piece dividing us, and my towel-wrapped body comes to rest sideways in his lap.

I take both sides of his face in my hands, and press a soft kiss to his lips, trying to do whatever I can to rid him of the nervousness he has. It has me worried.

"This," he says against my lips, "is me giving you the answers you've wanted. If you don't want to go in there right now, I understand. We can wait."

I already get creeped out at night, but I'm not about to refuse him.

This is apparently some big revelation, and I'm not going to risk him losing his nerve.

I was hoping we'd be going to a candlelit house with rose petals everywhere. And then I thought he might say he wanted to be in a relationship. I didn't have unrealistic expectations of him admitting he loves me. However, I was willing to accept whatever he was going to offer, because he's worth it.

But a cemetery? I didn't expect this at all.

"Do you have a flashlight?" I ask hopefully.

"I have two of them."

He reaches into the back seat and pulls out the first one to hand to me. Then he grabs a jacket and hands it to me. It wasn't all that cold until I got wet. Now the night wind isn't nice.

I take the jacket happily, and he grabs another flashlight. When he opens his door, he helps me down first, and I wait for him to get out before I glue myself to his side.

Every time there's a sound, I fight hard not to squeal. This is by far the creepiest thing I've ever done, and I have no idea why we're here.

"I didn't think this through," he says nervously, looking down to the towel still attached to my waist and his jacket that is trying to swallow me whole. "We can do this tomorrow."

This isn't exactly cemetery-after-dark attire, but I have a feeling this has something to do with his mother. There's no other reason we would be here. He's never said that she was dead, but I assumed she was either dead or out of the picture. Tria finally explained that she died a long time ago, but she didn't elaborate because I shut her down. Given our destination, I could have easily assumed it's the former of the two even without knowing.

Tria offered to tell me everything she knew about him, but I refused. I was hurting at the time, and there wasn't anything that I wanted to know from anyone else. I just wanted Rye to tell me. Now... Maybe I should have let her tell me what she knew.

I have a feeling he'll never do whatever he wants to if we leave now. So, putting aside my fear of dark cemeteries, I take his hand and point the beam of my flashlight toward the gate.

"I'm ready when you are," I say, not looking at him.

He starts walking, keeping my hand in his, but then he stops abruptly and turns before he crushes his lips to mine, soaking me in as though he's seeking courage. I think.

I don't know what he needs, but I try to give him whatever it is.

"Come on," he murmurs against my lips, his body still tense as he rethreads our fingers together and leads the way.

Dark, scary, and quiet enough to make every unseen rustle of motion sound ominous—it's like a scene from every horror movie ever made. But I trek on, following close to him as he navigates the way.

He only gets tenser the deeper we go, and I keep waiting on a wolf to howl at the moon right about now. Fortunately, no such thing happens—mostly because wolves aren't native to this area.

When he stops, I stop, too, and he pulls me beside him as he shines his light on a tombstone.

Marie Jenna Clanton

Loving Mother and Wife…

He's brought me to his mother's grave. But… why?

"I don't know why I felt like I had to explain this here, but for some reason… it just seemed easier to do it this way." He kneels and moves aside the dried flowers that rest on her grave. For some odd reason, there's a coffee cup next to the tombstone.

"They've apparently not cleaned up yet," he mutters to himself, but I don't question him.

"This is my mother," he finally says after a suffocating amount of silence.

What am I supposed to say? I don't want to ask what happened. She died several years ago, according to the date on the tombstone and Tria, so condolences would seem contrived. I don't know what to do. Nothing seems sufficient, so I just stand quietly and wait.

"It's no secret that she died. But there are only a few people in Sterling Shore that know *all* the details, and not just parts of them. Six to be exact. My old therapist, my father's therapist, my father, Wren, Ethan, and me. Now you'll be the seventh."

He snorts derisively before adding, "Usually the number seven is considered lucky. Sorry I'm about to ruin that for you. And honestly, you're the only one who is going to know the entire story besides me—all that I can manage to divulge."

He goes quiet again, as though this is actually painful for him to do. I start to tell him we can do this some other time, but he breaks the silence again before I can.

"She died when I was almost eleven. She was sick—very sick. Since no one knew she was sick until after she died, she was never diagnosed properly. Theories have spawned over the years, but it's nothing more than conjecture based on her symptoms. You'd be surprised at how many mental illnesses carry different aspects of her symptoms. Everything from severe depression to bipolar disorder to schizophrenia have been mentioned. But no one can say definitively what she suffered from."

Now I really don't know what to say. None of this is making sense, even though I appreciate him opening up to me.

"I'm sorry," I say lamely, leaning over to kiss his arm.

"I was the one who found her," he says suddenly, ignoring my pathetic attempt to comfort him as his body almost trembles. "She went to the bathroom, climbed into the tub, and she used a knife from the kitchen to open her veins."

Oh dear God. My heart, head, and stomach all constrict and roil in unison. He found his mother dead when he was a kid?

"Rye, I—"

"I remember falling," he says, interrupting me again, saying the words in a rush like he's trying to get it out while he can. So I hold back anything I want to say to comfort him as he continues.

"I slipped on her blood, and I hit my head on the edge of the tub. It knocked me out, and when I woke up, I was covered in her blood that had kept flowing out on top of me. I was scared, and we were home alone. She always sent them away. Always. Every time he was gone, she'd send the staff away. So I was alone and didn't know what to do. I just remember her being so cold and pale. Her skin was like ice. And no one heard my screams for help because we were alone."

I'm really trying to be strong so that he doesn't feel the need to comfort me when I should be comforting him, so I hold back the sob that rests on the tip of my tongue. But my tears burn my cheeks as they roll out, refusing to stay dormant.

"How long were you left with her?" I ask in a hoarse whisper that betrays my attempt to sound strong.

"Seven hours after I found her. My dad came home that night, and I was huddled in the corner of the bathroom where she was. I remember rocking with my knees tucked under my shirt and my head tucked down. But everything is such a blur. Everything was so red, including me.

"I don't remember him coming in, but I remember him holding me. I remember him yelling something to someone I couldn't see. And I remember all the sirens and police who came, but no faces or actions are in those memories. It's all a big... it's fuzzy. And honestly, I don't want to remember it any more clearly than what I do."

I want to ask so many questions, but I don't. He takes a breath, pausing to keep himself in control and doing what he can not to break.

"She killed herself because of the disease," he says, reciting it as though he's trying to convince himself. "She would be so happy some days. On those days, I was happy. I bring her a picture every year for those memories. But the bad days... She didn't do it often, only when he'd be gone for longer than five days at a time. He'd leave or one of her boyfriends would break things off, and she'd hit that lowest point that did the worst things to her mind. I became a problem—one she couldn't deal with on those days. Or maybe she was just sane enough to worry about what she might do if she didn't hide me. So she'd lock me in the closet until dad called to tell her he was coming home.

"She always apologized, and she'd cry and rock me in her arms. But for two or three days at a time, I'd be hungry, scared, thirsty… The worst was the last time she did it to me. Eight days. I was dirty and had to use the corner of the closet as a makeshift bathroom. She slid some water and food through the door. If she hadn't been lucid enough to do that, I would have probably died. Then she made me clean up my mess in there when she finally let me out. I hated her. I hated her so much."

He chokes back a sob and turns away from me, but he keeps holding my hand. I never imagined this, and my heart is breaking. I want to say the right thing right now, but I have no idea what that is.

After a moment of recomposing himself, he clears his throat and continues.

"She'd say she loved me, and I fucking hated to be loved if that's what it meant. My father would tell me he loved me, and I fucking hated him for his love if he was willing to leave me alone with her. And she'd cry and tell me that she loved him, that she missed him. That was usually what her bad days were like. She didn't always lock me up. Those were just the worst times.

"Usually she'd stay in her bed for days at a time. The covers would stay over her head. She never hit me, or yelled at me, or even threatened me. It was always a calm process when she hid me away. It was only wild and out of control when she'd hurt herself. She hurt herself a lot more than she ever hurt me. And she always lied about how it happened.

"I kept her secrets. She'd always beg me to keep her secrets, and I did. But I honestly thought everyone else saw it. She'd scream and yell at my father. Once she even went after him with a knife. He called her crazy, but he didn't realize she was actually mentally ill and needed help. With a case as severe as hers… She needed a lot of help. And medicine. And supervision."

I can't help it when my sob escapes. I try to stop it, but it just comes out again. All I can see is a terrified child version of Rye huddled in a corner with no one coming to rescue him. His hand tightens on mine, and I quieten down quickly, trying not to make him feel that urge to console me. I want to be here for him right now; I just wish I knew how.

"How did you deal with that?" I ask quietly when the silence begins to weigh too heavily in the air. "Why didn't your dad do something?"

"He didn't know how bad things were, and I didn't deal with it. Not in a healthy way. I didn't speak for six months after she died. He took me to the best psychologist he could find. He gave up traveling and started working from home, and he hired nannies that almost forced food down my throat when I wouldn't eat. For six months I was numb. On the seventh month… I grew angry. And I stayed angry.

"When I finally broke and told the shrink what all had happened to me, my dad turned pale for three straight days. I didn't cry when I relived the memories. I didn't break when I told them the horror stories they didn't know existed. I was just angry."

He looks down to our joined hands for a moment, and then his eyes stroll back across the grave.

"That closet is no longer in his house. He tried to make up for it, but he blamed himself as much as I blamed him." He says it so quietly that I almost think that part wasn't meant to be heard.

"I started getting into fights—all the time. Twice I was sent to detention centers for more than two months at a time. By the time I was sixteen, I was out of control. Alcohol was my best friend, and I toyed with drugs. I just wanted to escape the anger that had consumed me. And nothing was working.

"Dad almost sent me to military school just because he didn't know what else to do. But Ethan's parents convinced my dad to let me stay with them for a while, and things changed. I was still angry, but I wasn't in that house. I wasn't trapped with those memories staring me in the face. And I didn't have to see my father every day. It made a difference."

I wish I could just hold him right now. I want to be somewhere safe and warm and holding him.

"I eventually learned to live with the anger and even channel it. I actually have better control of my temper than anyone I know because of how long I've dealt with all that rage. It's damn near impossible to set me off. Or it was."

I'm not sure what he means by that, and I don't want to interrupt him to ask.

"It's always kept me detached," he says softly, squeezing my hand again. "From everyone. Everything. I keep everyone just close enough to push them away. But you…"

He pulls me to him, wrapping his arms around my waist and resting his chin on my head, forcing our fronts to push together. I don't waste any time in reciprocating the embrace.

"For a really long time, I've blamed everyone. I blamed my father—hated him for it. I blamed the doctors who came to the house and cared for her after she'd hurt herself, because they never saw it. I blamed her for not going to get help. Hell, I even blamed the school system for not looking into my many unexplained absences. But mostly… I blamed myself. I guess I still do."

I lean back so I can see into his eyes, but I can't see. The flashlights aren't giving enough light up here.

"Why do you blame yourself?"

He doesn't move or make a sound for too long, and I curse myself for pushing him for answers.

"Because," he says on a painful breath, "I could have told someone what she was doing to me, and they would have seen that she needed help. They could have stopped it after the first time she locked me up. They could have saved her life. She would have gotten the medicine she needed, and we might have had the chance to be happy. But instead of getting her help, I prayed for her to die. And she did. I hated my mother so much that I prayed for her to die. Now all I can do is come here, decorate her grave, and try to atone for my sins by giving her coffee, flowers, and pictures."

This time I pull him down to meet my lips because I don't know what else to do to take away this pain. "It wasn't your fault," I whisper against his lips. "You were a scared kid who was terrified, and you had no one there for you. It wasn't your fault." When he doesn't say anything back, I repeat the words for a third time, annunciating each one to punctuate the meaning as best as possible. "It. Wasn't. Your. Fault."

He stifles another sob as he picks me up and presses his face against my neck. I feel his tears against my skin, and I start stroking his hair with my hands. It makes sense now. I can't say I fully understand his mind and what he's suffered, but I can see why he'd be reluctant to get close to anyone, and I've been pushing him, and pushing him, and not giving him the time he needed.

His life was beyond fucked up, and that's the only family he's ever really known. How does someone move on from that?

"I'm sorry," I murmur softly, kissing his cheek as his hold on me tightens.

My feet are dangling several inches from the ground as he clutches me to him, but I don't care. He can hold me like this for as long as he wants to.

"I shouldn't have pushed you for more. If I had known… Rye, I'm sorry. I didn't know."

His lips press against my neck, and he kisses it, moving slowly around in small, patterned circles. "If you hadn't pushed me for more, I'd still be angry," he almost whispers.

I try to dissect that and analyze what it can possibly mean as he continues trailing small kisses all over my neck.

"I wouldn't have wanted more," he says, squeezing me almost too tightly. He puts me down gently, and he turns toward the grave once more.

He sits down on the ground, and I join him without regard for my shivering body. His arm comes around my shoulders, and I lean into him. For at least thirty minutes, we sit silently, just listening to the sounds of the graveyard.

It's actually not as creepy as it sounds.

It's a sea of tombstones that tell brief stories with a few simple endearments—some are truths, some are lies. All are insufficient if you're looking for true insight into a person's life.

Most say *loving mother*, just as his mother's tombstone. But it doesn't stain the present with pain from the past by telling that she lost her control in her life. It doesn't show the scars she embedded deep inside of her son's mind when the sickness ruled her. And it doesn't tell the story of how their home was broken because of a disease they couldn't see without physical manifestation.

Some stories are buried with the bodies those tombstones represent. Secrets hide amongst the layers of memories that still rest on the surface. Each soul has a different story that may or may not be told. And we're here, listening to the resting souls that have left behind both good and bad stories to be shared.

I never thought I could sit silently in a graveyard without being terrified, but I feel an odd sense of serenity seeping from Rye as it runs

337

over me. It's as though his whole demeanor has shifted in a matter of weeks. And it's as though this was some sort of closure that he needed.

He's blamed himself. For years he's blamed himself. He's still blaming himself, and that breaks my heart. But I'll make sure to remind him as much as necessary that it wasn't his fault.

No matter what happens between us, I'll never stop being his friend. Especially not now. He trusted me with this, and now I'll make it my mission that he never carries this burden alone again.

"Let's get out of here," he whispers, breaking the silence at last as he stands and helps me to my feet.

He stares at the picture of a small boy being held by a loving mother—the memories from a good day. Then he threads our fingers back together, and he tugs me toward the car. Our footsteps are slower, heavier, and much wearier as we make it to the vehicle.

"Can I ask why you decided to share this with me?" I ask when we reach the gate.

He smiles tightly as he opens the door, and ushers me in on the passenger side. Just as I make it into the seat, he answers me.

"You brought me the peace I haven't ever had. I just thought you might want to know what you saved me from."

He shuts the door while my lips part and a confused breath of air slips free. Even now he's the most confusing person I've ever met.

He climbs in and cranks the car, and with the streetlights, now I can see his face. His eyes are glossy, but his tears are gone.

"What peace?" I ask as he pulls out onto the road.

His grin grows, and he reaches over for my hand once we're on the straightaway.

"No anger, tiger. None. You broke it down little by little, and now it's just… gone. I never thought it was possible. Even when you were pissing me off with your vicious, unprovoked attacks, you were drawing out the real anger that I never thought would leave."

My attacks were completely provoked, but this hardly seems like the time to joke. Especially since I'm crying harder now and exerting a tremendous amount of effort not to start bawling like a baby.

He grins over at me, and I reach over and take his hand, wishing I could just climb onto his lap. He pulls his hand back as he turns onto the road that takes us home, but I hope he doesn't plan on taking me to my house.

"So you're not angry anymore." It's not a question. It's just me recapping his words and slowly processing it all.

His smile only grows as he pulls up to his side of the curb, parks, and turns the car off. My eyes lift to find his house as he answers.

"No. It started off subtle. I thought maybe you were just a fun distraction, but the more time I spent around you… I kept changing, and I didn't even know it. I've never laughed as hard as I do with you. I've never been laughing and pissed at the same time. I've never smiled so much as I do when I see you, and I've never felt so damn good about being me. You make me enjoy being me."

My tears drip for a new reason, and I finally give up and cross over the center console to be in his lap, leaving my towel and his jacket behind. He grins as he pushes his lips against mine, and I cling to him for a minute before pulling back just enough to speak.

"I guess that makes us even," I murmur softly, watching him tilt his head questioningly. "You make me enjoy being me, too."

His responding grin could slay me if I wasn't already completely and utterly his.

Rye

Perfect. No one could have ever been more perfect for me, and fate dropped her off right across from me. Maybe this is my reward for the shitty cards I was dealt. All I know is that I don't want to lose her ever again.

I honestly can't believe I was able to tell her about everything, but more importantly, I can't believe how free I feel right now. I can breathe so easily, and for the first time since I can remember, there's nothing holding me back. From anything.

"Will you come inside?" I ask her as she hugs me a little tighter.

"Yes," she says in a near whisper.

I swear I could never get tired of holding her like this.

"Will you stay the night?"

She grins as she kisses my neck, and I pull her closer, letting her do that divine thing with her tongue against my skin, imagining her doing that somewhere else, especially since I know how heavenly that mouth is.

"Yes," she whispers again.

"And tomorrow morning, afternoon, and night, too?" I ask in quick succession, smiling as she giggles against me.

"Yes, yes, yes."

I open the door, but I don't let her go. Instead, I keep her held to me, and she clamps those small but strong legs around my waist as I carry her toward the house.

"Have you been with anyone since me?" she asks, surprising the hell out of me with her seemingly random and offensive question.

"No. Of course not. Why would you ask that?"

She just grins again, but I'm confused.

"I want to feel your piercing," she says with that sultry voice that makes my knees wobble.

If she doesn't want me to drop both of us to the ground, she can't say things like that when I'm trying to walk. She laughs when she sees what she's doing to me, and the sound reverberates and carries through my bones.

I never would have been able to do this with anyone else. But she's done so much to me—for me.

Getting the door open while holding her is a pain in the ass, but I refuse to put her down. The more I struggle, the more she smiles.

"I missed you," I murmur against her grinning lips, feeling my stupid smile grow as well.

"Good," she says simply when I finally get the door open.

"Good?"

She kisses me harder, making talking an impossibility. When she moans into my mouth, I drop to the first thing that won't collapse— the sofa. I sit with her still wrapped around me, keeping her straddling me.

"Yes," she says while pulling her lips away from mine. "Because

I've missed you, too. It wouldn't be fair if I had been the only one missing you. I'd have to do something to get even."

She just keeps proving to be more perfect for me.

"I want to do this." The words come through easily, surprising me. I really expected that to be so much harder to say.

She tilts her head as an amused smile plays on her lips, and she leans back to pull at the strings of her bikini top. Swallowing becomes incredibly difficult when the strings fall, and gravity pulls the small garment down. Though I have no idea where it falls to.

"I would hope so. You've already got me here."

My eyes stubbornly stay on her chest for another second. Or ten. But I finally find her eyes again, and ignore her devilish smile.

"I mean I want to do *this*—us. For real this time. No holding back."

Her smile falls, and for a very long five seconds, I worry that I've messed up and waited too long. But then her smile that is only reserved for me breaks across her face, and she undoes the side of her see-through wrap thing.

Now breathing is becoming as hard as swallowing.

"Why?" she asks, bending down and pressing her chest against me.

I really regret the decision to put my shirt back on. I want to feel her against my skin.

When her lips find my neck, I realize her game. And she's really, really, really good at this game.

"I think you know why," I answer in a strained tone as she shifts in my lap, pressing herself even closer.

My hands slide up and down the bare skin of her back, and I tease the top of her bikini bottoms, ready to have her naked. It doesn't matter where we do this anymore. I just have to have her.

"I don't know why," she says, taking a breath that worries me. She looks serious now. So this isn't actually a game.

"Because you make me miserable."

Her eyebrows lift up, and I laugh at her confusion. I love that adorable little wrinkle her forehead gets when she's completely baffled. That little wrinkle gets a lot of exercise around me.

"I've never felt so irresistible," she mutters dryly, and I can't help but laugh while picking her up.

I lay her down on the floor, push her back, and cover her almost bare body with mine. When her breaths become more labored, I restrain a smirk.

"You *are* irresistible. My anger was gone, as I said. Somehow you got rid of it, but I didn't notice until you were gone what you had put in its place. While you were gone, there was nothing but misery."

She smiles bashfully as a tear rolls down her cheek. "Then I'm glad I make you miserable."

I grin and kiss her, but she starts tugging my shirt over my head, forcing me to break the kiss. When she unties the strings of her bikini bottoms, a feral sound escapes my mouth, forcing her little smirk to appear.

"There's another reason I want to do this," I say in a reverent breath as she slowly tugs the bottoms away.

My eyes go down, taking in her small body beneath me now that she's completely bare.

"Oh?" she muses, her delicate, deft fingers going to work on the strings of my swimming shorts.

I take a minute to truly admire her. She looks like mischief wrapped up in an innocent package that is ready to deceive the naïve. She's perfect.

"I also want to do it because I'm a little bit in love with you," I murmur, taking a deep breath as I find the courage to meet her blue eyes again.

She gives nothing away with the expression she's wearing right now. I really don't like that expression. Finally, a few more tears fall from her eyes and she pulls me to her while kicking my shorts the rest of the way down.

I grin when I feel her frantic feet trying to free me completely, but I shuffle out of them to help her out.

"Just a little bit?" she asks as I push against her.

I can't help but enjoy the little moan she gives me.

"A small, barely unrecognizable bit," I lie, and she grins against my lips when I push my tongue into her mouth.

It feels like years since I've been inside her, and I can't wait any longer. So I don't.

With a hard, swift motion, I slam into her, forcing her pleasured cry to escape, and I bite back a groan. I forgot how good she fucking feels. I'm fairly certain she was somehow crafted and molded specifically for me in every way.

It feels like my dick is sliding into a wet vice that has a thick rose petal lining. Fairly positive this defines the word *heaven*, and I never want to leave.

"I love you," she whispers, her words ending in another moan as I push deeper inside her, and she repeats herself. My restraint breaks.

I wanted to take this slow, but I can't. Not when her body is bowing to mine while she says those words over and over. I never want her to stop saying them.

No misery. No anger. Nothing but completion. I've never felt whole until her.

I thrust powerfully, gripping her hips tightly. As my fingers dig into her flesh, her nails slide across my back, and her heels dig into my ass, driving me forward. Her chest bounces, moving with the motions of our bodies.

My thumb slides over, finding that spot that has her gasping and cursing, and I start spinning circles, pushing down just hard enough. Her sounds tell me when I've found the right rhythm, and dual stimulation has her grabbing at my hair.

I don't care if she turns me bald or mars my back for life, watching her face go through numerous phases of ecstasy is worth anything I have to offer. Unable to help myself, I lean in to kiss her, needing to swallow some of those sexy sounds escaping her.

With every stroke, it gets hotter inside her tight sheathe. Her tongue tangles with mine, fighting for dominance in a way that has my balls tightening too soon with an imminent release.

Her hips arch as her walls tighten, and when my name comes out in an almost unrecognizable scream, I explode inside her, wishing we could just stay joined all night.

My entire body goes stiff before utterly lax and languid, and it takes all my strength to continue holding myself above her, knowing I'll crush her tiny frame if I drop.

"Do you love me more than a little bit now?" she asks teasingly, breathless as she drops her arms from behind my neck and lets them collapse to the floor beside her.

Despite the fact I'm completely exhausted, I want her again. And again. And then again.

I smile as I pick her up, refusing to fully separate our bodies, and she rests limply on me as I carry her to the bedroom.

"By the end of the night, I have a feeling I'm going to love the hell out of you," I say, even though we both know I already do.

She giggles, and my stupid, painful grin stays on my face. So this is what it's like to be happy. I could get used to it.

"What's in the present you sent me?" she asks randomly, and I pause.

"You haven't opened it?"

She shakes her head, laughing lightly as I make it to my room with her still firmly strapped against me.

"Would you open a present I sent to you?"

I think about that for a second, weighing it in my mind. "Good point. Is it at your house?"

She nods, and I drop her to my bed while rushing back into my living room. I hear her asking me what I'm doing, but I don't respond.

After pulling on my discarded swimming trunks from my living room floor, I jog outside and across the street. The door is unlocked to her house, and Maggie and Carmen both jump when I barge in.

"Sorry," I say distractedly, scanning the living room.

"Brin's not here," Maggie scolds, glaring at me. "She's on a real date with someone who can hopefully get his head out of his ass long enough to appreciate her the way she deserves."

I really thought getting Brin's car back would make Maggie like me again.

"I know where she is," I say, walking into her room and flicking on her light.

"What the hell are you doing in her room? You can't just—"

"Where's the present I gave her?" I ask when I don't see it in plain sight.

She follows me into the room, her arms crossed disapprovingly over her chest.

"I said she's not here, so you shouldn't be in her room. Your pranks are only giving her hope, and I can't allow you to break her anymore. She never cried before you, and now that's all she does."

That makes me feel like shit. But I'm about to work really damn hard to make it up to her.

"I know she's not here. She's in my bed. We're together—for real this time. So where's the present I sent her?"

Her mouth falls open, and she stares at me in shock. That's insulting. I think. I really don't understand women. And Brin thinks I'm confusing. Her whole fucking gender is mind-boggling.

"It's in the kitchen," Carmen says, grinning as she starts pulling a still-stunned Maggie from the room.

I quickly walk around them and rush to the kitchen. The red package is on the counter, and I snag it and walk back out while Maggie still stares, dumbfounded.

"I love her, Maggie," I say on my way out.

Just as I make it to the end of her yard, she yells, "You'd fucking better. I'd hate to have to roast your balls over a fire."

Why do girls always threaten a guy's balls? So unnecessary.

I just grin at her over my shoulder, and she works really hard not to smile back. Then I devote all my attention to getting back to the naked girl in my bed.

Brin

Rye walks back into the room where he abandoned me, and he's holding the red package that I still don't trust. "Shorts off," I demand, smiling at him when he laughs.

He complies though, and he gets as naked as I am before joining me on the bed.

"Here," he says, handing me the item of suspicion.

It's a long box, like something you would put clothing in. But I'm still not opening it.

"You open it for me," I say very warily, handing him the box and waiting for him to put me out of the suspenseful misery this *gift* has caused. It doesn't stink, so I'm assuming there isn't anything dead inside.

"No trust," he says with a playful sigh, and I snuggle up closer to his back, peeking over his shoulder and letting his body shield me… just in case.

He peels open the paper to reveal the white box, and then he opens the top. Inside rests something white, and I lean up to get a better view. It's a note on top of white tissue paper.

I miss you. And I bought things that make me think of you.

Really glad I didn't open this before. I would have melted and begged him to take me back. Then we might not be in this new place where a future is possible between us.

"You're crying," he says with a frown.

"They're not bad tears this time," I say, smiling at him as he shifts and kisses me sweetly on the lips.

I pull away and peel back the tissue paper, and I burst out laughing at the simple white cotton panties that rest on the top layer.

"Really?"

He shrugs as his grin grows. "They suit you. And I love you the way you are. Everything is always different, fun, and sexy in an entirely new way. These damn things shouldn't be sexy, but you looked so fucking good that night you were letting me pull those shorts off you for the first time."

Those words… He really does love me, and he's saying it aloud. I never thought it would happen. I keep expecting to wake up and realize this was all a torturous nightmare.

I smile and return my attention to the present, trying not to show how completely excited I am over something so simple. Then I pull out a white sundress. I grin bigger as I look at him, and he shrugs in response. On the next layer, there's a bottle of food coloring, and I laugh.

Under that are several other things. There's a Camry keychain hooked to a Porsche keychain, and I grin while I continue snickering. The box of baking soda and bottle of Febreeze makes me chuckle louder, and he pulls me to him.

"I was trying to make you play with me. I was pretty damn desperate."

I smile up at him, and put the things aside. Then I wrap my arms around him while he falls to his back, dragging me down with him.

"I'm glad I didn't open it. We wouldn't be here right now if I had. We'd be in the loop your father warned me about."

He tilts his head in confusion, and I realize he apparently hasn't talked to his dad about our visit, so I try to elaborate without all the details.

"I would have played. You wouldn't have ever thought of anything more with me," I say to clarify.

His eyes soften, and he presses his lips against mine.

"Then I'm glad you didn't open it."

I push my hips back, slowly sliding down on him, impaling myself, and feeling the full, stretching sensation moments before that metal bar does that divine thing of touching a place that has never felt so stimulated before him.

Ruined. He's ruined me forever, and I love it.

When I rock my hips, he groans. Each breath exchanged is a new breath of a freedom I never thought I could feel.

And he's mine.

Epilogue

One week later…

Rye

"We should probably get out there," Brin says breathlessly against my lips, but she feels too good to leave right now.

"One more time," I murmur, still panting.

"No. We have guests, and this is your house. It's rude, and I'm starving. We can continue this when everyone is too drunk to notice we're missing."

I frown, but she laughs, and I can't help but smile. With a reluctant sigh, I stand and pull my jeans back on while she wraps the sheet around her.

"This could be your house, too," I say, trying to make this sound as casual as possible while I grab for a shirt.

She's silent. I hate it when she's silent.

"What does that mean?" she asks in a hoarse whisper that forces her to clear her throat directly after.

I keep my back turned, shrugging as nonchalantly as possible.

"You could move in." I pull on my shirt, still refusing to look at her. "You're here every day and night, so it only makes sense for you to move in."

I turn to see her frowning. She has that confused wrinkle on her brow. This is moving fast, but I love her, so it only makes sense. I've spent my entire life playing it safe and staying detached from anything that could pose a threat. I want to live now, and there's no reason to waste time. I know exactly what I want, and for the first time in my life, there's nothing stopping me from having it.

"I'm not moving in for the sake of convenience," she says, still wearing her sweet frown.

I lean over, tug the sheet away from her body, and press a chaste kiss to her lips. "I'm not asking you to moving in for the sake of convenience. I'm asking you to move in because I want to take the next step. It's fast. I know. But I love you, and you love me, so this is next. We can do this."

She's fighting hard not to grin. Sure it's crazy to move in after only being in a committed relationship for a week, but we've been together for over a couple of months. Even when we were split up, she consumed me, so we might as well be living under the same roof. It would definitely make my life better.

"What happens if I say no?" she asks, failing miserably in her attempt not to grin.

As she stands, I lean back, watching her naked body slowly become clothed under a white sundress. Innocent mischief; it's an oxymoron to most. To me, it's the girl I love.

"I torture you until you say yes," I say absently, smiling as she goes to grab the top drawer.

She grabs those sweet cotton panties, and I grin like a fool as she slides them on under her dress. Then she grabs a white strapless bra and pulls down the straps of her dress to put it on.

353

We're never leaving this room.

"Stop," she giggles when I try to wrap her up in my arms.

"Then stop teasing me with a reverse striptease and answer my question."

She sighs playfully, feigning exasperation as she reaches a hand up and tugs on my neck.

"What happens if I say yes?"

I grin as I start pressing small kisses on her neck, and she arches to lean into me.

"Then I torture you daily, but it'll be fun."

She laughs, and the sound vibrates throughout me. I wonder how long it'll feel this good, because I'm pretty sure it's going to be impossible to ever get anything done if it's always like this.

"Then yes," she says at last, and I spin her in my arms to kiss her hard, pressing her up against the dresser and silently counting how many times I've had her right here.

It's not enough. One more time is necessary.

"No," she says through a laugh. "Guests. You have guests."

"*We* have guests. You live here now, too," I remind her, enjoying the way that sweet blush creeps across her cheeks.

"Well, *our* guests are waiting on us. Go on while I finish getting dressed."

I pout, but she shoves me out, somehow managing to withstand the power of my puckered lips. But I'm grinning when I walk out.

Dad is talking with a woman when I reach the outside, and he nods in my direction while smiling. Looks like Ash is still trying to play matchmaker, but at least this woman is my dad's age.

I smile back at him, and he takes a breath that appears to be easy. Everything is so much easier. I never thought it was possible. The relationship I have with my father is by no means a normal one. Not yet. Possibly not ever. But I can stand to be around him, and he's coming out of the house more.

I guess he decided if I was going to start healing, then it was okay for him to start healing, too.

Wren walks up with a small girl at his side, and I grin at the kid who looks so much like Wren and his family.

"You must be Angel," I say, kneeling in front of the little girl.

She nods and says, "You must be the guy with tattoos my momma stitched up."

I thought she was six. She looks six.

She points to the small scar on my hand, and I nod.

"Yeah," I say, confused as I look up at Wren.

"She's really smart, really observant, and really blunt. Oh, and she eavesdrops on any conversation she can," he explains dryly.

Angel walks toward Ash who is calling for her, and Angel thanks her when she offers her cake.

"She just turned six, right? Not eighteen?" I ask, looking at the back of the kid who very properly thanks Ash.

"Yeah. She's used to living with her mother and Bella—Allie's roommate and best friend. Like I said, she eavesdrops. I've learned the hard way to keep my mouth shut if I want to keep secrets, because she could be under your bed without your knowledge. And she's quick to

catch on. I think she's aware that I was a dick to her mother. So…
Yeah… It's a struggle, but I'm working hard to build a relationship.
Right now she's not too thrilled with me."

I sigh long and loud. This is fucked up no matter how you slice it.
No one is a winner in this. Allie was a single mom who didn't know the
name of her child's father; Wren is the guy who missed six years of his
daughter's life because he messed up once and acted like a jerk; and the
kid is stuck in the middle.

"Does Allie talk bad about you around her? I know you said she
hates you."

I feel bad for not being there for him as much as I should have
been this past month. I got too involved with my own drama, and I let
him down.

"No. She doesn't talk about me at all, according to Angel. This
sucks. Allie is actually trying to help us have a relationship, but she
resents me—possibly hates me. Angel is smart enough and observant
enough to realize that without Allie vocalizing it. She's loyal to her
mom, and I don't stand a chance until I get on Allie's good side. And
that's not working out so well."

Sighing, I take a sip of my beer. I suck in this department. I don't
know the first thing about kids.

"Tag got any insight?"

"He has tons of advice. But his kid is much, much younger and
loves him. His new one will love him, too, when it's born. But he can't
help me build a relationship with an estranged daughter. No one can.
It's on me, and I'll figure out a way to fix this, because I want to make

this right. And I really, really want to get to know her. She looks at her mother with such pride and adoration. But she looks at me with disappointment and the same resentment Allie has. I paved the road, now I have to try and drive down it despite the damn crater-like potholes that are on it."

I smile weakly in an attempt to seem encouraging. Angel sits down next to Ash, eating her cake, and we both watch.

"I should get her out of here. Her mom only gives me so long to keep her without supervision. It's sad that she trusts me that little. But she doesn't know me. I guess that's on me to change."

I frown as he ruffles his hair and sighs.

"She can't stop you from seeing your daughter. You have rights. You should talk to your lawyers."

He shakes his head. "I don't want to do anything like that unless I have to. The more amicable this thing is, the better. She's raised Angel on her own because I never gave her my name. The least I can do is take it at her pace. If she insists on continuing this limited time thing after I've proven myself, then I'll involve the lawyers."

I've seen guilt—struggled with it for most of my life. Still struggle with it.

His guilt is different than mine, but I see it.

"I'll come back after I drop her off," he says, clapping my back on his way over to his daughter.

"Are Wren and Angel leaving?" Brin asks, suddenly beside me, and I wrap my arm around her shoulders to bring her closer.

I wish Wren had someone to help him through this right now. I wish it was me, but I don't know what to say. But I'll be there as much as I can, just like he's always been for me.

"Yeah," is all I tell her. I'm not sure how much Wren wants divulged to everyone. He just announced he had a kid to our entire group a few days ago, and then he brought Angel over to introduce her to all of us at the last barbeque.

Until then, it was only a few of us who knew. No one is asking him a lot of questions right now, out of respect.

"You want a beer?" I ask Brin, smiling down at her wearing the white sundress I bought her.

"I do, but I'll get my own," she says, eyeing me like she still doesn't trust me.

I don't blame her. I have three bottles of green food coloring in my pocket.

She walks away to grab us both a beer, and I watch her with the same amount of suspicion as she watches me. I really love this girl.

Kode and Tria are hugged up, lost in each other—as usual. Tag and Ash are playing with Trip, and Tag reaches over to rub his wife's small, barely pudgy stomach. Dane and Rain are trying to convince Carrie, their daughter, to eat the vegetables on her plate. And Kade and Raya are walking through the gate, their eyes locked as though they don't need to see the world around them.

Brin comes up and tugs at my shirt, prompting me to bend so she can kiss me, and I smile while taking my beer from her hand. Before I drink it, I push it to her lips.

"You first," I order, eliciting a soft chuckle from her.

"No trust," she mocks, sipping the beer and then handing it back.

I inspect her mouth, and then sip the beer as we walk toward a table. I really don't like dark beer, but I needed it today to hide the food coloring. It's only natural that I would want to celebrate our one-week anniversary with a recycled prank.

Maggie and Carmen are eating the burgers I made as I sit down, and she points to the two plates in front of the two vacant chairs.

"I made your plates. Eat before it's too cold."

I smile at her, and she grins while rolling her eyes. "Yeah, yeah. I know. I'm too damn sweet," she says dryly.

I laugh while sitting down, and Brin snickers softly while joining me. Ash calls her name, and she turns to answer her. I capitalize on my opportunity, and empty all three small bottles of the food coloring into her beer.

Maggie chokes on her bite, and I glare at her in warning as I discreetly toss the bottles far, far away. I manage to finish just as Brin turns back around.

"You okay?" she asks Maggie, who nods while sipping her own drink.

Brin shrugs as she takes a sip of her beer, and I turn just as Tag comes up beside me.

"Poker next week?" he asks.

I really don't feel like hanging out with the guys all night. Not now. But I gave them immortal hell for the same thing for so long that I don't have a choice.

"Sure," I say noncommittally, not naming a day or time.

"Good. No Raya," he says, glaring at her just as she opens her mouth to speak.

"Why not?" she asks, affronted.

"Guys only."

Her glower grows, and she shakes her head. "Hell no. My girls' night was invaded by all of you men, so I'm coming to poker if I damn well choose."

"My wallet will lose some weight," Dane grumbles from behind us, and I smirk while turning back and sipping my beer.

"I think Raya should only play a few hands because we'll all be broke otherwise," I say, laughing, but everyone is wide-eyed and staring at me with horror seconds before their cackles break free.

What the hell?

Then I hear *her* laughing, and I turn to glare at her. But her green mouth is too funny for me not to start laughing at.

"You two are incorrigible," Maggie says, coughing on her own laughter.

Brin frowns when she sees everyone is laughing at her instead of me. She grabs Maggie's purse from the table, and searches for a mirror. The second she has it, she turns it on her face, and I'm rewarded by the shocked intake of air.

"You bastard!" she says in a whisper.

I just laugh that much harder, and Tag says, "Don't know what you're laughing at, Dracula."

My laughter ceases immediately as Brin's lips curl up in a green-stained smile. I grab the mirror, and groan when I see the red coating my lips and teeth. My tongue looks like it caught on fire or something.

"Fuck," I grumble, and everyone only laughs that much harder, including the two of us.

"Twisted minds think alike," Brin says mockingly.

"Are you two even yet?" Rain asks, amused.

Brin looks at me with a challenging glint in her eyes, and at the same time, we both say, "Never."

As the laughter continues, I pull her to my lap and kiss her, letting our mouths turn to Christmas colors as the red and green mingle together. She smiles against the kiss even as her devilish tongue provokes scandalous images of things I want to do to her.

I'm going to love spending the rest of my life trying to break even.

The   **End**

ABOUT THE AUTHOR

What does C.M. Owens write? A little bit of everything as long as the central focus is romance.

C.M. Owens is an escapist, and loves to stretch the imagination. Writing is more than a passion – it's a necessity. It's a means of staying sane and happy.

Where do her ideas come from? Usually it's a line in a song that triggers an idea that spawns into a story. Though she came from a family of musicians, she has zero abilities with instruments, she sounds like a strangled cat when she sings, and her dancing is downright embarrassing. Just ask her two children. Her creativity rests solely in the written word. Her family is grateful that she gave up her quest to become a famous singer.